Bones of Fire

A Spiritual Warfare Novel

The Fire Series

Eric M. Hill

Published by SunHill Publishers
P.O. Box 17730
Atlanta, Georgia 30316

Bones of Fire

www.ericmhill.com

ISBN-13: 978-1519196224
ISBN-10: 1519196229

Cover design by Cora Graphics.

A Note from the Author

Hello! If this is your first time reading one of my stories, I welcome you and thank you for choosing my book to read among the millions that are available. If you have read at least one of my stories and have returned for more, that says it all! I can't think of a greater compliment and vote of confidence than for someone to read one of my books and ask for more. ☺

May I Ask You A Favor?

Once you read the book, if you find that you enjoyed the story, would you mind going online to Amazon.com, iTunes, Kobo, Barnes and Noble, or wherever you purchased the book and writing a review? Many people determine from book reviews whether or not a story is worth their time. Your review (even a short one!) can help convince others to join the fun!

Let's Stay In Touch!

Readers who sign up for my mailing list receive and/or do the following:

Receive advance news of stories I'm working on.

Receive ***free*** portions of stories before they are published.

Receive whatever wonderful written ***freebie*** I can come up with.

Provide me with feedback on what they liked or disliked about a story.

Share ideas about what they'd like to see in future stories.

Join my newsletter at www.ericmhill.com/newsletter. Here's my contact info: ericmhillauthor@yahoo.com or Twitter.com/ericmhillatl.

God bless you!

Other Books by the Author

Spiritual Warfare Fiction

The Fire Series
Book 1: Bones of Fire
Book 2: Trial by Fire
Book 3: Saints on Fire

The Demon Strongholds Series
Book 1: The Spirit of Fear
Book 2: The Spirit of ??? (Coming March 2016)
Book 3: The Spirit of ??? (Coming June 2016)
Book 4: The Spirit of ??? (Coming September 2016)
Book 5: The Spirit of ??? (Coming December 2016)

Other Fiction

The Journey Series
Book 1: The Runaway's Journey (Part One)

Non-Fiction

Deliverance from Demons and Diseases
What Preachers Never Tell You About Tithes & Offerings

Chapter 1

The demon sat upon the neck of its unwary victim the way a small child would sit upon the neck of his father. His slanted eyes darted in different, unsymmetrical directions, each of the three following its own course. Its neck and head resembled a turtle's, bobbing in and out of its crusty socket with cat-like speed, hiding from and spying on something, some enemy, real or perceived. His small paw-like hands were covered with tiny suctions. He poised his hands, ready to grip the man of God and torture him with debilitating thoughts of guilt and fear. But he had to wait for an opening.

Pastor Edwin Styles was oblivious of the demon that had been perched atop his shoulders for the past thirty-five years, since he was just a boy of five. He didn't believe in demons. Or more accurately, he didn't think about demons. Or angels. Or anything supernatural. He was from the theological school of thought that believed the supernatural element of Christianity had existed at one time. But with the success of world evangelism in the first century, the writing of the Bible, and the death of the last apostle, supernatural occurrences had ceased.

As a seminary graduate, he had read the writings of the early church fathers: Tertullian, Origen, Polycarp, and others. He had even read Eusebius. He was aware that some of these writers made references to miracles, demons, angels, and those sorts of things as common occurrences. But as Professor Stuart in seminary had said so many times: "These are only eccentricities of the early church. As the church grew in knowledge, it discarded its silly superstitions. It began to trust more and more in the ways of God: education, medicine, science, and empirical data."

Pastor Styles stared at his bookcase. He could almost see Stuart's chubby face and bald head. He chuckled. The students had been right. He really did look like Humpty Dumpty. His gaze broke and he looked at the Scripture again. Yep, still there. As irksome and confusing as ever. "And Stephen, full of faith and power, did great wonders and miracles among the people."

He pushed away from his desk and stood up. "No wonder we stayed out of the book of Acts," he said. It wasn't a statement born of new insight, just frustration. "It just doesn't fit."

With what? My Word or your theology?

"Huh?" Pastor Styles turned around, startled at the question. There was no one there. *Of course, no one is here,* he quickly thought. Yet he knew that he definitely heard someone ask him that question. The voice was full of authority. It sounded foreign, yet deeply familiar, but it was a totally new voice. Too new for Reverend Edwin Styles. "I'm getting out of here," he said.

"Ed," he heard his wife call.

"Now I *know* who that is. Yes, dear?"

"Food's on the table. We're running late for church," his wife answered.

"Coming right down." His stomach growled in anticipation of dinner. He wore a smile as he entered the kitchen. His wife was a great cook. "I'm starved," he said, and was immediately sorry he had said it. His wife was seated, and so were their two sons, Andrew and Christopher. But good heavens! Sharon was standing at the side of the table with a big smile.

"Come on, Daddy. You sit here," she said, as though he were a special visitor. "I've made your favorite."

"Ugh...oh...yeah, yeah. Okay sweetheart," he groped. He looked at the boys. They were loving it. Christopher was only three years old, but he had a goofy smile on his face. A you're-in-for-it-now-Dad smile. He was only three. How could he be so ruined already? And Andrew, he looked like he wanted to explode with laughter, but his mother's cutting eyes convinced him that was a terrible idea.

"Hey, Dad," said Andrew, "she made your favorite."

Edwin made his face smile. It was a tight, rebellious smile. He looked at his daughter. "My favorite?"

"Yes. Chicken and dumplings," his wife added. "And she's put a lot of time into it." That was the hint that a cruel, torturous death awaited the first one who said or did anything to hurt Sharon's feelings.

Edwin could still taste the last chicken and dumplings his daughter had cooked. But the memory of that terrible meal faded as he looked into her eyes. Sure, Sharon was not a good cook—actually it was a crime any time she cooked—and it would probably be years, light-years, before she could cook an edible meal, but one thing she didn't lack was love. She was the most loving, caring person he knew. Her love was so complete. So trusting and vulnerable. She thrived on doing good for others.

Edwin's eyes watered a little. "Honey," he said with deep affection, "thank you for preparing the meal. You're the loveliest daughter a father could have." He almost looked forward to eating.

Sharon saw the softness in her father's eyes. It was as touching as his words. She knew she wasn't a good cook. "Oh, it's okay, Daddy," she tried to say matter-of-factly. But she was clearly moved by her father's appreciation. *I love you so much, Daddy.*

*****

An urgent and frenzied meeting was in session. Far above the Atlanta city lights in the spiritual dimension of wicked spirits, where natural and supernatural laws mysteriously intertwined, the four tiers of demon spirits that governed the area gathered. Principalities, powers, rulers of darkness, and wicked spirits from high places.

The emissaries of darkness found their places inside the giant structure. Every demon sat according to rank. An eight-foot-tall warrior spirit approached the raised lectern. He placed his large pad onto the lectern and raised his hand to silence the nervous murmuring of nearly five hundred devils. The chattering ceased at once. All eyes riveted to the warrior spirit.

Bashnar's piercing gaze searched the ugly audience. Those seated closest to the front had mixed emotions of being scrutinized by this great warrior. They wanted him to notice them. They wanted their faces to be seen and remembered. Recognition meant promotion. But there was a downside to recognition. It could sometimes lead to humiliation. Sometimes it meant terrible, excruciating pain. In extreme cases, it could mean banishment to the Dark Prison.

Nonetheless, the most distinguished rulers had insisted on first row seats. Many of them were well connected with powerful sponsors. They had that kind of arrogant swagger that silently, yet loudly, identified them as demons who knew they were important. Yet for all their brazen pomp, more than a few were visibly shaken when Bashnar fixed his piercing gaze on them.

He never seemed to merely look at you. To be looked at for any length of time by the Mighty Bashnar was to be studied. One always went away from this encounter with the overwhelming sense that the depths of one's soul had been thoroughly searched for the slightest trace of weakness, something the great warrior could use against his competition in the future. *Everyone was competition.*

But there were more immediate reasons to tremble in Bashnar's presence. All warrior spirits were ruthless, ferocious, and utterly evil. Yet there were some, such as Bashnar, who excelled in these hellish qualities. His exploits of cruelty against humans and even demons were well known throughout the ranks of darkness.

There was hardly a wicked spirit who didn't know of Bashnar. Yet his meteoric rise to the position of power and influence he enjoyed wasn't conferred upon him simply because he was a great fighter. There were many great fighters. No. Bashnar's legendary battlefield victories were only part of the reason he was a favorite of the Council of Strategic Affairs. He was favored for his fighting skills, but he was revered for his strategies.

Bashnar was indeed unique. His peers knew it. His superiors knew it. His enemies knew it. But most of all Bashnar knew it, and he was determined to never allow anyone to forget it.

He hoped the assembly of demons would fully comprehend the severity of the threat that he was about to disclose to them. He knew that some would treat it as a routine matter. Or worse, as a false alarm. He admitted that there were many false alarms. Nevertheless, those who didn't take Bashnar seriously would most assuredly taste his wrath.

Others with better sense would understand that the security of the entire state of Georgia was at stake. He hoped they were up to the imminent confrontation.

Bashnar glanced at his notes and looked at his audience. "You have been summoned here because we believe the Georgia region will soon be attacked." His deep baritone voice filled the large room. "Prince Krioni has—"

Every demon shot to his feet. "Prince Krioni reigns! Prince Krioni reigns! Prince Krioni reigns!" they all said in unison and took their seats.

Bashnar's stony, cratered face showed no emotion, but he seethed at the adulation given the prince. "I have been selected to prepare all of you for battle."

He motioned for the lights. The room went black. A large screen rolled down and a picture of a thin-haired black man appeared. He looked to be about fifty.

"This is the present threat," Bashnar's voice declared in the darkness. "This man is a dagger!"

Nervous shivers went over many of the wicked spirits. Some turned their faces away from the picture. For even the still photograph of a consecrated man of God was unsettling.

"His devotion to Jesus Christ has become most troublesome in this region. He has only returned to Georgia from South Africa a little over a month ago, and already his fervent, fiery prayers," Bashnar's face twisted in contempt, "has directed the forces of heaven against us."

Bashnar took a noticeably deep breath and wished he didn't have to reveal the next part. "He prays and worships Jesus Christ no less than two hours a day." His voice trailed off weakly. "Sometimes more."

The effect was explosive. Pangs of terror shot through the hearts of the villainous creatures. Daggers were fierce warriors who mercilessly tormented the dark powers. What were they being asked to do? Some in the audience had had the misfortune of battling daggers—men, women, and even children—who knew the power of prayer and faith in Jesus Christ. It was always nasty.

Win or lose, the demons knew from their own experiences and the horror stories of others that many demons would suffer tremendously in the upcoming battles.

Bashnar had deep reservations about revealing so much about this Jesus lover. He didn't want to scare his army, but he knew the mindset of the assembled demons. Unless they saw how dangerous this man was, they would never give Jonathan the attention he deserved. So reluctantly, yet purposefully, Bashnar continued to paint a picture of horror.

After he graphically described the threat for two hours, Bashnar commanded a spirit to turn on the projector. "I have told you with words. Now I will show you the dagger in action."

The setting was a small South African village. Thirty or forty people were gathered around the dagger. They listened desperately to his every word.

"Jesus Christ loves all of you. Your lives are important. Your destinies are important. Jesus Christ wants to enter your lives and become your Life. He wants your world to center around Him." The dagger's voice changed from a conciliatory tone to a confrontational tone. "Around Him Not around these worthless witch doctors who bind you with chains of religious darkness! Come out from among these workers of iniquity!"

Bashnar spoke over the dagger's voice. "You see," he said, pointing to the murderous group of witch doctors who were on the sidelines, ready to pounce on the man of God and hack him to death with their machetes, "he speaks the word of God boldly, without any fear, even in the face of such danger. This attracts the power of God, as you will soon see exhibited."

Bashnar had studied this film repeatedly. Yet, he was again strangely fascinated by this dagger's faith.

One of the four witch doctors had heard enough. He pulled out his machete and stepped forward. His long, unkempt hair was matted with dirt. He looked like a wild animal. Murder danced in his eyes. He yelled something, raised his machete over his head, and wildly charged the man of God.

That's when it happened.

The dagger stepped forward and extended his hand to the attacker. Only a few feet separated him from being hacked to death. "Yes, brother, come forth."

And come forth he did. He swung the long, razor sharp blade.

The man of God stood there peacefully, as though he were a spectator and not a participant in the unfolding drama. Inches before the long blade would have taken off his head, it was knocked to the ground by an unseen force.

Bashnar had the projector stopped. "Turn on the lights," he ordered, and stepped to the lectern. "I will explain what you have just witnessed. You have seen the beginning of an invasion. This man is the tip of the spear. Wherever he goes, there is revival. I mean real revival."

This caused some murmuring.

"Shut up!" Bashnar ordered.

The crowd hushed into cemetery silence.

"Before this dagger arrived at the village, it was baptized in darkness and despair. We gloried in the pain, suffering, and despair. We wrecked lives. We deceived the dumb idiots to pay homage to idols that could neither hear nor taste nor smell. We randomly crushed whomsoever we desired."

Pause.

Bashnar's eyes turned from fiery red to pitch black. His eyes always did this before he murdered. He slammed his heavy arm on the lectern. "Everything was going fine. Then this madman popped out of nowhere and preached the glory of the wretched cross of

Christ. When the villagers heard how much God loves them, and when the man of God explained to them how they could be forgiven of every sin, even the most vile and perverted sins, the putrid scum trusted Jesus Christ to give them a better life, one filled with hope and joy and acceptance from the God of heaven. We lost everyone. Even our witch doctors."

This meeting initially was designed to be a briefing and pep rally combined. Sure, the mighty Bashnar would have to detail the realities of the threat, but he would also remind them of how other daggers had been destroyed. However, his presentation had the opposite effect of discouraging every demon there.

Bashnar's description of the man of God was so one-sided in favor of the dagger that the assembly of wicked spirits felt as though their leader was like a suicide bomber instructor telling them to strap on their bombs. The assembly wasn't feeling quite that suicidal just yet.

Bashnar perceived this and knew that he had to encourage them. He had to say someth—no! he had to do something. He must do something to show that even this dagger could be destroyed.

"Do not be discouraged, my warriors. We will draw first blood, and I will be the first to do so. We will meet again shortly. And when we do, I will have struck a significant blow against this Christ-lover. On your way out, do not forget to take your case files. Study them. They will help you prepare for this Mr. Jonathan Banks."

Chapter 2

Sometimes the ride from Stone Mountain to Doraville took forty minutes or so if the traffic was bad. But tonight Interstate 285 had only light traffic and there were no wrecks.

This is great, Edwin thought to himself, as he enjoyed the quiet and flowed with the fast moving traffic. *We should make good time.*

There were very few things that could upset Edwin Styles. Yet one thing always bugged him, and that was to arrive anywhere late, even a minute late. According to him, as everyone in the house knew and was reminded periodically, "There is no better way to tell a person he isn't important than to arrive late."

Edwin looked at the clock in the dash. Six o'clock even. Good. Suddenly, there was a clap of thunder and the light drizzle turned into a blinding downpour. He flipped the lever to turn his windshield wipers from intermittent to fast. Nothing happened, except that the wipers stop working altogether.

Edwin feverishly worked the lever to try to start the wipers again.

"Daddy, turn on the wipers. You can't see!" Little Christopher's plea sounded older than his three years.

"Honey, what's wrong?" Barbara asked. Fear gripped her heart.

Edwin didn't answer. He looked nervously out the side windows. He couldn't see anything except the vague outlines of the cars around him. He wanted to slow down to minimize the impact should they wreck, but that would probably cause one. His eyes strained to follow the dashed lines and stay in his own lane.

Baaooonk! Baaooonk!

An eighteen-wheeler directly behind them tried to get them to change lanes so he could speed up. The truck's horn sounded to their other son, Andrew, like the call of death. He gripped his seat belt until his knuckles almost popped, his face frozen in a timeless trance of horror. "We're going to die," he said, with helpless resignation.

Everyone in the car was locked into their own world of horror and fear. They knew the loud crash and the twisting of metal against their flesh was coming. Everyone except Sharon.

Sharon often seemed out of place in the Styles household. At times she appeared to be in a world all her own, oblivious to the clamor and confusion of life, following the dictates of an inner peace that caused her to shine in the darkness.

Sharon wasn't in the least bit moved by the dangerous predicament they were in. As her family ordered tombstones and grave plots, she bowed her head in prayer to the Comfort of her life. She prayed silently. *Lord Jesus, help us.* An angel appeared over their car. *Please don't let anything bad happen. We are your workmanship, created unto good works. What good can possibly come out of our deaths? I don't believe you want us to die like this. Spare us that we may continue to bring glory to your wonderful name. Thank you for delivering us, Jesus.*

Sharon lifted her head. Her face radiated joy and serenity. An unexplainable buoyancy coursed through her soul that eliminated every trace of apprehension.

There was a muffled popping sound and the car pulled to the right. Edwin slammed on the brakes and immediately regretted it. The Explorer spun a full 360 degrees. Everything was in slow motion.

The sounds of horns blaring echoed through the car and added to the stark panic. Out of the corner of her eye, Barbara caught a glimpse of Kentucky Fried Chicken as the car spun. *Is that the last thing I'm going to see before I die?* She thought.

The demon never saw it coming. Trin's fist shot through the air with magnum force and caught the unwary spirit directly under the chin. The crushing force of the blow snapped his head upward. For a microsecond his neck tightened just before his head left his body.

Trin spread his multicolored wings over the car and guided it across two lanes to a safe resting place on the side of the highway and disappeared.

It was like a mausoleum inside the car. Edwin sat stoically. His face was ashen white and his lips were tight. Barbara's attractive features were hidden behind sculptured shock. Andrew's and Christopher's faces looked like they had been to hell and back.

Sharon appeared completely unruffled by their close brush with death. "Wasn't Jesus great?" she asked a non-listening and shocked audience. "Dad, you better change the tire," she said matter-of-factly.

The windshield wipers started working.

Edwin didn't hear a word. He could still see that big truck making hamburger meat out of all of them.

Sharon gently shook him on the shoulder. "Dad, do you want me to help you with the tire?"

"Uhh, no. No, thanks, sweetheart." He was coming out of his trance. His words came out slurred. He sounded as if he was drugged. "I'll fix the tire so we can go to church."

He opened the door and stepped into the cold rain. The frigid January air cut through his clothes and chilled him back into this world. He opened the trunk, pulled out the spare, and rumbled in the darkness for the jack. "Where is it?" he said, as he shifted things here and there. He couldn't see the jack because an angel had hidden it.

It hit Sharon that her father was in the soaking rain getting drenched without his coat. *He'll get sick,* she thought. She got his coat and opened her door.

"Where are you going?" her mother asked.

"To give Daddy his coat." She stepped out before her mother could say anything else. "Here's your coat."

"What? What are y—?"

Sharon cut him off. "Put it on before you catch the flu or something," she said, helping him with it. "Can I—?"

And now he interrupted her. "No. Get in the car, young lady."

*****

"Jonathan, look at that man in the rain." Elizabeth pointed to Edwin.

Stop and help him.

Jonathan Banks didn't hesitate to obey the faint inclination. He knew it was the Holy Spirit. "Alright, Lord, what are you up to now?"

Jonathan was a seasoned Christian. He knew that God was always up to something. He had seen many miracles happen simply because he aggressively followed the promptings of the Holy Spirit. He pulled over to the side and stopped in front of their car. Jonathan got out of the car and walked toward the Styles.

"Thank you, Jesus," said Sharon, when she saw the help that God had sent.

"Oh, my God!" said Barbara, when she saw his black face. "Quick, Andrew tell your father tha—"

But it was too late. Jonathan made his way to Edwin before Andrew could get out of the car.

Edwin's head was still buried in his trunk when the man walked up. He tapped him on the shoulder. "Excuse me. Can I be of some help?"

Edwin raised up and looked into the face of the unexpected stranger. *Oh no. If I don't get run over by a truck, I get murdered by a...* His silent vocabulary failed him. "We had a flat," he said nervously.

"Oh, that's no problem. We can fix that. You have everything you need?"

He reluctantly answered. "No, I don't seem to have my jack."

"Okay," said the stranger and walked towards his own car.

"Pray," Barbara exhorted frantically to her children.

Her childhood environment was surfacing. She was not immune to the racial prejudices of her parents. Barbara had always been taught that black people didn't have the same values and moral sensitivities as white people. Since she didn't personally know any black people, all she knew about them came from other white people or from the media. She knew her views were flawed, and she was often ashamed of herself, but it was hard to shake prejudices she had been taught all of her childhood.

Barbara watched the man pass their car. "Is your father alright?"

"I don't believe this," Sharon muttered softly.

"What, honey?" said her distracted mother.

"I said I don't believe this."

"Don't believe what, honey?"

"We almost get run over by who knows how many cars and trucks. Our tire blows out and we spin all over the highway. The car conveniently," she emphasized *conveniently*, "lands here on the side of the road out of harm's way, and you're upset because God sent a black man to help us. I don't believe you, Mom."

Sharon had said much more than she had planned to say. She knew that her words weren't only a response to her mother's behavior this evening. It was an involuntary response for the many times she had silently suffered her mother's irrational prejudices. But even though she knew her mother was wrong, she suddenly felt a terrible heaviness in her heart for speaking harshly to her.

"I'm sorry, Mother. I didn't mean to hurt your feelings."

"I know you didn't mean it, baby," she said, wiping a tear from her eye. "You're just too young to understand racial issues."

Sharon grimaced, but held her tongue.

Edwin and Jonathan got everyone out of the car and fixed the flat.

"How much do I owe you?" Edwin asked, still not totally convinced that he and his family weren't in danger.

"Ohhh, I'd say five, maybe six hundred dollars."

Edwin's mouth dropped open.

The stranger laughed when he saw that the man didn't have much of a sense of humor. "Just kidding. You're a mighty serious fellow Mr...."

"Styles. I'm Edwin Styles."

"Jonathan Banks," said the man, with his hand outstretched.

Edwin timidly shook the stranger's hand.

"May the Lord's light shine upon you and your family." With that the man left.

Edwin got into the car with the man's name on his tongue. "Jonathan Banks. Where have I heard that—? Oh, what a coincidence?" he chuckled. "That's the name of our guest speaker."

Chapter 3

Edwin slowed down and flashed his high beams so that the oncoming car would switch from its high to low beams. He stole a quick glance at his watch. 6:40 p.m. His stomach tightened as he turned into the church's parking lot and saw all of the cars. There wasn't a parking space available anywhere. Some cars were double-parked. Others were crammed onto the grass.

"Honey, who's speaking tonight?" Barbara asked, noting all of the cars.

"Some guy named Jonathan Banks. A missionary from South Africa or New Guinea or somewhere. Supposed to be a good speaker. Terrance Knox recommended him."

"We don't have this many people even on Easter," said Andrew.

"What's he like?" Barbara's curiosity was aroused that so many people would come out on a Wednesday night to hear this man.

"I don't know. All I know is his name is Jonathan Banks."

"Good thing you've got your own parking space, Dad," said Sharon.

As they approached the church door, Edwin looked down at his shoes. "Great," he said in disgust. They were covered with mud, and there was also mud on the bottom of one of his legs.

A grim-faced usher met the Styles at the outer door.

"Hey, Bob. How's it going?" Edwin asked, smiling.

The usher didn't return the smile. He didn't appear to want to return a reply either. "Oh, I'm doing fine." His intonation implied that Edwin wasn't doing fine.

The usher's awkward response puzzled Edwin, but he shook it off. Bob was known to be moody.

"How are you, Barbara? Andrew? Hi, Sharon. And how about you little Christopher?" asked the usher, with genuine interest.

Everyone responded positively.

"See you right after the service." Edwin gave his wife a peck on the cheek.

"Okay. Let's stop for ice cream on the way back." Every season was ice cream season for Barbara. That was her one dietary weakness, although there wasn't the slightest hint of this in her figure.

Inside the sanctuary, over eighteen hundred people were crammed into facilities designed for fifteen hundred. There wasn't an inch to spare on the cushioned pews. People sat practically on top of one another.

Folding chairs were lined along the center aisles. The walls were lined with people—several of them very dignified looking. Ushers hurried up and down the aisles looking for room that wasn't there. Chairs were set up at the front of the altar by harried ushers for some stragglers, to the consternation of others that had been standing for quite a while.

The atmosphere was festive. It was like a circus and a Super Bowl rolled into one. Something that this church was definitely not accustomed to experiencing.

Its usual services were without exception as predictable as the sunrise and as dry as desert sand. The church's bulletin was meticulously adhered to at all costs. Every Sunday of every week was exactly like the Sunday before. An unfunny joke. A few lifeless songs. A stale sermon. A merciful benediction. Boring. Boring. Boring.

Everyone knew it, but it seemed that no one was discontented enough to do anything about it. They were like sick people who refused to take medicine for fear of getting well. Health was feared more than sickness.

Tonight was different. The faces of most of the people were the same, but their attitudes were different—livelier, expectant. Some even appeared to be enthusiastic. Enthusiastic about church? This was totally foreign to this church.

After cleaning his shoes and pants in the bathroom, Edwin opened the door and literally bumped into Harry Thompson, the chairman of the deacon board.

"Excuse me, I didn't s—"

The chairman was getting ready to apologize until he saw who it was. "That's the first and last crazy stunt you'll ever pull!" His old, lined face wore absolute scorn. "You'll be sorry, Ed. You wait and see. You'll be sorry." The old man walked away in a huff before Edwin could get a word in.

"What was that all about?" Ed asked himself. "That's the second person that...." His mind drifted off into confusion and searched for an answer that eluded him. *What's going on here?* he thought.

There was nothing discernible to the naked eye that would have given a clue to the frantic angelic and demonic activity that was taking place inside and around the church. Angels and demons flew here and there, securing strategic positions.

There were roughly as many angels as demons encamped around the church. This didn't escape the attention of Oreon, a demon who considered himself a lawyer of sorts. It appeared to be an illegal gathering of angels.

Oreon sent a courier to arrange a meeting with the captain of the opposing army. The Lord of heaven considered Himself a righteous being, and as part of His deception He gave the appearance of ruling by law and order. *I will use this to my advantage,* thought Oreon.

The meeting was set apart from each army, but in full view of both.

"Rashti, what is the meaning of all of these soldiers?" asked the wicked spirit.

The big warrior was fearful to look upon and not to be trifled with. He ignored Oreon's sarcasm. "We are here on behalf of Jonathan."

"But you have no right to be here! All of you," he said, pointing to the legion of angels.

When the angels saw Oreon's hand rise in the air, they mistook it for an attack on their captain and rushed forward, weapons drawn.

Oreon's bloodshot eyes bulged twice their normal size.

"Hold!" commanded Rashti. The angels came to a reluctant stop.

Oreon's anxious eyes returned to normal. He pasted a phony smile of confidence on his face before Rashti turned to look him in the eye.

The legal challenge continued.

"I could say the same thing about you and your soldiers."

"But we have every right to be here. The people in this church have rejected your God, if not with their mouths, then with their lives. They sing praises to the Christ, but they live like the devil. Their hearts are filled with our desires. When they sin, they do not ask God for forgiveness in brokenness and contrition. They make excuses for their conduct and make a mockery of the contemptible blood of Christ."

Rashti stepped forward, bent down, and pressed his nose against the nose of Oreon. "Like you, we have a right to be here. You know as well as I do that according to the righteousness of God, the angelic host is released to work for the saints in direct proportion to their prayers." Rashti smiled. "And as you can see, Jonathan prays a lot."

*****

Edwin walked down the hall and placed his hand on the doorknob of the side entrance to the pulpit. Before he could open the door, a stabbing pain of realization shot into his gut like a bolt of lightning into an unlucky tree.

A terrible, sinking feeling brewed in his stomach until he thought his innards would drop to the floor. He opened the door and almost sank to the carpet. His eyes had to be playing a cruel trick on him.

He closed the door and hurried down the hall and into his office, happy that no one had seen him.

"What am I going to do?" he said. He fingered desperately through his hair. "That's why Bob acted the way he did. And Harry. Oh, Lord," he whined desperately.

Listen to him, he heard inwardly.

That Voice! That was the Voice Edwin had heard when he first came to Christ. It had told him that he would be used by God to do a very important work that would lead tens of thousands of people into the kingdom of God. He hadn't heard that Voice in years. He didn't know then, and he didn't know now, what this Voice meant. And after several years of Bible college, he no longer believed God directly communicated with anyone. He convinced himself that it was nothing.

He opened his office door and walked down the hall as though his last hope of a reprieve was lost and he was about to be fried in the electric chair.

Edwin opened the side door to the pulpit again. He saw the crowd and hoped his legs would carry his weight. He ascended the few stairs and sat the only place he could, next to Jonathan Banks.

Jonathan didn't see Edwin. His head was lowered between his legs in prayer.

Edwin looked at the ocean of faces. Many of them he had never seen before. The large number of visitors stole away the familiarity he normally felt with his congregation. Tonight he felt as though he was on exhibit. *Like an animal in the zoo,* he thought. His eyes fell on Harry Thompson. He quickly found another more friendly face in the crowd.

Time torturously stood still for Edwin and the other stone-faced deacons. It seemed like the service would never end. Actually, it was only just beginning, but to them every minute was an hour.

Finally, it was time for the introduction of the speaker. Jonathan was still enraptured in a prayer of spiritual ecstasy. The

Holy Spirit was filling him, infusing him, overwhelming him, revealing to him the needs of his audience.

An unearthly love rose up within him. A love that transcended the limitations of his humanity, a love that could only come from the very heart of God. It rose within him like a tide responding to the gravitational pull of celestial bodies. Unstoppable. Unbreachable. Irresistible.

Jonathan felt in his heart that the Spirit of God wanted to move...and quickly. He leaned over and tapped the assistant pastor on the hip. "I'm ready now."

Larry McGuire was befuddled. This was the first time someone had interrupted him in the middle of an introduction. He was basically being told to shut up and sit down. Not knowing what else to do, he shut his mouth, picked up the biography he was reading, and sat down.

Jonathan stood to his feet and surveyed the congregation. Over the years he had noticed a definite pattern to how God used him to minister to others.

Sometimes the Spirit of God came upon him as he earnestly looked upon the people. At times like these he felt as though God was inside of his body looking out through his eyes. He had often felt the Omnipotent One yearning to use his body as a vehicle to manifest His greatness, but most of all His love.

This was one of those times.

Jonathan undeniably sensed the craving of his Father to bless His children. "I have been sent here by God to introduce you to His essence and His ways. This is a night you will never forget."

*****

Oreon felt a nervous rush. He barked last minute instructions to his hyperactive demon soldiers. "Attack their minds with vehemence. Bombard them with foreign thoughts—holy or unholy—just so long as they are not allowed to think on his words. You religious spirits, rationalize his words. Explain away his message with human intellect and experience. Demons of racism, get busy!"

Rashti knew that this night of battle would be the flint that the God of heaven would use to spark a raging inferno of revival. He shouted out his own last minute instructions.

"Get the demons of doubt first. Then take care of those demons of religion. They cannot be allowed to complicate the glory of the Cross. Fight for the Lord and the sons of men!"

And the battle began.

Inside the church, angels and demons grappled in spiritual warfare. The combatants moved with lightning speed as they fought for strategic positions.Spirits of racism crisscrossed the sanctuary and spoke words of bigotry and prejudice into the ears of many in the pews.

Harry Thompson didn't know that directly in front of him, less than two feet away, was the demon that would eventually cause his death. Most demons were grotesque monsters of horrific ugliness. But the hungry demon that stood before Harry had a special, odd kind of ugliness. His ugliness set him apart from the others.

He didn't have the appearance of a man or monster, but a thing. His body was not a body, but many bodies. It appeared human and was meshed, connected, and hinged into one awkward creature. His color was that of every color of humanity. His features were as the features of every race and ethnic group in the world.

This thing entered Harry just as he said under his breath," I'm not going to be preached at by a black man."

Jonathan sensed the warfare all around him. "There is a tremendous battle raging here. It is a battle for the souls of men, women, and children. It is a battle for your souls. God has spoken to me and sent me here to deliver you from the hand of the devil."

Except for a few visitors, that statement did not go over well. If there really was a devil, who was he to accuse them of being under his power?

"God told me that you would not accept what I say unless He first demonstrated Himself. How many of you believe the Bible to be the Word of God?"

A few people raised their hands. Most simply answered with sighs or awkward silence.

"How many of you believe this verse?" He turned to the book of Acts. "And Stephen, full of faith and power, did great wonders and miracles among the people."

Edwin grabbed his butterfly-infested stomach when he heard that verse. The evening was going from bad to worse. He wanted so badly to stand up and take over the service before anything bizarre happened, but he couldn't. Neither could the assistant pastor or the deacons. Trin stood between them and Jonathan.

"Stephen was not an apostle, yet he performed great miracles. How is that possible? I'll tell you how. Jesus Christ did not limit Himself to the apostles to work His mighty acts of mercy and power. He made Himself available to all." His voice dropped and he got to the part he was itching for. "And he *makes* Himself available to all—to you."

"Think how you're going to look when your friends hear about your little charismatic miracle service," a demon laughed into Edwin's ear.

What are my friends going to say when they hear about this? A miracle service in my church! thought Edwin.

Jonathan searched the audience, ever sensitive to the prompting of the Holy Spirit. *Who is it?* he thought. He looked up and down the center aisles, where some sat in folding chairs.

Nothing.

He looked along the walls where many stood.

Nothing.

He looked at those seated in folding chairs in the back of the church.

Nothing.

"I love you, Jesus," he said softly. "Thank you for what you are going to do, Faithful God." He stood there waiting on the Lord. His eyes were upon the congregation, but he saw only the beauty of his Savior.

One minute passed.

The congregation was half disgusted by the unorthodoxy of this man; he was so unlike their pastor. Yet they were mesmerized by the powerful aura of spirituality that emanated from this strange man.

Two minutes passed.

Curiosity heightened. Something was going to happen.

Three minutes. Four minutes. Five minutes passed.

The congregation's curiosity was turning into restlessness. Some fidgeted in their seats. Some wondered out loud what in the world was going on.

Thirty minutes passed.

Trin knew what the Holy Spirit was doing. He sadly anticipated what would come next. Any moment now people would begin to leave the sanctuary. It would begin with one brave soul. Then others would follow. *Why are you Americans so impatient with God? Why do you require God to work within the boundaries of your shortsighted time limits? Do you not realize that the Lord of all creation yearns to answer your prayers? To break the yokes and chains of your oppression? To deliver and bless and exalt you above your highest expectations? No, you do not. Oh,* Trin groaned in his heart, *if you only knew how close you were to true liberty. If you only knew the secret of living on God's schedule instead of your own cursed schedule.*

"Hmp!" said a well-dressed lady as she stood to leave. "I'm not going to sit here all night like a bird on a perch." She didn't know that her whisper was loud enough for others to hear.

Someone followed her lead. Then another. A few more popped up and left. Now a steady trickle of people headed for the doors.

Edwin couldn't believe what was happening. He would be the laughingstock of the city. This man was destroying everything he had worked so hard to accomplish. Respectability. Acceptance. Praise. All were being lowered into the graveyard of ridicule. Each passing minute shoveled more dirt on his dead dreams.

Larry McGuire's eyes pleaded with the pastor. *Do something. Do something before it's too late. Make this idiot shut up.*

Edwin caught the look. He knew what Larry was thinking. *I want to do something. Oh, God, how I want to do something, but I can't. I can't move my hands or feet or any part of my body. I'm paralyzed all over. Everything is in slow motion. My mind.... I see everything that is going on around me, but I can't respond.* A long moment challenged Edwin's mental equilibrium. *Am I dying?*

Finally, the small exodus ended. The room was emptied of those judged unworthy by God to behold His glory. Thirty minutes of silence had passed since Jonathan had thanked God for what He was about to do. But now his eyes were fixed, anchored to a young child who was seated among the crowd at the altar, just below the podium. She was a darling. No older than four years old and the perfect picture of a child movie star. Her long, brown hair was decorated with curls that gave her a Shirley Temple look.

"Are you the child's mother?" Jonathan asked the lady seated next to the little girl.

The lady's mouth opened and her lips moved, but for a few seconds no words came out. She was caught off guard by Jonathan's sudden attention. "Yes...yes, I'm her mother." She hugged her child protectively.

Jonathan walked past the immobilized pastor and associate pastor without looking at them and descended the stairs. The bunched-up people made a path for him as he made his way to the little girl.

A surge of compassion rushed through Jonathan like a warm, soothing river. It flooded every inch of his being with heaven's love. He reached out and grasped the little girl's hand. When their hands touched, Jonathan felt as though he had stuck his soul into an electricity socket.

The love became almost physically unbearable. Jonathan's insides quaked as the undiluted compassion of Christ invaded his humanity with an intensity that shook him to the core.

In the back of his mind, he saw, or rather, perceived the cross of Calvary. There was Jesus, the Son of God, the Master of all creation, hanging on a tree. Huge nails pierced His hands and feet, exposing crushed bone. Blood ran down His arms to His torso. Jesus moved

His head from one side to the other. Agony was sculptured on His face.

A Roman soldier mocked, "This is the King of the Jews—hanging on a cross! Ha, ha, ha." His laughter ceased and a maniacal expression of demonic hatred replaced his look of derision. He lifted his spear and thrust it into the limp body on the tree.

I did it for you. I did it for you, Jonathan heard the Spirit of God say to his heart. *I gave my life for you...Sarah.*

"Honey, your name is Sarah, isn't it?" Jonathan asked.

The mother's mouth dropped. "Yes, her name is Sarah. But how did you know? We're not from this church. Nobody here knows us. We're not even from this state."

"That's okay. God knows who you are and where you live."

Jonathan hadn't noticed it before, but he did now. Behind the coke bottle glasses Sarah wore were a pair of badly crossed eyes. Apprehension wrapped itself around Jonathan. This would be a visible miracle. He had hoped that God would choose an internal malady to heal. A bad kidney, a malfunctioned heart, a blood disorder, or something of the sort. Yet, he knew all along that God wanted to do something visible.

It wasn't that Jonathan was opposed to outward manifestations of God; he wasn't. He loved them, and if he could've caused them any time he wanted, he would've caused them not only every day, but every second of every day. But he wasn't the cause, only the conduit, and he knew this all too well.

The problem was this was America. This was the land of mega-ministries, mega-personalities, and mega-egos. This was the land where God's servants were turned into men's heroes, and more often than not with the agreement of the servant.

Jonathan had long ago promised God and himself that he would never fall victim to the I'm-God's-man-of-the-hour syndrome. But he knew that the more God displayed Himself, the more people would display him.

Cursed flesh! he remonstrated inwardly. Why do God's people always help to destroy His servants with idolatrous praise and misdirected glory? *Oh, God, help me to remember that I am the clay and you are the Potter.*

Jonathan placed his hand on the little girl's forehead ever so lightly. "Jesus Christ heals you," he said softly, almost inaudibly.

Those seated around the girl didn't know what to think or expect. Most had no idea what was going on. Some in the back of the church stretched their necks to catch a glimpse of what the black preacher was doing to that little white girl.

"My God!" shrieked Sarah's mother, as she clutched her chest and looked at her child in disbelief.

Several people jumped out of their seats to see what the commotion was about. Some rudely pushed their way to the front.

"I can't see," said the little doll, squinting her eyes as she tried to focus.

"Of course you can't, sweetheart," said Jonathan. "You're wearing glasses you no longer need." He took her glasses off and picked her up. "Now you're more beautiful than ever."

Sarah's mother stared into her daughter's soft eyes and tenderly stroked her little face with trembling hands. "Baby...baby..." she managed to say, "you can see without your glasses." It was more a question than a statement.

Sarah beamed a toothy smile. "Jesus fixed my eyes."

The mother looked at Jonathan, then at her daughter. She put her face close to Sarah's. "You can—" Her hands shot into the air like a football fan celebrating a touchdown. "Thank you, Jesus! Oh, thank you, dear Lord!" She closed her eyes and jumped in the air and twirled unashamedly. "I never—oh, thank you! Oh, God!"

A demon of vainglory shouted into her ear. "The preacher healed your baby! The preacher healed your baby! You must thank him! Tell him how much you appreciate him!"

Suddenly the lady stopped praising God and began to praise Jonathan. "Thank you so much, so much for healing my little girl." She caught her breath and swallowed. "She's been—" she placed her hand on her chest, and then through tears of gratitude—"you healed my baby."

Jonathan smiled and hugged Sarah tighter. He felt a burden lift, not his own, but the mother's. He knew exactly how it felt to have a loved one healed, and he shared her joy.

However, he couldn't help but recoil inwardly in utter horror at her praise of him. Very softly he said, "Satan, I reject your praise."

The demon of vainglory trusted too much in his cohort's ability to protect his blind side. Humility felt the Holy Spirit shoot him like a projectile into the direction of the proud demon.

"Aaaagghhh," gurgled the demon, as Humility thrust a silver blade into his back. Vainglory's proud look contorted into an expression of surprised pain. He sank through the floor. Down. Down. Deeper and deeper to the Dark Prison to await the Judgment Day.

Again the lady directed her praise to Jesus. "Thank you, Lord, for healing my baby!"

Jonathan went up the stairs and took his place behind the podium. The congregation watched him with rapt attention. It was as though he would disappear if they took their eyes off of him. Some were awed. Some were puzzled. Most were dubious.

As far as most of them were concerned, this was one of those faith healing gimmicks. No one here knew the lady or her child, and who could say that this was not a stunt?

Jonathan slowly waved his hand. Almost every standing person in the church slumped to the floor in a Holy Ghost stupor. Some people panicked at the sight of so many bodies strewn on top of one another. Hesitantly, a small number of gawkers stood to their feet to get a better look.

"Sit down and be still," Jonathan politely, but firmly demanded. "God is not finished yet." He paused for a few seconds. "Look at me."

Almost no one did. They were focused on the people on the floor. "Look at me," he repeated a little louder.

This time everyone except a few obeyed. Not because they wanted to, but because they were awed by the strange powers of this man.

Jonathan looked squarely at a lady in the left section. She was seated about four rows back. Her attire was immaculate, very fashionable and expensive. A dotted mink stole hung on her shoulder. The jewelry she wore could have financed a soup kitchen for a year. Her cold, stern expression contrasted her external fineries.

"Ma'am, the Lord Jesus Christ would like to serve you."

People began looking around. Some hoped that he was speaking to them. Others in the area hoped that he was speaking to someone else.

The lady looked straight at Jonathan with that frigid face of tight muscles. She was still. Defiantly still.

"No, no, the other lady. The one...yes, her," he pointed.

She did not respond.

"He's talking to you," someone offered.

No answer. No response. No movement. She had not even blinked since he had first spoken to her.

Carol.

Thank you, Holy Spirit. "Carol," Jonathan implored.

She blinked.

"Carol, Jesus Christ wants to become real to you. He knows of your dilemma, and He has heard your prayers." Jonathan spoke as though he was trying to talk a jumper from a suicide ledge. "Will you let Him take care of you?"

The granite lady felt herself softening, but she resisted the strange warm feeling that slowly enveloped her. *Leave me alone. I don't want His help...He would never help me anyway.*

"You feel that you are beyond God's help. And even if He could, He wouldn't. Isn't this true?"

The hardness left her face. *I've done so much wrong.*

"It doesn't matter how much you've sinned; God loves you."

There was a definite softness in her face now. *What do I do?* She thought. *How do I—? I don't know how to do what You're asking. I don't even know what You're asking.*

"You must confess with your mouth that you are a sinner and believe in your heart that Jesus Christ lives. You must turn from your wickedness and walk humbly before Your Lord," said Jonathan.

I'm not strong enough, she thought.

"God will be your Strength," Jonathan offered.

The mental battle was over. God had won. Carol Lockhart did something that she hadn't done in two years. She lowered her head in her lap and cried. The reservoir of pain and abuse was finally draining.

Normally Jonathan would have spoken to the lady privately, but God wanted to deal with this woman openly. "You are hard and resentful. It's because you've suffered so much. You can't give love because you've never received love. You're afraid to trust because you've been bruised. Your marriage is in shambles. Your son is into Satanism. And your business is virtually bankrupt. On top of all of this, the doctor told you today that you have only six months to live. Carol."

She looked up at her rescuer.

"Your marriage is healed. In three days you will receive the largest order your company has ever had. And, Carol...the cancer is gone."

"Jesus, save me!" Carol yelled. "Oh, God, I'm Yours if you'll have me!"

The next several minutes were punctuated with outbursts of praises from this once stoic lady. Some cried with her and shared in her joy. Others wished she would behave in a more dignified manner. Church wasn't the place to show such emotions.

Jonathan now turned his attention to the others. He looked at them with a mixture of disgust and tender love. "I told you that God sent me here to introduce you to His essence and His ways."

The audience was attentive now.

"God is holy. He hates sin. Yet you play with it as though it's a toy. You are like the graves Jesus spoke of. On the outside you appear clean and wholesome, but on the inside you are full of death."

He had taken them to the heights of the heavens. Now they were being made to explore the depths of hell.

"Jesus shed His precious blood that you might live free of Satan's power, but you would rather feed upon the pleasures of poisonous sins than to live a life acceptable unto God." Jonathan stretched out his arms and surveyed the sanctuary. "Such a lovely building," he paused, "for such a rebellious people. Behind your religious facade and choreographed piety are hearts full of envy and strife, gossip and maliciousness, lies and hypocrisy," he turned and looked Larry McGuire, the associate pastor, squarely in the eyes, "lust and adultery."

Larry was still in a semi-trance, along with Edwin and the deacons. But the threat of exposure didn't stop him from almost trembling out of his shoes.

Jonathan turned back to the audience. "God is claiming Atlanta for Himself, and He is beginning with this church. You can ride the crest of God's mighty wave of revival, or you can resist it and be swept into the torments of everlasting hell!"

Chapter 4

Harry Thompson and the others sat stone-faced and silent. The others were Edwin Styles, Larry McGuire, Henry Jennings, Carl Briarwood, Scott Bridges, and Terrance Knox. This was another of Harry's get-over-here-right-now meetings. He liked to have the church business meetings at his oversized home. The place unabashedly reaffirmed his enormous ego and reminded his guests that he was an important man. At least he liked to think that he was important.

Harry controlled the church because he controlled these men. Edwin was at the mercy of the deacon board, and the board belonged to Harry. Larry's adulterous affairs had long been known to Harry, and he never hesitated to remind the wayward minister. Henry was engaged to Harry's daughter. Carl's plumbing business received a good portion of its contracts from Harry and his contacts. Scott was Harry's nephew. And Terrance was just a cantankerous old man who Harry was content to let stay on the board until the old man died. That couldn't be too far off.

Edwin, Larry, and the four deacons sat in silent subservience. They were like school children awaiting the principal's paddle.

Finally, Larry broke the awkward silence. "How's the home business?"

Everyone shrunk at this out of place question.

The demon inside of Harry was furious for the events of the night before. "We didn't come here to talk about Harry's, err, my business." The words were gurgled, as though something was stuck in Harry's throat. "We came here to talk about what happened last night."

He was the only one who wanted to talk about last night. The others would gladly have put all memories of that horrid evening in the basement of oblivion. But as much as they would have liked to have forgotten, they knew that if they ignored last night's fire it would eventually burn down their tranquil religious structure.

"How did this dagger gain entrance to our church?"

Bewildered expressions hopped from face to face.

"Jonathan! How did Jonathan get in our church?" he corrected himself.

Almost all eyes went to Edwin.

"Ohhhh, no. I'm not taking the blame for this. This was cleared by you." He pointed to Harry.

"Me?" The demon was incensed beyond his own intelligence. "You idiot! Do you think I would authorize a man of God to speak in our church?"

Edwin didn't know what to say. Neither did the others. Harry seemed beside himself. His words didn't make any sense.

"Do you think I would let a servant of Christ disrupt our peace and bring spiritual anarchy to our church?"

Edwin didn't answer.

"Do you!?" he yelled.

Edwin was thoroughly unnerved now. "Terrance said you okayed it," he cowered.

Harry spun on his heels. "Is this true? Did you use my name to further your own warped plan?"

"Nope."

"You most certainly did!" Edwin defended.

"Nope, I did not."

The demon in Harry peered at the old man. There was something strange about him. Something foreign.

"You approached me about this Jonathan guy and said that Harry approved," Edwin recounted.

"No, I told you the boss approved."

"That's what I said. When I asked you if Har—"

"Shut up!" demanded the spirit that had invaded Harry.

Edwin was used to being manipulated by Harry, but he was finding it hard to swallow his new brashness. He looked at Harry with a touch of defiance and reluctantly closed his mouth.

"Yes. That's what you are—one of His," the spirit said.

"One of his?" someone asked.

"You're of the Enemy. He's put one in my own backyard!"

"What are you talking about Harry?" asked Carl. "What enemy?"

"Yeah, what enemy?" his nephew Scott wanted to know.

Harry flicked his wrist in disgust at the old man. "Let Terrance tell you."

All eyes were upon the old deacon. Finally, they'd find out why Harry was speaking so crazily.

If Terrance was afraid or nervous it didn't show. Actually, he was more calm and confident in the midst of this storm than he'd ever been in his life. It could've been because of the Scripture that was insulating his heart from the roar of fear.

And when they bring you unto the synagogues, and unto magistrates, and powers, take ye no thought how or what thing ye shall answer, or what ye shall say. For the Holy Ghost shall teach you in the same hour what ye ought to say.

Or it could've been because an angel named Peace had both of his hands on the old man's shoulders.

Both of these reasons played their part in giving the deacon his inner strength. But the main reason that Terrance was strong now was because he knew he was right. He knew that Jesus was pleased with him, and that He was smiling upon His servant. In this, he was right.

"I will tell them, Satan." Terrance was surprised at his own words.

"Now wait just a doggone minute, Mr. Knox. You can't talk to my uncle like that." Scott was incensed.

The deacon ignored the young man.

"I've been a hypocrite for as far back as I can remember, and I've got a pretty good memory. Always doing what others wanted me to do, even when I knew it was wrong. I never had the backbone to stand up for what's right. Whichever direction the wind blew," the old man theatrically blew a long breath and waved his weathered hand, "that's the direction I went. And none of you are any better. Our hands are bloody with the blood of God's people. And you," he pointed to Edwin, "you're in big trouble."

"Me?" Edwin asked incredulously. "I didn't do anything."

"You're absolutely right. You haven't done anything. That's why you're in trouble. You're as weak and spineless as I am. I doubt that I've ever heard you preach one single solitary sermon on holy living or the consequences of breaking God's law. You'd rather protect your salary and pension than rescue that bunch of intellectual heathen from the fires of hell."

"Now wait just a dang minute, Terry. That's enough!" Carl was incensed.

Terrance could literally feel the presence of God inside of him. He felt so full of God, like a balloon that was blown to full capacity. "No, that's not enough. Carl, what have you ever done for God? What have you ever done for His Christ?"

"What do you mean, what have I done? You know just as well as I do what I've done. I'm a deacon." He was satisfied with his answer.

But Terrance wasn't. "You're about as much a deacon as I am Babe Ruth. Do you know what you are? You're a farce. A phony, just like me."

"Speak for yourself," Carl retorted.

"I'm speaking for all of us because we're all guilty. Those people need someone to stand up and proclaim the Word of God to them without fear and without compromise." He paused, then continued his punishing confession. "That's why God sent Jonathan. He knew that neither Edwin nor Larry," Larry shuddered when he heard his name mentioned, "could be depended upon to preach the truth."

Larry dared not give a reply.

"Are you finished?" Harry asked contemptuously.

"Not as finished as you are." The old deacon got to his feet and smiled. "And one other thing. There will be revival. Starting with our church."

"Over my dead body!" Harry challenged.

*****

Bashnar's red eyes looked like openings to a volcano. His black cratered face was more hideous than ever. "You want to explain to me how you allowed the dagger to wreck our church?"

Oreon's knees could've started a fire they knocked together so badly. He swallowed hard and searched desperately for an explanation that would save him from Bashnar's wrath. "Mighty one," the condemned demon began, "the angels of God were there in great numbers. Rashti was their leader."

This touched a nerve. "Rashti was there?"

"Yes," he answered with a flicker of hope.

Bashnar's keen mind recalled, analyzed, and deciphered millions of bits of information about his opposite. He knew that the demon standing before him was no match for Rashti. A hundred demons like Oreon were no match for the angel they called the Sword of the Lord. *They never had a chance,* Bashnar mused.

Bashnar was feeling philosophical. He decided to lecture the unfortunate demon before he did what he had to do. "Rashti was there with Noah. He was with Melchizedek and Hezekiah...and David. He was with Elijah and Elisha. Does that tell you anything?"

The demon didn't have an answer, but he opened his mouth and hoped something intelligent would come out. However, Bashnar cut him off before he could begin his filibuster.

"Of course not." Bashnar pushed his chair back from his desk and stood up. "It tells you absolutely nothing. But it tells me that the God of heaven plans to take not only Atlanta, but possibly the entire state of Georgia. Maybe even the entire South." Bashnar's voice took on a lyrical tone as he stuck his defiant fist in the air at his Enemy. "Maybe the Lord God of heaven and earth seeks a confrontation!" His eyes dropped back to Oreon. "Yes, Oreon, that deceiver wants a confrontation, and He is going to get a confrontation."

Oreon was silent. He knew he shouldn't be. His silence only made him look worse. He wanted to say something that would win Bashnar's favor. Something to show that he shared his defiance of heaven. But caution kept his lips sealed for fear that he would say the wrong thing.

"What were your orders, Oreon?" Bashnar knew what his orders were, but he wanted this failure's condemnation to come out of his own mouth.

"My orders, Mighty Bashnar, were to neutralize the Wednesday evening church service at all costs."

"How many soldiers were under your command?"

"Ten thousand, sir, but—"

"Ten thousand demons and you failed."

Oreon noticed that Bashnar's voice had dropped dangerously low. Time was running out. "Mighty Bashnar," he hurried, "I did not have ten thousand. I mean—"

"Enough!" This time Bashnar didn't whisper. His red eyes turned a deep black. "I personally signed the authorization for ten—"

"But they were reassigned, sir," Oreon interrupted, and only because his neck was on the chopping block.

"Reassigned?" he yelled.

The shaking in Oreon's knees turned into a quaking of his whole vile body. His teeth chattered so much that it was almost impossible to get the words out. This display of dread both disgusted and pleased his interrogator. The Mighty Bashnar was a dauntless fighter who had never tasted the wine of fear, and he absolutely abhorred anyone with its smell on his breath. Yet there was something orgasmically intoxicating to his sadistic nature to be able to rape Oreon of his courage.

"Yes, Mighty Bashnar. A courier brought me a message that countermanded your orders."

"Countermanded my orders? Who would dare countermand my orders! My authority was granted by the Council of Strategic Affairs."

"Mighty Bashnar, just moments before the battle began, the courier gave me written orders signed by Prince Krioni himself. The orders directed more than two-thirds of our warrior demons to immediately report to Seoul, Korea to stop the relentless attack of Pastor Woo. That left me with less than one thousand warrior demons and the standard contingent of harassing demons for a job of this magnitude."

Bashnar stopped listening when he heard the name Krioni. *Chairman or not, he had no right to jeopardize the success of this operation,* he fumed to himself. *Bureaucratic idiot! Armchair tactician! What could be so important to justify a last minute change in battle plans?*

This battle was pivotal. How could he be expected to stop this revival if he had to listen to bureaucrats who were going to fight this thing the way the Americans had fought the Vietnam war? How he hated Krioni!

"Oreon," Bashnar beckoned.

"Yes, Mighty Bashnar?"

"You never stood a chance."

Oreon felt his respiratory system begin to work again. Was there hope after all? Could it be that this master of cruelty understood the impossible odds he had fought against the night before?

"We fought valiantly."

"I'm sure you did." There was a long, awkward pause. "I cannot hold you responsible for something you could not change."

Oreon breathed a sigh of relief and silently thanked the god of darkness for granting him mercy.

Bashnar's eyes returned to their normal fire red color. He twisted his ugly face into what Oreon recognized as a smile. "We are all in this together. You are not responsible for the actions of others."

Oreon could barely believe his leathery, pointed ears. He bowed his head in gratitude. "Thank you, Mighty Bashnar."

When he lifted his head, Bashnar snatched him by the throat with one hand and with the other he grabbed a handful of chest and slammed him against the wall. Bashnar's strong, hairy arms pinned the shocked demon above the floor. Oreon's frightened eyes strained to leave their sockets.

"You are not responsible for the actions of others, but you are responsible for your own." Bashnar's words squeezed through his clenched teeth. "No doubt you were as unprepared last night for the unexpected as you are my discipline today. Do you think it was a coincidence that the Christians in Seoul, Korea broke out in spontaneous prayer? You and that kindergarten tactician, Krioni, can't see two feet in front of you. That was a diversion to strain our forces. But you couldn't see that, could you?"

Oreon tried to answer, but Bashnar's iron grip was suffocatingly tight around his neck. All he could do was dangle his legs and vainly pull on Bashnar's powerful arms.

"You have disappointed the Mighty Bashnar, and now you will pay for your failure." He stretched his thick fingers and razor sharp claws came up from under the hair. "Look at my claws, Oreon. They are sharp. Lethal weapons indeed. But today they will not be used for war, but for discipline...and pleasure."

Oreon's legs danced desperately in the air.

"We're going to play a game. I'm going to carve you until I get tired, and when there is nothing left to carve, the game is over."

“Please, Mighty Bashnar, it was not my fault.” Oreon pushed the words out of his mouth. “There was nothing I cou—”

Bashnar began to play.

*****

Rashti and his most able guardian angel, Trin, exulted in their impressive victory. But like most victories, they were but preludes to the next battle. They knew that the forces of hell would mobilize all their fury against Jonathan, and that if he was not fully prepared to withstand the coming attack, he would join the ranks of King Uzziah. He had been a mighty conqueror for the Lord, who at his zenith was mightily conquered by the devil. It was one of heaven’s greatest failures.

They went down the character development list.

"Love?" began Rashti.

"Check."

"Joy?"

"Check."

"Peace?"

"Check."

They covered several other traits. All were good.

Rashti didn't doubt Trin's judgment, but it was highly unusual for a Christian to grade so well.

Trin detected Rashti's caution. "I don't blame you one bit. If I had not personally studied this man for myself, I would not believe it."

That was enough for Rashti. If Trin believed it, he believed it. "How about his immediate family?"

Rashti was afraid that maybe Jonathan had fallen prey to one of Satan's most lethal impulses. Satan, often with great success, encouraged God's ministers to neglect their families for the cause of Christ. What the duped ministers didn't realize was that God required them to take care of home first.

Trin answered happily. "She is the treasure of his heart. He allows nothing to come between him and his wife. Not even religion. He also allows nothing to come between him and God. Not even his wife. He's no Adam."

"Excellent!" Rashti was catching Trin's happy mood. "And his finances?"

"No problem there. He's very conscientious."

Rashti's exuberant mood lowered. "Jonathan has opened many doors for us through his prayers, but," he prayed that the answer would be positive, "can he be depended upon? Is he a consistent prayer warrior?"

This was a valid concern. Most American Christians were terribly inconsistent with their prayers. How many battles had gone amiss because even the Holy Ghost could not tear His people away from their televisions?

"Jonathan prays more than two hours every day. He allows nothing to distract him from his prayer time. Chores, telephone calls, visits...nothing. We can depend on him."

Rashti could hardly believe his ears. Could it be that they had actually found a man who took the Bible seriously? Rashti's combat mentality involuntarily went into overdrive. What exploits could be done for the kingdom of God! But he made himself calm down. *There must be something we've overlooked,* he thought. "Trin, hand me his case file."

He handed it to him.

Rashti studied every detail, every event of this man's exemplary life. There was nothing. He closed the book and paced back and forth a few times. *Think like the devil.* Several more minutes of deep contemplation. *Of course!* He opened the book and raced to a particular page. "Here!"

Trin looked at where Rashti's finger pointed. "Yes...yes, I see it. Captain, you're brilliant!"

"Not really. The devil doesn't have any new tricks. It's the same old game. If he can't exploit your weakness, he'll exploit your strength." The captain's face turned ominously sober. "Jonathan is in great danger."

Chapter Five

Edwin's mind spun as he drove up to his garage. He stopped the car and rested his pounding head on the steering wheel. He needed a few moments to relax and gather his thoughts before he entered the house. Edwin knew that he had a lot of questions to answer, and no answers.

Tap. Tap. Tap.

Someone interrupted his fleeting reprieve.

It was Sharon. She was beaming.

“Daddy! Daddy!" she bounced in hyper-animation, "Come in. Everybody's waiting on you."

Edwin raised his troubled head and looked into the radiant face of the only person he knew whose kindness and love toward him was constant. Oh, he knew that Barbara loved him. Truly, she did, deep down inside. But sometimes it seemed that her love for him was controlled by either her mood or his performance—or lack of it. It was a love that only heightened his insecurity.

Yet, like an oasis of love in Edwin's lonely desert, Sharon's selflessness and giving nature provided his parched soul with living waters that never dried. Somehow, now, just looking at her had an anesthetic effect on his headache. The slow waves of pain subsided to tolerable ripples. He felt a slight breeze of refreshment in his mind. *Thank you, Sharon. Thank you so much!*

He got out of the car and Sharon took him by the hand and hurried him to the open door.

"Daddy, we've been waiting on you." Her words were rushed, excited. "I could hardly wait to get home from school to talk to you."

As Edwin neared the door, he could hear the sound of several voices, all going at once. When he entered the room and saw how many people there were in his living room, the ripples of pain left and the waves returned. He massaged his left temple.

Sharon couldn't wait to hear her father's explanation of what had happened the night before. "Here he is everybody!"

Edwin entered the room with about as much enthusiasm as a deer entering a den of lions. He really didn't feel up to enduring another question and answer session. Harry's prolonged interrogation was enough. *Okay, who is going to take a bite out of me first?* he thought.

"Reverend, we want some answers," came a forthright demand from a man in a dark suit. He wore a pair of clear designer glasses. They seemed out of place on his fifty-plus face.

It figures it would be you to draw first blood, thought Edwin.

Wallace Reynolds was a businessman who knew only one direction. Straight ahead.

"Yes, we're appalled at that man's conduct, and at you for allowing such a blasphemous display of ridiculous antics in our church." His wife, Marjorie, was a successful commercial real estate agent who was never at a loss for words.

"That a girl, Marge," one of Bashnar's demons laughed. "It appalls me, too," he said, as he gave her a doggie's pat on the head.

Edwin sat down. "I believe there are some of you here I haven't met before," he said, with his best pastor's smile, ignoring King and Queen Reynolds.

He was referring to a young couple, perhaps in their late twenties or early thirties. The man had a full head of curly, brown hair. He wore circular, wire-rimmed glasses that gave him the appearance of a 60's hippie from Berkeley, California. The lady with him was plain-looking, with a bright smile. Edwin noticed that she had exceptionally white teeth.

"Hi. I'm Adam Chriswell, and this is my wife, Sherry."

"Are you—?" began Edwin.

Adam anticipated the question. "Yes, we're members. We've attended now...." He looked at his wife.

"Next Sunday will be exactly one year," she helped.

Edwin blushed, ashamed that he didn't know his flock better. "I'm very glad to...." *What do I say? Meet you? No, that's not appropriate. I met them when they joined the church.*

"Reverend Styles, we don't expect you to remember every face," Adam chuckled. "We're only two of several hundred people."

His disposition was sincere and congenial. Edwin appreciated that, especially now. "Thank you for understanding. Tell me, what can I do for you?" Edwin was attracted to this couple's warmth.

"We're friends of Jessica," said Adam. We told her what happened last night, and she offered to introduce us to you."

Edwin hadn't noticed her until Adam mentioned her name. Her face was obscured by a plant.

"Hi, Ed."

A cloudburst on a summer picnic.

"Hello, Jessica." His voice was noticeably strained.

Whatever warmth Edwin had found in Adam and Sherry Chriswell left as soon as he saw his kooky, charismatic sister-in-law. The two could not occupy the same room without getting into a theological sparring match. She was so spaced-out and subjective in her interpretations of the Bible. Edwin simply couldn't stand her.

Well, Miss high and mighty, what new revelation have you acquired from your CD library? I must be very tired, he thought, when he heard his uncharacteristic sarcasm.

"Hey, let's get on with this," said Billy Mitchell in an irritated tone.

He and his wife, Karen, frequently contributed significant sums of money to the church, and because of this they felt they should have a say in how the church should be run. Their suggestions usually met with no opposition.

"Get on with what?" Sharon was alarmed that everyone sounded so angry with her father. She had thought that her father's visitors were as happy about last night as she was. Obviously she was wrong.

"This doesn't concern you, sweetheart," said Wallace Reynolds, the businessman.

"It most certainly does, Mr. Reynolds," Sharon answered respectfully. "This is my father he is talking to."

Edwin smiled slightly. *That's Sharon. Always quick to support her father,* he thought.

Billy Mitchell ignored the sassy teenager. "Edwin, what's the meaning of bringing in a speaker without going through the proper channels? That man spoke heretical things last night. I doubt that the church will ever recover from the terrible things he said about us." He looked at the others for moral support. There were nods of approval.

"I didn't bring him in," Edwin retreated.

"What do you mean you didn't bring him in? Did he just walk in off the street?" That was Marjorie Reynolds.

Edwin gave her a tired look. "No, he didn't walk in off the street. He was invited."

"Invited by whom?" demanded Wallace Reynolds.

"By Terrance Knox."

"That's absurd," said Billy Mitchell. "Terry wouldn't invite a—" he was going to say a black man, but he reworded it so that it wouldn't sound so bigoted"—someone like that."

She cried, "What a terrible thing to say about Terry," exclaimed Marjorie.

"It's the truth," Edwin stated listlessly.

Sharon was puzzled by her father's lackluster defense.

His temperament was basically non-confrontational. She knew that he hated to upset anyone. But surely he would not let these people trample upon something so good, so right, so... holy.

But Sharon was wrong. She didn't know it, but she and her father had very different perspectives of what had happened the night before. Sharon felt that Jesus Christ had visited His people in an unusual, but scriptural way. Never before had she witnessed such manifest power and glory. Never before had she beheld the goodness of God the way she saw it last night!

It was as though God Himself was in that church. And the people who were helped—the little girl, and that lady.... Last night had opened a door of reality that Sharon had never known existed. After she had seen God's glory manifested in such a real and powerful way, she knew that she would never again be satisfied with spiritual mediocrity. She would have none of God or all of God, but nothing less.

However, Edwin had seen things differently. Jesus Christ was in heaven and people were on Earth, and there was no spectacular interaction between the two. The Bible was the most blessed, but most abused book in the entire world. It had been used in the Old South to justify slavery. It had been quoted by bloodthirsty Popes during the Dark Ages to justify their lust for blood. And the last few decades had seen many religious groups—Pentecostals, Charismatics, Holiness, and other spurious groups—use the Bible to justify damnable heresies, such as miracles, healings, and tongues. Last night, Edwin surmised, was an attempt by the devil—if there really was a devil—to infiltrate his church with false doctrines.

"Why is everyone so bent out of shape? I mean, wow, man, people were helped."

Billy Mitchell and his wife and Wallace and Marjorie Reynolds turned in almost perfect unison. They stared at Adam as though he had just stepped off of a Martian spaceship.

"I beg your pardon!" said Marjorie.

Adam was unruffled. "I mean you guys act like the guy did something wrong. It seems to me that you ought to be happy that people were touched."

Marjorie looked at the man's battered jeans and holey Georgia Tech sweatshirt with disgust. *They are not the only ones that are touched,* she thought. "He did do something wrong."

"What?" asked Sharon.

"He insulted us!" answered Marjorie.

"That's just what Timothy says," said Sharon.

Marjorie frowned her face. "What? Timothy? Who's he?"

"His letter says, 'For the time will come when they will not endure sound doctrine; but after their own lusts shall they heap to themselves teachers, having itching ears; and they shall turn away their ears from the truth, and shall be turned unto fables.'"

Marjorie wasn't sure, but this sounded like something that could be from the Bible. "Who are you, young lady, to judge me?" she challenged Sharon.

"Okay, this is getting out of hand," Edwin said.

"Getting out of hand? It got out of hand when you let that false prophet speak in our church!" This was Billy Mitchell again.

"I told you I didn't invite him."

"False prophet?" Adam asked incredulously. "I didn't hear him say anything that was false."

Wallace, Marjorie, and Billy launched verbal tirades, but Marjorie's voice rose above the rest. "He called us hypocrites and liars!"

"I don't mean to offend anyone," said Adam, "but if you claim to be something you aren't, well..." He hesitated. *Oh, go ahead. What've you got to lose?* he thought. "That would make you a hypocrite and a liar."

Marjorie was shocked that a dusty vagabond would call her such terrible names. For the first time in a very long time she was at a loss for words.

Edwin filled the vacuum. "We are getting a little bit too emotional here." He looked at Marjorie. "I'm sure Adam wasn't calling you a hypocrite, were you?" he asked, sure that the man would reword his statement.

An angel of truth descended through the ceiling with a golden tray in his hands. On it were two smooth stones that glowed with the fire of God. The angel held the tray with one hand and with the other he used a pair of golden, jewel-embroidered tongs to pick up one of the fiery stones. He placed one on Adam's tongue. There was a singeing sound, like a piece of meat frying. Dark smoke came from his mouth and rose to the ceiling, carrying with it a suffocating stench. The angel smiled and repeated the process with Adam's wife.

On the other side of the room, the demons that hovered over Marjorie and her crew watched the cleansing with jealous fury. But that was all they could do.

Adam felt a rush in his head that rivaled memories of his greatest cocaine high. But this rush was different. It didn't pervert his senses; it enhanced them. He felt an invasion of deity, a clarity of thought he had never experienced before.

“Christianity is not a religion of carnal excesses and unbridled debauchery. It is not a religion of convenience to be used to justify your sinful passions Monday through Saturday and to appease your guilty consciences on Sunday. We are told in the book of 1 John that those who live in and enjoy sin do so for one reason: they are sons and daughters of Satan."

There were gasps in the room.

His wife, who had been silent up to this point, now took up where her husband ended. She felt the same energizing sensations in her head. "We have attended this church for almost a year now, and I must admit that it is the deadest church I've ever been in."

"Glory!" howled Jessica, Edwin's sister-in-law.

Edwin lowered his head in embarrassment and rested his forehead in his hand.

Sharon watched his resignation in disbelief. *Why don't you do something? Take a stand for Jesus. You're the pastor*! she thought.

Adam's wife continued. "Thus saith the Lord, He who knows the secrets of our hearts, I know your works, that you are neither cold nor hot: I wish you were cold or hot. So then because you are lukewarm, and neither cold nor hot, I will vomit you out of my mouth. Because you say, I am rich, and prosperous, and have need of nothing; and do not know that you are wretched, and miserable, and poor, and blind, and naked—"

Edwin's head snapped up in alarm. *My God, she's prophesying!* "Wait a darned minute," he interrupted. "We are not going to have any of that stuff in here!"

"Any of what stuff, Daddy?"

"Prophesying, that's what."

Sharon had no idea what prophesying was, but if it was what that lady had said, she didn't see anything wrong with it.

"And what's wrong with prophesying," asked Adam.

"It's of the devil," answered Barbara.

Edwin looked at his wife, surprised that she would enter the fracas. She usually confined her superficial interest of spiritual matters to Sunday mornings.

She looked at him. "I overheard you tell someone on the telephone that prophesying and tongues are of the devil."

"Look, what are we going to do about last night?" Billy Mitchell tried to get them back on the subject.

"Do what the preacher said: repent." When Sharon received incredulous looks, she added, "What's so wrong with obeying Jesus? We're Christians, aren't we?"

"Of course we are, dear," answered Barbara confidently.

Adam took his wife by the hand and they both stood up. "There really is no need to prolong this meeting. All of you have already made up your minds to resist God. I hope—"

Marjorie found her tongue. "That wasn't God. That was...witchcraft or something."

"I think it was Something," Adam said, smiling, as he and his wife walked toward the door.

Sherry turned and faced the group for one final word. "I never did tell you why we chose to become members of this country club." There was no cynicism in her voice, only disappointment. "The Lord instructed us to affiliate with the church so that we could pray for revival."

Oh, no, thought Edwin.

"Of course, we could have prayed for the church without becoming members, but that would have been like praying for those Christians being persecuted by ISIS. Unless you are there with them, you can't really feel the sense of urgency." There was a determination in her voice as she said, "The Lord sent us here to pray for revival, and there will be revival."

Adam, Sherry, and Jessica left.

Edwin watched Adam and Sherry leave with mixed emotions. Although they were spiritually misguided and had said some rather hard things about his church, they didn't do it in a self-righteous or judgmental way. Strangely, he felt an affinity with these people.

Jessica Lyons was a different story. She was the personification of self-righteousness and judgmentalism. It was virtually impossible to reason with her. Her mind was closed to everything except the teachings of her favorite prosperity preachers, whom she followed robotically. Edwin felt something between euphoria and ecstasy when the door closed behind her.

The lone dissenting voice now was Sharon.

The meeting continued.

"Harry's seen this kind of thing before," Edwin told the group. "He said that these faith healers use creative gimmicks to give the appearance that they have some kind of special power."

"And what about the people who were healed?" Sharon asked.

"What people?" asked Edwin.

Sharon couldn't believe her father's blindness. "What people? Dad, you saw Jesus heal that little girl and that lady with cancer."

"Harry said they sometimes plant people in the audience with fake illnesses. They pray for them. They are healed. And the offerings roll in."

Wallace chuckled at that. He could appreciate a good marketing plan.

"But, Daddy, that little girl wasn't sick; she had crossed eyes. I saw them go back to normal."

"Honey," Edwin said tenderly, "have you ever seen that little girl before?"

Sharon was reluctant to answer. She knew where this question was going. "No," she answered softly.

"So how do you know she was ever really in need of healing?"

That question took the wind out of Sharon's sail. Her momentum of faith came to a slow halt. "I don't know," she answered weakly.

Edwin was getting ready to say something when Sharon spoke up again. He let out a deep breath. His embarrassment was noticeable.

Sharon saw it, but she didn't let it deter her. "How do you explain all of those people falling to the floor as the preacher waved his hand over them?"

Everyone looked at Edwin, hoping he had a good explanation.

"Harry said that we witnessed mass hypnosis last night."

"Mass hypnosis?" Sharon asked incredulously. She didn't want to hear what her father would say next. She knew that no matter how ridiculous his explanation was, it would put doubts in her mind about the most wonderful display of God's love and power she had ever seen.

"Did you notice that the only people who fell to the floor were those who stood against the wall?"

"I don't see what that has to do with anything."

"Don't you see, honey? That was the reason he waited almost twenty minutes before he waved his hand. Those people had stood there for quite a while. They fell not because of some mystical power, but because they were tired."

The answer was obviously weak, contrived, a desperate and elaborate excuse. Edwin knew it. The Mitchells knew it. The Reynolds knew it. Barbara didn't care. Yet it was the only excuse they had, so they went with it.

Sharon knew that her father's explanation was weak, but it still caused unwanted doubts in her mind. She was hurt and betrayed by her father's unbelief. The man who was supposed to lead her into spiritual lands of plenty was instead forcing her into dry lands of spiritual famine. He was robbing her of the most wonderful night of her life. *How could you steal my faith? How could you destroy something so beautiful?* The thoughts came from deep within her heart. They rolled around in her subconscious mind like the spiked wheels of a farmer's machine, poking holes in her faith in God.

A tiny demon that resembled a five-pound fly flew around Sharon's head and whispered something into her ear.

I hate you, Father.

Sharon shuddered when she heard the thought. This was the first time she had ever had such a terrible thought about her father. It repulsed her.

The demon in charge of those assigned to monitor the meeting was incensed at the smaller demon's failure. He smacked him across the room.

"You idiot!" he thundered. "You spoke too loud. How do you expect to plant a seed of hate if you announce your arrival? Get out of here!"

Something else was whispered into Sharon's ear, but this time by an angel.

But what about the words he spoke?

"But what about the words he spoke," she asked, with renewed vigor.

Edwin was getting angry now. His own daughter was grilling him. "Sharon, we can talk about that later."

"We need to talk about it now." Sharon was insistent.

"It's late." Edwin's voice had a slight cutting edge to it.

The angel whispered something else into her ear. "It's later than you think, Dad."

Edwin was astonished at his daughter's behavior. She had never before defied him. "Sharon, what's come over you? Why are you doing this?"

Sharon looked at her father with sad eyes. Disillusionment filled her heart as she saw the transparency of her father's religion. She felt something for her father leave her heart. Was it love? Respect? She didn't know, but she feared that it was a little of both.

"That's what I'd like to ask you," said Sharon and left the room.

One hour later the last of the guests were gone. *Good!* Barbara gave Edwin a pat on the behind and an inviting look.

The turtle-like demon that had sat upon Edwin's shoulders for years fidgeted with excitement. It was time.

Chapter 6

When Edwin saw the desirous look in his wife's eyes, that's when he struck. The demon lifted his small hands into the air and screamed in rabid anticipation of what would come next.

He smashed his open hands down onto Edwin's head and massaged furiously. His uneven three eyes rolled in his head in a devilish ecstasy of evil. Yellow slime oozed from the open suctions in his hands. Some dripped down the sides of Edwin's face.

Haunting thoughts of inadequacy ripped Edwin's mental equilibrium to a million shreds. The thoughts were like projectiles of lethal fear that threatened the core of his masculinity.

The demon was in a frenzy now. His crusty head rocked back and forth like a creature experiencing the heights of hallucinogenic rapture. Every squeeze of his hands sent irresistible waves of guilt into Edwin's mind. Edwin was like a desperate animal cornered by a hunter. There was no way of escape.

Leave me alone! Stop tormenting me!

But the attack was merciless. Its intensity increased a hundred times with each torturous second.

Barbara's hormones danced eagerly. She smiled alluringly and took him by the hand. "Oooww...your hands are so cold and sweaty."

Their eyes met.

Edwin's body went rigid with stark terror. A rigor mortis of fear snatched away his motion. *She knows...my God, she knows!* He felt as though a giant spotlight was shining on his dark places, exposing his shame...his nakedness.

I can't do it. I can't go up there!

Barbara stopped suddenly, unable to pull his weight up the stairs. She didn't notice the expressionless face or the blank look in his eyes. Her arm went around his waist. Then slowly her hand ascended his back, slowly rubbing and massaging.

"You're soooooo tight," she said, in an exaggerated whisper. She rubbed his back some more. "That nonsensical impromptu meeting has upset you," she said with the authority of a doctor. "I'll fix that," she purred.

The more she spoke, the smaller he became. She was asking the impossible.

Edwin's face was fully covered by the slime. More massaging from hell's emissary. More terror in his soul. Somehow his legs forced him up the stairs.

The children were all in their rooms with the doors shut. Sharon's room was strangely silent. Usually, the sound of a Christian song could be heard coming from her room. It was most often a Vineyard love song to the Lord. But tonight nothing.

Barbara led Edwin by the hand into their spacious bedroom. Edwin felt like a condemned criminal in a court of law. Tonight the bed of marital delight appeared as an angry judge, ready to inundate him with the cruel truth. Edwin could hear the verdict reverberate in his mind and echo in his soul. *Misery without parole!*

How could I have ever let it happen? I could have stopped it. I could have—

Scenes of his shame bubbled up into his mind.

They were alone, he and Uncle Ted. So vulnerable, so trusting, so defenseless. What could he have done? He never suspected his own uncle would do something like that. The thought never entered his naive mind. But it happened anyway. First a pat, then a touch...a stroke...nakedness. Edwin hated to even think about it. Each time he did, he felt filthy all over again. *If anyone ever found out—*

"Ed," he heard Barbara call him through the fog, "you look a little spacey, dear."

"Oh, I'm alright."

Barbara's warm hand pulled him closer to the bed. She started with his shirt.

No, Barbara, please...don't, he thought.

But she did.

Barbara looked at her husband's body with satisfaction. She could see the effects of his strenuous daily exercise routine. He wasn't a Hercules, but he was firm and there was not the slightest hint at a spare tire around his waist. Everything was perfect, except for the obvious sign that he desired her as much as she desired him.

Nothing that a few minutes won't remedy.

But nothing she did had any apparent effect on him.

"Come on, Ed," Barbara coaxed playfully, "you're acting the way I acted with you our first time. Remember? Like a scared virgin. And you're certainly not *that.*"

Ordinarily Barbara had only to think sex and Edwin was like a runaway train. But over the past several months Barbara reluctantly watched her once mighty locomotive come to a sputtering stop.

Their sex life was now sporadic and unpredictable. She never knew when Edwin would be up to it. At times he seemed so sexually aloof and uninterested. Sometimes he was overtly disinterested. Tonight she didn't know what to think of him. She wore a smile, but her patience was wearing thin. *I may as well make love to a mannequin*, she thought. "Honey, what's wrong?"

Edwin didn't hear her.

Do it just this once, insisted his uncle*, no one will know.* Edwin tried to pull away. He wanted to leave, but his uncle was too strong. When it was over his uncle made him feel that it was his fault. He told him that if he ever told anyone, they wouldn't believe him. And that even if they did, he would tell everyone that Edwin had wanted to do it.

Edwin kept this dark secret to himself and tried to bury the memory. But he had never been able to get rid of the guilt. And lately the sporadic guilt that surfaced every now and then had turned into a tormenting and debilitating guilt that was driving him crazy.

"Edwin?"

"Please, I don't want to—"

"You're going to do it or—"

Submission. Again and again. Until finally there was nothing left to resist, only the compromised shell of the hollow soul of a child.

"Edwin?" The irritation was noticeable in her voice.

But it didn't matter. She was only talking to herself. Edwin was locked in a chamber of horrors, far away from the sound of his wife.

"I don't believe this!" There was no mistaking her irritation now. "You don't hear a word I'm saying! I'm sitting here on the bed naked, and you act like you don't even know I'm in the room!"

He didn't answer.

"Edwin!" she screamed. "I don't know why you are doing this to me, but you better stop before it's too late!"

The mist of painful memories slowly and mercifully dissipated enough so that Edwin could hear what Barbara was saying.

"...before it's too late!" he heard.

The vivid pictures of the past disappeared from Edwin's mind, but the crushing weight of it all still controlled his body.

"I can't," Edwin admitted, his ego buried in a coffin of dejection.

"You can't or you won't?"

"I can't...I can't."

"Why can't you? Why...what's—?" The room was warm, but a chill covered Barbara's nakedness. "Are you..." she was afraid to ask, "having an affair?"

Edwin hesitated.

I wish I could tell you. But just as quickly as the thought entered his mind, he dispelled it. He knew that Barbara wouldn't understand.

"You are, you are ha—"

"No, Barbara. I'm not having an affair. I'd never do that to you."

Barbara's expression showed her relief, but it also reflected the frustration of not knowing what was destroying their once trouble-free marriage.

Edwin took his wife in his arms and held her tightly. He tried to tell her with a kiss that she was the most beautiful, most exciting lady he had ever known.

Barbara yearned for this reassurance and delighted herself deeply in and around her husband's mouth. Her lips were moist and soft against Edwin's. For a brief moment everything was right again.

Suddenly, the demon pounded Edwin's head. A horribly wicked and indescribably powerful thought of perversion filled his mind. He seemed to actually be doing the act.

He snatched away from Barbara in disgust, leaving her kissing air, but the filthy thought was still there. It was not only in his mind. It was in the core of his being. It seemed to course through his very veins. For a moment it seemed that the air he inhaled was the breath of vileness. He was dependent on that which he hated.

Barbara was stupefied and humiliated as she watched Edwin hurriedly put on his clothes and leave the room in a panic.

The spirit was just a worker, a common, insignificant demon that was simply following orders. He had no idea that he was doing much more than tormenting a weak man of God. He was destroying a family and quite possibly stopping a catastrophic revival.

*****

Sharon felt a warning in her heart.

Don't call her!

She picked up the receiver and held it until a loud beeping sound began. Sharon put it down and lied across her bed for a few minutes.

Her eyes were red and puffy from crying. "God, why are you doing this to me? Why can't You be experienced? Why do I have to wait until I'm dead before I can begin to live?"

Two nights ago Sharon would not have been able to imagine herself praying so desperately for a closer walk with Jesus. She had always enjoyed an intimacy with God that lifted her soul above the heights of nominal Christianity. But for some reason there was a dearth in her heart, a leanness in the core of her being that she hadn't felt since before she surrendered her life to Christ.

"Oh, God, if only it was true. It felt so real." She spoke of last night's church service.

Myla was the angel tasked with Sharon's safety. He guarded her life with a tenacity that pleased Rashti, but infuriated the demons who sought to destroy her.

Her life before Christ had been a testimony of teenage rebellion and waywardness. She loved wild parties and occasionally smoked marijuana. However, even in her hell-bent days no one could have accused her of being promiscuous. That was one line she had not crossed yet, although she had come dangerously close many times.

Myla found her no more difficult to protect than any of the hundreds of people he had guarded since the Fall. Actually, in many ways she was easier to keep from harm. Her father's walk with God—although it was almost weak to the point of nonexistence—gave her added protection.

Once she had received Christ, it became even easier to protect her than the average Christian. This was because she was not an average Christian. She took the words of Jesus seriously, and did her absolute best to do whatever He desired.

However, this guardian angel who had come to love Sharon, and to admire her devotion to Christ so much, looked at her with grave concern. He knew what was going through her mind, and he knew what was going through the sick mind of the hairy creature that followed Sharon everywhere she went.

Sharon's keen spiritual intellect had been awakened by Jonathan's apostolic ministry. She would never be the same. Not after having seen the reality of God. It was as Sharon had said, "I want all of God or none of God." She stood at the crossroads. One sign said Fulfillment; the other said Disillusionment.

The next few days are critical, Myla thought. *I'll have to work extra hard to keep her.*

The hairy demon that stalked Sharon had similar thoughts.

An icy breeze blew into the room. The intensity of the cold caused Myla's wings to shiver. *What is that*?

A terrifying thought entered the angel's mind. He recognized that cold. *It was the cold of—No! It couldn't be. That demon shouldn't be here. What could possibly have attracted him?*

Myla searched his mind for any breach in Sharon's spiritual armor. Besides the usual weaknesses and mistakes of baby Christians, she had no significant deficiencies that should have attracted such evil.

The angel looked through the walls of Sharon's bedroom with the hope that he would not see what he dreadfully expected. The room's temperature was dropping fast. It was changing from uncomfortably cold to unbearably cold. The cold stabbed at Myla with such intensity that it felt like he was being punctured with frozen needles.

You announce your arrival with ice. Myla thought about the return of Christ. *The Lord shall announce His arrival with fire.*

The guardian angel still did not see him, but he knew he was out there. Somewhere. Why else would the air—?

There. In the horizon. Myla could see him approaching. He backed up to Sharon without taking his eyes off the demon and closed his wings. He removed the spiked glove from his belt and placed it on his left fist. Next, he pulled his sword from its sheath and gripped it tightly.

"Saints, I hope you are praying," he said, not relishing the predicament he and Sharon were in.

The figure was getting closer and closer, more discernible now. There were no escorts or guards with the unwelcome visitor. If it were any other demon besides this one Myla would have thought it odd for him to travel alone. But the approaching demon had no need of escorts or guards. They could only get in the way of a demon like this. Besides, there weren't very many angels in this area that were equipped to confront a demon of such stature.

If only I had more prayer support, I would....

The demon descended through the roof and landed in Sharon's bedroom. She stopped crying and looked around the room. Something was odd. She could feel it.

"You are her guardian angel?"

"That is correct."

"I am Witchcraft."

He flicked his wrist and the hairy demon that was always with Sharon hurriedly left the room.

Myla knew that he was at a disadvantage. The only way he could beat such a demon was through the fiery prayers of God's people, and he hadn't received any significant prayer support since last night—there was always a surge of prayer power on Wednesdays. Too bad the American saints didn't pray that way every day.

Throughout the kingdom of darkness there were no demons among the myriads that were like the spirits of witchcraft. They were truly a distinctive class of evil entities.

Before the Rebellion they had occupied the most prestigious and influential positions in all of heaven's infinite expanse. They were the official worshippers who had access to the very throne room of Almighty God. The worshippers not only inspired and directed adoration to the Creator, they carried and displayed His manifest glory to the innumerable host.

The official worshippers, which Lucifer—now called Satan—was chief, were specially designed to be carriers of the essence of God. Their bodies soaked in the holy presence of the Creator like sponges. When they walked among the angels, they released the sweet aroma into their midst. An intoxication of praise and adoration for the Lord filled their hearts and minds. Ecstasy! Climax! A trillion times more intense and fulfilling then anything ever experienced by humans.

Myla rehearsed his intelligence briefings. Captain's Rashti's words came to mind.

"A terrible thing has happened to our"—he was going to say brothers, but chose a more appropriate word—"enemies. The Rebellion has caused a repugnant mutation among them. It was inevitable. The blessings of God can only remain blessings when we are faithful to Him. Without union with the Creator, the blessings will turn into dreadful curses."

"So they will not lose their powers?" someone asked.

"No, they will be as powerful as ever," he said, *as he contemplated the misery the rebels would inflict upon God's beloved creation. "The Worshippers will become our worst enemies."*

There were incredulous gasps of shock among the angels.

"Their ability to inspire and direct will turn into a tragic weapon of manipulative coercion and hypnotic delusion," said the captain.

Myla focused on the present threat. "What do you want?" His voice was brave and demanding.

Witchcraft was surprised at the confidence of Sharon's guardian angel. "I want Sharon," he answered without a moment's hesitation.

"She hasn't given you permission to destroy her life," answered the angel. "Her heart is closed to your dark occult practices. She doesn't even read horoscopes."

Myla opened and closed his hand into a tight fist. There was only one way Witchcraft was going to get to Sharon, and that was through him.

Witchcraft took one step forward. Before his foot touched the floor, Myla's sword whizzed over his head. A lock of Witchcraft's hair fell to the carpet.

"Next time it will be your head." Myla felt the energy of God burn in his right arm. *Thank God, someone is praying*.

He was right. Someone was praying. A Marietta car salesman was praying for revival as he prepared to leave work.

Witchcraft was stunned by the lightning-fast action of Myla's sword, but he didn't allow his face to show it. He picked up the lock of hair and rolled it around in his hand. "You are fast."

The unknown Marietta car salesman's prayers strengthened Myla by the second.

"That was nothing. It gets better." He was anxious now to mix it up.

"I will have her," Witchcraft declared confidently.

Myla beckoned him with his gloved hand. "Come and get her."

The angel's bold stand against the dark spirit momentarily confused Witchcraft. What Witchcraft didn't know was that his words, "I will have her," had nearly paralyzed Myla's heart with fear until he had received the unexpected prayer support from the car salesman in Marietta.

Innately he knew that this was no idle threat. The pompous demon across the room from him wasn't mouthing off pipe dreams. There was something about his words that alarmed Myla. There was something prophetic.

Witchcraft lunged at Myla. There were two brilliant flashes of light as Myla swung his sword at the demon's head. He missed his head, but two more locks of hair and a piece of ear fell to the floor.

Witchcraft's retreat was faster than his attack. The muscles in his monkey-looking face were tight with surprise. He was sure that this guardian angel could not defeat him. *Unless he has prayer support,* mused Witchcraft. *But the reports were that Myla's prayer cover was insignificant. Obviously the intelligence was wrong. He has more than enough prayer power.*

A blue flame erupted upon Myla's sword.

Witchcraft looked at the flaming sword as though he was looking into the mirror of his own destruction. *Prayer! Fervent prayer!*

He backed up gingerly and floated to the ceiling. "You win guardian...this time." He looked at Sharon with a menacing scowl and opened his mouth. Rows of sharp, jagged, and uneven teeth tainted with nasty discoloration filled his wide mouth. "Daarrrling, we shall meet again on my terms, playing by my rules. I will have your soul."

Myla watched the spirit of witchcraft ascend into the sky until he was just a dot against the black night.

Witchcraft abruptly turned and let out a thunderous bellow of rage. Myla fell to his knees with his hands over his ears. Finally, after what seemed an eternity, the eardrum-bursting roar of defiant fury ended and Myla wobbled to his feet.

The other demon that Witchcraft had dismissed earlier returned to the room. When he saw the flaming sword, he tried to appear as passive as was demonly possible.

Myla looked at him with no deference whatsoever. This demon was the least of his worries. Witchcraft's words echoed in his mind.

"I will have your soul."

*****

Edwin drove through the midtown section of Atlanta for forty-five minutes with no particular aim in mind. Filthy thoughts of perversion screamed in his mind. "No!" Edwin screamed. "I am a Christian! I will not do this! I am not a homo—"

"Prove it!" the demon on his shoulders taunted. "You're not a man of God. You're a dirty, filthy, rotten hypocrite. You like it. That's why you're here. Admit it. Admit it!"

Edwin pulled over and parked in front of a house. The wicked thoughts that tormented his beaten mind drowned out the loud music and frivolous debauchery of the house party. He heard nothing except the demon that mercilessly dug his crusty nails into his head.

He rolled his window down to get some air.

You will never get away from your past," said the demon. "You can't hide behind a pulpit all of your rotten life."

"It's not true!" Edwin countered. *Oh, God,* he thought, *what if it is true? What if I am—No! God! You must help me. It wasn't my fault. I didn't want to do it.*

The demon kept squeezing his head.

Call on Jesus, Edwin heard in his heart.

"God, help me, please." Edwin was desperate. He felt like he was in a quicksand pit of filth and degradation. The more he struggled to get out, the deeper he sank.

Call on Jesus.

"God, where are You? Why don't You do something?"

Call on Jesus.

A light came on in Edwin's troubled mind. "Jesus," he whimpered, but it was sufficient.

"That is enough!" the demon heard someone say. He saw no one, but he knew all too well who it was—Trin. Immediately, he stopped his torture.

Edwin breathed heavily. His head rested on the steering wheel. "Thank you, God."

Trin could only look at him and shake his head sadly. When would he ever learn the power of that Name? If he only knew the power that was unleashed against the dark forces when Christians boldly used the Name of Jesus.

Someone at the party spotted Edwin sitting alone in his car. "Hey, honey, you look like you could use some company."

Trin touched Edwin's eyes to allow him to see the homosexual demon that possessed the man who was trying to pick him up.

Edwin looked up. "Aaaaahhh!"

The face he looked into was a contortion of diseased rot. Yellow pus dripped from open sores that emitted a rancid, garbage can smell. Maggots crawled in and out of his mouth. One eye socket was empty, except for the maggots, and the other had an eyeball hanging by its stem past his eaten-away nose.

The tires squealed and Edwin was gone.

The homosexual shouted an obscenity and went back to the party to find someone whose vision wasn't as clear as Edwin's.

Chapter 7

Bashnar had faced many crises in his dark and infamous past. Yet he couldn't remember ever feeling such intense urgency. It was an overwhelming mandate to crush God's revival in the womb. He was beginning to feel the unfathomable magnitude of his task.

He put Jonathan's file down on his desk and rose to his feet. Bashnar's office was a showcase of trophies, plaques, and awards that commemorated his legendary accomplishments. There were several pictures of him at various ceremonies receiving accolades. He folded his hands behind his back and slowly walked around the room and reminisced.

He looked first at two certificates that were signed by the demonic governor of America. They were placed side by side for their irony. Bashnar smiled at the stupidity of humans as he read the commendations. One he had received for creating a national organization for white racists. The other had been awarded for creating black organizations that respond to white racism with black racism.

He laughed at how ironic it was that many black Americans embraced Islam, but cursed Jesus Christ. The warrior smiled darkly at his own brilliance. "Jesus," he said with utter disdain, "because of me you're the *white* man's God, and those who should love you the most love you the least. Suckers don't even know that Islam was one of the greatest enslavers of Africans. How can you love such a stupid creation?"

Bashnar walked past several trophies and stopped at a picture of a preacher who had been revered as a miracle-working prophet. "You weren't much of a challenge, miracle man. Should've listened to your buddy, Gordon Lindsey."

He looked at another picture.

"Aaahhhh, now you had fire." He spoke of John Alexander Dowie, the Chicago preacher who had caused a revival of healing and miracles in the early 1900s. "I am sorry that you had to come to such an ignominious end, Elijah. But that is what happens when you think too highly of yourself."

Next, a spot he had reserved for Billy Graham.

"What a prize you would have been!" He spoke with the involuntary resignation of a failure that could no longer be denied, but would never be admitted. Now that the famous evangelist was so old and feeble, anything less than him claiming to be a closet homosexual or an atheist would mean nothing for Bashnar's reputation.

Bashnar glanced at the rest of his collection and sat pensively at his desk. Past victories were like food eaten long ago. One could remember the meal, but not taste it. The warrior was hungry. He looked at Jonathan's thick file, several hundred pages of biography.

"But you are not like the others, are you? Your motives are pure, your agenda inspired of heaven. You have no love of money, not a covetous or materialistic bone in your holy body."

Bashnar mentally compared Jonathan to the hundreds of daggers he had fought. Without emotion, he objectively concluded that he was of the most lethal of daggers. Some daggers were exceptionally gifted with miracles and healings. Their characteristic ember-hot oratory, coupled with the manifest power of God, rained havoc on the kingdom of darkness. Yet—a self-assured smile came across Bashnar's face—most of them had this one glaring weakness: lack of wisdom.

He thought of Aimee Simple McPherson, William Branham, Alexander Dowie, Franklin Hall, A. A. Allen, and a host of others. For all their daring spiritual exploits, they usually fell for the most obvious traps.

Most of them had never learned the secret of the body of Christ, the church. They never came to understand—until it was too late—that the ministry gifts of God were given not to lift up personalities or to secure hidden agendas, but to build up the church and to magnify Christ in the hearts of mankind.

The daggers usually were quite easily convinced that they were special people with special liberties. An alarmingly high ratio of them had actually held the church in contempt. And most of them had absolutely disregarded the opinions of pastors. Surprisingly, most of them had been spiritual mavericks who had chosen to operate outside of the traditional church. These had been the easiest to seduce.

Bashnar flipped through several pages of Jonathan's case file. He lost count of how many times he had read the section *Character Development*, but his instincts told him to read it again. There was something he had overlooked, something hidden in the obvious.

He read out loud. "The man of God is consumed with Christ. As it was with Paul—yuuk!"—the mention of that name brought back terrible memories"—so it is with Jonathan. He presses toward the mark for the prize of the high calling of God. He will not be distracted nor deterred...."

He skipped some. His bushy eyebrows touched together angrily when he read the next entry. "Jonathan has exceptional spiritual vision. He sees things as they are and not as we would like them to appear. For this reason, the customary tactic of side-tracking promising black preachers has failed miserably. He refuses to hate white people for their many atrocities against his people. This dagger correctly understands that hatred and racism cannot be conquered through natural methods."

Bashnar then read Jonathan's answer to a critic who questioned his understanding of the plight of black Americans.

> *There is nothing wrong with boycotts, protests, marches, and the like. If something is evil—and we all agree that racism is evil—it should be vehemently protested. But, sir, where you and I*

differ is that you do so with anger and malice in your heart toward your white brother. You see him as your enemy and do not understand that his racism, and your racist response to his racism, has chained both of you to the wrists of your master.

When the young man had asked, "Who is our master?" Jonathan had replied, "Satan."

Bashnar slammed the book shut. "So you refuse to put Band-Aids on cancer." He pulled out his knife and gripped it tightly. His knuckles bulged under his hairy skin. "You prefer to deal with the root of the problem. To cut the cancer out! It is only a matter of time—" he slammed the knife into Jonathan's picture—"before I hang you on my wall."

*****

Jonathan's eyes lazily opened. They burned from lack of sleep. He blinked a few times to get rid of the grogginess. He took a deep breath and stared at the ceiling. Even after so many years of waking up early for prayer, he still found it physically difficult. Especially after a night like the previous one, a several-hour counseling session with a waiter he had met at *Carrabbas*, an Italian restaurant. He didn't get to bed until 3:00 a.m. It was now a few minutes past 6:00 a.m.

The usual contingency of demons who sought to keep him from his early morning prayers showed up again.

Jonathan sat up and took another deep breath. "Well, Satan, I hope you're ready, because I am."

The four small demons that hovered in the room shared here-we-go-again expressions. There was no mystery to what was going to happen next. They had been through this routine with Jonathan hundreds of times before.

Jonathan got out of bed and went downstairs to the kitchen. He wrapped some ice cubes in a towel and took a pitcher of water out of the refrigerator and soaked the towel.

"Aahhhh," he said, as he rubbed his face and neck with the icy towel. He felt refreshed and invigorated, ready to pray. But first his morning coffee. It helped him come alive. A couple of cups of the black brew and he was ready.

The demons fired the standard lies at him as he walked toward the garage. They told him that he wasn't worthy to pray; that he was too sinful to receive an answer from a holy God. They told him that God didn't answer prayer.

One of the demons recited his lies in a tired, monotonous tone of voice and was obviously dissatisfied with being there. He felt it was a waste of time and didn't mind wondering out loud why they were ordered to bang their heads against a brick wall. But he had to fill the squares. So he banged away with the rest of them.

Jonathan welcomed the coolness of the garage. It would help him awaken. He loved his garage, not for the reasons that most men treasured garages. There wasn't the usual clutter of junk and sentimental debris. Except for a few tools and some fishing poles, the garage was bare. Just the way Jonathan wanted it.

The garage was his refuge of tranquility, his designated doorway into the heavenlies. This is where Jonathan customarily stormed the gates of hell every morning from 5:00 a.m. until 7:00 a.m. Today he was an hour behind his written-in-concrete schedule. *Oh, well, wake up an hour late, pray an hour longer.*

Jonathan stretched his arms over his head and let out a tired yawn. One of the demons placed a thought in his mind. "You forgot to brush your teeth." *I forgot to brush my teeth*, thought Jonathan.

For a split-second, he contemplated brushing his teeth before he started to pray, but he decided against it. "I'll brush my teeth after I pray," he said, for the benefit of the invisible trespassers he knew were there.

"I knew it wouldn't work," the demon said. He was in mid-sentence of another gripe when he read his obituary on Bashnar's face. *Where did he come from?*

Jonathan felt a sudden oppressiveness in the room.

Bashnar's eyes were black with death. He placed his hands on his hips and stuck out his chest. His menacing presence towered over the four puny demons. Bashnar stood eight feet tall, more than twice the height of the tallest of the four demons.

The warrior spirit stepped forward. All of the demons awkwardly, but quickly descended to the ground. They bumped into one another like bowling pins after a strike. The four of them stood at attention in the presence of the Mighty Bashnar.

Bashnar looked at the despicably worthless spirits with utter disdain and contempt. As far as he was concerned—all warrior spirits felt this way—there was nothing lower than the class of demons known as helpers. The only thing lower than a helper demon was an insubordinate helper demon.

"Step forward." Bashnar's low, gruff voice carried the dread of a million murders.

The four terrified spirits obeyed instantly.

"Not all of you!" The befuddled demons panicked in disciplined silence. They didn't know what to do. Bashnar helped them. "I want the little demon with the big mouth."

The other three knew who he was speaking of. They immediately and with great relief stepped back, leaving the talkative demon up front.

Bashnar didn't ask, but the other three helper demons began to spill their guts. They rehearsed every gripe and complaint of their colleague.

"Shut up!"

Silence.

Bashnar took another step forward. The dwarfed demon looked up with begging eyes into the black holes that glared at him.

"Little demon, who has filled your small mind with grandiose thoughts of rulership?"

"Mighty Bashnar—"

He waved his index finger and the demon cut short his explanation.

Bashnar slowly reached down and gripped the demon's neck. He lifted him into the air. "You have spoken against me and now I will respond. Not with words, but with discipline."

He slowly tore off one ear, then the other. The tortured demon desperately sank his sharp claws into Bashnar's arm. He wildly and futilely kicked the big demon in his torso. This pleased Bashnar. *At least he has the heart to fight.* Nevertheless, he tore off one of his arms for daring to assault the Mighty Bashnar.

"...revival," Bashnar heard Jonathan say.

A paralyzing chill shot down Bashnar's spine. He dropped the wailing demon to the floor and cautiously walked over to where Jonathan stood. He was careful to not get too close. He knew there were powerful angels hiding in cloaks of invisibility. They would pounce upon anyone or anything that threatened this dagger.

Jonathan stopped praying. He sensed the change in the spiritual atmosphere of the garage. "I rebuke you, Satan!"

A powerful blow struck Bashnar in his midsection. It knocked the wind out of him and sent a wave of nausea over him. He wanted to double over and throw up, but his pride would never allow it. He would never give his enemies the satisfaction of seeing him in pain. Instead, he absorbed the blow and said, "I hope that wasn't your best."

The other four demons weren't so fortunate. They had neither the spiritual attributes nor the will to absorb such punishment. All of them were scattered on the floor holding their bellies. Their breathing was raspy and forced, as though they were all hooked to bad respiratory machines.

Bashnar looked at them with disgust. *Pitiful.*

"Atlanta will never see revival!" he boomed at Jonathan.

Jonathan suddenly felt very weak and alone. *What happened?* One minute he had felt the Presence of God and the power of the Holy Spirit, and the next minute he felt as though he was on stage in front of a million people naked and with no place to hide.

"There will never be revival in Atlanta! I will destroy everything you hold dear first!"

Jonathan dropped to his hands and knees. He couldn't explain it, but he suddenly felt that his wife was in grave danger. He started to get up and run in the house to check on her. He was on one knee when the almost imperceptible thought rose up within his spirit. *Praise Me.*

Tears coursed down Jonathan's face. "Jeeessusss! I love you, Jesus! I love and magnify everything You are. You are so worthy of my praise and adoration. Take my life as an offering. Do whatever you will. Without You I am nothing. Life has no meaning without You."

Bashnar's posture was less defiant now. He pulled out a mammoth sword and turned in small circles, hunched over, awaiting the imminent attack. The odds were against him and he knew it. That's why he smiled. Any second now the cowardly angels of God would show themselves and there would be a clashing of swords. Might against might, strength against strength. But in the end, the Mighty Bashnar would be the victor. He always was.

But nothing happened. No one appeared.

Bashnar didn't stop circling. He was too smart for that. But he did slow down. He waited several minutes and still no one showed up. This was most unusual.

The praises of the saints was their most awesome weapon. Bashnar had lost count of how many works of darkness—some of which had taken years to establish—had been completely obliterated by praising saints. Something was wrong. Perhaps this was a trick to get him to put down his guard. If it was, it wouldn't work.

He waited several more minutes. Still nothing happened. As highly improbable as it was that Jonathan's worship and praise had not attracted the power of God, Bashnar found himself wondering if perhaps his own forces had been able to ambush the reinforcements.

Something broke in the spirit realm. Jonathan felt it. He began to praise God even more earnestly.

The little demons were on their feet now, though still gasping for breath.

"What will you do—?"

POOOFF! A blue flame engulfed Jonathan.

This stopped Bashnar in mid-boast. He stumbled back at the intense heat.

POOOFF! POOOFF! POOOFF! POOOFF!

The four demons shrieked and wailed and wildly thrashed about as the flames erupted upon them.

Bashnar struck out at the tortured demons with his sword whenever they got too close. He tried to stay, to show the heavenly cowards why he was called Mighty Bashnar, but the heat was stifling. He would have to leave.

But wait. Why had he not been enflamed like the others. Was it not because he was the Mighty Bashnar? His pride would not let him go.

The thought had no sooner crossed his mind when a flame erupted on him too. Unlike the others, the flame that engulfed Bashnar lasted only a second.

"AAAaagghhh!" Bashnar screamed in pain. His sword dropped from his hand and he fell to his knees in a stupor. In a few moments his senses returned. He was astonished to find that he was still alive. Instinctively, he reached for his head. His mane was gone and so was the rest of his hair. Bashnar was furious.

He floated above the garage. "You will curse the day you were born, man of God!" He shot into the sky. He was almost ten miles up when he circled and stopped. He shook both his fists at the Most High God and said, "You have hurt me. Now I will hurt you!"

The humiliated demon hurled himself at Atlanta with a vengeance that shook the city. His opposition was fierce, for not everyone was easily within his reach, and some not at all. Nonetheless, Bashnar proved again why he was known as the *Mighty* Bashnar and not simply Bashnar.

The police reported a shocking sixteen murders committed that day. Most of them inexplicably appeared to be random shootings. The most bizarre and shocking of the murders, however, was the bludgeoning of a woman who was walking down Atlanta's most recognizable street, Peachtree Boulevard.

A man waiting in his car for the light to turn green suddenly got out of his car. He popped open the trunk and grabbed a thirty-pound, thirty-six-inch wrecking bar—a tool used to demolish walls and cabinets and to pull up floors. What he did next could never have been anticipated and would never be forgotten by those who witnessed the horror.

He calmly walked behind a young woman who had made the unforgivable mistake of leaving her hotel room and going across the street to get something to eat. She had long flowing hair and a cute, youthful bounce in her step that was as much the result of her recent marriage proposal as it was the unbelievable job offer she had received earlier that day. She smiled as she contemplated her good fortune.

Behind her the man lifted the demolition tool and ended her life with one powerful blow. But the savage attack didn't end until some of the dazed onlookers got over their initial paralysis of shock and fear enough to tackle the killer from behind. By then the killer's ten or so blows to the woman's head had all but reduced it to mush.

Bashnar stood over the bloody mess. He peered intensely at the awkwardly crumpled victim and savored the taste of his revenge for several deeply satisfying moments. He closed his eyes to heighten the sensation. His breaths were long, slow, and deliberate, as though he was meditating. It was glorious. The horror. The panic. The tears. But most of all the fear.

And yet for all this, Bashnar's wrath wasn't appeased. He returned to his ethereal office and opened Jonathan's file once more.

Chapter 8

It was scary at first, when she had been a little girl, only seven years old. Her mother had been dead for only a week when he entered her room one night and took off his clothes and got into bed with her. She had not wanted to do it.

Daddy and Mommy had always told her to never let anyone touch her private parts. She had known by the serious looks on their faces that it was terribly wrong for grown-ups to touch little children there.

As a young child, Toni had not understood why her father did dirty things to her. She was sixteen now and she still didn't have all of the answers to her dilemma, but she concluded that somehow she must have been to blame. Why else would her father abuse her?

But Toni's dilemma went far beyond sexual abuse. When Toni's mother died, her father became extremely depressed. He sat for hours at a time and grieved. Nothing anyone said helped him. This went on for several weeks until one day he entered his bedroom and closed the door. He stayed there for two days without coming out. On the second day while Toni had her ear to the door, she heard her father scream at the top of his voice. There was a long silence and then, "I hate you!" he yelled at someone.

The door opened suddenly. Toni looked into her father's face with frightened eyes. His expression made her little body go rigid with fear. He had never before looked so evil. Her father went from room to room and snatched certain pictures off of walls. He busted and ripped them to pieces.

That evening was the first time Toni's father violated her. It was also the first time she had heard him speak glowingly of Satan. That was over nine years ago, but his words and the hatred on his face...the eeriness of the moment was still so real, so vivid in her mind.

"Satan," she recalled him saying on his knees, "to hell with that holy bastard! If He can't save my Cissie, then to hell with Him! From now on, I'm with you."

Toni sipped her bourbon and lit a cigarette. She laughed sardonically. "That must have been his first command," she said, thinking back to that first humiliating night. A lonely tear coursed its way down her cheek. Soon others followed.

Beeeep! Beeeep!

Toni guzzled the rest of her drink and hurried to the window. It was Rick, her date. After a few moments of reapplying her makeup, she was outdoors and down the steps.

Rick's adrenaline rushed when he saw what Toni wore. *Jerry was right. You got it all. In all the right places!*

"You look really nice, Toni." Rick's eyes burned furtive holes through her tight blouse.

"Thanks. You too, Rick," she said, smiling when she saw his approval. "What do you have on your mind?"

You'll find out soon enough, sweetheart. Rick's answer was perfectly camouflaged in benign innocence. "Oh, I don't know. Maybe we can go to a movie or something, and get something to eat somewhere, maybe Bennigan's."

"Okay, yeah. Let's go see *The Adjustment Bureau*." Toni did like the Bourne trilogy, but was not a big fan of Matt Damon. She could take him or leave him. But there was something irresistible about a man, any man, fighting and risking his life for the woman he loved. Toni's despondency was lifting fast. Rick seemed to be a nice guy.

The Adjustment Bureau? Why don't we go see Toy Story 3 instead? "Sure," Rick answered enthusiastically, "I've been planning to go see that," he lied. Actually, he had hoped they would go see something with lots of skin.

Toni's smile lit up the dark street. It was going to be an enjoyable evening.

Rick glanced at her and smiled also, but for different reasons. He gave the Boxster S Black Edition some gas and the Porsche engine flexed its mighty muscles. This was a limited edition model. Only 1,911 were made. Rick owned *NR.* 0534/1911.

The convertible top of the totally black car was down. A cool breeze made Toni's hair dance with aimless abandonment. She closed her eyes and stretched her neck backwards and delighted herself in the cool wind and in the gorgeous car. Rick tried to make some small talk, but Toni's responses were all short. Not terse, just short. She was relaxed and transfixed in the calm and comfort of the Porsche's soft black leather interior. The farther away from home she got, the more relaxed she became.

Toni loved the movie; Rick suffered through it. However, he was encouraged by the small advances she allowed him in the dark of the theater. He could hardly wait to leave the movie and fill the square of dinner so that he could make his expenditure of time and money worth his while. He would see whether she was as talented as he had been told.

He made his move after they had eaten and gone to a couple of bars in the *Virginia Highlands* area. This was a small, yet popular Atlanta night life community with several bars and restaurants. Part of its appeal was that it was in the heart of a residential community.

"What does your dad do?" he asked, although he knew the answer to this question. But this was all in the game.

Jerry, his sycophant, had told him a lot about Toni. Things he had solemnly promised Toni he would never tell anyone. To his credit he had actually planned to keep her secrets to himself, but that resolve lasted only until his first opportunity to impress Rick.

Toni stiffened at the unexpected question. Even with the amount of liquor she had drunk, his inquiry effectively put a damper on her buoyancy. Her high spirits crashed into a mountain of harsh reality.

Rick saw her reaction and congratulated himself. Jackpot! "What's wrong? I—I'm sorry. I didn't mean to intrude." Rick feigned embarrassment.

For a few moments Toni said nothing. She felt terribly alone and dejected, even though she was surrounded by many people and sat across from a great looking guy who really knew how to have a good time.

"It's okay," Toni answered weakly.

"I'm really sorry," Rick repeated. "Boy, am I a jerk."

Toni looked into Rick's face. All she could see, all she wanted to see, was kindness and concern. All she had ever wanted was for someone to care for her, someone to appreciate her as a person. Maybe Rick was that person. She knew that was a presumptuous thought, but it felt good to fantasize something good about herself. It seemed that was the only way anything good would ever come her way.

"No, no, really Rick. It's okay. It's just that—" Toni fished for the right words, something appropriate. She couldn't just say, My dad's a weird freak who prays to the devil and has sex with his daughter.

"My dad and I don't have a very good relationship," Toni managed to say. She was embarrassed to discuss such personal matters with a stranger. Although as each second passed she felt more and more that Rick was a friend. A true friend.

"Yeah, I know what you mean."

Toni knew there was no way he could possibly know what she meant. Yet he spoke with such compassion, such sympathy, as though he really did know and share her pain.

He reached across the table and gently took her hand. It was small and dainty, covered by his. A smile came across her face.

"Dimples!" Rick exulted.

"Yeah," Toni blushed.

"Wow, I love dimples. My little sister has the cutest dimples. Of course I'd never tell her that."

Toni laughed.

"You're very pretty when you laugh. You should laugh more often."

Toni knew that her face must have been beet red. "I would if I had something to make me laugh," she heard herself say, then winced inwardly for having been so honest. She felt her soul open with those words. A discomforting sense of vulnerability descended upon her like a rude trespasser.

Rick put on his most polished act. He had learned long ago that it was more effective to let the girl proposition him. They loved it when a guy played the part of *The Last Decent Man Alive*. He began his performance.

"You're blushing," Rick teased.

"Quit it, will you?" Toni answered, enjoying the moment.

"Okay, but only if you promise to laugh more."

A picture of her father flashed across her mind's eye. She saw her and her father naked in the bed. His angry face looking down at her with contempt.

Her face lost its brightness; the cheer evaporated. "I have nothing to be happy about," she said dryly. Her admission was uncharacteristically true, and subconsciously she wondered why she was being so honest and open about her tortured life. She had become quite skilled at plastering a phony smile and displaying an everything-is-great disposition. However, only she knew how many times she had thought about killing herself.

Toni's abrupt honesty threw Rick off balance. He knew that the lovely lady who sat across from him was baring her soul to him. It made him feel awkward. He had slept around with many ladies, but this was the first time he had actually tasted intimacy. He knew that Toni hadn't simply shared a secret. She had placed her heart in his hand. Her admission was really a cry for help.

For a brief second, Rick felt a tinge of compassion. A slight urge to halt his sex safari and answer her cry with real friendship. Something he had absolutely no experience doing. This alien thought was shown to the door the moment Rick glanced at the fullness of Toni's tight-fitting blouse.

I'm no psychiatrist. I'm a lover, he corrected himself.

"Please don't take this the wrong way," Rick feigned nervousness. He knew he had everything under control. All he had to do was hit the right keys at the right time and there would be sweet melody in just a short while. "Toni, I would really like to be your friend. I don't have many friends." He thought for a second. "To be honest with you, I don't have any friends—not real friends. You know what I mean."

"Yeah, I know what you mean. I don't have any close friends either. I used to have one, but she flipped out."

"Drugs?"

"Worse than that."

"What's worse than that?"

"Religion." The word tasted like rancid trash in Toni's mouth. Rick's expression told her that he wanted to hear more. "We were really close; like sisters," Toni's voice dropped off, "only closer." Toni didn't like to think about it. Thinking about it only depressed her. She put on a phony smile. "Anyway, now we aren't. Let's talk about something else."

"That's a good idea. Let's talk about something nicer." Rick took her other hand into his. "Like you."

Toni looked into her date's eyes. They were a crisp blue. The darkness of the dimly lit bar accentuated his sharp features. His face was masculine, but with a hint of pretty. She liked the way his hair fell over his forehead and curved to the right. One of his gorgeous eyes was almost hidden by a defiant bang. Rick wasn't a kid like the other guys she had been with. He was a man. Twenty-two years old. A senior at Emory University, and incredibly warm and sensitive.

Toni felt her heart beat furiously against her chest. "That would be a short conversation. There isn't too much to me. Nothing spectacular."

"That depends on what you consider spectacular." Rick leaned back in his chair. "There is a girl in one of my political science classes who plans to become a United States Supreme Court justice. That's a pretty tall order for anyone. If it were anyone else..." His voice trailed. "You know, one of these days that lady will be one of the ten most powerful people in the United States."

He spoke of the president and the Supreme Court justices. Everyone else—the Senate, the House, the myriad of appointed offices—were second-stringers. Their power was too diluted to mean anything. Rick appreciated real power.

Rick's eyes danced with excitement. Golf was his hobby. Women were his adventure. But law was his passion. He loved it. "People expect me to dream big. My great grandfather was a Solicitor General. My grandfather was a state attorney general. My father has his own firm—a rather large firm. I'm expected to do something, to be somebody great. But this lady will most likely be greater than I'll ever be."

Toni was fascinated at Rick's heritage, but even more at the lady of which he spoke.

"Do you know what's so special about this lady?"

"What?" Toni's curiosity piqued.

"She's blind and crippled. The lady has only one eye and she's in a wheelchair." He looked thoughtfully into a bottle of liquor on the wall's shelf. "And yet one day she's going to be a Supreme Court justice."

Toni didn't know what to say. She had never before heard of anything so touching. She had never before witnessed such tenderness in a man. "That's...that's beautiful."

"Yeah, it is." Rick saw that Toni's eyes were moist. He smiled. "I believe we were talking about you before I got on my soap box."

Toni didn't speak. She didn't want to speak. All she wanted was to bury her head into his chest, to be held close to him. She knew that she was rushing things, and she felt guilty and stupid about it. There was no rational reason for her to feel this way about a stranger, even one as beautiful as Rick. But as she sat next to him and listened to him talk, she was painfully aware of all that she didn't have. Love. Security. Friends. Someone to believe in her the way Rick believed in this blind lady. What a crappy, pathetic life.

Toni inwardly shook her head at the cruel irony of life. Without arrogance or conceit, she mused how someone as beautiful as she could have no one, nothing, and a blind cripple could have everything.

"Toni, life means nothing if you have no one to share it with."

"I agree," she assented, wondering where that statement would—or could—lead.

"Jerry told me that you didn't have a boyfriend, but I know that—"

"No, no, I'm not seeing anyone," she answered before he could finish. Toni knew how eager she sounded, but she didn't care. She was tired of being alone, and she was tired of being used. It was time for her to start enjoying the life she knew must exist somewhere.

"I hope I don't sound too brash or presumptuous, but I have never met anyone like you." The would-be attorney was making his closing remarks. "Something inside of me tells me to swallow my pride and tell you how much I've enjoyed this evening, how much I enjoy your company."

Toni looked deeply into Rick's eyes. "I've enjoyed myself, too." Her voice was soft, almost inaudible.

"Toni—" the sound of him saying her name was hypnotic—"please forgive me for asking, and I understand if you never want to see me again." Rick was impressing himself. He knew that everything was right. His words, his expressions, his timing—everything! "But I don't want to see this night end. Will you come home with me?"

This wasn't the first time she had been asked to spend the night with a man, but this time it was different. Rick was different. He was caring and thoughtful and mature. He had a way of making her feel valued.

"Yes," she answered.

Rick smiled and lifted her hand and kissed it. As he and Toni walked to his car hand in hand, he couldn't help but think, What kind of a dizzy chick would swallow that crap about a blind cripple wanting to become a United States Supreme Court justice?

Chapter 9

Adam turned on the television and plopped down onto the vinyl bean bag. He loved his bag and fully intended to take it to heaven with him when he went. However, he knew that heaven wasn't big enough for his bean bag and his wife. One of them would have to stay. Adam chuckled. He was going to miss his wife.

Really, he didn't know what the fuss was about. But if he didn't, his wife did. Sherry was a study in contrasts. Like her husband, her taste in clothes was anchored in the 1960's. She still wore headbands, beads, and tee-shirts with political messages. But that is where their similarity in tastes ended.

Adam's sense of fashion was across the board nonexistent. Sherry, on the other hand, was only fashion blind when it came to clothes. Her appreciation for nice furniture and fine art was commendable, and every inch of their home reflected her handiwork. Every inch, that is, except for the orange bean bag that sat in the middle of the floor like a tomato plant in a rose garden. It clashed terribly with the black and white scheme of the great room's decor.

"Sherry, we gotta get going, honey. The preacher's getting ready to rev it up."

Rev it up was what Adam called the preacher's oratorical climax. How he loved black preachers! And especially this one. They were so emotional and spontaneous. It seemed to Adam that black television preachers were much livelier than white preachers. Most white preachers were so deliberate in their movements and careful with their words that they appeared to be robotic. But not the black ones. Their attitude was if you don't like what I say and the way I say it, let the door knob hit you where the dog should've bit you. He heard one of them say those exact words. Adam loved it!

"I'm coming. Adam, have you seen my Bible?" Sherry asked.

Adam took a quick glance around the room. "No, it's not in here."

Something flashed in the corner of his eye and he turned to see what it was. Nothing. He shrugged it off and returned to his program. Pastor Kidd was really letting them have it.

"Some of ya been a slippin' and a slidin' on the Lawd. You thinkin' that singing in the choir or shaking the preacher's hand gone get you in. But I'm here to tell you that nobody," the organist pounded a few keys, "nobody," the preacher bent over and the organist hit those keys again, "gone make it in unless their name is written in the Lamb's book of life."

Adam was caught up in the movements of the preacher and the sound of the organ when he saw another flash. This time it was much brighter than the first. He turned his head and again saw nothing.

I know I saw a light. What's going on here?

He stood up and when he did the light appeared again. Adam saw it clearly this time. It was small, about the size of a quarter, and extremely bright. Adam walked toward the light and stopped when he was within two feet of it. The light grew larger. As it did, Adam's strength drained. His muscles could hardly hold him up. He wanted to collapse, but he managed to keep standing.

Adam's mouth dropped open at the unbelievable scene that unfolded in his great room. This was like no acid trip he had ever been on. He would not have believed it in a million years had he not seen it himself. And even now he still wondered at the Star Trek-like event that was happening right before his incredulous eyes.

A—?—man stepped out of the light. That was just too much. Adam's weakened body collapsed to the floor in what seemed to him as slow motion. He could feel his heart pounding wildly, dangerously against his chest. A sharp, piercing pain shot through his upper cavity and he closed his eyes. Suddenly, the searing pain was gone. His spirit separated from his body and rose to the ceiling. Adam looked down at his crumpled body. *I must've had a heart attack.*

He felt a gravitational pull from above. Then it dawned on him. *I've died! I'm dead!* For a split second a wave of panic washed over him. But just as quickly, the panic subsided and an indescribable joy that could never be captured with words flooded his being from head to toe. *Heaven! That's heaven calling! I'm going to heaven!*

The angel looked up at Adam and their eyes met. He didn't say a word, but Adam sensed what was to come next. "No! No!" he begged. "Please let me go."

"It is not yet your time." And with that he reached down and touched Adam's limp body. When he did, Adam's spirit felt an irresistible pull downward. He fought it with all of his might, like a fish fighting to get off of a hook, but it was to no avail. The pull was too great. His spirit united with his flesh and he regained consciousness.

"Adam," he heard the angel call. His unearthly voice pierced the grogginess like the whistle of a locomotive in the dead of night.

Adam strained to raise his head, but his muscles wouldn't respond. He felt a touch on his shoulder and instantly his strength returned. Trembling, he stood to his feet. Adam studied every detail of the man who stood before him. He wore no shoes and his clothes were like something from the era of the Roman Empire. Everything about this man was big. He stood at least a full foot higher than Adam.

Adam looked into the man's face, and when he did he had the sensation of being x-rayed. He knew that this man knew everything there was to know about him. All the sins of his old life, as well as the new. He ashamedly recalled how just the other day at work his eyes feasted on a co-worker's breasts as she bent over. He guiltily sank to his knees before the angelic visitor.

"The blood of Jesus has cleansed you of that sin and every other. Stand to your feet and worship only the Lord your God, for I am but a messenger of the Most High." Adam stood up. "You must stay here and pray, you and your wife. The revival for which you have sought is coming to Atlanta, but not without the enemy's resistance. Pray for Pastor Styles and the man, Jonathan. Satan has plans for both of them. Only the prayers of the saints can neutralize his attacks."

"What is your name?"

The angel looked at him incredulously. "What difference does it make? I have told you all you need to know. Obey the words of Christ and prosper." He punctuated his exhortation by vanishing right before Adam's eyes.

"Where...is...my—Adam! I thought you said it wasn't in here," Sherry said, as she entered the room. She picked the Bible up from the end table. "Come on. We're going to be late."

"We're not going."

Sherry looked at him as though he had lost his mind. "What do you mean, we're not going?"

Adam was like a wrung out rag. He was expressionless and emotionless. His mind was sedated with the reality of the other world. "We can't go." He stared emptily at a painting, seeing nothing on the canvas, but reliving everything that had just happened. *Why did God appear to me? Who am I?*

Sherry interrupted his thoughts. "Adam, what's wrong with you? Why can't we go?" Her question was more a demand than a question.

He turned and looked his wife in the eyes. "God told me not to go to church."

She looked at him like he had just told her that he was born on the moon. "God appeared to you and told you not to go to church?"

"Yeah."

Sherry looked at him searchingly. "You're serious."

"Yeah, God—"

"You're really serious," she blurted. "God took the shuttle from heaven to come here and tell you not to go to church. I don't believe this." Sherry was exasperated.

"I know what it sounds like Sherry, but someone stepped out of a light. I died and he stopped me from going to heaven. He told me—"

"Waaait a minute." Sherry waved her hand. "What did you just say?"

"He stepped out of a light and—"

"No. No, after that. About dying."

Adam gave her an I'm-not-crazy look. "I said I died and the angel wouldn't let me go to heaven. He said my time wasn't up yet. He told me—us—to stay here and pray for pastor and Jonathan."

Sherry's independent streak stood as tall as the Statue of Liberty now. She didn't know what to make of this crazy story. Maybe it was a flashback from his LSD days. But she knew that she was going to church with or without her husband. "Adam, I'll see you after church." She kissed him on the cheek and left the house.

A few moments passed and Adam heard a terrifying scream. It was his wife. He jumped to his feet. She burst through the door and grabbed Adam. "Close the door! Close the door!"

Adam ran to the door and looked outside. It was a lovely morning. The sun shone brightly. Melodic songs of birds danced on the air. A slight breeze intermittently coursed through the trees. "I don't see anything." He closed the door and turned to his wife. "What's wrong?"

Sherry's teeth chattered so badly she could hardly talk. She hurried to the window and peeked out. Nothing. "A thing appeared."

"A thing? What thing?"

"A big black thing—a monster or something." She placed her shaking arms over her chest and began to cry. "It was so ugly. It came after me."

Adam took her in his arms. "It's okay. It's gone now." He lifted her chin. "Honey, God let you see that to confirm what I'm saying. Do you see? God—"

Sherry dropped to her knees. "Let's just do what the angel said and pray for the pastor and Jonathan."

There were only two angels present when they began to pray. One half hour later ten warrior angels surrounded their home with drawn swords and prepared for battle. The stakes were too high. Nothing would be allowed to interfere with these prayers.

*****

The mood was solemn. Grimness was on every angel's face, especially Rashti's. He didn't want to do it, but he knew that he had no choice. He had read the report of the meeting at Edwin Styles's home, and he agreed with the observing angel that Wallace and Marjorie Reynolds were major players in Satan's scheme. They were a threat that had to be dealt with.

Rashti stood. "I wish there was another way." He hesitated for a couple of seconds. "I've received approval from the Lord Most High to order the mercy angels to withdraw their support from the Reynolds's family. All of you know what this could mean for the Reynolds. Keep your eyes open for the slightest trace of repentance. Maybe we'll be able to save them."

The angels knew all too well the gravity of the situation and the inherent weaknesses of this tactic, but there was no other way. God had only two ways of leading men and women to repentance: mercy and judgment.

Mercy was always the first method used. God considered mercy to be infinitely greater than judgment. Mercy displayed His essence—love, while judgment only displayed one of His attributes.

It always hurt God immeasurably to deal harshly with His people. But some of them were so blind, rebellious, and stubborn that they mistook His mercy as a sign that they were free to sin without consequences. Often the goodness of God seemed to only harden sinners' hearts.

Usually, God's next move was to put pressure on the sinner to face reality and consciously decide for or against Jesus Christ. Most of the time He exerted the pressure Himself, but often—for reasons only He and a few of His closest angels understood—He allowed

Satan to put pressure on them. Of course, the great danger in this was that Satan's motive was not to cause repentance, but destruction. Nonetheless, this was the method chosen to deal with the Reynolds.

Marjorie looked at herself in the mirror. Unfortunately, it was a large mirror and it reflected the cruel truth. She looked at least fifteen years older than her forty-three years. She turned sideways. Her borderless belly and jiggly thighs mocked her distant memories of being thought attractive. She was disgusted with herself. Why, her thighs had been in a civil war for years, one slapping the other with each fat step she took. There wasn't the slightest hint in her mirror that she was once one of the most sought after girls in college. Back then she was fabulously beautiful and incredibly smart. Now she was fabulously fat and too dumb to stop eating.

"I simply have to go on a diet," she mumbled to herself. *Who am I kidding? I've been on every diet there is. I'm never going to lose weight.* She felt an all too familiar depression descend upon her as the finality of her thoughts sunk in. She wiped away a threatening tear and valiantly fought her way into a girdle that could've killed her.

Marjorie never carried a Bible to church; she didn't own one. But her husband always carried his Bible. He was proud of it. It was a seventy-five dollar Scofield's Study Bible. In the two years he owned it, he had opened it exactly three times. Once when his appendix burst and he almost died. Once when their son, Scott, was in a bad car accident. And Thursday afternoon in a futile and embarrassing attempt to find some scriptures to justify his outrage at Edwin's surprise speaker.

Wallace paced back and forth with his unruffled Bible under his arm. *This thing has got to be nipped in the bud. We can't let some fanatic get us off on a charismatic tangent.*

"I'm ready," Marjorie said, as she entered the living room.

"So am I," her husband snapped.

Marjorie's face registered surprise.

"I'm sorry," he apologized. "It's just that the more I think about what happened Wednesday, the madder I get. Reverend Styles better make good on his promise to set things straight or he's history."

"Everything will be fixed today," she said.

As Wallace and Marjorie spoke, they had no idea what was taking place in and around their home. A lone demon spirit floated in and out of their home in a methodical fashion. He darted here and there.

The two angels of mercy who watched understood what the demon was doing. Like a wild animal that marks its territory to keep intruders out, the evil spirit was establishing a perimeter. This was nothing new. Demons always established perimeters. And the angels of God, as their custom was, violated these presumptuous boundaries with great frequency. But there was something about the cocky smile and smug confidence of the demon that struck one of the mercy angels as odd.

"Something's wrong. Look at his face."

The other angel noticed it also. "Yeah, he looks like he has won the race before it has even begun." He stepped forward. "Hate to bust up the party, but—"

"But nothing!" the demon snapped at the startled angel, who was unaccustomed to being spoken to so rudely by demons of such inferior ranking as harassing spirits. He reached into a pouch that hung around his neck and pulled out a scroll. The ugly spirit thrust it into the angel's face.

The mercy angel peered angrily at the brash demon. *Be careful little devil. I've never violated protocol, but you tempt me.* He snatched the scroll and read it. His eyes widened in disbelief. This had to be a trick.

"What is wrong my friend?" asked the other angel, taking the scroll from his stunned partner. He read it and dropped it to the floor in shock.

"You were saying?" the demon mocked. "Hate to bust up the party? Why, gentlemen, the party is just beginning. And I am so sorry you must be leaving." The demon picked up his scroll and smiled triumphantly. "You know where the door is."

"We're not going anywhere until this is verified," one of the angels answered.

The demon jumped up and down and flailed his long, hairy arms wildly in mad protest. "But you must go! The Most High God has ordered it!"

"That's your copy. We've received no such orders, and until we do, we stay."

"Minka," someone called.

The mercy angels turned toward the call and saw Rashti, captain of the host. They looked at him the way an army private would look at his commanding general.

Minka had once caught a brief glimpse of the legendary hero at the Parade of Triumph. This was the official welcoming home of Captain Rashti and his warriors after they had won the Battle of the Resurrection of Christ.

The mercy angel could still vividly see Rashti as he appeared that day. He had worn battledress made of pure silver and transparent gold. Rubies, emeralds, and diamonds lined his breastplate, signifying his many accomplishments. Yes, that was an awesome and memorable day. But the thing that burned indelibly in Minka's mind was Rashti's speech. It had been a masterpiece of picturesque beauty and eloquence.

Rashti had described in great detail what the Resurrection would mean to God's fallen creation. He had spoken with such passion that it seemed he was speaking of his own. "This is a glorious day of new beginnings," Minka recalled him saying. "Our Lord Jesus has turned tears into triumphs, grief into glee, fear into faith. The prayers of the saints are no longer simply prayers. They are realities. The kingdom of God has—"

"Minka," Rashti called. His commanding voice sifted through the angel's fond recollections.

The mercy angel stuck his chest out. "Yes, sir!"

"You have done well to question the legitimacy of this order."

Minka glowed inside at Rashti's commendation. *I knew something wasn't right about these orders.*

"However," Rashti continued, "the orders are from the Most High. Both of you are reassigned to help guard Jonathan Banks."

"But, sir, what will happen to the Reynolds?" Minka knew the answer before he asked the question. Without the mercy of God to act as a buffer between Satan and this family, the enemy would fill the vacuum and rain havoc upon their lives. He looked questioningly to Rashti for an explanation.

Rashti did not have to tell the mercy angels anything. But he knew the pain that these creatures of extraordinary compassion were capable of feeling. He knew that behind the stalwart appearances of the mercy angels were hearts crushed by the news that they must leave the objects of their love.

The captain placed his big hand upon Minka's shoulder. "Go to region six headquarters. Tell the guards that I sent you. The intelligence officer will fill you in on the details."

"Yes, sir. Thank you, sir."

The mercy angels left at once, sure that their cloud of confusion would disappear once they were briefed by the intelligence officer. Yet they were also sure that no matter what the reason was for this tactical move, it would definitely open a cage of demonic horrors for this stubborn family.

Chapter 10

Pastor Styles put his hand on his nauseated belly and closed the bathroom door. He was beyond butterflies. Squirrels maybe, but definitely not butterflies. His stomach felt like a rumbling volcano about to explode. He was dizzy and utterly drained by this whole Jonathan ordeal. He leaned over the toilet and emptied everything but his organs. That helped a little, but the squirrels were still there.

He rinsed out his mouth and brushed his teeth again. The sour taste was gone, but as he looked at himself in the mirror, he could distinctly taste disaster. This wasn't the disaster of Wednesday's church service or of Thursday's surprise meeting, or even of his emasculating episode with his wife. No, what he tasted was not the residue of past meals, but the foretaste of an even greater calamity.

Edwin couldn't explain it, but deep down inside he knew that if he followed through with his promise to Harry Thompson and the others to speak against the words of Jonathan Banks, he would be force fed a miserable diet of remorse.

But why? Why did he have such foreboding thoughts about doing something he knew was right? It was his duty to expose heresy and to save the flock of God from fanatics like Jonathan Banks. Where would the church be if men like Banks went unchecked? They simply couldn't be allowed to raise such false hopes in the congregation. Healings and miracles had long ago passed away with the last apostle. Everyone knew that. Everyone of higher learning, that is.

That's the trouble with these guys, Edwin thought. *They turn up their noses at education. No wonder they don't know what they are talking about.*

The other great unsettling thing that worried Edwin was Jonathan's pompous, holier-than-thou attitude. What gave him the right to barge into his church and point an accusing finger at some of the finest people he knew? Jesus didn't accuse and offend people. He loved them.

This Jonathan is a mess, and he's created a mess. And I'm supposed to fix it. Just like that: fix it. Easier said than done.

Resignation rose up in the troubled pastor. But this feeling gave way to another when he recalled how Jonathan had stopped in front of his associate pastor, Larry McGuire, and all but accused him of adultery. How could he? Larry was one of the best Christians he knew. He was a dedicated servant of the Lord. No! He would not idly stand by and watch his good friends be publicly attacked by some ignorant mad man.

Edwin stepped out of the bathroom like a determined quarterback making a comeback drive, but when he saw his wife, he fumbled. The shame of Thursday night was bad enough, but to make matters worse it had happened again the night before.

This time Barbara was explicit in her dissatisfaction with him. Her words cut Edwin to the core of his masculinity. He felt all of two feet tall in her presence. But he was sure that this wasn't going to last forever. He'd get over this problem and their marriage would return to normal.

This is what he kept telling himself, but he couldn't help wondering what would happen if his impotence was permanent. Barbara took the mystery out of an impotent future by telling him flatly that he was crazy if he expected her to live like a nun. Edwin didn't know exactly how to interpret that, but he was sure that his wife was merely speaking in anger. Tomorrow after the anger subsided, he had told himself, she would apologize. But this was tomorrow, and the look on her face told Edwin that if an apology was coming, it wasn't going to be today's tomorrow.

"Good morning," Edwin offered, almost in a whisper.

"What's good about it, Edwin?" Barbara was clearly not in a repentant mood.

He didn't know what to say to that, so he didn't say anything. He left the room and rounded up the boys and herded them downstairs. He didn't bother to knock on Sharon's door. She was probably already in the car. She was always the first one in the car to go to church.

When Edwin and the boys got to the car and saw that Sharon wasn't there, Edwin said, "Go on. I'll be right back."

Why did he get a sick feeling when he saw that his daughter wasn't in the car? And why did his heartbeat quicken when she didn't answer the door the first time he knocked? And when she did answer and he opened, why did he feel his world collapse when he saw his daughter lying across the bed with her night clothes on?

"Sharon," his voice was weak with a fear he didn't understand, "honey, we're ready for church."

She didn't answer.

Edwin repeated himself.

Sharon turned and looked at her father the way Jesus must have looked at Judas on the night of His betrayal. Edwin saw a lone tear on her cheek.

"What's wrong, baby?" he asked.

Sharon's soft answer rocked his parental equilibrium. "You."

Edwin looked into his daughter's sad eyes and read her heart. He wanted to ask her what she meant, but he reluctantly acknowledged that he knew what she meant. He had betrayed her trust. His performance Thursday night—or his lack of it—had shamed and disappointed his daughter.

She had always been his precious, innocent little angel. He had always been her *he-can-do-anything* dad. Her hero. And how he loved her approval and admiration! It seemed like only yesterday that he had taught her how to ride a bicycle. But now as he looked upon her, he conceded to a mind that didn't want to admit it. His treasured relationship with his lovely daughter was forever altered. Her eyes told him that he was no longer her hero. This was too much to bear.

"I'm going...I'll be..." he stammered, then turned and went downstairs, sure that he was the loneliest, most despised man in the world.

Sharon's guardian angel looked on with great sympathy, but with even greater alarm. Edwin and his daughter needed each other. This rift would weaken both of them and put them at a disadvantage to the forces of darkness. But he took comfort in the fact that Trin was a mighty warrior. Edwin would be safe.

Right now his concern was for Sharon's welfare. Witchcraft had not been seen in the area since his threat. However, there had been numerous sightings of his spies: thirteen on Thursday, twenty-two on Friday, fifty-seven on Saturday, and already today there had been close to one hundred sightings. This could only mean one thing. Attack was eminent.

The angel pulled out his sword and got as close to Sharon as he could. With both hands he lifted his sword over his head and said, "For the glory of God and His Christ!" He began to twirl around and spin his sword. Slowly at first, but then faster and faster, until he moved so fast that one movement was indiscernible from the rest.

Witchcraft looked at this defensive maneuver with great derision. Ordinarily this brainchild of the hated Rashti was impenetrable, but Witchcraft was not ordinary.

He pulled out his sword and held it the way a baseball player holds a bat. His eyes tightened as he studied the tiny openings. He would have to swing at just the right time, and his blade would have to hit at just the right—

Cling!

The angel's sword flew out of his hand and landed several yards away. Sharon's guardian came out of his defensive spin and found himself looking into the red eyes of Witchcraft. Witchcraft's sword was at his neck.

"Surprised?" The guardian said nothing. His eyes told it all. "Don't be. I told you I would return."

The angel was deathly still. He didn't want to provoke Witchcraft. He knew that he wouldn't do anything to him just yet. He had to have time to savor the moment, to enjoy his moment of triumph. A Scripture of the saints came to his mind. *Pride goes before destruction, and a haughty spirit before a fall.*

Faith rose in the angel's heart. This was not the end. Something was going to happen. He didn't know what, but something was definitely going to happen.

"Are you frightened, little angel? You should be. You have smitten my honor and treated me as the vilest of my kind."

"What do you want, Witchcraft?"

"What do I want?" Witchcraft parroted contemptuously. "You know what I want."

"You can't have her."

Witchcraft laughed. "You are in no position to tell me what I can't have." He pressed the razor sharp blade against his neck until the angel thought for sure he was cut. "I will tell you what I will have. Sharon is mine!"

Sharon lay across her bed on her back with her hands folded behind her head. Why was her father fighting against what was so obviously the hand of God? Why was he so fearful of something he should be praying for?

"Do you see her? Do you know what she is thinking? She's wondering what's wrong with her father. By the time I am finished with her, she will hate that weak-kneed shell of a man. Then she will be mine."

Witchcraft spoke with such conviction that the angel found himself involuntarily believing his words. "You will never have her," he answered, but his words seemed hollow.

"And who will stop me?" Witchcraft spoke condescendingly as he added, "Don't build your house on the sand. There will be no prayer support for you today. All the Christians are in church doing their thing. You're on your own."

*****

"God, in Jesus name, send us revival! Help us, oh God!" Adam cried in desperation. "Roll back the forces of darkness! Send forth your mighty angels to fight in our behalf! For it is written in Your Word, are they not all ministering spirits, sent forth to minister for them who shall be heirs of salvation?"

Sherry prayed with as much fervency as her husband. "Help us, Jesus!" She rocked back and forth as she prayed. "Help us, Jesus!" The lightnings of God broke loose in her spirit. She leapt to her feet. "I bind you, devil! In Jesus' name, I come against the spiritual wickedness in high places. Loose God's property!" she screamed, with an authority inspired of heaven.

*****

"I will turn her against her mother," Witchcraft spat. "This fragile facade of a family will crumble before me. I will drown this home with tears of—"

Witchcraft's throat constricted.

*****

"Every tongue that rises up against us in judgment I do condemn!" Sherry was intoxicated with the eloquence of the spirit of prayer. The thoughts came fast and furiously. "The devil who comes against us one way shall leave seven different ways! We shall be a terror unto our enemies! Get out of our city, Satan!"

*****

Sharon felt an infusion of unexplainable optimism and lightness. It was as though her burdens were mysteriously lifted. She sat up, wondered at the sudden buoyancy she felt in her heart, and prepared for church.

Witchcraft's eyes tightened with alarm. He still had the sword pressed hard against the angel's neck, but it was getting harder and harder for him to breathe. He strained and pushed the words out of his wide mouth, "I will spare you so that you may languish in my victory." He shot through the air and was almost instantly out of sight.

Edwin waited patiently in the car for Sharon and his wife. This was a small miracle of sorts. He had always found it extremely difficult to wait patiently for anyone who made him late. But this morning he felt like he could wait a million years. He was in no hurry to face Barbara or Sharon.

However, his million years expired in a matter of minutes.

As Sharon approached the car, Edwin thought he saw a bounce in her step. Not the usual joyful bounce, but a bounce nonetheless. His heaviness lifted a little.

A few minutes later his wife was ready. She approached the car. Edwin searched her face for the slightest sign of softness. What he found were eyes red from crying, and a coldness in her countenance that turned his heaviness into despondency.

The ride to church was an awkward experience for the Styles family. Christopher was too young to know that anything was wrong. But Andrew knew that all was not right. Sharon's faith had made a resurgence, but as she mused over what might take place at church this morning, her buoyancy gave place to sadness and disgust. She could only hope that the dad driving her to church this morning was not the same dad that had cowered before those awful people Thursday. Barbara wasn't thinking anything. She was locked into a void of anger and resentment.

Edwin's emotions swung to the right and left as he drove into the church parking lot. He didn't know which was more endurable: sitting in a car with a family that despised him or preaching to a church that despised him.

Unlike Wednesday night Bible study, tonight there were many empty parking spaces. Edwin shook his head at the fallout of that fanatic. Why had Terrance done this to him? It took every ounce of strength to open the car door and get out. He walked around to Barbara's side to let her out, but she opened it herself before he could get there and walked away. Edwin sighed.

"Ed," someone called across the parking lot.

Edwin cringed. He knew who that was.

Harry Thompson strutted across the parking lot.

"Andrew, take your brother in. I'll see you after church." He kissed Christopher on the forehead and looked at Sharon. She didn't look him in the eyes; she couldn't. Sharon walked away before Harry got there. This was no coincidence.

"You know what to do, don't you?" Harry asked, with his arm on Edwin's shoulder. Edwin opened his mouth to answer, but Harry cut him off. "Tell the people that Jonathan Banks is a false prophet. Tell them that biz about miracles and healings dying out with the last apostle. They'll believe it." Harry looked around as though he were a spy under surveillance. In a low, conspiratorial tone, he added, "Above all else, erase that garbage about sin and hell fire. Jesus came to make us feel good, not guilty. He understands our shortcomings."

There seemed to be no limit to how miserable and wretched Edwin could feel. Harry's words only increased the sinking feeling in his belly.

"You do understand how important this is?"

Edwin read Harry's message loud and clear. If he wasn't satisfied with his performance today, he would be voted out by the board. And for all practical purposes, Harry Thompson was the board. No one would dare raise a voice of dissent. Not even his good friend Larry McGuire, the assistant pastor.

"Yes, I do. Don't worry, I'll take care of it."

Harry said, "Good," and patted him on the head. "I knew I could count on you." He abruptly turned and walked toward the church.

Edwin didn't know why he felt like he had just been raped. Neither could he understand why he felt like he was selling his soul to something evil. He should've felt good about taking a stand for God and His people, but he didn't. Instead, he felt as though he was about to make matters even worse. But what could be worse than what already was?

As he walked across the lot, two scriptures floated up in his mind: *They shall put you out of the synagogues. Yea, the time cometh, that whosoever killeth you will think that he doeth God service. And these things will they do unto you because they have not known the Father, nor me.*

Edwin nervously asked himself what could that possibly mean? It certainly couldn't be speaking of him. If anyone knew God, it was him. He had the degrees to prove it. He dismissed the thought and entered the church.

*****

Witchcraft's eyes bore through Sharon with an intensity that could've cut through granite. He was hungry for her soul. White, frothy spit dripped down the sides of his wide mouth. Soon her father would get up and go to the podium and push her closer to Witchcraft than she had ever been. Witchcraft would then destroy her mother's credibility. Once this was done, he would consummate his plan and capture Sharon's heart.

Edwin went directly to the pastor's study. He had to do something that he didn't do much. He had to pray. His deficient prayer life was a product of his training. The liberal seminary that he had graduated from didn't speak much of prayer. God was portrayed as a mystical, unreachable, impersonal figure who was interested in the welfare of mankind, but was detached from it. So there really was no practical purpose of prayer, except to ease the mind. The world would get better not by passive exercises of prayer, but by the acceleration of knowledge.

Yet Edwin knew that his problems were beyond his knowledge. As useless as it might be, the only thing he could think to do was pray. He closed his office door and got on his knees.

"Thou, God, most high," he began. There was a long silence as he tried to think of something to say. “Thou who hast created the heavens and the earth." Silence again. "Whence art thou Spirit?" was the only thing he could think of. He hoped that he was praying properly, saying the right words. But he felt like he was making a fool of himself.

He stammered and stuttered like this for a few minutes. Finally, in desperation he threw aside his feeble Elizabethan English and prayed from his heart.

"Jesus, help me! I don't know what to do!" Tears rolled down his cheeks. "Everyone is pulling me in different directions. What am I supposed to do? I'm only a man."

Edwin expressed his worries through his tears. He cried as never before. His tightly clenched fists vibrated under the intensity of his desperate prayer.

"I'm losing my daughter. I'm losing my wife. I'm losing my church. Oh! God, I'm losing my mind!" Edwin rocked back and looked up to the ceiling. Before he knew what he was doing, his hands went up and reached for the heavens. This was something he had never done before. "What do You want from me?" he begged the God he scantly understood or knew. "Why are You driving me insane?"

I love you.

Edwin opened his eyes and took a deep breath. What was that? He didn't hear it with his ears, but he distinctly and unmistakably heard it—*I love you.*

He rose to his feet and blew his nose. Who loves me? Then it dawned on him. It must be God! God had spoken to him? It had to be Him!

Courage rose in him. He had never felt this confident and sure in his life. He looked at the ceiling again. "God, I'll do your will, and not because of Harry Thompson. I'll do it because it's right." He then thought about Sharon. He had never been put in this position before. He had to choose between his daughter and his God.

As he left his office with his Bible tucked securely under his arm, he said, "Oh, God, please help her to understand."

Sharon suffered through all of the religious preliminaries. She watched her father approach the pulpit with a mixture of disdain and affection. Her heart was torn and bruised and she was confused. She didn't know what to believe about her father, herself, or her God. But one thing she did know: if her father didn't stand up for Jesus today, she would never speak to him again.

Edwin put his Bible on the pulpit and opened his notebook. He would use a lot of notes today. The title of his sermon was *The God of Yesterday and the God of Today*.

"I have been deeply troubled since our last gathering," he began. "For those of you who were not here, you have no doubt heard of the strange happenings that occurred in our midst."

Edwin scanned his audience. Such a diversity of faces! Some were pleasant. Most of those were probably visitors. Others were angry and hard. His wife was in this group. He looked at Sharon. Her expression wasn't hard, but it wasn't soft either. It was hurt and withdrawn. Harry had a blank look on his face.

A spirit whispered into Edwin's ear and he continued his sermon. He had never experienced such eloquence and freedom of thought and speech. Every word he needed was on the tip of his tongue. He quoted scriptures he never knew he knew. With the eloquence of an ancient Athenian orator, he explained in great detail why Jonathan's concept of God was heretical.

He told them how God had used miracles and healings only in biblical times to establish Jesus's claim to messiahship and to evangelize the world.

He asked rhetorical questions and then answered them himself. “If God does heal the sick, why do so many precious Christians die with cancer and other dreadful diseases? We do not understand nor can we ever understand the mysterious ways of God. We cannot question the unfathomable wisdom of our great God."

Sharon placed her Bible on the pew and left the church.

Witchcraft followed close behind.

Edwin watched his daughter rise and leave. He wanted to take her in his arms and tell her how sorry he was for letting her down. He wanted to tell her how much he loved her. But he didn't. He couldn't. Any step toward her would be a step away from his responsibility to God. He mentally acknowledged his past weaknesses and determined to be strong for the God who had supernaturally reaffirmed His love for him.

As Edwin concluded his sermon, he saw Harry beaming, and so were Wallace and Marjorie Reynolds. Ironically, their approval made him feel uneasy. He felt as though he was a juror who had condemned someone to death only to find out after the execution that the defendant was innocent.

Wallace and Marjorie were the first to commend him after the service.

"Fine job, Reverend," said Wallace, shaking his hand vigorously. "Just what they needed to hear. All that nonsense about miracles and holiness should be kept on the other side of the tracks."

"Oh, my, what a fantastic sermon! I never knew you were so eloquent," Marjorie added.

It was Harry's turn now. "Great job! Great job! You preached like a devil. A few more weeks and everything will be back to normal."

After the small crowd of satisfied customers dispersed, someone else walked up. Oh, no! It was his sister-in-law. What was she doing here?

"You quoted a lot of scriptures," she said haughtily, "but you forgot one: Woe unto you, when all men shall speak well of you. You can find that one in Luke 6:26."

Edwin didn't answer. He had learned that to respond to his sister-in-law only prolonged the agony of being in her presence.

However, it wasn't so easy to casually dismiss the next person who approached him. The old man placed his hand on Edwin's shoulder and looked him directly in his eyes.

Edwin always felt uneasy when someone looked at him like this. For some ridiculous reason, direct eye contact of more than a couple of seconds made him feel inexplicably inadequate. Inadequate in what way, he could never determine.

He had read in a book that when speaking to someone face to face, if you looked at the person's nose, the person couldn't tell that you weren't looking at his eyes. He focused on the nose that was attached to the man who was responsible for this whole mess, Terrance Knox.

"Son, I know you mean well," he began, his voice tired with advanced age, "but you are fighting for the wrong side." The old man smiled and squeezed Edwin's shoulder. "I suggest you do some soul searching. God will reveal Himself to you...if you really want Him."

The old man walked away, but his words lingered. *If you really want Him.*

Chapter 11

Nerod was Oreon's replacement. He stood at the Mighty Bashnar's door and swallowed hard. Even though he had news of a great victory, he wondered if his promotion was really a demotion. He swallowed hard again and knocked on the door.

"You may enter," said the intimidating voice.

The newly promoted demon clutched his report and opened the door. Nerod had attended the emergency meeting where Bashnar had informed them of the threat of revival. He recalled how frightening an experience it had been to be seated only four rows from the front and dead center of Bashnar's lectern. But at least there he could hide in the crowd. Here he had no place to hide. He was face to face with the Mighty Bashnar. This was the most terrifying moment of his life.

Nerod stepped forward, saluted by pounding his chest once, and hoped his trembling wasn't noticeable. It was no secret that this great warrior hated displays of weakness. Although it was widely known that he got some kind of sick satisfaction out of seeing subordinates cower in his presence.

"Mighty Bashnar, here is my formal report of the proceedings of this morning."

The proceedings of which he spoke was the battle that had taken place at Edwin Styles's church only two hours earlier.

Nerod stood at attention as Bashnar read his report. Thirty minutes. Forty-five minutes. An hour. An hour and a half. Two hours! What was taking him so long to read a ten minute report? How hard could it be to see that Nerod's first battle was an astounding, almost unbelievable victory?

Finally, Bashnar put the report down. "You completely routed the enemies of light?"

Can't you read? "Yes, that is correct." There was no trace of disrespect in his voice.

Bashnar's eyes cut through Nerod. He could hardly stand the gaze. This pleased Bashnar. "Have you ever heard of Rashti, the angel they call The Sword of the Lord?"

Nerod swallowed hard again. So hard that he feared Bashnar had heard it. Who had not heard of Captain Rashti? Just answer the question. Don't add anything. Don't get hung with your tongue. "Yes, Mighty Bashnar."

"You made no mention of Rashti."

"No, sir, Mighty Bashnar. He was not there."

For what seemed like eternity to Nerod, Bashnar said nothing. Finally, still peering at his subordinate, Bashnar asked, "What is your appraisal of the effect of Edwin's sermon?"

"He has caused many doubts and questions. I believe his church will remain passively detached from spiritual warfare."

He knew Bashnar would be pleased at his next revelation. "Sir, the thorn, Sharon, uughh...she seems to have lost her faith not only in her father, but in God."

Bashnar sat up straight at these words. He did not smile, but he wanted to.

"Witchcraft is stalking her now," said Nerod.

The thought of smiling vanished. Warrior and witchcraft spirits were in a constant state of contention. Each group hurled accusations of glory-seeking and connivance at the other. And both were correct.

"Trin?"

"Sir?"

"Trin—he was there?"

"Yes, sir. But he made a tactical error and we capitalized on it. We outflanked him and routed his forces." Nerod was proud of his accomplishment. He waited for a word of praise from the Mighty Bashnar.

"He made a tactical error?"

"Yes, sir."

Bashnar put Nerod's battle report next to Jonathan's file. "Dismissed."

Disappointed, the demon saluted his superior and did an about face. As he walked toward the door Bashnar said something that caused Nerod's knees to buckle.

"Yes, I can."

"Sir?"

"Yes, I can read."

*****

"How is your arm?" Rashti asked Trin.

"Superficial. It'll heal quickly."

"Do you think they bought it?"

"The soldiers on the field, I know they bought it. They celebrated wildly afterwards. That new commander, Nerod, he danced himself silly."

"Excellent! All is going according to plan," said Rashti. "Unless there is a cataclysmic reversal, Edwin's seeds of doubt will spring up into trees of everlasting life."

Trin could only admire the brilliance of his leader.

The plan that Rashti spoke of was a classic ambush. Rashti had directed Trin to concentrate his forces in one area. He knew that Nerod would seize the opportunity and move to his flank and surround Trin's army. The only risk—and it was a very real risk—was that if anything went wrong, specifically if there wasn't enough prayer support, this ambush would turn into a massacre. As it turned out, Adam and Sherry gave them more than enough prayer support to fight their way out of Nerod's grip.

The result? The defeat of Trin's army allowed Nerod and his wicked spirits to do as they pleased in that church service. And it pleased them to overwhelm the place with their most skillful demons of religion. An extra detachment of these spirits was called down from Utah to help deceive the congregation.

A religious demon with an enviable string of great successes—the deluding of Charles Taze Russell, Mary Baker Eddy, Joseph Smith, Jr., Jim Jones, and others—helped Edwin reclaim some of the ground he had lost to that dangerous man, Jonathan Banks.

He gave Edwin the thoughts and eloquence to persuade his flock that holiness was more a mental disease than a commandment of God. He energized his sermon so powerfully with devilish logic that most of the church accepted Edwin's explanations.

This is exactly what Rashti wanted. He wanted Edwin's anti-holiness, anti-supernatural position to be so strongly stated that once it was disproved, he and his church would be left with the smoldering ruins of a bankrupt theological system.

Rashti would then fill this theology vacuum with the Word of the Lord. Revival would break out in his church and spread into Atlanta and the surrounding cities. Hundreds of thousands would be swept into the kingdom of God!

*****

Toni didn't want to admit the real reason why she went to church this Sunday. She tried to make herself believe that she went because she was feeling low for not being able to contact Rick. Why didn't he call her?

She shuddered at the thought that he might be like all the others who promised anything to go to bed with a girl. No. Rick wouldn't do that. He wouldn't hurt her. But even as she tried to convince herself that Rick was different, a cruel voice in the pit of her gut told her that he was just another bip! bam! thank you, ma'am.

Yes, she was hurt and her heart did ache for Rick, but that wasn't why she went to church this morning. Deep down inside, as much as she hated to admit it, her real reason was Sharon. She wanted to see Sharon.

Sharon was the only real friend she had ever had. Toni had never known anyone who loved her so unconditionally. Her memories of Sharon made her feel stupid for being so bitter towards her. How could anyone not like Sharon? Why did she try so hard to dislike her?

Toni admitted to herself what she had known all along. She was bitter because she felt rejected and left out. After Sharon had given her life to Jesus Christ at a Teen Mania, *Acquire the Fire* concert, things just weren't the same.

Sharon changed so dramatically in the following weeks that they had little left in common. She stopped going to parties. She stopped drinking. She stopped smoking marijuana. She stopped cursing. She even stopped going to movies! Why did she have to take this Jesus thing so far?

Yet, with all the abrupt changes in Sharon's life, one thing didn't change: her love for Toni. If anything, it intensified, and Toni could feel it. But it made her uncomfortable. Whenever she was around Sharon—which was becoming less and less—she became painfully aware of the emptiness of her own dismal life.

Sharon never pushed Jesus on Toni, but she never apologized for Him either. She unwaveringly refused to compromise her devotion to Jesus Christ for anyone, and it was only natural that she talked about her new heartthrob to everyone who would listen.

Toni remembered their last conversation.

"You shouldn't feel threatened, Toni. Jesus didn't come to pull us apart, but to put us together."

"Well, He's doing a lousy job! You're in another world." Toni put her hands to her face and added through tears, "A world that I can never be a part of."

"But you can, Toni." Sharon's heart broke for her friend. "Jesus loves you."

"He could never love me," she said, dejectedly.

Sharon hugged her friend tightly. "Oh, but that's not true, Toni. You have to believe me. That's not true."

They both cried.

"Sharon, there is so much about me you don't know."

This was no surprise to Sharon. She knew that her friend had serious problems that she kept to herself.

"Toni, whatever it is, it isn't bad enough to keep you away from God," Sharon pleaded.

"I hate your God and I hate you."

Sharon dropped her arms from Toni's shoulders and looked at her incredulously. "You don't mean that. I know you don't."

Toni's eyes tightened. Her face hardened. "I do mean it, Miss Priss." She added by punctuating each word with a pointed finger to Sharon's face. "I hate you and I hate your God."

Sharon was shocked. The voice came from Toni, but it wasn't Toni. Neither was the expression on her face. It was so evil that it nearly made her perfectly beautiful face ugly.

"You can't...I know—"

"I mean it!" Toni screamed.

Sharon had taken a couple of awkward steps backward and turned and ran away as she loudly cursed her then best friend with the most vile, filthy language she could think of.

Toni looked back on that episode and wondered why she had said those things. What had gotten into her that she could say such things to someone like Sharon?

Sharon tried to contact Toni several times afterwards, but Toni was too ashamed to speak with her. Then there was the frequent unexplainable revulsion that rose up inside of her belly at the very thought of Sharon. Actually, it was more than a feeling of hatred. It was more like a personality—a *thing*. Something inside of Toni hated Sharon. She shuddered as she contemplated what that *thing* was. It would never let her and Sharon be friends again.

Something made Toni look at her watch.

Four o'clock. Only eight more hours. She had to talk to Sharon. Toni picked up the phone.

Sharon was in her room with the door locked. She sat in a spaceless void, suffering in the silence of her unbearable confusion. She didn't know what was right or wrong any more. Had she given her life to a myth? A religious figure whose decayed remains lay trapped in a Holy Land crypt?

Jesus. Now the very sound of His name seemed to mock and tease her. A rubber steak thrown to a starving dog! "I hate You! I hate You! I hate You!" she screamed in agonizing emptiness.

Myla's alarm was immeasurable.

Suddenly Witchcraft's voice thundered. "I always make good on my word."

Myla snatched out his sword and got in a low, crouching position. Give him a small target, he told himself. But it was unnecessary. Witchcraft only wanted to taunt for now.

Sharon's telephone rang. She let it ring until it stopped.

"Call again," a demon instructed Toni.

The telephone rang again. Sharon let it ring several times before she picked it up.

"Hello."

Toni heard Sharon's voice and almost hung up.

"Hello," Sharon repeated.

"Sharon?" Toni's voice was timid.

"Toni?" Sharon sat up. "Is that you?"

"Yeah, how's it going?"

Sharon wiped her eyes. She could hardly believe her ears. "It's going. What about you?"

"Oh, life's a blast," she answered cynically.

There was an awkward silence as both of them quickly ran out of small talk.

"Sharon...I didn't mean—I'm sorry. I don't know why I acted the way I did. I really don't know what came over me."

Ordinarily Sharon would have been quick to receive the apology and gloss over the gravity of the offense. This time she didn't. Instead, she was silent.

Sharon was uncharacteristically unmoved by Toni's penitence. She wanted to reach out to her friend. (How she missed her!) But she was spiritually and emotionally drained. There was nothing left in her to reach out.

The silence both alarmed and confused Toni.

"Sharon, I really am sorry." *I really am. Please believe me.*

"I believe you." Toni was further thrown off balance. Sharon's words sounded perfunctory, insincere.

"Hey, could we get together and talk?" she asked Sharon.

There was a momentary spark of hopeful and jubilant fire in Sharon's bosom. But it failed to catch and burn. The mist of her crushing disillusionment put out the fire that would have been.

"Yeah." Sharon's answer was robotic, without a trace of emotion.

An hour later they met at *The Joint*, a restaurant and bar that was more bar than restaurant that was a favorite of the high school crowd. The music was lively, the atmosphere festive, and the waitresses wore very little clothes.

The meeting place was Sharon's idea.

Toni lit a cigarette. "Sharon, I met this guy—one of Jerry's friends—a great guy. His name is Rick. He's a senior at Emory. He's going to be a lawyer."

Toni went on for five minutes telling Sharon how wonderful her new boyfriend was. The more she spoke, the more at ease Sharon became.

"Sounds like a great guy." The robotic tone was nearly gone.

Toni smiled. "He is."

Toni's smile brought one to Sharon's face. Sharon took Toni's hand. "I'm so happy for you."

Toni smiled widely. "Thank you," she said, happy that the old Sharon was back. A few moments passed. "I have something else to say."

Sharon looked at her friend compassionately. She found herself listening to thoughts of a Sharon that was. *She's so unhappy, so unfulfilled. She's so tossed about. She's never going to find peace and satisfaction until... Until what?* she asked derisively. *Until she meets Christ?*

Sharon shook the intrusive thoughts and tried to listen to Toni without analyzing her.

"Lately I've been thinking about some of the things you used to tell me." Sharon's expression told her that she didn't know what

Toni was talking about. "You know, those things about Jesus and all."

Sharon felt sick to her stomach. A demon of self-pity whispered into Sharon's ear. *Oh, Toni, please not now. I can't help you. I can't even help myself.*

"Hey, girl!" a waitress said.

They both looked up.

"Marcy!" Toni beamed, "I didn't know you still worked here."

"I don't," she quipped. "I just shake a little butt and collect big tips."

All three girls laughed.

"Hey, Marcy," Sharon said.

Until now Marcy had not noticed that the girl with Toni was Sharon. "Hi." Her surprise at seeing her and Toni together was clearly written on her face. Sharon's conversion and subsequent falling out with Toni was no secret. "Are you going to the dance?" the waitress asked Toni.

"Wouldn't miss it. You?"

"With my party shoes on. I hope I see you there. You want to order anything?"

"I only want a sweet tea," Toni answered.

"Sharon, what about you?"

Sharon's face turned mischievous. "A strawberry daiquiri. Can you get it?"

The waitress was stunned. So was Toni.

"A virgin?"

"No," she answered. "Can you get it?"

Marcy smiled. "Yeah, I think I can get it past old four eyes. I'll be right back."

“Hey, Marcy,” Sharon added, “have them strain it for me. And go light on the lime. Okay?”

Marcy tilted her head and raised her brows with a half-smile as she looked at Sharon, then Toni. “Oh, oh, okaaayyy.”

Toni stared at Marcy as she walked away. "When did you start drinking again?" Toni asked, unwilling to believe what she had just seen.

"Just now."

Their conversation rambled here and there for a number of minutes. Then Toni steered it towards religion. "I went to your church today," she said, knowing she would get a favorable response from Sharon.

Sharon could hardly believe her ears. How many times had she invited Toni to church only to be rebuffed? How many prayers had she offered for the salvation of her friend? How many tears had she cried on her behalf? And, now, of all times she goes to church.

"You went today?"

Toni smiled. "Yeah. I didn't see you."

"I was there," Sharon said, with a touch of remorse. "I left early."

Toni noted Sharon's response, or lack of it, and asked, "Is everything all right? You seem to have something on your mind. Maybe I can help."

How things change. Just a week ago I was the helper. Now I'm the one who needs help. "Yeah, I do have a lot on my mind," Sharon admitted.

"Want to talk about it?"

Sharon hoped Toni couldn't see the moisture that was building in her eyes. "Thanks, Toni, but right now I don't understand enough about it to even begin to tell you." And before Toni could press her further, she added, "There is one thing you could do for me."

Toni was eager to help. "What's that?"

"Be there for me. Be my friend."

Toni put out her cigarette and clasped Sharon's hand. "Oh, yes...yes! Just like old times!" she giggled.

"Just like old times."

They spent the next hour reminiscing and catching each other up on their lives. Although their friendship had been put on hold for a year, this meeting lacked none of the energy that had made their relationship special. The cords that bound them together appeared as strong as ever.

Suddenly Toni's smile faded. She looked at her watch and placed her elbows on the table. She rubbed her hands together nervously.

Sharon noticed the abrupt change in mood. "What's wrong?"

Toni's mouth opened and she started to say something, but she closed her mouth. She again looked at her watch and took a deep breath and looked at Sharon with troubled eyes.

Sharon could see the pain. "Toni, what's wrong?" she asked once more.

"This is my problem," she answered. "I don't want to trouble you with it." But she did want to trouble Sharon with it, and she hoped Sharon wouldn't let it drop.

This is where Sharon excelled. Nothing fulfilled her more than helping others. She felt herself rising to the occasion even though she felt in as much need as Toni.

"No, it's not your problem. It's our problem."

"Oh, thank you, Sharon," Toni said, infinitely grateful to have such a friend.

Sharon waited impatiently while her friend gathered her thoughts.

"Tonight I have to do something. Something for my father."

"What?"

Sharon and Toni looked at one another for several moments. Whatever it was, Toni was having a hard time getting it out. Sharon beckoned her on with a raised brow.

Okay. Here goes. "My father's a...a...Sharon, he worships the devil." She had to force the words out of her mouth.

Sharon's mouth dropped open. She scarcely knew what a devil worshipper was, but it sounded evil enough. "What does he want you to do?"

"Tonight I'm going to be coronated as a high priestess."

"A what? A high priestess of what?"

"The Family," Toni said, shaking her head at the irony of her father's concept of a family.

"What do you guys do?" asked Sharon.

"We pray and have ceremonies...and other stuff."

"To the devil?" This all sounded so bizarre to Sharon's sheltered mind.

"Yes."

Neither of them said anything else for a long while. Then Sharon spoke up first. "Toni, none of this makes any sense to me. What is it all about? I mean, why do you guys pray to the devil?"

"It wasn't always this way," Toni answered. "I can remember as a little girl we used to go to church. We were so happy then. Everything seemed so right." Toni's recollections of her early childhood brought back vividly fresh sensations of the security and love she used to enjoy. She smiled into the mirror of her memories and experienced them anew. But in a few moments reality cracked her mirror. "I have to go," she said, as she stood up.

"Wait a minute," Sharon stated. "Where are you going?"

Toni put some money on the table. "This will cover your drinks. I can't explain right now, but—" she looked into Sharon's eyes—"I want you to know that I love you. You're the best friend I've ever had." She turned and walked a few steps and turned again to Sharon. Toni was crying. "You're the only friend I've ever had."

*****

At exactly twelve o'clock midnight Toni, her father, and ten others were in a large barn somewhere close to the Georgia-Tennessee border. It was an uncommonly warm night for this time of year.

Ten hooded figures dressed in long black robes stood in a half-circle. A man in similar attire faced them. He lifted his right hand over his head and read strange words from a worn book.

Behind him stood Toni. She was dressed in a beautiful white bridal gown that glowed even in the darkness of the dimly lit barn. Her head bobbed from side to side under the heavy influence of the drugs she had been given.

The apparent leader of this robed group placed his book on the altar that was behind Toni. He then faced her and put his hand to her throat. Toni floated in and out of reality. She could see the man standing before her, but the drugs distorted his body. His arms and face and torso stretched beyond their human limitations.

RIP!

He violently tore Toni's gown off of her. She stood before the group unaware that she was naked. Two men took her by the arms and guided her to the altar. She was placed on her back. The men tied her hands and feet to posts.

The leader then ascended the three altar steps where Toni was lain. He faced a large picture that hung on the wall of the barn adjacent to the altar. It was a picture of a star within a circle. All five points of the star touched the circle. Inside of the star were two small dots.

With both hands, he held over his head an inverted cross. "Prince of darkness, father of the underworld, we beg your pardon and presence." He turned to the group and repeated himself. This time they responded in kind.

Someone brought a small goat to the altar and tied his legs in twos. Then the leader went to a small table with a black cloth draped over it and picked up a shiny knife. He went to the goat and routinely slit his throat. The blood poured into a large silver chalice.

He took the bloody knife and slowly pulled its sharp blade across his inner hand. He mixed his blood with the goat's blood and everyone else did the same. The leader took the chalice and sipped its ghastly contents. He gave to the others and they sipped also.

The leader now slowly poured the warm blood over Toni's naked body until the chalice was empty. One by one each member of the Family discarded their clothes and had communion with their new high priestess.

After the last communion was complete, the leader again faced the picture of the star and with both hands lifted the inverted cross over his head.

"Prince of darkness, father of the underworld, we beg your pardon and presence."

The others followed their leader and repeated these words. Over and over they called to the nether world. Suddenly, the temperature in the barn dropped drastically. The leader jerked violently a few times. A voice not his own emitted from his throat. "There will be no revival in Atlanta! Atlanta is mine!"

Chapter 12

Toni's internal alarm clock awakened her. She rolled over on her side and looked at the clock. Her eyes burned for lack of sleep. She had to squint several times to make out the time. Seven o'clock. She jumped up. Seven o'clock! "Oh, God, I have to hurry."

Toni hurried through the morning mumbling to herself that she was going to miss homeroom. She took a five-minute shower and almost fell in her frenzy to make up for oversleeping. She put on her clothes and make-up in record time and headed for the door. She stopped dead in her tracks and grabbed her head. "My hair!" Toni dropped her books on the bed and frantically doctored her hair.

She was loathe to leave the house looking the way she did this morning. Anything less than a magazine's cover was out of the question. Toni usually spent an inordinate amount of time in front of the mirror. Everything had to be perfect. Hair. Make-up. Clothes. Perfume. Nails. Jewelry.

Toni's appearance was her therapy. It compensated somewhat for her being a rotten, unlovable, unwanted person with nothing to offer except her body.

Her coronation as the Family's high priestess didn't come to mind. She wouldn't let it come to mind. The humiliation and degradation of last night was placed in the basement of her sub-consciousness. Thinking about her problems was simply too much for Toni to handle. So she just acted as if they didn't exist. This was Toni's way of staying sane.

"There!" said Toni, looking at her hair. "That will have to do." She stuck out her chest and examined her appearance. *I can't wait to see Jerry so that I can ask him about Rick.*

She hurried out the door and made better time than she could have imagined. It wasn't long before she found out about Rick. At lunch she was told that Jerry was near the snack bar. She could see him as she approached. There was a small group of people around him.

Toni smiled and shook her head. *Animals must have gotten their hands on a Playboy magazine,* she thought. As she got closer to the crowd, she saw that the guys were ooohhing and aahhing about something Jerry was showing them.

There were a couple of girls in the crowd too. Toni frowned as she recognized one of the girls: Andrea Singletary.

This was a girl in whom Toni could find nothing worth liking. No one noticed Toni as she approached.

"Jerry," she called, smiling, "what have you little boys gotten your grubby little paws on?"

A hush fell on the crowd. There was a mad shuffling of hands. Someone dropped a photo and it landed face down at Toni's feet. She smiled mischievously as she stooped to pick it up.

Toni turned the picture over in her hand and froze. "What...what is this?" she demanded. "My God! How did you—?"

She pushed her way through the crowd and snatched pictures from several hands. They were pictures of her and Rick naked. *How could this be?* she thought. *We were alone. Who could have taken these pictures?* She looked at another picture and gasped. It was a picture of her and Jerry! She dropped the pictures to the ground and put her hands over her mouth. She backed away, shaking her head in shock.

"I don't believe this. I don't believe this." Then it hit her. She remembered the dizzying sensation she felt after Rick gave her the drink. She remembered the noise in the closet. I was drugged. "You were there! You and Rick planned this whole thing!"

"Like you didn't know!" Andrea spewed.

Toni couldn't hear her above the deafening noise in her head. She felt dizzy. She had to get away. She turned and ran away as fast as she could. Later that evening she called Rick several times. He never answered. Toni sat in a daze with the phone to her ear. She called once more. It rang incessantly. Toni's mind was in neutral and pointed downhill. Each unanswered ring brought her closer to a terrible crash.

Finally, someone picked up the phone. Toni lurched forward and sat on the edge of the sofa. "Hello! Rick?" Toni heard a clicking sound. "Rick! Rick, I need to—"

Dial tone.

Toni let the phone fall to the floor. Once more she had been used. Walls of rejection closed in on her and her foolish dreams. Her mind went numb with yet another realization of a dashed hope.

Ring! Ring!

Toni slowly picked up the phone. "Hello." Her voice was void of life.

"Toni, Toni, I have to talk to you."

"Who is this!" Toni yelled. "Jerry?" she asked, unbelievingly.

"Yeah. Toni—"

Click!

The telephone rang again.

"What do you want?" Toni asked angrily.

"Toni, we have to talk," said Jerry.

"Jerry, I thought you were my friend. How could you do this?"

There was a long silence.

"Toni, I'm sorry," he apologized. "I've never truly been your friend." The words were hard to say, but he had to say them. He had no choice. His parents were standing over him. "Toni, I don't know why I did something so stupid." Jerry looked at his father's angry glare and his mother's fraught expression. "I...I told my parents," he offered.

Nothing he said helped the pain of betrayal. She would have hung up again had he not mentioned his parents. "How did they find out?" This didn't make sense.

"I told them."

"You told them," Toni said, unbelievingly.

"Yeah, I—"

Click!

Jerry turned to his father. "She hung up."

"Call her back," he demanded.

Toni picked up the phone. "Don't ever call me again, Jerry. Please, just leave me alone. I can't take all of this." Her voice was no longer defiant and angry, just pitiful, defeated.

"Please don't hang up," Jerry begged. "My parents are standing here listening to this whole thing."

"You just won't stop, will you?" The anger was back. Jerry's parents were Christians. She knew that he would never tell them what he had done."

"Toni?"

Toni blinked hard. "Yes," she said, cautiously.

"This is Jerry's father."

Toni recognized the voice and could hardly believe it. "Hi, Mr. Woods."

"Toni, our son told us what happened. Young lady, I don't know what to say, except that I am extremely sorry," he looked his son in the eyes, "and I am extremely disappointed and shocked by my son's behavior."

"Toni?"

"Yes." Jerry was back on the phone.

"I never wanted to hurt you." Jerry's voice had the sound of true penitence, but his after-the-fact sorrow was too little, too late.

"Yeah," Toni said, and hung up, her miniscule self-esteem and growing self-hatred seemingly more justified than ever. She buried her face into the sofa and cried until she could cry no longer.

If Toni could have seen the slithery intruder enter her living room, she would have screamed in morbid fear. She was terrified of snakes and would not even look at pictures of them. But there wasn't the slightest chance of her seeing it.

It was a demon spirit of suicide attracted by the intensity of her self-pity. His long tongue darted in and out of his mouth as Toni's depression pulled him toward her. The spirit wrapped his long body around her neck several times and constricted. A barrage of suicidal thoughts flooded her mind with a ferocity that paralyzed her sensibilities.

"No one loves you," the suicide demon said seductively. "Your own father believes you're a tramp and a whore. You have one thing and one thing only to offer anyone. And what is that? Your body. What does that make you? Are you any better than the strip dancers at Mardi Gras or Cheetah's? No! You're worse! At least they're paid for what they do. You do it for nothing more than pain and rejection. I don't blame them for playing you for the fool. You are a filthy whore unworthy of anyone's love. Your whole life is a mess and it will never get any better."

On and on and on he went until he felt her will weakening and becoming more pliable under his onslaught. This energized him. His eyes were as close to hers as he could get without entering her. "How long are you going to live like this? How long are you going to be a doormat? There's only one thing to do, Toni. Kill yourself. Your father's gun is in his dresser drawer in the bedroom. Go on! Go get it and blow your brains out." When he felt her resistance rise, he said, "Who's going to miss you? Your father? Rick? Jerry? Not even Sharon. Do it and see how many people shed a tear at your funeral. If they even give you a funeral!"

Toni stood up and slowly walked hypnotically to her father's bedroom. She opened his top drawer and pulled out the pistol. It was cold and heavy and dark. *The story of my life*, Toni thought. "Where should I die?" she asked the silence. She took the gun and walked robotically from room to room. "How about the kitchen?"

She left the kitchen and went into the family room. "What about you!?" she screamed. "Do you want a whore to splatter her brains on your walls?" She slumped to the floor, emotionally exhausted.

Toni tried to cry, but couldn't. This only added to her frustration. She lifted the gun to her head, and like a dope addict who hates the needle that feeds her death, but can find relief no other way, she said, "I don't want to die," and pulled the trigger.

*****

Sharon was in her fourth period trigonometry class when she heard about what Jerry and Rick had done to Toni. Rick had talked her into going to his apartment where Jerry had been waiting in the bedroom closet, camera in hand. Her friend had been drugged and used like a slut. The pictures seemed to be everywhere. God, she hoped none of them ended up on the Internet!

Sharon slammed her books on the floor and stormed into Jerry's chemistry class. This was the first time in over a year that Sharon cursed, but curse she did. She called him every name she had erased from her vocabulary. Afterwards, Sharon looked everywhere unsuccessfully for Toni. Tonight she hoped Toni would be at home.

She called her and let the telephone ring several times before hanging up. "Toni," Sharon whined. A bad feeling came over Sharon as she said Toni's name. Instinctively, she prayed for Toni and asked God to help her, and then felt foolish for asking anything of a God she wasn't even sure existed.

A mercy angel took Sharon's short, but urgent prayer and shot to Toni's home. Two demons of fierce appearance met him. There were brilliant flashes of light as sword met sword. In a moment too brief to be measured with human tools, it was all over.

The demons lay crumpled on the ground. One ripped to shreds. The other, the biggest one, clutching his chest with the one talon that was left of the battle. His innards dropping to the ground.

*****

Toni looked at the gun befuddled.

Click. Click. Click. Click.

Five times she pulled the trigger. And five times nothing happened.

The mercy angel took his sword and came down hard on the serpent. The blade stopped a fraction away from Toni's neck.

The depression lifted. Toni shook her head as though she was coming out of a trance. She looked at the object in her hand. When she saw that it was a gun, she gasped and dropped it on the floor.

Boom! exploded the gun. The bullet ripped a hole in the huge grandfather clock.

Toni screamed and jumped back. The busted glass and shredded wood of the clock was strewn on the floor. Toni's eyes were wide as she saw what could have been. What almost was.

She lit a cigarette and walked to the huge arc shaped window in the living room. Toni took short, nervous puffs on her cigarette and blankly stared out the window.

Her mind searched for some course of action. One part of her knew that Rick was now nothing more than a pain of her past. Another part of her wanted to believe that he was yet the joy of her future. Facts meant nothing now. All that mattered were feelings. Hers, and hopefully his.

Toni grabbed her keys and headed for the car. Her drive from Duluth to Atlanta was one long near miss. Toni parked her car next to Rick's Porsche. She lowered her head and gripped the steering wheel tightly. The adrenaline that had helped her get in the car wasn't there to help her get out.

What if he doesn't want me? she asked herself. Then a thought that made her shudder. *What if he is in there with someone else?*

Toni took a deep breath and got out of the car. It was chilly. She wished she had brought a sweater. She folded her arms in a vain effort to warm her sleeveless arms.

She ascended the stairs to his apartment and very slowly approached the door. She was going to knock when she heard laughter on the other side. She wasn't sure, but it sounded like a female. Again she heard laughter. This time she was sure. It was a female's voice.

Toni knocked hard on the door.

Silence.

Toni felt someone looking at her through the peep hole.

In a few minutes the door opened. Rick wore a black silk Majestic Herringbone robe. His feet were bare. "Toni!" Rick said, excitedly. "How are you doing?" He pulled her into his apartment.

"Fine," was Toni's stoic response. Now that she was face to face with Rick, she found herself leaning more toward the reality that the handsome, smiling man that stood before her was a polished liar.

"What are you doing here?" he asked with a smile.

"I tried calling."

"Yeah, I've been out of town. I went to visit some relatives."

"I missed you," Toni said. She wanted to see what his response would be.

He took her in his arms and hugged her tightly. "I missed you, too," he said. He cupped her face in his hands and put his nose lightly against her own. Their eyes were closed. For a few seconds he did nothing. He just breathed on her with open mouth. Then he began to kiss her, lightly, ever so tenderly. He took his time and tenderly sucked one lip and then the other. His tongue coursed the circumference of her mouth. He nibbled. He flicked. He teasingly probed.

"Mmmmm, is there more where that came from?" Toni asked, pulling him toward the closed bedroom door. Toni felt his body stiffen.

"Oh, I want to baby, but I'm beat. I've been driving all weekend."

"Come on," she coaxed, with a pouty face.

"I can't. I can’t, baby."

"Can't? You? Can't? I know why you can't," she said, in a playful tone.

"And why is that?" Rick joined in the play.

Toni stood directly in front of him and looked him in the eyes. He was so cool. So smooth. The perfect actor.

Slap!

It was a solid blow that came from nowhere. Rick grabbed his face. He looked at her wide-eyed. “Why’d you do that?” he yelled.

Toni stormed to the bedroom and busted open the door. "This is why you can't!" she screamed, pointing to the girl lying on his bed.

The girl didn't even look up. She simply lifted her hand towards the pathetic figure, flicked her fingers goodbye, and went back to admiring her nails.

Rick followed after her, snatched her by the arm, and threw her to the floor. She landed hard. "What's the matter with you? What I do in my place is my business."

Toni's toughness vanished. All that was left was a lonely, hurt girl who wanted someone to love her. "But what about us?" she cried.

"What about us?" Rick answered, holding his nose.

"I thought you loved me."

"You thought wrong."

"You can't mean that." Toni knew she was hoping against hope.

"I can mean it, and I do mean it." Rick's words cut like a dull knife. His voice was low and resolute. "Get out of here, Toni." You shouldn't have come here." He pointed to the door.

Toni refused to believe what she was hearing. Rick wanted her. She knew he wanted her. He had to want her. Toni looked up from the floor. Her eyes begged Rick to let her stay.

He grabbed her roughly and jerked her to her feet. "Come on. Go on home to mommy."

"No!" Toni screamed hysterically. "Let me go!" she demanded, her arms and legs flailing wildly.

Rick couldn't get a firm grip on her. "Elaine, open the door!" he yelled, as he tussled with an adrenaline-pumped Toni.

The girl nervously inched her way around the fracas and bolted to the door and swung it open so hard that it hit the wall and closed again.

"Open the door!"

"Okay! Okay!" Elaine opened the door again.

"Let me stay! Rick, you said you loved me! Please, Rick, I need you!" Toni pled. "You said you loved me!"

Rick carried her wriggling body to the door and threw her against the hallway wall. She crumpled to the floor. "You said you loved me," she whined over and over. Tears streamed down her face.

Rick looked at her scornfully. "I lied," he said, without any sense of shame or regret.

The door slammed shut.

"You'll be sorry!" Toni yelled. "We'll get you for this!"

Toni's father was waiting for her when she arrived home. She explained everything to him and was surprised when he hugged her and did his best to coax away her tears. He placed his hands on Toni's shoulders and looked her directly in her eyes. "The Family will take care of this. He will regret the day he was born."

Toni knew that her father's words were no idle threat. He and the Family had strange powers. She could only hope that they wouldn't hurt him permanently. But she knew that the Family would show no mercy to the man who had hurt their new high priestess.

Chapter 13

This was a special meeting of the Council of Strategic Affairs. The Council was a five-demon panel that deliberated matters of extreme importance. They were the Pentagon of the Georgia region. Their recommendations were almost always accepted by Prince Krioni.

The setting was a dark room, heavily fortified with thousands of demon soldiers outside to prevent the forces of Jesus Christ from capturing such a rich booty. This gathering of eminent spirits was almost too tempting a prize to ignore. The nervous edginess of the soldiers accentuated the threat.

Ruler spirits were exceedingly domineering and suspicious. The slightest gesture, expression, or dissident word could be taken as insubordination or treason. Therefore, the chairman of the Council, a ruler spirit, was the only member of the Council permitted to speak and ask questions. The other members could say nothing without his permission.

The five demons sat in a semi-circle, elevated several feet above the floor. Petitioners had to look up to them. This served to satisfy the enormous egos of the Council who used every opportunity to promote themselves.

The members of the Council gave new meaning to the word ugly. This was the collective opinion of both angels and demons. They were not simply ugly. They were terrifyingly ugly. Their ghoulish outward appearances were birthed at the Rebellion. Those who were the most beautiful angels before the war against God became the ugliest demons afterwards. Their inner corruption and wickedness expressed itself in hideous and disfiguring ways. The morphed condition was like a spiritual leprosy.

The chairman was easily identifiable not solely because he sat in the center chair, but because he looked the part. His monstrous features were keen and foreboding. His intense eyes were a wild red that burned with evil passion. Battle scars decorated his face, arms, and chest.

"Witchcraft, step forward," ordered the chairman untactfully. He was no fan of witchcraft spirits. They enjoyed the presence of Satan like no other demons. The chairman felt that only ruler spirits should be allowed in the presence of the Evil Master.

Witchcraft stepped forward. His footing was unsteady. Bashnar's trained eye saw the lack of confidence in Witchcraft. A wave of revulsion rose up into his chest. He wanted to spit in his face for his weakness. (How Bashnar hated weakness!) If he had noticed the lack of confidence, surely the chairman, a hero of the Rebellion and many other lesser wars, had seen it, too. This embarrassed the Mighty Bashnar. He determined in his heart to destroy Witchcraft for his humiliating display of weakness.

Bashnar took his eyes off of the pathetic spirit and stared intently at the pentagram in front of him. It was not permissible to look the chairman in his eyes until he directly addressed you. Bashnar would not allow himself to make a costly mistake.

"You are here to state your case concerning the Atlanta revival."

Bashnar smiled inwardly. He knew that Witchcraft's position was weak. After this meeting Bashnar would be granted exclusive authority to destroy the would-be Atlanta revival.

"Chairman," Witchcraft began, "it is the contention of Bashnar that I have no right to destroy Sharon. He believes that my work interferes with his own. Sir," he pointed at Bashnar, "his work interferes with my work. I can destroy Pastor Styles through his daughter. She belongs to me! Her mother went to a fortune teller when she was pregnant with Sharon."

This information had a visible effect on the Council. If someone in Sharon's family was involved in the occult, Witchcraft did have a valid claim.

Bashnar was unruffled at this news.

"*Mighty* Bashnar," said the chairman. The chairman's contempt for Bashnar's title was no secret.

Bashnar stepped forward, incensed that the chairman called him mighty just to spite Witchcraft. He was mighty.

"State your case."

"Chairman, my accomplishments are a matter of public record. Unlike Witchcraft, I do not wait for my enemies to open their doors to me. I rip doors from hinges and take what I want. What I did to that PTL crew is no secret! What I did to that Louisiana preacher is a matter of public record. Has Witchcraft any comparable victory? No, his trophies are my refuse!" Bashnar moved closer to his scrutinizers. "Chairman, we must move with lightning speed. The forces of God are stirring the saints to prayer. The dagger, Jonathan, has vowed to God in his secret place of prayer to take Atlanta from us!"

The mention of Jonathan's name agitated the Council. They absolutely hated and feared any person who really trusted in Jesus Christ. This man Jonathan was a threat that could not be ignored.

"I will destroy Jonathan!"

The chairman stood up. "You will destroy Jonathan?" he asked incredulously, yet hopefully.

"I have discovered a weakness," Bashnar declared, his eyes wide with controlled excitement.

"How will you destroy such a man?"

Bashnar asked permission to speak to the chairman privately. This odd request was enthusiastically granted and Bashnar explained in detail what Jonathan's weakness was and how he would exploit it.

The chairman and Bashnar reentered the room. Witchcraft was seething.

"You will leave the room while we weigh your arguments," the chairman told Bashnar and Witchcraft.

In only five minutes they were summoned.

*****

Rashti left the presence of God with the prayers of the saints. He wished there was more, but this would have to do. He entered his camp with a scant hope that this mission would prove successful. But his real concern was for the safety of the soldier that would try to penetrate the formidable defense of the Council of Strategic Affairs.

There was only one angel who could possibly get in and out alive. Rashti met privately with Enrid, a trusted and fearless fighter, but one who was revered even more for his stealth and resourcefulness. And one known for loving to make impossible missions possible. Rashti smiled gratefully. *My friend, you will have a lot to love*, he thought.

The captain had no ego to get in the way of truth. So he had no problem acknowledging the enemy's strength. "A strategically critical meeting is planned," he said to Enrid. "The Mighty Bashnar is petitioning the Council of Strategic Affairs for exclusive authority to destroy the Styles family. We can't allow this."

Enrid knew that whatever the captain had in mind would be exceptionally dangerous and brash. His eyes lit up with excitement. "What do you have in mind?"

"They are meeting at the old fortress."

"The castle?"

"That's the one," Rashti answered.

Enrid was quite familiar with the castle. It was a defender's dream. Situated on the top of a hill and surrounded by thick, high walls it was virtually unassailable. One could not get within five hundred yards of the walls without being seen by the sentries. Flying was an impossibility in an area of such dense evil. This was one of the many inexplicable realities of spiritual warfare. There were so many limiting variables of spiritual warfare that often angels and demons seemed to be as limited as humans. Enrid would have to travel by foot.

"How are we going to stop the Council from giving Bashnar everything he wants?"

Captain Rashti looked at the angel intently. "You're going to stop the Council."

Enrid almost laughed in astonishment, but the seriousness in the beloved leader's eyes kept him from doing it. "How?" he asked, without a trace of fear, but exceedingly curious to know how he would be able to do what ten thousand angels couldn't do in a frontal attack.

Rashti loved Enrid. He was everything Rashti was at that same level of experience and responsibility. Daring. Courageous. Bold. Youthfully presumptuous at times. Intensely devoted to God's creation.

"The Spirit of God is creating a hunger for revival in the Atlanta saints. Most are satisfied with the present weakness, but some—" he changed that—"a few have become uncomfortable with their spiritual listlessness." Rashti pointed to the table. "Here are their prayers."

Enrid looked at the container in amazement.

Rashti said, "I know it's not much, but it's all we could spare. We had to loan some to our brothers in Egypt. The dark powers there are ferociously resisting us."

Rashti's apology was unneeded. He had misinterpreted Enrid's expression. The brave angel wasn't disappointed at the small amount of prayers, but instead was awed by the small crystalline container.

Enrid walked slowly, reverently toward the prayers. His feet touched the floor with the lightness of a feather falling to the earth. He reached out his trembling hand and gently stroked the container. Never before had he been so close to the prayers of the saints.

He lifted the lid and looked at the bubbling contents. A sweet aroma filled the air and both Enrid and Rashti enjoyed its smell. As Enrid looked into the bowl, he thought of how dynamic and immensely powerful the liquid was. A tablespoon of prayer was more powerful than man's atomic bomb.

"Captain, I've never actually seen prayer before."

Rashti appreciated Enrid's awe. He smiled, recalling how dumbfounded he must have appeared to Michael the archangel when he was first shown prayer.

"If only the saints knew how powerful their prayers were," Enrid said wistfully. "If they only knew how God used their prayers to rule the world."

"They're learning, Enrid." Rashti got back to the business at hand. "You must take the prayers into the very room where the Council is meeting. Once there you will throw the prayers to the floor and flee for your life."

"What diversion will we use to get me in?"

"There will be no diversion. That would only complicate matters. The Council would make it to the bunker before you could get to them. This is a very dangerous mission. It is practically impossible. We don't have enough prayer to take care of all of the hazards you will encounter. You will have to use some of the prayers to get you in. However, if you make it to the Council—"

"When I make it," Enrid added.

Rashti's heart lifted. "Yes," he agreed, "when you make it to the Council you will use the remainder of the prayers on them. That will leave you in a very bad position." Rashti paused. "It may be necessary to save just a little for yourself to assure your safety."

"We don't have enough to waste on me. That would weaken the effects on the Council."

Rashti knew the young warrior was correct. "I leave that to your discretion."

Shortly thereafter Enrid applied some of the prayers to himself and his armor. He used just enough to get him in without being seen. He'd worry about getting out later.

*****

Bashnar looked at the wicked spirit to his far right. Crucifix was his friend. The other members of the Council had no idea that

Bashnar's private meeting with him was the reason for this public petition. Crucifix and Bashnar shared furtive smiles.

The chairman spoke. "We have studied your petitions and grievances and heard your oral testimonies. It is the decision of the Council to forbid the interference of Wi—"

CRASH!!

Every demon pulled his sword. Anxious eyes darted around the large room. They waited for the sound of the siren, but there was none.

Bashnar watched Witchcraft drop to one knee and fall on his face. Siren or no siren, they were under attack! Bashnar crouched low. He gripped his sword so tightly he almost crushed the handle.

The chairman dropped his sword and grabbed his belly and threw up. Intense muscle spasms exploded in his wretched body. His arms and legs involuntarily twisted in rigidity.

One by one the spirits fell to the floor in excruciating pain. Bashnar was the last to fall. His muscles, too, were in rebellion. His eyes burned so badly he could hardly keep them open. He wanted to fall to the floor like the others—the pain was so acute—but his pride would not allow this show of weakness. He fought his way through his delirium and made it to a bench.

Ten minutes later Bashnar and the others began to come out of their painful stupor. Witchcraft was the last to revive. Bashnar's hatred for Witchcraft increased. *How despicable*! he thought. *The first one down and the last one up*!

The Council chairman called the main gate and asked for a state of affairs. The sentry told him that no angels of Christ were in the area. The chairman seated himself and groped for words. He didn't know what to say. He looked around the room and wondered what he was doing there. The other demons were suffering different degrees of amnesia themselves.

Bashnar didn't know why he was there either. He strained to regain his mental faculties, but they wouldn't focus on any one thing. He remembered the crash, but that was all. He felt like an idiot. Yet, through the smoke of confusion Bashnar could see clearly that whatever had just happened was a result of one thing.

Prayer!

Enrid ran as fast as he could down the long, dark corridor. Were it not for the thickness of wickedness in this place, he could fly, thus saving valuable time. His legs burned as he turned the corner and ran up what seemed to be an endless staircase. He covered his mouth to conceal his heavy breathing. When he reached the top of the stairs, he leaned against the wall and tried to catch his breath.

Enrid heard footsteps coming down the dark hall. He thanked God that demons loved darkness. He removed the dagger from his leg strap and inched as close as he could to the edge of the wall.

The two demons neared Enrid.

His motions were swift and precise. The demons clutched their abdomens and sank to the cold floor. Enrid pulled them to the steps and pushed them both down. He couldn't afford to be discovered this early in the game.

He looked up and down the hallway. Nothing. That's what he wanted to see. He ran to the end of that hallway and came to a screeching halt.

Voices. Several of them!

Enrid stood motionless, temporarily paralyzed by indecision. He was too far from the other end of the hallway to run back without being seen. But to not run meant certain detection. He waited until the voices got closer.

"For the glory of God and the salvation of men," he said under his breath and leapt upon the three demons.

Enrid's backhand took off the first demon's head. He came around with his right hand and thrust his dagger into the second demon's chest. But before he could retrieve his knife, the third demon struck him in the head with his fist. Enrid stumbled backwards under the blow. Another shot to his face and he heard his sword hit the floor.

The demon snatched up Enrid's sword and swung it wildly. He missed badly. This demon was clearly nothing more than an administrative spirit. Nevertheless, he had a sword and Enrid a twelve-inch dagger.

Enrid held his hands close to his body. A basic rule of hand-to-hand combat. Soldiers who forgot this rule often lost a hand or arm. The dark spirit who circled Enrid didn't know this. He held the sword so awkwardly that it limited his mobility.

Enrid tested his theory. He lunged to the left, slowly enough to let the demon respond. The demon took an amateur swipe at his enemy. Enrid tested the right side with the same results. It was time to do it for real.

The demon knew he was a deer in a lion's jungle. *Why me?* he thought.

Enrid shot his left hand above the demon's head. The demon took the bait and swung the sword at Enrid's arm. Enrid ducked into his swing and buried twelve inches of silver into his side.

Enrid quickly pushed all three bodies against the wall and placed them head to toe. He picked up his sword, sheathed it, and trotted down the hall into the darkness. He thought how differently this job would be if the Atlanta saints had offered more prayer for revival. Or at least more fervency to the prayers they did offer.

*****

Bashnar asked permission of the chairman to speak. His request was granted. "We should go to full alert. Something is wrong."

The chairman's eyebrows raised. His voice was full of angry skepticism. "What is wrong, Mighty Bashnar?"

"I don't know exactly, but my instincts tell me that the security of the castle has been breached."

"Breached?" the chairman yelled. This was an insult to the chairman's intelligence. He was part of the team that certified the impregnability of the fortress. "The fortress can't be breached!"

Bashnar gritted his teeth. There was no such thing as an impregnable fortress. He had a room full of trophies to prove that point. "Chairman, I am not questioning the quality of our security."

The chairman's eyes narrowed and his massive frame stood up. He looked down at Bashnar contemptuously. "What are you questioning?"

"The prayers of the saints."

This had a sobering effect on the chairman. "Prayers?" he gurgled.

"Yes, prayers." Bashnar's irritation was thinly disguised.

"But there has been no significant prayer offered by the Atlanta saints."

Bashnar was tired of the niceties. "All prayer is significant." His voice had a cutting edge.

The chairman knew that Bashnar was right. "How much would be needed to breach the security of the castle?"

Bashnar knew he was being set up. "Five pounds."

The chairman had him now. "Five pounds?" he screamed. "Do you know how long—?"

"For a frontal assault," Bashnar interrupted.

"There is no frontal assault!"

Checkmate.

Bashnar stood silent. To say anything would spoil this verbal coup.

The chairman knew he had been outsmarted. If he declared a full alert Satan would be immediately notified and his credibility would be questioned. Yet, if he admitted that a smaller force had infiltrated the castle, he would become the butt of every joke. However, the end result would be no laughing matter. There was only one thing he could do to save his skin.

"I will consider your fears," said the chairman. "Unfounded though they may be."

Bashnar could have exploded, but he didn't. Instead, he put a little more pressure on the chairman. "Sir, why are we here?"

The chairman didn't answer.

"No one in this room, including myself, knows why we are gathered here. The last thing I remember is a loud crash. It is obvious that we have been attacked. Someone filled this room with prayer."

Pangs of rage and fear shot through the chairman. He was enraged at Bashnar's total disregard for authority and protocol. He was afraid because Bashnar was right. Someone did detonate a prayer bomb in the very chambers of the Council!

"We must search for the infiltrator at once!" declared Bashnar.

The chairman hit his gavel. "Dismissed!"

He was the last one to leave the room. He called the gate and gave instructions to relax the security for a special exercise. If there were any dead demons lying around, that could always be attributed to demon-on-demon crime. Everyone knew that problem was getting out of hand.

The anxious chairman sat sulking, his large head in his crusty hands. He never thought he'd see the day that he would cheer for the enemy, but that's what he found himself doing. *Whoever you are angel, run. Run like hell*!

*****

The little pastor shrugged off his sense of failure and thanked God for the faithful few that had shown up for prayer meeting. *Who knows what we've accomplished tonight*? he thought, as he turned off the lights.

Chapter 14

Anthony Righetti was a very serious man. Two days ago his daughter and high priestess, and his Family were violated. This was a serious matter. Fire would be answered with fire.

Today had been a tough day at school for Rick. However, Katrina's physical therapy had made it all worthwhile. Not bad for a first date.

He opened the door to his apartment and stepped inside the dark room. He flicked the light switch. Nothing happened. A crushing blow to his abdomen doubled him over. He gasped for air that wasn't there. A jarring knee to the face snapped his head back. He bounced off the wall and slumped to his knees. Two pairs of strong hands lifted him up and threw him forward to the floor.

Rick floated between consciousness and unconsciousness. Someone tied his hands behind his back. His legs were tied together at the ankles. Someone stuffed a rag in his mouth and tied another rag around his head and over his eyes. A powerful hand gripped his hair and jerked him to his knees.

Rick's eyes tried to focus in the darkness. He could see outlines of three people through the thin rag. They wore hoods and robes. Rick's bladder released involuntarily. His eyes bulged with fear under the cloth. What was going on? What were these people doing in his home?

One of the hooded figures stepped forward. "Rick, how are you?" He spoke with a slight accent. "I would have come to see you earlier, but I had important business out of town. I am out of town a lot nowadays." The man spoke as though he and Rick were the best of friends. "How was Katrina?" he asked.

Rick answered with silent words caught in his throat.

"Was she as good as my daughter?" The man's friendly tone was gone. "I am sure you haven't the slightest idea. You have so many girlfriends."

Rick's mind searched frantically for possibilities. Jenny? Adrian? Darlene? Toni? Yvonne? Toni! It was Toni! He shook his head vigorously at the faceless man.

"Rick, I am not angry with you for going to bed with my daughter. I am angry with you for humiliating the Family. You have no knowledge of the Family, do you? Well, allow me to introduce us. I am Anthony Righetti." He took off his hood.

Rick's eyes strained to leave their sockets. *Oh my God! He took off the mask. He's going to kill me.*

Anthony Righetti pointed to the man on his right. "This is a very good friend—Andy Novak. You may recognize him. He's running for congress." The man removed his hood. "And last, but certainly not least, we have Donny Sanford. Donny's only been with us for two years, but he's risen quickly." This man also removed his hood. He had a big head and a thick neck. The rest of him was thick, too. But this wasn't from overeating. It was from a mixture of genetics and weight rooms.

Another of the men turned on a lamp.

Rick's eyes raced from face to face. He was surprised to see that the men appeared normal, congenial, even friendly. He had expected them to look like something out of a horror flick.

"I organized the Family several years ago. It was just me and a couple of friends and relatives." Anthony smiled. "Now there are over two hundred of us." He shook his fist at Rick in triumph. "Over two hundred!" he said, through clenched teeth. "Policemen, housewives, teachers, politicians, businessmen, merchants, preachers. Over two hundred!"

Anthony got on his knees and faced Rick. "We are growing, Rick. Our recruiters are exceeding their goals." There was an accent of evil in his eyes as he said, "Soon Atlanta will be ours. The Christians have their Jerusalem. Our holy city will be here—the Olympic city." He stood up. "Rick, what you have done is a grave sin. We are here to pronounce judgment upon you."

Rick struggled furiously to free himself. He fell clumsily on his side. He squirmed and kicked desperately. His captors watched with amusement for several seconds. The thick guy propped him up on his knees.

Anthony pulled out a large, shiny knife.

Rick fought and jerked and squirmed against the two men who held him. His face was sweaty with fear. His shirt was drenched in musty perspiration.

Anthony ripped open Rick's wet shirt. He smiled at his victim. There was nothing nice about his smile. He gripped his neck, and pushed him backwards so that Rick was lying on his own feet. He lifted the knife toward the ceiling. "Lord Satan!" he yelled. He gave Rick a maniacal look and thrust the knife into his chest.

Rick closed his eyes and waited for the pain. His muscles tightened when the tip of the knife slammed against his chest.

Laughter. Uproarious laughter.

Anthony grabbed Rick's hair and violently jerked him back and forth. He pulled the knife from his chest and began to laugh hysterically. Finally, he stopped. "Open your eyes, Casanova."

Rick's body quaked. He opened his eyes.

Anthony held the knife to Rick's face and put his finger on its tip. He pushed the blade into the handle. "It's not real, Rick. I bought this knife at a theatrical shop—San Francisco. See, I can even make it squirt blood."

Anthony pulled out another knife from under his robe. He rubbed the smoothness of the blade across Rick's face. "Lover boy, this one is real." He put the tip against Rick's chest. "I could rip out your heart if I wanted to. I could chop you into a hundred pieces."

Rick almost fainted. *Please, just kill me. Kill me*! he thought.

The man's voice was calm again, conversational. "But I'm not going to kill you." Rick looked into his eyes and saw livid hatred. It was like looking into the eyes of Satan. "You are going to kill yourself. That's right, Rick. Death will be your only way out of agony." Anthony stood up. "Take the gag off."

One of the men untied the rag around his head and took the other out of his mouth.

"We know who your father is. We know his strengths and his weaknesses." Anthony paused. He had the power of life and death in his hands. It felt good. "We know your mother. We know your brothers." An evil smile. "Your little sister, Erica, is a freshman at the University of Georgia. We have a number of people there."

"Please don't hurt my sister."

"What about the rest of your family?" Anthony asked, with a chuckle. "Aren't you concerned about their safety?"

"Yes. Yes. Please don't hurt them," Rick begged.

"Untie him."

They did so.

Rick's arms and legs were free, but his mind was still tied. He didn't move an inch.

"You will be dead by midnight tomorrow. Our spirits will do it," Anthony said, matter-of-factly.

The men took off their robes and left.

They were ten minutes away before Rick got up. His pants were drenched, but not from sweat. He locked the door and put the chain on. He went to the bedroom and fell upon his bed. *I can't tell my folks. They'd kill them,* he thought.

*****

The mercy angels had their orders. BRING RICKY WILLIAMSBURG TO REPENTANCE!

*****

Rick couldn't take it anymore. How could he sit through another class with so much on his mind? He got up in the middle of Dr. Kirk's class and left. He felt for his phone. It was gone. Rick went to one of the few telephone booths left and called Elaine. Her first class didn't start for another hour. There was no answer. He hung up.

There was a piece of paper on the counter.

"Pick it up," the angel said.

He picked it up.

In big, bold print the paper read: IF YOU DIED RIGHT NOW, WHERE WOULD YOU SPEND ETERNITY?

Rick balled up the paper and threw it on the ground. He dropped another fifty cents in the slot. Maybe Adrian was at home.

She wasn't.

He slammed the phone down and cursed. He had to go somewhere. Rick reached in his pocket for more change and came up empty. He cursed again. "Say," he called to a guy who was walking by. "You got change for a dollar?"

The guy smiled and shuffled his books.

Rick didn't like his smile. He was a freakin queer. *Just give me change and get your tight butt out of here.* The man looked in his hand. Fifty-five cents. "Nope, I don't have it. But you can have this." He gave him the money.

"Thanks." Rick dropped some change in the slot and turned away. "Jenny, hey, what's cookin'?"

"Oh, hi, Rick. Nothing. I'm working late shift today."

She didn't seem too happy to hear from him.

Rick was baffled. She was one of his most available girls. "Why don't we get together?" Rick offered.

"Uuuhh...I don't think so, Rick. I got saved last night."

"You what?"

"I met a man named Jonathan who led me to Christ. He's a real nice guy. Uuuhhh, anyway, that's why I can't see you anymore. I belong to Jesus now." Her last couple of sentences sped out of her mouth as though she was trying to say them before her mind could be changed.

Rick grimaced. He couldn't believe what he was hearing. One of the wildest and kinkiest chicks he knew had just told him that she had become a Jesus freak.

"Okay, Jenny. I'll talk to you later." What else could he say?

"Rick...."

"Yeah?"

"Jesus will save you, too, Rick. He really will. I can give you this guy Jonathan's telephone number." Jenny's voice was hopeful that he would take it, but she knew that he wouldn't.

"Naw, naw. That's okay, baby." In a stupor, he slowly hung up the phone. He let out an exasperated breath and turned around. The guy who had given him change was still there. He had a huge Bible in his hand. It was open.

"I want to talk to you about Jesus Christ."

I don't believe this. What do I look like? Harry Heathen?

"My name is Glen."

"Rick," he answered curtly. *Is this what I have to go through for some change?* "Look man, I don't—"

"Rick, do you know that Jesus Christ loves you?"

Rick extended his neck. "Huh? Yeah, I haven't pissed Him off lately."

The man smiled. Rick was disappointed that he wasn't offended.

"Have you ever pissed Him off?" the guy asked.

"Yeah, I guess so. Hasn't everybody?"

The man's face lit up at his answer. Rick knew he had given the wrong answer.

"Yeah, Rick, everyone has. I guess the only question is what have you done since you've pissed Him off?"

"Look, man, I really have to go." Rick walked away.

"Rick," the man called out, "you can't just piss God off and walk away. You have to make it right."

But he did, and he didn't.

*****

Bashnar watched the ceremony with a mixture of delight and derision. From the beginning, the powers of darkness were limited to expressing themselves in the earth through willing men and women. Without humans to work through, Bashnar and his kind were like ships without water. They needed something to facilitate their movement. For this reason and this reason alone, he appreciated the work of the Family.

Even so, like all humans, he hated them. As wicked, depraved, and cruel as the Family was—attributes Bashnar greatly admired—they were still objects of God's love. This was reason enough to hate them.

The other reason he hated them was because they sought to control him. Idiots! The Mighty Bashnar was master of his own destiny. He could not be controlled by hexes and curses and sacrifices. Everything he did for the Family, he did because it served his purpose. But for the cause of evil in the land he would destroy every member of the Family.

However, Bashnar knew that he was locked into this love-hate relationship. He had to work with the Family, and others like the Family. Their alignment with evil allowed him to show his greatness.

Tonight he had been asked by the Family to torment and destroy someone who had violated their high priestess. Bashnar's first act was to determine the amount of prayer support, if any, this young man had.

He had none. This would be a routine task.

Bashnar never did routine missions. He summoned three demons: a spirit of death, a spirit of torment, and a spirit of suicide.

He heard the knock. "You may enter."

All three spirits waited for the others to enter first. No one was in a hurry to enter Bashnar's presence.

Death opened and motioned the others inside.

Bashnar nodded approval when he saw Death. Suicide and Torment increased his satisfaction.

"Mighty Bashnar, we are here as ordered, sir," said Death.

Bashnar had no respect whatsoever for helpers and other demons who indirectly supported the mission of evil. Glory was the fruit of front-line soldiers, warriors who faced the enemy head on.

Death, Torment, and Suicide were front-line soldiers. He respected them all. However, he was especially impressed with Death. Death was the only demon in the dark empire that did not have a body of solid mass. He was a faceless, bodiless, black mist of evil.

Bashnar showed a picture to Death. "I want this man dead by midnight."

A voice came out of the black mist. "Will we encounter mercy angels?"

"At the most, one. He has no one praying for him."

"Consider it done, Mighty Bashnar."

Death's confidence pleased Bashnar. "Torment, I want you to drive this man mad with pain. I want him to pulsate with such grievous pain that he begs for death. Suicide, when this putrid scum cries for death, fill his mind with yourself. Death will then finalize the job."

The evening closed upon Rick like a curtain of dread. An evil foreboding gripped his quaking heart. Anthony Righetti's words haunted him. “You will be dead by midnight tomorrow. Our spirits will do it.”

Rick understood the part about being dead by midnight all too clearly. But what did he mean by, “Our spirits will do it”? His mind chilled as he recalled the scene of Anthony raising the knife to the ceiling and yelling, “Lord Satan!” Rick looked at his watch. Seven thirty-five. Less than five hours to live.

I've got to get to a phone, he thought.

There was one across the street. Rick stepped onto the street and was stricken by a bolt of fear. He clutched his chest and jumped back on the curb. His eyes searched vainly for an oncoming car or truck. All he saw were a few people looking at him strangely.

"Get a hold of yourself, Rick," he told himself. He crossed over and trotted to what had to be one of the last telephone booths in Atlanta.

"Sharon, hold on for a second, okay? I have another call." Toni pressed the button. "Hello."

Rick held the phone with both hands to control the trembling. Thank God that her father didn't answer. "Toni..." Rick's voice was weak with fear. "Please, can I talk to you?"

"Rick?" Toni felt an involuntary desire for him swell up in her heart.

"Toni..." he groped for coherent thoughts. "I...you have to believe me—I'm sorry. I didn't mean to hurt you."

Toni swept her feelings aside. "I trusted you. I gave you my heart and all you gave me was a sack of lies. You're not sorry for me. You're sorry for yourself. You're sorry I told my father."

Rick nervously looked up and down the street. He was sure that something evil was watching him. "Toni," his voice was hushed, "I don't know. I'm just sorry, that's all."

Toni put the phone to her chest and looked up to the ceiling with eyes that had quickly filled with water. She took a deep breath and made herself sound strong. "Don't ever call me again."

Click.

Rick hung up. "What now?" he asked the chilled March wind. He certainly couldn't call the police.

"Call Jenny," the mercy angel told him.

He didn't know why, but he decided to call Jenny again. "Hello, Jenny?"

"No, this is Kristy, her roommate."

"Kristy, this is Rick."

"Hey, Rick."

That was the happiest reception he'd received all day. He knew Jenny's roommate had a crush on him. Too bad he never had the opportunity to follow up on that. "Kristy, is Jenny there?"

"Yeah. She's in the shower. Hold on Rick, I'll tell her it's you."

The few minutes he waited seemed like eternity. Finally, Jenny came to the phone. When she did, Rick didn't know what to say. "Jenny...I...uuhhh—"

"Rick, would you like to come over? Kristy's got a date tonight. You know her. She won't be back until the morning."

Rick couldn't believe his ears. That was the best thing he had heard all day. "Kristy tells me you just got out of the shower."

"Yeah?"

Rick felt his confidence returning. "Sounds good."

"Can you be here in about half an hour?"

He was there in thirty minutes. Rick knocked on the door.

Jenny opened. Rick was disappointed to see that she was fully clothed. "Come in," she said.

Rick stepped into the scantily furnished living room and was shocked to see there were two other people there. A man and a woman.

Jenny took Rick by the arm and guided him to the man. "Rick, this is Jonathan. The man I told you about. Jonathan, this is Rick."

"Nice to meet you, Rick." Jonathan extended his hand and they shook.

"Nice to meet you, too," said Rick, angry that Jenny had set him up.

"This is my wife, Elizabeth," said Jonathan.

Rick's surprise showed. She was the most beautiful black woman he had ever seen. She had to be at least twenty years younger than this guy. "Hello," said Rick.

"Hi."

"I have a son about your age," said Jonathan. "He's in heaven now. How old are you, son?"

"Twenty-one. Almost twenty-two.

"My son would be twenty-one."

"Rick," said Elizabeth, "Jenny tells us you are a senior at Emory, planning to become a high-priced lawyer."

Elizabeth's sparkling smile abated his anger. "Yes, my father is an attorney. So was my grandfather. I guess I really don't have a choice but to be a lawyer." Rick's charm was natural.

"Something tells me that parental pressure has very little to do with your decision," said Elizabeth.

Rick was delighted at the attention this beautiful lady was giving him. He smiled sheepishly. "I'm guilty as charged. Dad used to take me to see him in action. I thought Dad was better than Perry Mason. Law's exciting. I caught the fever as a child and never recovered."

"Wise father," Elizabeth added. "You'll love it. My brother is an assistant district attorney. There's no money working for the state, but—"Elizabeth made a playful face—"he has political ambitions. This way he gets to rub elbows with the big boys."

To Rick, every expression of Elizabeth's was more lovely than the one before. "I'd like to enter poli—"

"Honey, are you all right?" Elizabeth asked Jonathan.

He was rubbing his temples. "Yes, Nurse Liz. I'm fine. Just a little tired, that's all."

She sat next to Jonathan. "You've been running too hard, honey. Even Jesus took time to rest."

Jonathan mimicked a wimpy, "Yes, dear."

Jenny laughed. "Would anyone like something to drink?"

Everyone politely declined.

"Rick," asked Jonathan, "did Jenny tell you what happened to her?"

Oh, no. Here it comes. "Yes."

"What do you think about it?"

"If it makes her feel better, cool."

"What do you think about Jesus Christ?"

Everyone's eyes focused on Rick. He felt like he was on trial. "What difference does it make?" His answer didn't come across as rude.

"The difference between heaven and hell," said Jonathan.

Rick let out a chuckle born of ridicule. "I don't believe in hell. A God of love wouldn't send anyone to hell."

It was time to cut through the facade. "Do you believe in death?" Jonathan asked.

The color drained from Rick's face. "What do you mean?"

"Young man, Satan has marked you for death. Tonight, before the clock strikes twelve, you will enter life or death."

Elizabeth and Jenny were shocked at Jonathan's words.

Midnight! How did he know? Rick looked at his watch. Eight forty-five.

"What? Are you trying to scare me into religion or something?" Rick's veneer of confidence was now transparent to everyone.

"No, I'm trying to save your life. When you entered the room, I heard God say, 'Tonight, before the clock strikes twelve, he will enter life or death.'"

The room was cool, but Rick was sweating profusely. Death was closing in on him. He could feel it.

Before Rick could refuse, Jonathan grasped his hand and began to pray.

"That's the place," Death said to Torment and Suicide.

"What's that?" Torment asked his cohorts as he came to an immediate halt.

There was a dull, white haze emanating from the apartment.

"The presence of God!" shrieked Death.

They shot to a higher, safer elevation and peered down at the light like deer looking into the headlights of an oncoming car.

"Lord, open Rick's eyes so that he might see his need of salvation. Reveal the wickedness of sin. Give him understanding of his condition. Tear the scales away from his eyes that he might see the love of Christ." Tears coursed down Jonathan's face. He stopped praying and looked up.

Rick was trembling in awe of the power that he felt come upon him as this man prayed. It was a strange sensation. He felt as though he was being washed with gentle currents of electricity.

"What will it be young man? Life or death?" asked Jonathan.

Everything within Rick yearned for this...whatever it was he was feeling right now. "What do I do?"

"Surrender. Give your life totally and completely to Jesus Christ. Live for Him."

"Okay."

"Praise the Lord!" exulted Jenny.

"Thank you, Jesus," said Elizabeth.

Jonathan looked intently into Rick's eyes and listened for the voice of God. Their praise was premature. "Rick, your motives are wrong. You want to take refuge under the wings of God, but only for a season, until the danger has passed. You are full of lust and adultery, Rick. Are you willing to sacrifice your sex life for Jesus?"

Rick felt abandoned by a hope he knew could not be real. He looked at Jenny and Elizabeth—Elizabeth! He stood up and walked towards the door.

Jenny began to softly cry. Elizabeth held her in her arms and consoled her.

Rick opened the door and looked back at Jonathan.

Jonathan felt an implosion of compassion for the young man. He knew the terrible cravings of sin. He wanted to get on his knees and beg Rick to reconsider. He wanted to make living for Christ appear easier, less stringent than it really was, but he knew he couldn't do that. It was hard. It was stringent. It was demanding. True Christianity was one long sacrifice unto God—although it was a sacrifice of love and not compulsion.

Rick closed the door and stepped out into the night.

"There he is," said Suicide.

"You're coming home," said Death.

"After I get through with him," added Torment.

One hour later Rick sat crouched in a corner of his bedroom in a fetal position. His arms were wrapped tightly around his legs. He shook with terrifying fear. His eyes raced around the room looking for the intruder he knew was there.

Torment raised the knife again and came down hard on his victim.

"Aaaagghh!" Rick fell to his side and panted heavily. His eyes rolled back in his head until the whites could be seen. His mouth opened widely. He needed air. "Oh, God."

Torment went into a rage when he heard Rick call upon God. The invisible assassin slashed and cut and ripped his victim with all the fury of hell. Rick's body convulsed with such excruciating pain that he could no longer find relief even in a scream. His mouth moved, but nothing came out. He simply jerked with each invisible blow.

"That's enough!" Suicide yelled with envy. "It's my turn."

"Be quick about it," Death snapped.

Suicide wrapped himself around Rick's neck and head. The yellow, snake-like demon constricted until he grunted. A flood of suicidal thoughts rushed into Rick's mind and overpowered his reason. Rick crawled to the kitchen and took a knife to both wrists. His desperation added to his thoroughness.

Death waited impatiently for the life to ooze out of him.

Rick lost consciousness. Ecstasy flooded the misty demon. The pleasure he felt was beyond description, even for a demon. He moved closer to the motionless victim.

Rick's spirit rose from the floor. He looked at his corpse. It was a mess. He was dead. He knew this for a fact. Yet, he was definitely standing in the room looking at his dead body. Rick now focused on the body that was allowing him to see his other body. He was confused. He reached out his arms and looked at the front and back of his hands. This didn't make sense. There were two of him.

His musings were interrupted by animal-like sounds in the room. Rick's eyes bulged when he saw the hideous creatures. "No! This can't be!"

His protests came from a new instant understanding of the message of Jesus Christ. He had rejected the only person who could have saved him from his sins.

Death latched himself onto Rick's chest. Suddenly Rick felt himself descending. He didn't know how fast, but he sensed faster than anything on earth could ever travel. The deeper he went, the darker it became. Finally, the darkness seemed tangible.

Claws and hands grabbed at him in the darkness, ripping at his spirit. Shrieks. Screams. Howls. Hideous laughter. Anguished moans. All around him. They filled this horrible place.

Rick inhaled and his mouth, throat, and lungs caught fire. Or at least they seemed to catch fire. He tried to hold his breath, but he was just as dependent on breathing now as he had been before dying. Each breath sucked the fire of eternal vengeance into his body. The searing pain! The burning of flesh that refused to be consumed!

This can't be happening to me, he thought. He closed his hot eyes and tried to will himself awake from a terrible nightmare. When finally he opened his eyes, he saw that he was approaching a dull flicker of light. In a moment he was there. He stood before stone walls that were incredibly high and fortified.

Death unleashed himself from his victim's torso and approached one of several guards. "His name is Rick. Have fun." And he was gone.

The guard had pale white skin and sunken eyes. He spoke with a hatred that could only exist in such a place as this. "You will enter the gates of hell and be tormented forever. Pray! Cry! Scream! No one will ever come to your rescue. This is a prison of no escape, no hope, and no Christ!"

Chapter 15

Larry McGuire looked across his black mahogany desk at Edwin and Barbara. This was no easy case. He was as embarrassed as he knew his friend had to be.

"How long have you...eehhh...? When did you first...eehhh—?"

"He's been impotent for several months," Barbara answered for her husband. She was tired of diplomacy. She needed answers.

Edwin's face turned red. Larry shifted uncomfortably in his chair. Barbara maintained an angry calm.

"What could have possibly happened to cause this?" Larry's question was to both of them.

Barbara turned in her seat and faced her husband. "Tell him what I did to cause this, Edwin."

"Barbara, you know you are not to blame. You have absolutely nothing at all to do with this."

"Something's to blame," Barbara responded.

Edwin caught the accusation. "There is no one else. How many times do I have to tell you this?"

"Please calm down, both of you." Larry got up and locked the door. No one else was at the church, but he couldn't take any chances. He sat down and looked earnestly at Edwin and Barbara. "I am going to show both of you something that can help you. It's going to be shocking, but you must promise me that you will not be too critical before hearing me out."

Barbara's curiosity piqued. "I promise."

"Edwin?" Larry asked.

He hesitated, then answered, "Yes."

Larry unlocked his desk drawer and pulled out several magazines, books, and a couple of videos. He spread them out on the desk.

Barbara gasped and covered her mouth.

Edwin stood up. "What's the meaning of this?" he demanded.

"Edwin—"

"Let's get out of here," Edwin interrupted Larry. He motioned for Barbara, but she didn't budge. "Are you going to look at this trash?" he asked her.

"We need help!" she yelled.

"She's right, Edwin. Sit down, please."

He looked at his wife disbelievingly and slowly sat down.

"I know what it looks like, and you are right. It is trash, and I wouldn't be caught dead with any of this if it were not for one reason."

"And what's that?" Edwin asked cynically.

"Roman's 8:28."

Edwin had never heard such a twisting of Scripture before in his entire life, unless he considered Jonathan. "How can you use the Bible to justify pornography?"

"Romans 8:28 says, 'All things work together for good.' We know that some people use pornography for lustful purposes, but we also know that God can use negative things to bring about good."

Edwin imagined that Larry meant well. He was only trying to help him and Barbara. There was no telling what she had told him to make such a good man go to such lengths to help them. He thought about this for several long seconds.

This was sick. He wasn't biting. He wanted to get up and walk out. However, he knew that if he did so, Barbara would probably leave him. He'd then be kicked out of the church for not ruling his own house well. He thought about the irony of having to participate in porn to remain pastor. What a mess.

"What should we do?" Barbara asked Larry.

Edwin was shocked and dismayed by her eagerness. He knew that Barbara enjoyed sex—she really enjoyed sex—but he never knew sex was so important to her that she'd consider something so perverted.

Larry picked up two thin paperbacks. He gave one to each of them. "These are manuals. Read them word for word. Explore. Get in touch with one another." He pushed the magazines and videos to Edwin. "These will help stimulate you."

Edwin knew it was wrong. It was way beyond wrong. But what choice did he have? "Okay, Larry, I'll do it," he said gloomily.

"Do you have a bag, Larry?" Barbara asked. He put the material in a bag. "Thank you so much."

Edwin wasted no time leaving Larry's office.

"Barbara, if none of that stuff works, call me. Maybe we can think of something else."

"We appreciate your concern," she answered gratefully.

*****

Sharon jumped up when she heard the car in the driveway. She looked out of her window. It was her parents. She called Toni.

"They're home. I'll be right over."

"I'll be ready," said Toni. She hung up the phone and poured herself a drink. Witchcraft descended through the roof and sat beside her on the leather sofa.

"Sharon is your best friend," he said. "She is the only one in this entire world who really loves you. She is the only one who cares about what happens to you." He let Toni think on that for a while. Then, "What would you do without her?"

Toni knew the answer to that disturbing thought. She had only been reconciled to Sharon for about a week now. Life without her best friend wasn't a life at all. It was merely an existence. No one Toni knew genuinely cared for her like Sharon.

Toni tried to push this unwanted possibility out of her mind. However, Witchcraft was relentless.

"Why did Sharon leave you the first time?" the invisible visitor asked. "Was it not because of Jesus?" Toni shook her head in a vain attempt to empty her mind of these troubling thoughts. "Isn't it funny that now that Jesus is out, you're in? And when He's back in, where will you be? Back out in the cold!"

The thoughts came so forcefully that Toni could almost audibly hear them. A growing sense of vulnerability overtook her mind. She felt like her happiness was trapped in quicksand, and unless she did something fast it would soon go under.

Witchcraft saw the worry in her eyes.

"She has a family that loves her," he continued. "You haven't had a family since your mother died. Sharon has a future. What kind of future do you have? None! You are a tramp, and you will always be a tramp! But Sharon—look at Sharon." He paused to give her fears time to rise. "Pure, innocent, perfect! There is only one way to make sure she stays your friend forever. Destroy her purity! She has to become like you!"

Witchcraft smiled at Toni. She was weak. Lonely, bruised hearts were so easy to manipulate. There was no need to stick around. He had said enough.

Twenty minutes later Toni's doorbell rang.

"Come in, girl."

"I like that dress," said Sharon.

"What about yours? I haven't seen you in something that tight in over a year."

Sharon looked down at herself self-consciously. *Is it really that tight?* she wondered.

Toni saw the concern. "Just kidding, Sharon. Lighten up. You're okay."

"Are you sure?"

"Sure, I'm sure. Let me grab my bag and we can get out of here." She went to her room and opened her drawer. She picked up the capsule and kneaded it guiltily. Toni loved Sharon more than words could express. It hurt her to do this, but there was no other way to make sure that nothing would separate her from her friend again. Toni put the capsule in her purse. She had to do it.

Friday nights at *The Glass House* were once a given for Toni and Sharon. Toni was so excited about partying with Sharon that she got out of the car before Sharon turned off the ignition.

"Toni, don't kill yourself getting out of the car."

"Let's go party!"

"Does T's cousin still work the door?" asked Sharon.

"No, there's another guy named Boo-boy. He's cool. He'll let us in."

"Boo-Boy?"

"I didn't name him, Sharon."

Toni took Sharon by the arm and hurried her towards the small line at the door. The crisp air, the starry night, the alcohol she drank before she left the house, they all added to the freeness Toni felt tonight. There was a bounce in her step and a twinkle in her eyes.

"There's Boo-Boy," said Toni. She hoped he remembered her. It had been several months since she had come to *The Glass House*.

"Toni," he said eagerly, "how ya been? Haven't seen you around for a while?"

Toni smiled. "I haven't been around." She handed him her driver's license. He took it and gave it back without looking at it.

"Who is your friend?" he asked, with every tooth exposed.

"My name's Sharon."

He took her driver's license and looked at it closely. He looked her in the face. "I know you," he said, thumping the card on his hand.

Sharon politely took her license. "I don't think so." It was obviously an amateurish attempt to talk to her.

"No, no...I mean it," he persisted. "I know you. Manhattan. You were with the David Wilkerson group. The witnessing team," he said excitedly. "You talked to me. I was strung out on crack. You don't remember? You and those other folks prayed for me?" He sounded a bit ashamed. "I only do this on Fridays. I'm looking for another job."

Sharon stood petrified in a thick forest of condemnation. "I don't know you," she lied. "You have me mixed up with someone else."

"But I—"

"You have the wrong person," Toni snapped.

Boo-boy thought about it. “Yeah, you’re right. I'm sorry," he apologized to Sharon. "You couldn't be the one. The girl who prayed for me wouldn't be caught dead in this place."

That pierced Sharon's heart.

Toni saw the pained look on Sharon's face. She knew there was no mistake about it. Sharon was the one he had met in New York. She remembered that she had spoken to Sharon after that trip to New York. Sharon had told her about this guy.

"Come on," Toni said. She glared at him as they passed by.

Sharon stepped inside the club. Everything within her rebelled at the unholy atmosphere. She felt as though she would've been more at home on Mars.

The music blared. It sounded like Prince. She couldn't stand him. He was filthy. She tried to ignore the pornographic lyrics that blasted through the huge speakers.

"Where are they?" she screamed into Toni's ear.

Toni scanned the darkness. "I don't kn—there they are." She pointed to the bar.

The two guys she pointed at were Jeffrey and Kevin. Jeffrey was someone that Toni dated infrequently. He wasn't a heartthrob, but he was fun to be around. Kevin was Sharon's blind date.

"Let's go meet him," said Toni. "You'll like him. He's cool."

Sharon's feigned enthusiasm was weak.

The smile didn't fool Toni. *When Jesus is back in, where will you be? Back out in the cold*! Toni heard the thought echo in her mind again. Her insecurity heightened. *That jerk*! she thought of Boo-Boy.

Sharon proceeded as though she were walking through a mine field. A battle raged within her angry, confused soul. Why was she here? Why was she doing things she knew were wrong? Why was she seeking answers in all the wrong places? Why was she compromising and destroying her relationship with God?

She angrily answered her own questions. She was here because she had no better place to be. She was here because being miss perfect had taken its toll on her. She was here because she was angry at God. She was here because she had been brutally robbed of her faith in God.

Nonetheless, her mental protests couldn't quiet the loving voice of the Holy Spirit. His voice drowned out Prince. His voice drowned out the voice of self-pity and anger. She heard Him calling for her, beckoning her with His irresistible love. Even now she knew that He cared, that His love for her was as great as it ever was. She wasn't condemned; she was loved.

"Sharon, snap out of it," said Toni. She knew what was happening to her friend, and it scared her. She was only a short while from being abandoned again. Toni would have to move fast.

Sharon blinked. The love trance was broken. "Hi," she said.

"Hi, Sharon," said Kevin. "I've seen you a couple of times at school."

She smiled. "I've never seen you before," she said, then cringed when she heard how that sounded. "I didn't mean it like that. I mean—"

"It's okay. We moved down from Vermont only a month ago."

"Jeffrey, let's hit the floor." Toni pulled him to herself. "Show me what you got."

He looked at Kevin and shrugged. "What can I say? The lady knows what she wants."

"Sharon, you wanna dance?" asked Kevin.

She wanted so badly to say no. She wanted to free herself from the stickiness of this web of sin. *No! No!* her mind screamed. *Leave! Leave now!*

"Yeah, sure."

It was a slow record. Kevin pulled her closer than she wanted to be. His face was next to hers. Sharon thought she felt his lips touch her neck, but she wasn't sure. She endured this dance like a lady would a slow rape.

Toni stretched her neck to monitor Sharon's reactions. She could see that Sharon wasn't into it. Her mind was somewhere else. Probably heaven.

Sharon agonized through another forty-five minutes of superficial partying and lyrical raunch. Kevin's antsy hormones only added to the moral nausea of the place. She felt like she was in the pit of hell.

I have to get out of here.

Toni saw the mood swing. Her heartbeat quickened with fear. "Sharon," she said, trying to hide the anxiety that had taken over her, "I'm not feeling too well. Would you mind if we went to my place. We could play cards or something. My father is out of town on business."

Sharon didn't want to go there either, but it would certainly beat this filthy place. "Yeah, let's go."

"You guys follow us," Toni told Jeffrey and Kevin.

Once they were there, Sharon did her best to keep her distance from Kevin. Somehow he always managed to end up practically on her lap. As bad as it sounded, she heard herself wishing her blind date really was blind.

It was only nine-thirty, but Toni knew Sharon would be leaving soon. After several hands of cards, Toni fixed herself a drink and offered one to Sharon. Sharon hesitated, then took what she knew would be her last alcoholic drink.

Toni hoped her face didn't betray her. She tried to act normal, but it was impossible to do so. Her whole future was in Sharon's glass. If she didn't consume the drink, Toni would lose her friend forever.

When Sharon took her first sip, Toni closed her eyes and lowered her head. Violent, conflicting emotions tore at her heart. Crushing, debilitating guilt; joyous, liberating freedom. She thought how cruel life was that she was forced to hurt the one person who truly loved her. Yet, this was the only way she could keep her.

After a couple of more sips, time seemed to stand still for Sharon. She felt lightheaded and free. Toni walked across the room in slow motion.

"Sharon just needed to loosen up a little bit," Toni whispered to Kevin. "I think she likes you."

"She has a funny way of showing it," he retorted. "She hasn't given me any play all night."

"No, I'm serious. I know her. That's just the way she is. Sharon's a slow starter, but..." she smiled, "she's a good finisher."

"You serious?" he asked excitedly, his hormones awakening from their forced nap.

Toni nodded.

Sharon saw Kevin approach her in her dream state. She saw it in his eyes. He told her his desire and she gave him a groggy, mindless smile.

Toni and Jeffrey disappeared, leaving Kevin alone with Sharon.

An hour later Toni sat alone on the sofa. She had a drink in one hand and a cigarette in the other. This was her third drink since their dates had left. She gulped it down and poured another. *The night's a success*, she thought cynically.

Toni hurriedly gulped down the drink. She wanted to pass out into nothingness, oblivion, a place where she would not have to remember how she had treacherously crushed such a lovely flower. A flower whose sweet, aromatic fragrance had filled her empty, worthless life with such meaning and joy. A flower named Sharon.

Would anything good come of this? Or had she stabbed Sharon in the back for nothing? Toni blew a smoke ring and followed it until it disappeared. "You're the best friend in the whole world," she taunted herself, in a pitiful voice that couldn't carry the weight of the enormity of her betrayal.

Sharon opened her eyes and looked up at the trey ceiling. The ceiling fan twirled slowly. Where am I? She struggled to raise her head from the pillow. She looked down and gasped in horror. Her dress was raised and her panties were missing.

"My God!" she screamed. "What happened? Where are my panties?" Sharon tried to scuttle off of the bed and winced in pain. Her crotch seared. She touched herself and pulled up a small amount of blood. There was also a little blood on the bedspread.

Sharon sat stunned. She slowly shook her head at what she knew had happened. She got off of the bed and frantically searched for her panties. They were in the corner under the aquarium. She put them on and slumped to the floor and cried in unbelief.

"Toni," she cried. "Toni..."

Toni bit her lip and clenched her fists when she heard the wailing cry. "I'm in here," she answered normally.

"Toni, please come here," she begged.

Toni heard the desperate voice and knew she would have to tell Sharon what happened. She didn't know when she would tell her. But she knew that if she tried to keep this a secret her heart would burst with guilt.

"I'll be right there," she said innocently.

She walked in the bedroom and saw Sharon crumpled in the corner. There was no life in her eyes. No spirit in her countenance.

"Sharon, what's wrong?"

Sharon looked up with sad eyes. "What happened, Toni? What happened?"

"What happened? What—what do you mean what happened?"

"With me and Kevin? What did I do with Kevin?"

"You had a few drinks," she lied, "and partied with him."

"Partied with him?" Sharon yelled through her tears. "Is this what you call partying?"

Toni didn't look Sharon in the eyes. She knew that if she did, her curtain of lies would be ripped to shreds.

"Well, yeah," she answered weakly.

Sharon looked up at Toni with the helplessness of a little child. "Toni, you knew that I was a virgin. You knew that I was saving myself for God." A deluge of tears burst forth.

Toni didn't know what to do or say. What could she do? What could she say? Sharon was broken because of her. "Did it hurt?" she asked lamely. "It won't last long."

"Did it hurt?" Sharon screamed. "You don't understand, do you? You can't understand! You're used to this kind of thing! I'm not!"

"You'll get over it, Sharon." She went to hug her and was brushed aside.

"How do you get over something like this? I came over here because I trusted you. I wake up not knowing where my panties are? How do I get over that? He didn't even take off all of my clothes. He just lifted my dress and took what he wanted. Like I was some kind of..."

"Like some kind of tramp?" Toni slipped.

Their eyes met and Toni quickly turned away.

Sharon slowly and awkwardly stood to her feet. The last thing she said to Toni was, "I thought you were my friend."

Chapter 16

Bashnar did not look forward to addressing the assembly. They were here to be told of the great advances he had made against the man, Jonathan. The Mighty Bashnar had confidently pointed to this next meeting. He had intended to tell them how he had drawn first blood.

However, it was Jonathan who had drawn first blood. Bashnar's glorious mane now consisted of nothing but a smoldering residue of physical pride. Jonathan was a worthy opponent. His prayers were explosive. His holiness a perpetual sore. Bashnar appreciated these qualities in his opponent. He even admired them. They made for a worthwhile fight.

Nonetheless, not everyone shared Bashnar's sentiments. Bashnar knew and understood the nature of war. Wounds came with the turf. No one was immune to them. Even the Evil Master, Satan, had suffered grievous wounds at the Great War and then later at the Battle of the Resurrection.

Yet, Bashnar knew that many of the assembled demons would see his scorched mane and concede that Jonathan was superior.

This reaction was something he had no control over. Time would show who of the two was the greater. Nonetheless, Bashnar determined to severely discipline anyone who questioned his generalship. Already there were rumors that a witchcraft spirit had done more to stop the threat of revival than the Mighty Bashnar.

Bashnar approached the lectern.

There was a hush.

"This meeting is to inform you of the state of affairs of the Enemy's planned invasion of our territory. As I stated to you in our last meeting, Jonathan has been chosen to spearhead an offensive against our region." Bashnar stuck out his chest.

"I have been chosen to counter the threatened revival of holiness and power. As you can see," he pointed to his head, "Jonathan and I have met."

It sounded to the assembly like a joke, but no one dared laugh.

"Make no mistake about it," Bashnar continued, "Jonathan and I will meet again. I promised you that I would destroy him, and I will. He has a major weakness that I have discovered. Presently, this weakness is being fully exploited. He will fall!"

*****

Sharon opened the door and went straight to her room. She immediately took a shower and tried to wash away her immorality with soap and water. She scrubbed herself so vigorously that she bruised her skin.

Sharon went to bed, but not to sleep. This evening she would get no rest, but would instead spend the entire night and next morning questioning her own morality. Did she do something to cause this? Did the alcohol cause her to act sexually suggestive? A million questions and not one good answer.

Edwin and Barbara heard Sharon enter her room and take a shower. Neither noticed how long the water ran. At the moment, neither of them would have noticed if their home was burning to the ground.

For over thirty minutes Edwin and Barbara had verbally wrangled about his problem. It seemed to Edwin that this problem was acting as a spotlight. Each day its light revealed things about his wife that he did not know existed. Things that he did not know could exist in his wife.

After seventeen years of marriage, he only now realized that the lady he married had evolved into a woman who could rationalize anything. He had ignored her racial prejudices, attributing that to her parents. He had always laughed off Barbara's suggestions to cheat on their income taxes, choosing to believe that she was only kidding. And there were other things that came to mind that compelled him to look at his wife in a different light. It was a scary reflection.

"Barbara, this is wrong." He spoke of the pornographic paraphernalia.

"That's irrelevant. You heard what Larry said." She put a DVD in the player, but didn't push the start button.

"Since when is right and wrong irrelevant?"

"Since you became impotent."

That hurt. Edwin was momentarily stunned by his wife's cutting words. He waited. He hoped for an impassioned apology. It never came.

Edwin was silent in troubled thought. Barbara interpreted his silence as a concession. She pushed the start button.

Edwin was offended by the very first scene. *How on earth can Larry justify this? This is filthy!* Edwin hopped up and turned the DVD off. He ejected the disk and broke it half and threw it on the floor. "I don't care what Larry says! This is filthy, and I'm not watching it!"

Barbara was surprised by her husband's rare display of fire. "What are you doing?" she demanded, once she got over her surprise.

Edwin's eyes flashed with anger. "I am not going to watch a pervert rape some deluded, masochistic, Dolly Parton look-alike!"

"Whheeww!" Barbara grunted angrily.

Edwin snatched his clothes off the chair and put them on.

"Don't you leave me," Barbara demanded sternly. "I mean it."

"Is that another threat?" Edwin asked, as he buttoned his shirt.

Barbara didn't know what to say. He rarely stood up to her or anyone else. She was ill prepared to deal with an Edwin who stood his ground.

"Where are you going?" she asked.

"Someplace where I can think without having to be subjugated to dirty books and filthy movies."

"Edwin, don't you dare leave this house!"

He left.

*****

Jonathan put on his reading glasses. "Look at Romans the fifth chapter, verses six through eight."

Jenny turned the pages of her new Bible frontwards and backwards trying to find Romans.

Jonathan smiled. "Let me help you." He found it for her.

"Okay," said Jenny, a little embarrassed that she couldn't find Romans.

"Read it out loud for us."

"For when we were still without strength, in due time Christ died for the ungodly. For scarcely for a righteous man will one die: yet perhaps for a good man someone would even dare to die. But God demonstrates His own love toward us, in that while we were still sinners, Christ died for us."

"Do you understand what you've read?" asked Jonathan.

"Well, yeah. Sort of, I guess."

"Let me elaborate on this a little." Jonathan sat back and searched his heart. *Help me, God.* "Jenny, God is in love with you. He has always been in love with you. Do you remember when we first prayed that you told me God could never love you because you had done so many bad things?"

"Yes."

"Do you remember what my response was?"

"Yes."

"What was it?"

"You said, 'Good! You qualify'" Jenny smiled.

"Jenny, Jesus Christ died for you before you were born. He paid the price for your sins before you committed any sins. Now, if He loved you before you committed any sins, and if He died for you before you committed any sins, and if He extended His love toward you while you were yet in sin, what is greater? Your sin or God's love?"

Jenny gave it some thought. "His love."

Jonathan grasped her hand and looked into her eyes. "Never forget that, Jenny. Never measure God's love for you by your emotions or your success rate. Measure it by the sacrifice of Jesus Christ." He stood up. "Well, I guess it's time to get going. I have some reading to do."

Elizabeth and Jenny stood up.

"Jenny, it has been a pleasure studying with you," said Elizabeth. "I'm sorry we kept you up so late."

"That's okay," Jenny answered. She didn't want the Bible study to end. "I have to work tonight anyway. Hey, why don't you guys follow me in and we can have a coke or something before I go on?"

Jonathan answered. "I love those hot fudge sundaes."

"Good! Let me get my purse."

When Jenny left the room, Elizabeth said, "Jonathan, do you ever say no? We're going to end up staying up all night." She wasn't angry, but she really didn't want to stay up late for the third night in a row.

Jenny bounced back into the room. "You guys ready?"

Jonathan smiled guiltily at his wife.

Elizabeth gave him a playful evil eye. "We're ready," she answered.

Abby's was a low priced, late-night restaurant whose breakfast bar had attracted scores of new customers. However, the night traffic was sparse, and the late night traffic was even lighter.

Jonathan led the way to a window booth. "You guys are really packing them in here," he teased. Everyone ignored his jibe.

Jenny sat down and opened her new Bible. She thirsted for more of the God that Jonathan had introduced to her.

Elizabeth was dead tired, but Jenny was a new Christian and her enthusiasm was contagious. So she tried to hide her exhaustion.

"I have twenty minutes before I'm on," said Jenny.

Jonathan opened his Bible and for the next twenty minutes he did what he did best. He made the love of God real to a ready listener.

"Jonathan," said Elizabeth, in a startled hush, "there's that man."

"What man?" Jonathan turned around in his seat. A smile crossed his face. God was at it again.

The man they spoke of sat down with his back toward them. His expression was tired and worrisome. He ordered a coffee and rested his head in his hands.

"Excuse me," he heard someone say.

He looked up. *I don't believe this.*

"How are you?" Jonathan greeted him. "My wife saw you come in."

The man didn't answer. He had a dumbfounded look on his face.

"Do you remember me?" asked Jonathan, not believing that anyone's memory was that short.

Jonathan's question was a cruel joke. How could he ever forget the man who was destroying his church and his family? "Yes, I do," he answered without pretense.

Jonathan ignored the man's apparent displeasure. "Would you like to come sit with us?"

Edwin couldn't believe the audacity of this man. This was like the robber casually stopping by for a chat. No! He did not want to sit with Jonathan. He wanted to put as much distance between him and Jonathan as possible. But Edwin was uncharacteristically angry. He was angry at his wife and he was angry at Jonathan. He had left the house to get away from Barbara, only to run into someone who evoked even greater anger.

He decided to sit down with Jonathan and do something that he had never done before. He would release the fire that burned in his chest. If someone's feelings were hurt, so be it. Edwin sat next to Jenny and across from Jonathan and Elizabeth." Do you have—?"

"Oh! I have to go," Jenny interrupted Edwin.

Edwin stood up, and she rushed to sign in to work. He tried again. "Do you have any—?"

"Excuse me," Elizabeth apologized to Edwin for interrupting," I need to go to the restroom."

Jonathan stood up so that his wife could get out. She left and Jonathan said, "You were saying...?"

"I was saying," Edwin said with emphasis, "do you have any idea what you have done to me?"

The waitress interrupted with their coffee and Jonathan's hot fudge sundae. Edwin let out a long, tired breath.

Jonathan thanked the waitress. Edwin opened his mouth to blast him, but Jonathan said, "Excuse me," and bowed his head to pray. After a silent blessing, he said, "Now what were you saying?"

"Do you have any idea what you have done to me?" Edwin's words rolled out quickly with irritation.

Jonathan took a bite of the sundae. It was delicious! He chewed slowly to savor its taste. "Have you ever had one of these?"

"No!" Edwin snapped.

"No, I don't know what I've done to you. Please tell me."

Jonathan's calm added to Edwin's irritation.

"My church was a good church, and I say was because it may not ever recover from the things you said and did. Do you know how long it took me to earn their respect and trust? Years! And in one night you destroyed it all."

Jonathan took another mouthful. Whoever had prepared it tonight had done it perfectly. There was lots of syrup. He was careful to not lose a drop.

Edwin was incensed that while he spoke, this false teacher expended such energy on his dessert. "Everyone is mad at me," he continued.

Jonathan swallowed another bite. "Does that bother you?"

"Why, of course it bothers me."

"It shouldn't," said Jonathan, rather nonchalantly.

"Maybe that's the way you operate, but that certainly is not the way I operate!"

"Obviously."

Edwin sat back and looked at Jonathan. "What do you mean by that?"

Jonathan took a big spoonful of his sundae. It was time to put down his feather. "I mean there really is a difference in the way we minister, and that difference boils down to one thing. I worship God and you worship man."

Edwin was aghast at Jonathan's arrogance.

Elizabeth returned. When she saw the anger on Edwin's face, she thought, *That's my Jonathan, Mr. Tactful.* "And how are the night owls?" she asked.

"Pastor Styles and I were just getting to know one another better," said Jonathan.

"Yes, much better," added Edwin. *She's a lot younger than he is,* he thought.

"Pastor, feel free to say whatever is on your mind. Elizabeth is used to it. She has heard it all."

Edwin said nothing for a few moments. When he was sure of his composure, he answered Jonathan's assertion. "Your husband was just telling me how he worships God and I worship man."

Elizabeth chuckled. "He didn't," she said, treating it more like a joke than an insult.

"He sure did," said Edwin.

"Well, don't let it bother you. He really likes you."

"He has a peculiar way of showing it." *How did he get her*? "I'm sorry, what is your name?"

"Elizabeth," she answered with a magnetic smile. "Honey," she said to Jonathan, "why did you say Pastor Styles—"

"Edwin," Jonathan interjected.

Elizabeth smiled. "Why did you say Edwin worships man?"

Jonathan looked directly into Edwin's eyes. Edwin fixed his eyes on Jonathan's nose. "I said what I said because it is true. Edwin, did God call you to the ministry?"

"Did God call me?"

"Yes, did God call you to the ministry?"

"Well..." he stammered, "of course He did."

"Do you know what God called you to?" Jonathan didn't wait for an answer. He had his own. "God called you to do what Jesus did."

Edwin picked up his coffee. *Oh brother*, he thought. Jonathan was obviously about to get on his charismatic soap box.

"And what is that?" he asked, with more than a trace of condescension.

"To destroy the works of the devil. To set people free. To...let me show you." Jonathan flipped through his Bible. He felt the fire of God rising in his soul.

Edwin felt like a physics professor being lectured to by a high school dropout. He took a deep breath and mentally braced himself for the ramblings of a madman.

Jonathan found his first passage. "Edwin, may I call you Edwin?"

"Yeah, why not?"

"Edwin, Jesus said something that I think you should consider? It's in Luke the fourth chapter." He began to read. "The Spirit of the Lord is upon Me, because he has anointed Me to preach the gospel to the poor; He has sent Me to heal the brokenhearted, to proclaim liberty to the captives and recovery of sight to the blind, to set at liberty those who are oppressed, to proclaim the acceptable year of the Lord."

Elizabeth mentally prayed as fervently as she could for Edwin's eyes to open to the truth of God's word.

"Edwin, He said something else that ties in directly with this." He flipped pages again. "It's in John 14:12."

Edwin took another sip of coffee. It was lukewarm and distasteful. Just like this conversation.

"Most assuredly, I say to you, he who believeth in Me, the works that I do he will do also; and greater works than these he will do, because I go to My father."

Edwin was unimpressed.

Jonathan looked at Edwin. He saw nothing, absolutely nothing to give him any reason to believe that Edwin understood one word of what he had just heard. It was hard to believe that this was the man God had chosen to challenge the dark powers in Atlanta. "God called you to be like Jesus."

"And your understanding of like Jesus means what?" Edwin asked suspiciously.

"Simply this: God has invested in the church what he invested in Jesus—power. Power to deliver people from the power of Satan."

Edwin looked at Elizabeth. She smiled and tried to look as objective as possible, but her silent prayers continued to rise to heaven.

"You mean miracles," Edwin stated skeptically.

"I mean miracles and anything else it takes to set people free. What do you have against miracles?"

Edwin scooted up. "What do I have against miracles?" His question displayed more anger than he cared to let Elizabeth see. "I'm sorry, Mrs. Banks."

"Call me Elizabeth."

Edwin smiled. He felt the anger drain slightly. "I don't have anything against miracles because miracles don't exist."

"What did you see when I preached?" Jonathan asked.

Edwin's voice was even. "I saw my church destroyed."

No one said anything for a few seconds. Then Elizabeth asked a question. "Edwin, how was your church destroyed?"

He didn't know how to answer this question without sounding bitter. Hopefully, Elizabeth wouldn't be offended. "My church was destroyed by false doctrine. Five years of work went up in flames. My people are now so confused they don't know what to believe. I've lost close to four hundred members since you preached, Jonathan. How do you explain that?"

"I agree with you," answered Jonathan. "False doctrine destroyed your church." He looked Edwin dead in the eyes. "False doctrine that you have taught."

This shocked Edwin. "Me? We were growing before you came."

"Numerically, yes. Spiritually, no."

"You have no basis to say a thing like that."

"Your church is drying up because you would not let it grow up. They're not used to the meat of God's Word and they're choking on it. This should not have happened. It wouldn't have happened if you would have taught the Bible instead of fabricating sermons that tickled the ears of your congregation. I'm not your problem. Your problem is Edwin Styles."

Of course, Edwin totally disagreed with everything Jonathan said. However, the accusations sank deep into Edwin's heart. They were seeds planted in fertile soil. He felt an immediate germination and was repulsed by it. His orthodoxy was being assailed by spurious charismatic doctrine. It greatly disturbed him that he was utterly incapable of protecting his heart from the effect of Jonathan's cancerous words.

"I don't believe a word you say," Edwin said, even though he heard the mockery of whisperings in his mind that told him he did believe Jonathan.

"That's really irrelevant," answered Jonathan. "God is going to free Atlanta from its deception and bondage to sin with or without your help." There was a fiery determination in Jonathan's eyes. "God is going to set your church free whether you like it or not."

Elizabeth looked at the two combatants and decided that it was time to step in.

"It's getting late and I really need my beauty rest. Edwin, I would really be honored if you and your wife had dinner with us tomorrow. My mother gave me some Cajun recipes that I just have to try out on somebody."

"I don't think—"

She cut him off. "Do you like Cajun shrimp?"

"Well..."

"That's an excellent idea, honey," said Jonathan. He wrote his address on a card. "Here's where we live. It's really easy to find."

Edwin was surprised at Jonathan's sudden change in demeanor. He accredited it to the man's general instability.

"Good! Then it's settled," said Elizabeth. "How does six o'clock sound?"

Edwin knew that if he accepted the invitation, he would change forever. As repulsive and abhorrent as Jonathan's so-called miracle ministry was, Edwin knew inexplicably that there was something inside of him that was sympathetic to this man's ridiculous understanding of God. He also knew that to be perfectly honest, he had to admit that things happened at his church when this man preached that simply couldn't be explained away. That little cross-eyed girl, for instance.

"Six o'clock will be fine."

*****

Bashnar put his latest trophy on his display shelf, right under the picture of the hated Louisiana preacher. His face carried an ugly frown of scorn for the vanquished man of God.

This enemy of darkness that had wreaked such catastrophic damage was now nothing more than another glaring example of Christian weakness. Bashnar spit on the floor in contempt.

"So much for your international ministry," said Bashnar to the picture on the wall. "What great delight I have in preachers whose ministries outgrow their spirituality."

Bashnar looked at the spot he had reserved David Wilkerson. He hated this man as no other. His ministry had done incalculable damage to the kingdom of darkness. The preacher's holy life and fearless denunciation of sin had turned many people from materialism to God. His church had been in revival for longer than Bashnar cared to remember.

What an embarrassment it was that Wilkerson had had such success right there on Times Square. And now the Mighty Bashnar would never have the pleasure of crushing such a loathsome dagger. A car wreck. A car wreck that they had nothing to do with! The warrior spirit noted the suddenness of the great man's death and fumed. Even his manner of death prophesied the message that he preached. *Live ready to meet your Maker!*

His musings were interrupted by a knock on the door. Bashnar seated himself and sat erectly. "Enter."

The jittery demon on the other side of the door dropped the report on the hallway floor. He scurried to pick it up.

Bashnar stared intently at the door.

The demon sorted the papers and almost knocked on the door again. "No," he told himself. He opened the door with a sweaty hand and entered. "Sir, Mighty Bashnar, I am here to report on the dagger, Jonathan." He didn't want to say this. "Sir, uh...Jonathan has made contact with Pastor Styles."

Bashnar shot to his feet. "When did this occur?"

"Tonight."

"When tonight?" Bashnar demanded.

"Ummm, sir, at exactly ten thirty-four."

He held out the report for Bashnar and he snatched it from his hand. Bashnar scoured over the report. His eyes bulged when he read the last line: Jonathan and Pastor Styles are scheduled for dinner tomorrow at six. "Is this an exact transcript of the conversation?" Bashnar asked.

"Yes, sir."

"What kind of angelic presence was there?"

"Pastor Styles's guardian angel, Maht-a'sah, was there, and Jonathan's angel was there, along with two other mercy angels."

"Dismissed."

The door closed and Bashnar sat down. He read the report several times. "They are having dinner? What exactly is the Enemy up to?" The obvious answer was that God was planning to use both Jonathan and Edwin to pull down the satanic strongholds over Atlanta.

Bashnar mulled over this possibility. A Scripture from the cursed Bible came to his mind. It was 1 Corinthians 1:27: *But God has chosen the foolish things of the world to put to shame the wise, and God has chosen the weak things of the world to put to shame the things which are mighty.*

That was it! The Enemy was going to use Pastor Styles to spearhead this attack. Even to Bashnar this seemed almost impossible. Styles was such a weak, vacillating man of God. How could the Enemy ever use him?

Nonetheless, Bashnar knew that the Enemy took great pleasure in using weak and ungifted people for His own purposes. His keen mind meticulously weighed the threat. Two things would have to be done immediately.

First, all outside interference would have to be stopped. That meant the destruction of Witchcraft. Second, Jonathan's ministry would have to be so discredited that pastor Styles would reject it categorically.

Chapter 17

The power brokers of the church met as most discontented church groups do: in secret. Harry Thompson loved secrecy. He coordinated this meeting with the utmost of urgency. Some of the attendees joked behind his back about his *The-Chinese-are-coming* meetings. However, no one joked about the seriousness of this meeting.

The people that sat in Harry's spacious living room, with the exception of Scott Bridges, Harry's nephew, were a factious, warring group who had nothing in common except their desire to control the church.

Appropriately, they were seated in two groups. On one side of the room sat the big four: Billy and Karen Mitchell, and Wallace and Marjorie Reynolds. The Mitchells owned a super successful restaurant in the swanky Buckhead area, as well as three other restaurants. Wallace was a manufacturer of plastics. And there wasn't any commercial real estate that his wife couldn't sell, although Atlanta's commercial real estate market had been hit hard when the real estate bubble burst. But even in such an austere market, Marjorie still found a way.

This group controlled through money.

Across the invisible boundary sat the participants of Harry's first secret meeting, minus two: Larry McGuire, Henry Jennings, Carl Briarwood, Scott Bridges, and of course, Harry. This was the deacon board. They controlled the church through the legal vote granted them in the church's bylaws.

Today both groups put all differences aside. They had a common problem that was more pressing than their political infighting. It seemed only a matter of time before there would be nothing left to fight for. Church attendance and financial contributions had dropped off sharply, and word was spreading among the religious community that their church was involved in faith healing and miracles.

Two people were conspicuously absent. Terrance Knox, the only dissenting deacon, and the topic of discussion, Edwin Styles.

"Now we got to do something to turn things around," said Harry. "If we let things go on as they're going, we're going to find ourselves with an empty church."

"Do you really think it could come to that?" asked Larry, more out of concern for himself than for anything else.

"You bet I do," answered Harry.

"Let's not get carried away," said Wallace. This sounded like another one of Harry's melodramatic panics.

"I'll tell you what's getting carried away. Our church! That's what's being carried away. And I tell you that if we don't do something about it, we're either going to lose everybody or turn into a foot stomping, chandelier swinging, tongue talking Pentecostal church."

Marjorie put her hand over her heart. "Oh, good heavens, I'd rather die a thousand deaths."

"I'd rather die ten thousand deaths than to see our church turn into a circus," Harry added.

"How many members have we lost so far?" asked Wallace.

Harry picked up a piece of paper. "We've lost four hundred and thirty-seven." He waved the paper in the air. "And these are people who told me personally or called the church." He looked at the paper again. "That equates to an average loss per month of $34,635.00."

This hit a nerve with Billy Mitchell. Money was something he understood. "That's almost thirty-five thousand dollars."

Carl Briarwood, Harry's staunchest ally, spoke up. "Someone asked me when we were having our next healing meeting." He said this with a chuckle, but no one thought it was funny.

"Carl is right," said Harry. "The secretary tells me that several people have called the church asking for someone to pray for them to be healed."

"Who do they think we are? Jesus?" This was Marjorie again.

The spirit in Harry was agitated. "We have to stop Jonathan!"

Several faces looked at Harry in bewilderment. What did he have to do with this? He was history.

"Jonathan is our problem! Miracles! Healing! Holiness! This man will take us down!"

"The old geyser is going crazy," Wallace whispered to his wife.

"How is Jonathan our problem?" asked Billy Mitchell.

A blank look came across Harry's face. Then, "Edwin's just not doing the job. He's not preaching against this stuff strong enough."

No one commented on his sudden change of thought.

"How strong do you want him to preach against it, Harry? The Inquisition is over. He can't do any more than he is doing."

"I agree with my husband," said Marjorie. "Ed has done all he can do." As an afterthought, she added, "Why don't we call in an evangelist or somebody? Maybe an outside voice will help."

"That's a good idea," said Karen Mitchell, who had been silent up to now.

"We won't be able to get anyone for tomorrow," said Harry. "We need someone for tomorrow!"

"We don't need anyone for tomorrow," said Billy. "I'm satisfied that Edwin is doing a fine job putting down this foolishness. I say we stick with him." Billy turned to Wallace to explain his position. He couldn't afford a crack in his coalition with the Reynolds. "An outsider is here for a day, or a few days and he's gone. We need continuity. We need someone who will reiterate our position over and over again."

"You have a point there, Billy," said Wallace, his ego satisfied that it was deferred to.

"There's been some talk in the church that that stuff about living holy is in the Bible," said Scott.

Harry's nephew wasn't a major player, and he rarely spoke at these meetings, except to say what his uncle coached him to say. This is why Harry was so surprised at his comment.

"Who said that?" Harry inquired.

"Just some people, visitors. I don't know them. They just said that without holiness no man shall see the Lord." Scott lied. He knew who it was. It was his girlfriend.

"You see there?" Harry said to everybody. "That's what we have on our hands. Our own people are running off and this, this bunch of kooks are coming in our church and echoing what that false prophet man said. We gotta stop it. And we gotta stop it now."

"I heard some other people say that the reason we don't reach out to the sick and the suffering is because our church is spiritually bankrupt."

"Who would say such a thing?" asked Marjorie. "We have a good church."

Harry looked at his nephew suspiciously. "And who said that? Those same people?"

"Well, yeah. Them and others," he answered. He shifted nervously.

"If you see those people again, tell them if they don't like it, leave."

Scott was nervous. He knew he was about to jump into a pool of alligators, but he jumped anyway. "What's the goal of our church?" he asked no one in particular. When no one answered, he timidly added, "I mean it would be easier to keep the false gospel out of our church if we knew what the real gospel was."

The alligators looked at Harry's not-so-silent silent partner in bewilderment. They wondered whether he was friend or foe.

"Just what do you have in mind, nephew?"

Scott knew that the only time his uncle called him nephew was when he referred to him as beneficiary of his will. He wanted to shut up, but knew that he couldn't. Too much had been said already. He would have to tread lightly.

"What I mean is Reverend Banks didn't just attack our doctrine. He attacked who we are. He accused us of being nothing more than a country club with a steeple on top."

*****

Until now the demons couldn't see who was approaching the door. But the soft white mist that obscured their vision lifted as he got closer.

"It is him!" one of them said. "I told you that's who it was!"

"What do we do?" asked the bigger of the two demons.

The smaller demon searched his dark mind for an answer that wasn't there. They had to do something. They couldn't just let this man of God break up their meeting uncontested. Not having any better answer, he said, "Draw your sword."

The bigger demon pulled out his sword.

As the man approached, he prayed under his breath. "Father, you said you would never leave me nor forsake me. I claim that promise tonight. Help me, Lord."

There was a clanging on the ground. The larger demon turned around and saw an abandoned sword. His rubbery neck stretched in shock against its limit. He watched his accomplice speed away, zig-zagging as he fled.

The demon that was left turned back toward the man of God. "Eeeeekk!" he screamed in terror, and stumbled backward and fell to the ground. Six huge angels surrounded the man of God. They carried swords of blue fire. Their stern expressions chilled the demon's heart.

The emissary of hell decided at once that he neither wanted to be a martyr nor a hero. He dropped his sword to the ground and joined his evil partner in flight.

*****

The spirit inside of Harry repeated Scott's words to himself. *A country club with a steeple on top*. He liked that.

The doorbell gave a hollow gong.

"Get that, Scott," said Harry.

Scott left the room and opened the door. The blood drained from his face.

"Hello. May I come in?" asked the man, as he walked past the numbed doorman.

Scott didn't answer. The words were caught in his throat.

"Where are they?" the man asked.

"In—" Scott cleared his throat. "In the living room."

Wallace and Billy were having a good time comparing observations about television faith healers.

"Yeah, but there's a rascal that comes on in the morning that tops him," said Wallace. "This guy preaches out of Texas somewhere. He spends the majority of the show telling you how you can have success in life by contributing to his ministry. I heard him say one time that he didn't like hundred-dollar donations. He liked thousand-dollar donations. It's amazing how those guys can link everything in the Bible to money."

Billy Mitchell laughed. "Maybe we're in the wrong business."

Marjorie joined in. "It's not too late. If we start now, by summer we should have enough money for a giant water slide."

That comment evoked laughter.

Wallace was surprised, but pleased at his wife's participation. She wasn't known for her sense of humor.

"And maybe there will be enough left over for an air-conditioned dog house," she added.

An eruption of laughter filled the room. The only person who didn't find it funny was Harry. But his sour expression didn't dampen the mood one bit.

Scott followed behind the man into the living room.

Wallace was the first one to see him. His laughter abruptly ceased. The others saw the man and also stopped laughing. He was not supposed to be there.

"Good afternoon," said the man. "I'm sorry that I'm late. My answering service has been on vacation. It won't record my messages. So I didn't hear of the meeting until half an hour ago."

Half an hour ago? thought Harry. *Who could have told him? We've been here longer than that.*

Carl Briarwood whispered a question to Harry. "How did he find out?"

Harry didn't answer Carl. "Terrance, who told you about the meeting?" he asked.

The old man sat down. "God," he answered.

"Excuse me," asked Marjorie.

"I said God told me."

"That's what I thought you said," Marjorie replied.

"Terrance, you were not invited to this meeting," said Harry.

"Oversight, I'm sure," answered the spunky old man.

"That was no oversight!" said Harry.

The old man was unperturbed. "Sure it was. You know that our bylaws do not allow secret or unadvertised meetings among the deacons if there are at least three in attendance."

"This isn't a meeting," Harry snapped.

"Why, of course it is, Harry. Your words to me when I stepped in were, who told you about the meeting?"

"I know you," said the spirit in Harry. "You are of the Holy One. We hate you!"

"In the name of Jesus, shut up!" ordered Terrance. "Sit down," he added softly.

Harry stood there rigidly. His body quavered back and forth in defiance of the command.

"In Jesus's name, sit down and keep quiet," said Terrance.

Harry went to a chair in the corner. His gait was stiff and deliberate. He sat down and folded his hands in a docile manner.

Volumes of confusion were written on every face. They looked back and forth at Harry and Terrance wondering what in the world was going on.

"Would anyone care to fill me in?" asked Terrance.

No one answered.

How did he do that? What did he say? In Jesus's name, shut up? the conspirators wondered.

"Harry," said Billy Mitchell, "what's going on here?"

Harry didn't answer. He couldn't answer. An angel stood in back of him with one large hand over his mouth and the other arm wrapped tightly around his body.

Billy turned to the old man. "What's wrong with Harry?"

"What's wrong with Harry is he has the same disease that all of you have. It's called terminal hypocrisy."

Several insulted egos blasted back.

"How can you call us hypocrites?" asked Marjorie angrily. "We've given tens of thousands of dollars to the church."

"That's right," added a deeply offended Billy Mitchell. "It's funny how spiritual you thought we were when the church needed a loan to build the fellowship hall."

The old man sat through the verbal tirades until finally he could get a word in. "You're right, Billy. When we needed your money, we tickled your ears and told you whatever you wanted to hear. We wanted the money, and we were willing to compromise to get it. But that was then; this is now. And I am no longer willing to play your games." Terrance looked at the others. "I'm through playing church."

Carl Briarwood had heard enough. "That's about the most self-righteous bunch of crock I've ever heard! Who do you think you are? What qualifies you to be our judge?"

"You have a Judge, Carl, and I am not He. But when He does come, you won't have a leg to stand on."

Carl didn't answer this.

"I take it this meeting was called in response to the alarming number of members we have lost."

"That's right," answered Wallace. "We've lost over four hundred members. Harry tells us that the church secretary is receiving ten to fifteen calls a day from disgruntled members."

"And what do all of you propose to do about it?" Terrance asked.

"Well, for one thing, eehhh, we—I don't know!" said Wallace.

No one else had any suggestions either.

"I have an idea," the old man said.

Wallace looked at him skeptically. "And what's that?"

"Repent. Repent, all of you and obey God."

Wallace didn't know what repent meant, but it sounded bad enough. "We don't need to repent!" he exclaimed.

"What all of you need is an encounter with Jesus Christ. You need to give your hearts to the Lord and let Him redirect your lives. I've been talking to Jonathan—"

"Jonathan?" more than one interrupted.

"Yes, Jonathan."

"He's the one who started this whole thing," said Marjorie.

"No Marjorie. He's not the one who started it. Jesus started it, and He's going to finish it."

"What do you mean by that?" asked a wary Billy Mitchell.

"Simply this, Billy. Our church is not really our church. It's God's church. And He's not pleased with the way we've been running it. So He's going to shake it up a bit."

"He's going to shake it up a bit?" said Marjorie. "I feel like a milkshake already."

"Harry," Wallace looked at the weird expression on his face. "Oh, forget it."

Marjorie was worn out with this whole thing. "Well, what does God want?" Her husband looked at her strangely. "Somebody has to come up with something. We're just going around in circles."

"Scott, could you get me a cup of water, please?" asked Terrance.

Scott looked in Harry's direction. Harry sat as erect and still as a statue. There was a smirk on his face.

"Just get him some water so we can get out of here," said Carl Briarwood.

Everyone waited impatiently for Scott to return with the water.

The old man felt a slight pain in his chest. He drank the remainder of the water and smiled at the unseen Presence he felt so strongly. "God wants all of you to repent," he said.

"What is that?" Marjorie asked.

The old man couldn't discern her motivation. He answered this question for them all.

"Repentance means to change, and in the context of Christianity it means to change from Satan to God."

"Well, are you saying we are of Satan?" Marjorie asked.

"You tell me," the old man answered. "Have you ever felt sorrowful for your sins? Have you ever asked Jesus Christ to forgive you of those sins? Is He the most important Person in your life?"

Marjorie didn't answer.

Wallace was insulted that his wife's Christianity was publicly scrutinized. "We'll let God judge whether or not we're filling all the squares."

"How did we get on this anyway?" asked an irritated Billy Mitchell.

"You asked me what I meant by saying Jesus was going to finish what He started," Terrance answered.

"Yeah, and you still haven't answered," said Mitchell.

"A reenactment of the book of Acts. That's what's going to happen."

Wallace quickly opened his new Bible to the Old Testament to find the book of Acts.

Larry McGuire emerged from his silence. "What exactly do you mean, Terrance?"

"Larry, just yesterday Jonathan told me something that struck a nerve. He said that American Christianity was weak. No, he said anemic. He said that materialism and comfort had replaced commitment and sacrifice. So much so that God got disgusted with us and let us go our own way. Jonathan told me that Americans don't know the real Jesus. He said the American concept of Christ is a Christ that sanctions everything and demands nothing." The old man's eyes sparkled with energy. "Those days are coming to a close."

"We're right back where we started from," blurted Billy Mitchell. "What do you mean by that?"

"Billy, the end is approaching rapidly. Soon Jesus Christ will appear in the skies for His faithful. But before that happens He's going to force us to decide for Him or against Him. It's going to become very unpopular to be identified with Christ." A forceful thought popped into the old man's mind. "There are no hypocrites in the Christian church in China or Saudi Arabia or North Korea. Do you know why? It's because the price is too high. No one is going to willingly suffer or die for a lie."

"What has that got to do with us?" Wallace was fed up with this foolishness.

"It has everything to do with us. We have a church full of hypocrites, pretenders. It's going to stop. It's going to stop one way or another. God will have a holy church or no church at all!"

"Then He'll have nothing at all!" came the shrill voice from the corner of the room.

Everyone turned in surprise at Harry.

"In Jesus' name, quiet!" ordered Terrance once more.

The silly smirk came on Harry's face again and his mouth moved from side to side as though his facial muscles were in revolt.

Terrance stood to his feet and parted with these words, "I suggest all of you read the book of Acts, because that is exactly what's going to happen to Atlanta, beginning with our church."

Once Terrance was gone, the room quickly emptied. No one was in the mood to continue this disturbing conversation or to contemplate the old deacon's threat. And most of all, they were rattled by Harry's weird behavior.

Wallace and Marjorie didn't speak much on the way home. Once inside Marjorie shivered with morbid apprehension.

"Wallace?"

"What?"

"Something is wrong."

Wallace looked at his wife. It wasn't often that she looked vulnerable and unsure, but right now she looked both. "What's wrong?" he asked.

"Go upstairs and check on Johnny. Make sure he's alright." She would have done it, but it was getting harder to carry her weight up the stairs.

"Okay, okay," he said, with a concerned look.

He went upstairs and heard sounds coming from his son's room. He opened the door. "Hey, Keith."

"Hi, Mr. Reynolds," said the boy.

"Johnny, has everything been alright?"

Johnny looked at his friend and then at his dad. "Yeah, nothing's wrong."

Marjorie was on the third stair. "Is everything okay?"

Wallace came downstairs. "They're fine. They're just watching movies."

"Oh, okay."

"Are you okay? You don't look too good," said Wallace.

"I don't know," Marjorie answered. "I guess it's just old man Knox. This whole thing is playing with my nerves. Did you see how Harry acted when he told him to be quiet in the name of Jesus?"

"Yeah, it was weird," her husband mused. "He acted like he had to obey."

"That was no act, Wallace. He did obey."

"Oh, come on Marge. What are you saying? That Terrance has some kind of magic power?"

Marjorie chuckled nervously. "Of course not. It's just that I've never seen anything like that before. Did you see his face move?"

Neither of the Reynolds were openly affectionate people. But Marjorie was so obviously shaken that Wallace took her in his arms and held her tightly. This was a welcome surprise.

"Who ever said Harry was normal? Don't let it bother you."

"You're right. He is a character."

Wallace looked at his watch. "I'm going to take the car down to Pep Boys and get a tune-up." Fifteen minutes later he was gone.

Marjorie huffed and puffed her way up the stairs. She stopped at the top and took some deep breaths. Her lungs wanted more air than she could suck in. Her flabby legs ached under the strain of their heavy load. “I simply have to go on a diet. I have to lose weight.”

She went to her bedroom and locked the door. She took off her clothes and stood before a full-length mirror.

"Pathetic," Self-Hate said.

"Pathetic," said Marjorie, as she examined her big body.

The demon went to her other ear. "You are a ugly, fat slob."

"You are an ugly, fat slob," she told herself. She turned away from the mirror in disgust and sat on the bed. Her husband's embrace came to mind and a warm feeling replaced the chill of self-pity. She couldn't recall the last time she had felt this way.

Her thirteen-year-old marriage had changed from a steamy romance to a parched contractual obligation. She and Wallace were no longer lovers, but simply partners in business who happened to live under the same roof. Yet now she wondered whether all was not lost. All the more reason to go on a diet.

Marjorie's hopeful mood vanished suddenly and a blanket of dread wrapped itself around her. *Johnny's in danger*! She quickly put on a robe and burst into his room.

Two startled eleven-year-olds looked up at her as though she was crazy.

"What's wrong, Mom?" Johnny asked.

"Uh...oh, nothing. It's nothing dear. Go on and watch your movie." She left the room, but the demons didn't.

Hordes of evil spirits scurried about the room in a mad frenzy of lust. These spirits were animated by the absence of the mercy angels. Fights broke out as every demon vehemently clamored for the unprotected boy.

A voice boomed out of the invisible sphere. The spirits heard it, but saw nothing.

"The boy has been turned over to the spirits of infirmity and dumbness for the glory of God. All others must leave."

Every demon was deathly still. They did not have to see who was speaking. They recognized the Voice. It was the Lord God Almighty! Even so, their rebellious nature wouldn't let them obey, so consumed with hatred were they for God.

A breeze blew softly through the room. The spiritual trespassers knew that meant trouble, but they stood stubbornly still. They were transfixed in defiance of the Holy One of heaven. There was a clap of thunder and a lightning bolt struck a spirit of murder and fried him on the spot. That was enough. The room cleared instantly. Only Infirmity and Dumbness were left.

They stood perfectly still for a couple of minutes, then cautiously approached the boy. Their eyes were hungry for him.

Chapter 18

The Battlefield Assessment (BA) was as thick as a telephone book, but Rashti read it three times and skimmed it once to prepare for the assessment meeting. Overall, there was nothing shocking in the report. Resistance to the Atlanta revival was as ferocious as anticipated. Casualties were a bit higher, but the upcoming Prayer-O-Rama at the Atlanta civic center would cause devastating losses to the spiritual wickedness in the area.

However, Captain Rashti wasn't allowed to relish in the future victories that the Prayer-O-Rama would provide. A precious child of God was wandering aimlessly through a harsh and dangerous wilderness of confusion and fear. Sharon was a joy to the angels under his command, especially Myla. Rashti knew how hard Myla was taking it.

You will smile again, Myla, thought the captain. *The Lord God Almighty will deliver the precious one once more.*

Rashti made himself consider another facet of the assessment. This one brought him joy. His friend Enrid had successfully infiltrated the security of the Castle, sabotaged the Council of Strategic Affairs' meeting, and returned to tell about it! The most daring mission accomplished in quite a while! He would definitely recommend him for the Medal of Valor.

"Thank you, saints, for your prayers!" he exulted.

He considered another development: that of Edwin and Jonathan. Much prayer had been used to coordinate their dinner date. A fierce and costly battle had been fought to rid the area of wicked spirits and to secure a perimeter around Jonathan's home. Yet Rashti knew that these accomplishments meant nothing unless Edwin received Jonathan's message.

*****

Bashnar knew what he had to do. His plan was ambitious, bold, and daring—Bashnar smiled—and extremely dangerous. It was a two-part, short-range, long-range scheme directed against Jonathan.

The short-range plan was simple enough. Discredit Jonathan at all costs. Edwin could not be allowed to enter the dimension of the supernatural. He had to remain a pawn of the devil and a slave of tradition.

Bashnar skimmed the pages of the History of Exploits and Defeats. This book was invaluable to the hordes of darkness. It gave comprehensive details and summaries of every major battle against the kingdom of God.

He closed the book. He would not try to reinvent the wheel. Bashnar would have only to highlight and emphasize the excesses of the charismatic movement. Edwin would be so turned off by the excesses that he would reject it all. Bashnar laughed. What was it that humans said? He would throw out the baby with the bath water.

Which extreme would he exploit first? How about the name-it-and-claim-it doctrine? Or the prosperity doctrine? That was one that shallow preachers loved. Bashnar grinned. Even mealy-mouthed Edwin would see through that farce.

Bashnar wrote a name on a piece of paper. This would be his spokesman. This would be the person to poison the charismatic well. One taste of its water and Edwin would throw up the putrid liquid.

Just the right person for the job, Bashnar thought. *A person with an ego almost as big as mine. Someone with more confidence than knowledge and more simplistic formulas than godly wisdom.*

The second phase of Bashnar's plan wasn't as cut and dry. It was a dangerous, career threatening plan that had all the elements of a death wish. So much could go wrong. Yet, so much could go right.

Bashnar remembered how he had destroyed Demas, the disciple of Paul—yyuuk!—the apostle. Very similar strategies with one dangerous twist. So far everything was working as planned. But it was now time to open more doors of ministry for the man of God. It was time to send him more hurting people than ever before.

Spit drooled lazily down the sides of Bashnar's mouth onto the desk. He could taste this victory. He knew that even the great Jonathan couldn't resist this bait.

"Heal the sick, mighty man of God. Cast out as many devils as you please. Show forth your God's glory. It will be your undoing!"

But first things first. He had to put his puppet in place. She was ready; he knew she was. The demons of strife that he had assigned to her weeks ago—great forethought!—had informed him that the road was paved for the spirit of divorce.

"Jessica, I'm counting on you."

*****

Divorce approached Jessica's home cautiously. It wasn't that she was exceptionally dangerous. She wasn't. Actually, she was relatively harmless. Her bark was much worse than her bite. Nonetheless, a demon just never knew when a Christian like this would suddenly decide to do the Word of God. That would be a most unwelcome surprise. Divorce hated surprises.

He glided to a soft landing in front of the house. When his webbed feet touched down, immediately three luminous beings surrounded him. Divorce stood deathly still. Crazy charismatics! You never knew what they would pray up next.

"What is your business?" one of them demanded.

"I am Divorce. I am sent of the Mighty Bashnar to tempt Jessica."

"Then you won't be needing this," said one of the angels as he took Divorce's sword and dagger.

"No, I guess not," answered the outnumbered demon. *No sword. What do I do for protection?*

"You are free to tempt the woman of God," said one of the glowing entities, "but that is all. We will watch you for any unauthorized movements."

The implication hung threateningly in the air.

Divorce walked past the three unexpected guards. *Surprises! Thank you, Bashnar. What else will I find?*

Jessica listened to preaching on her iPod as she washed dishes.

Divorce was curious to what she was listening to. He listened in. His face cracked a smile. *Hmmmmm...How to Get God to Do Anything You Want.*

"When will you fools ever realize that that is the same lie that Adam and Eve fell for in the garden?" He shook his head in amusement. "The creature is going to tell the Creator what to do—yeah, right. We tried that. It doesn't work."

Jessica was unaware that she was under demonic attack. And if someone would have told her that a demon was in her home, she would have angrily denied it.

Divorce had worked with these kinds of Christians before. They were know-it-alls. They had God and the devil and all of life reduced to a few simplistic formulas. Everything fit neatly into a little box.

Divorce's job was elementary. Convince Jessica to leave her husband in violation of 1 Corinthians 7:13: *And a woman who has a husband who does not believe, if he is willing to live with her, let her not divorce him.*

Easy enough task. All he had to do was deceive her into thinking that she could serve God more fully if she left her husband. Divorce knew this was a total distortion of Scripture, but most Christians could be manipulated rather easily.

*****

Anthony Righetti wore a calm, self-assured smile, but his intestines danced nervously. He could hardly sit still for the introduction. This was the biggest day of his life. The next hour or so would decide his fate, either as a frustrated, muzzled messiah with a large, but forever limited group of secret Satanists, or as the celebrated spiritual revolutionary who declared war on Christianity and won!

Christianity was a dead religion anyway. A monolithic corpse of structured fables and myths whose repressive stench cried for a proper burial. He determined to answer the call and push the obese body into a deep grave. People were tired of Jesus Christ. They were tired of being told what to do, what to say, and what to think. They were tired of repressing their true feelings. They wanted freedom!

Anthony felt the sweat build and drip under his arms. He looked out at his audience. There were more than one thousand people present. Satanists, Wiccans, Pagans, Spiritualists, New Agers, Reincarnationists, Psychics, Crowleyites, Voodooists, Punkers, etc.

Waves of exhilaration washed over him. He had hoped that the Family's ad would attract a crowd, but at the time he didn't really believe so many people would respond. Now he knew better. Atlanta was sick of Jesus!

Anthony chuckled in anticipation of the punchline. He had heard it before, but it was still funny. "And now, ladies and gentlemen, the man who taught me that the difference between Christians and babies is that babies are cute and dumb and Christians are just plain dumb."

Much laughter.

"Ladies and gentlemen, the founder and director of the Family, Anthony Righetti."

Anthony stood up and went to the lectern.

Everyone stood to their feet and clapped. Just as it began to die down, the clapping rose to a crescendo. Anthony looked down at his adoring audience. He felt the energy in the air. They wanted him. They wanted his message.

The time for the demise of Christianity had finally come!

"Good afternoon," he said.

The crowd responded vigorously.

"How was the lunch?"

An assortment of satisfactory answers.

"Before we begin, I'd like to introduce you to the high priestess of the Family. My daughter, Toni."

The audience clapped their approval.

Toni gave an abashed wave to the crowd.

"Now see what you've done?" said Anthony. "You made her blush." The audience responded favorably. Anthony's confidence soared. He knew deep down in his heart that today was his day. He could do no wrong. "How many of you saw our ad? Let's see your hands."

Almost half the audience raised their hands.

"How many of you heard about this meeting through word of mouth?" he asked.

Nearly everyone else raised their hands.

Anthony noticed an elderly lady wearing a red scarf. She didn't raise her hand for either question.

"Ma'am, how did you find out about us?"

The lady was delighted to be singled out. She stood up. Her eyes twinkled with strangeness. "My guide told me about this meeting. He told me that I should come. He told me that you were a great man and that you would free Atlanta from negative influences."

"Who is your guide?"

"The spirit of Edgar Cayce."

Several people clapped at the mention of his name.

Edgar Cayce had been a psychic of notable paranormal accomplishments who had died decades earlier. Anthony was well acquainted with him and his writings, as well as others such as Ruth Montgomery, Jeanne Dixon, Arthur Ford, and Peter Hurkos.

They were held in high esteem among fledgling psychics and would-be witches. But Anthony Righetti held them in the highest contempt. They were adolescents exploring their own puberty! Novices with a new toy! These soft sell children of the occult would never know the depths of Satan's power!

However, the time was not right to show his hand. He had to have patience. He didn't want to scare them away.

"Tell Mr. Cayce that I said thank you for the kind words," he said, with a politician's smile.

"I certainly will," said the lady and sat down.

Anthony was fanatical about proper preparation. Many of his ex-employees knew from experience that Mr. Righetti never compromised this issue.

Tonight he was as prepared as he ever was. He had lost count of how many times he had practiced this speech in his basement or in his bathroom mirror. He had a stack of index cards with notes on them to help him stay on track. There were even cards telling him what facial expressions to make and when to make them.

A demon spirit emerged from the multitudes of evil spirits that were in the hotel's banquet room. The spirit slowly opened his mouth and coughed into his hands. He coughed repeatedly until he threw up into his hands. He took the thick, lumpy substance and stuffed it into Anthony's mouth.

Anthony didn't see the spirit, but he knew he was there. He felt a sensation like warm honey sliding down his throat. Thoughts, powerful thoughts exploded into his mind at a furious pace. They came so fast that he could hardly tell where one ended and the other began.

He smiled evilly and turned his note cards over. He wouldn't need them today. "There are over one thousand of us here," he said. "One thousand intelligent and enlightened people. Over one thousand seekers of truth. As I look across the audience, I see one common trait on every face: hunger. Every one of you hunger for truth. Truth that can be attained only through nontraditional means. I, too, am hungry."

Anthony slowly walked across the podium, his head lowered in deep thought.

"I want to recount for you how I came to be and how the Family came to be." He paused. "I was once a Christian, a follower of Jesus. My family and I were model Christians. We went to church every Sunday and Wednesday, and sometimes more. We paid our tithes, ten percent of our income, to the church, and we gave offerings. Cissie and I won people to the Lord on a regular basis.

"We worshipped the invisible God with all of our hearts, Cissie and I. Toni was just a little girl then. I remember the good, mushy feeling I felt each time I sang the song *Amazing Grace*. Me, a rotten, depraved sinner having fellowship with a holy, righteous God. It was beautiful, fulfilling, as most fantasies are!"

Anthony maintained intense eye contact with the audience. His voice lowered and raised at just the right moments to emphasize his words.

"Blasphemous words, aren't they?" he rhetorically asked. "Blasphemous only to those who believe in the Christian lie! Blasphemous only to those who abdicate their inalienable religious rights to the Christian aristocracy! Blasphemous only to those with weak minds and faint hearts! Christianity is a world of fantasy, a cave of refuge for the weak!"

Anthony smiled at his enchanted audience. "Now," he said calmly, "what caused my transformation? What changed me from a pie-in-the-sky Christian to a hedonistic here-and-nower?" Hatred burned in his heart. "This is what changed me." Anthony's eyes stared into the past. "Cissie...my wife, began to lose weight. We...we took her to see a doctor. She was diagnosed with cancer."

There were muffled responses of empathy in the audience.

"We went to see our pastor. We asked him what we should do? Do you know what his answer was? Do you know what the man of God told us? The Lord giveth and the Lord taketh away! I could hardly believe my ears. Was he telling me that Jesus gave Cissie cancer? I asked him, Reverend, did Jesus give my Cissie this horrible disease that is eating her body away and turning her into a skeleton? He didn't answer me. I searched the Bible day and night for answers. I found several places where God healed people in response to prayer, especially in the New Testament.

"Matthew, Mark, Luke, and John, the narratives of Jesus's life, were filled with countless examples of miraculous healings. I was filled with hope. Cissie was going to live! My wife was going to be healed! I went back to my preacher, Bible in hand. Look! Look! I told him, showing him the many places in the Bible where Jesus had healed the sick. Won't Jesus do the same for Cissie? I'll never forget his answer. 'Jesus doesn't do that anymore?' Just like that. He doesn't do that any longer.

"I was devastated. How could He not do it anymore? How could a good, kind, merciful God not heal my wife? She had served Him so faithfully. I went to every Christian I knew. I wrote to every preacher on television. No one helped me." Anthony chuckled contemptuously. "I did get a response from a famous so-called faith healer. In response to my letter asking him to pray for my wife to be healed, I received a letter, a computer printout really, telling me that he needed me to make whatever sacrifice necessary to send him money to enlarge his ministry. Ministry my butt! He wanted money to satisfy his greed!

"My wife died! And with her died my dream of a world where Christ ruled. I turned to the only thing that made sense: Satanism."

Anthony knew that he would have to choose his words carefully lest he scare the New Agers, Wiccans, and other benevolent non-Christians. *Stupid idiots! Little did they know that they were all servants of Satan*. Yet he would have to reveal enough to win the Satanists, the Crowleyites, and others of his kind.

"Satanism—a word that denotes so much that is not true. A word that conjures up images of unjust crime and bloody sacrifices." He hoped the hardcore would take note of the word unjust. "Satanists are law abiding citizens. We obey the law of human nature. We obey the dictates and desires of our bodies. It is not criminal to be human.

"The real criminals are preachers who prey on the meager social security checks of the old and the infirm. The real criminals are those who legislate their immorality on those of us who are moral." Anthony saw that there were twice as many women in the audience than men. "The real criminals are the Christian Inquisitors who wish to infringe upon the rights of women and deny them the right to legal abortions."

Applause broke out from the women. The men quickly followed suit.

"The real criminals are the religious bigots of Christianity who have cursed the world with their Crusades and holy wars. Their

Inquisitions and Dark Ages. Their false morality and repression of sin. And bloody sacrifices. They accuse us of bloody sacrifices? Whose religion sheds more blood than the Christian religion? Sheep, goats, bulls, and even a person sacrificed—Jesus Christ."

The Wiccans and New Agers, you have to speak directly to them...and the other softies.

"I say the world has had enough of Christian absolutes crammed down our throats! Homosexuality is wrong! Adultery is wrong! Hate is wrong! Abortion is wrong! Everything good is wrong! But wrong according to whom? It's only wrong to those narrow-minded, finger-pointing Christians!"

The crowd's enthusiasm and radiant ungodliness fueled Anthony's speech.

"Today I stand before you not as a slave brainwashed with antiquated Christian fairy tales, but as a champion of hedonism and self-indulgence. If it feels good, do it! That's what the Family is all about. We're about self-gratification, self-indulgence, and self-exploration.

"I founded this great organization to serve as a refuge for those who have been raped and brutalized by Christian guilt trips. But more than that, the Family was created to protect the vital interests of the ungodly. Every day we're losing our rights to the vocal minority. Our division and inaction has given a green light to Christian bigots to run roughshod over our rights.

"The goals of the Family are to provide a solid front of ungodliness to impede and halt the influence of Christian thought in Atlanta. Our goals are to organize politically. To speak as one irresistible voice. A voice that cannot be ignored or denied." Anthony's clenched fist vibrated with tension. "We will drive the Christians and their bigoted God from Atlanta!"

Chapter 19

Jonathan sank into the soft, cushiony chair. It was one of those long, fancy chairs that added twelve hundred dollars to the price of the living room suit. Jonathan's burning eyes closed. His mind drifted back to the day his wife had talked—no, badgered—him into purchasing such an expensive piece of furniture.

"It's not a sin to buy something nice, Jonathan," she had argued.

He had looked at the chair and frowned. "I know, but how many little orphans could brother Balais in the Philippines feed with twelve-hundred dollars?"

"Quite a bit." Elizabeth turned to the toothy salesman. "Yes, we'll take it, and he'll love it later."

Jonathan had not protested. If this had been anyone else, he might have been tempted to think her to be another product of American Christianity: self-centered and materialistic.

But this was Elizabeth. She was the most selfless and devoted Christian lady he'd ever known. No matter where in the world God had called them, the Philippines, Mexico, Haiti, New York City—it didn't matter. His wife never complained. She was at home among the poor and the rich. Stuff just didn't have a hold on her. She was such a wonderful gift of God.

Jonathan smiled. Elizabeth was right. He did like this chair, all twelve hundred dollars of it. His tired body conformed to the contour of the chair. In a moment, he was asleep.

A couple of minutes later his eyes popped open. I have to write some letters. He got up softly and tried to creep out of the living room.

"And where are you going?" the unexpected voice surprised him.

"Uumm, uh, I"—he knew he was caught—"well, I was just going to write a few letters."

Elizabeth's mouth turned up in disapproval.

"Brother Giminez's church has been on my mind. You know, with the guerillas and all." His wife's expression didn't change. "Columbia has gotten even more dangerous since FARC...." His voice withered under Elizabeth's dispassionate look.

"You're not too big to be put over my knee," she said.

Jonathan opened his mouth to protest, but Elizabeth cut him off. She knew his defense better than he did.

"I know, the Lord is coming soon and we have to work while it is day, because the night cometh when no man can work. We are our brother's keeper, et cetera, et cetera, et cetera."

Jonathan smiled in submission. He knew he was licked.

"You can't win the world all by yourself, and even if you could, it couldn't be done overnight. My goodness, even Jesus rested. You think maybe there's a chance that Jesus wasn't as spiritual as you?"

Jonathan shook his head in mock agreement. Lady's on a roll. Just have to grin and bear it.

Elizabeth placed her hand on her hips. "Am I making myself clear?"

Jonathan looked at his wife. Her physical beauty matched the beauty of her spirit. She was such a lovely creature. She normally only wore pants when they were out of country, when the rigors of their missionary work demanded it. But sometimes she wore them around the house. This was one of those times.

"Am I making myself clear?" she repeated, smiling, aware that she was being surveyed. This was one of the things she loved about her husband. He thrived on making her feel special and beautiful and wanted.

She turned and began to leave the room. Jonathan admired the fit of her jeans and watched her departure with delight.

"Loud and clear," he said.

Elizabeth stuck her head back in the room. "Get your mind out of the gutter."

Jonathan spoke in an exaggerated tone. "I am a holy, sanctified, pious, heavenly-minded man of God totally incapable of thinking gutterous thoughts."

"Okay," Elizabeth said, smiling, "okay, Mr. Heavenly-mind, we'll see if that line lasts the whole night."

He waved his fingers. "Goodbye, Elizabeth."

She waved back. "Goodbye, Jonathan."

He waited a couple of minutes and then snuck to the edge of the kitchen and peeked in. Elizabeth was hard at work preparing dinner for their guests, the Styles. He quietly made his way to his den to write those letters.

*****

"I can't believe we are actually going to have dinner with that Jeffrey Banks," Barbara said as she applied her makeup. "It would make better sense for President Obama to have dinner with Trump."

"It's Jonathan. His name is Jonathan," said Edwin.

"Well, whatever. It just doesn't make sense. What do we do if he burns our church to the ground? Throw him a party?"

Since when do you care anything about the church? "We're just going for dinner," Edwin said, fully aware that his wife was right. When this thing was over, he would probably be an even bigger fool than he already was.

"Ed, we're going to dinner with the man who's going to cost you your job."

"My job?" Edwin said incredulously. "Is that what your concern is? My job?" The question was directed at her, but he suddenly felt that he was under a giant microscope being examined, his own inner fears shamefully exposed.

My God, why am I having dinner with this man? To somehow save my job? The thought made Edwin instantly sick. *If this is what I am, God help me.*

"Well aren't you concerned about your job?" Barbara asked, angry at his apparent disinterest, which she knew was phony. "Don't tell me you aren't."

Edwin didn't answer. He just went downstairs and started the car.

Barbara gave last minute instructions to Sharon and the boys and joined Edwin in the car. He tried to silence her incessant chatter by ignoring it, but it didn't work. She was irritating him to death.

"Momma and Daddy never had any black friends."

Where did that come from? he thought. But he didn't vocalize his question. He wanted to quench her ramblings, not encourage more of them.

"Momma was raped by a black man," Barbara said softly.

Edwin turned at this stunning revelation and looked at his wife in astonishment.

"You never told—"

"Look out!" Barbara screamed.

Edwin jerked his head around and looked squarely into the face of a UPS truck. He turned the wheel sharply. His wife grabbed her face to protect it.

Mudillus, who was Nerod's replacement, who in turn had been Oreon's replacement—it wasn't easy working directly for Bashnar—watched on in frenzied anticipation. If this worked...

CRASH!!

Edwin was doing forty-five. The UPS truck was doing fifty.

Mudillus's oblong eyes bulged at the wonderful sight. He and the several demons with him celebrated with acrobatic flying when they saw their orchestra of destruction.

The UPS driver was not wearing any type of restraint. The centrifugal force of the crash propelled her unwilling, but helpless body into and over the steering wheel and through the large window. The young lady's battered body landed several yards away.

Mudillus saw Edwin's body absorb the engine as it exploded through the dash. He and his wicked spirits examined the grisly details of the wreckage. Both bodies—if they could still be called that—were broken and bloodied.

Trin looked at Mudillus. Mudillus looked at Trin.

Mudillus saw the shock and horror of his bloody victory etched on his enemy's face. He ventured closer to the angel of God, but not too close.

"Is this the best you can do?" he screamed. He pointed to the strewn and contorted metal. "This is what will become of your revival!"

Trin and the other three angels, who were absolutely stunned, kept silent.

"Come," Trin told his detachment, "we must report this...incident."

"Go! Go you weak puppets of a weak God!" Mudillus yelled in derision. "We will stay to watch their bodies be scraped into little bags."

Their wicked laughter filled the air.

*****

Mudillus stepped into the Mighty Bashnar's office. He had the written report.

"What is this urgent news?" Bashnar asked, in his customary no-nonsense manner.

Mudillus's heart thumped wildly beneath his coarse, hairy chest. This would most certainly get him recognition with the Council of Strategic Affairs. Images of prestigious assignments danced in his wicked mind.

"Sir, Pastor Edwin Styles has been eliminated." Mudillus would like to have embellished his statement, but his excitement compelled him to be direct.

Bashnar shot to his feet. If this was true the coming invasion of righteousness would never materialize. Edwin was God's man for Atlanta, perhaps even more so than Jonathan. He was a weak man who knew he was weak and therefore extremely dangerous, for God's power was made perfect in weakness.

"Are you sure?" Bashnar asked, exhibiting an excitement that was inconsistent with his reputation of suppressed emotion.

"Yes, sir, your plan worked exactly as you said it would. I watched him and his wife get ripped to shreds. The others will verify that they were carried away in body bags. They had to use the Jaws of Life to cut them loose. They were totally crushed, Mighty Bashnar," he added with a triumphant smile.

"Excellent! This leaves only Jonathan. And that congregation isn't going to follow a black man. Even if they do, he won't last much longer. The seeds of his destruction are soon to break through the soft earth of his armor."

Mudillus waited for Bashnar's commendation.

"Give me the report."

Mudillus handed it to him.

Bashnar thumbed through it quickly, looking for particular items of interest. He looked up. "I know how difficult this assignment was. Your compensation will be just. Dismissed."

Bashnar sat and devoured the report. When he finally finished, he folded his large hands behind his head and leaned back in his chair and planned his next move.

No air bags. His eyes popped open. Alarm spread over him like a flash flood of an ugly possibility. Bashnar gritted his sharp teeth and pounded the desk with his powerful hands. He went to his bookcase and pulled out the *History of Exploits and Defeats*. He scanned the table of contents and stopped at Elijah: The Battle on Mount Carmel. Bashnar read the account and slammed the book shut in disgust. "Idiots! Incompetent, juvenile idiots!" he yelled.

*****

Trin handed his report to Captain Rashti.

"Head-on collision?" asked the captain.

"Yes, sir," confirmed Trin, his voice heavy with grief. "The enemy's booby traps were well concealed. This family never had a chance."

Trin didn't have to clarify what sounded like a fatalistic statement. The captain understood fully well what his friend and fellow warrior meant. Most of God's people miserably failed to appropriate His divine protection. They walked through life half expecting God to automatically do everything for them, whether they sought Him or not. When would they awaken out of their passivity and enforce Satan's defeat?

"No, my friend," said Rashti, "they never had a chance."

A thoughtful pause.

"The child in her womb was to be a great evangelist," Rashti added sullenly.

Ever since the Fall, angels had lived with the tragedy of human death. Multiple billions had died in every conceivable manner, many in horrific ways. Yet the angelic nature would not—could not—allow them to ever get used to the fact of death. It was so foreign to the original plan.

Rashti shook his head.

Five people killed. Two of them pastors, and a lady eight months pregnant with a yet to be born evangelist.

"You have the report on Edwin Styles?" Rashti asked.

"Yes, sir." Trin handed it to him.

"Sit down, Trin."

"Thank you, sir."

Rashti read the report and asked, "Everyone saw the accident?"

"Yes, sir. Mudillus and his soldiers all saw it happen."

"You left them there?"

"Yes. They wanted to stay and enjoy the carnage."

Rashti weighed the situation.

"With Edwin dead what do you anticipate Mudillus' next move to be?" he asked Trin.

"Mudillus is ambitious; he wants recognition. I believe he'll forego standard operating procedure and try to exploit this situation for all he can get out of it. He will most likely redirect the demons that are trying to break through the perimeter we have set around Jonathan's home, use them somewhere else. Somewhere where a breakthrough will get him an instant promotion"

"Like that outreach to homosexuals."

"Right," Trin agreed.

The outreach they spoke of was an affiliate of True Life International. This ministry was mainly the effort of people who had once been homosexuals and lesbians. True Life International was one of the most hated works of God among demonic strategists. It had caused great embarrassment to Satan's government. How disgusting that the grace and love of God had been allowed to deliver so many people from homosexual lifestyles. Many high-level demonic princes and generals had been banished to the Dark Prison for the effectiveness of this ministry.

"Reinforce them immediately," the captain ordered.

"Yes, sir."

"If he does redirect his forces, it will only be for a short while."

"Sir?"

"Bashnar is an avid student of warfare tactics and strategy. He knows his history, too. We'll probably have only a couple of hours of respite until Bashnar discovers what has happened. Use this time wisely. Widen the perimeter. Dig in. Fortify your positions."

"I'll relay this information to the officer in charge."

"And Trin..."

"Sir?"

"How much prayer did you have to use to create this illusion?"

"More than we could afford."

But both of them knew they couldn't afford to not divert Mudillus's forces. The meeting between Edwin and Jonathan had to work.

"Good job, Trin."

"Thank you, sir."

*****

It was Saturday night and Toni was alone again. Once more her father was out of town on some speaking engagement. He had really become a star since the Family's banquet.

Toni was accustomed to being lonely. She was accustomed to being alone. Though she had never liked either. She especially disliked the silence that accompanied being alone. It made her think about things she'd rather forget. But this evening she yearned for silence that was distressingly elusive.

She poured another drink to quench the thirst of her torment. Toni swallowed too quickly and choked. The liquid spewed sloppily out of her mouth.

How could she hurt her best friend? How could she let that animal do that to her? She'd have to tell her what she had done.

Toni knew that Sharon would hate her forever.

*****

Sharon lay sullenly on her bed and pushed the remote's button aimlessly. She didn't want to look at television. She wanted...she didn't know what she wanted.

Ever since that night, the night she lost her virginity, guilt ate away at her soul like acid. She wanted to call it rape, but she wasn't raped. She had been seduced. There was a world of difference in the two. Sharon knew she would never recover from this tragedy. She'd never again trust anyone.

She hated herself for letting this happen. It wasn't enough that she had begun to party again. She had to go to bed with a stranger.

"What got into me?" Sharon asked herself guiltily.

Not far from Sharon he stood.

Sneering. Delighting in her anguish.

Witchcraft.

"Pitiful whore," he spat. "Poor, pitiful whore."

Sordid laughter.

Myla stood between Witchcraft and Sharon. His weapon ready for action.

"Why are you crying?" Witchcraft taunted. "Did you think, like so many others, that you could play our game with your rules? Did the little virgin think she could flirt with sin and walk away unscathed?"

More laughter.

The wicked dignitary got too close and a flaming blue sword flashed under his nose. He jumped back.

"Careful, you could hurt someone with that," said the demon.

"I aim to if someone isn't careful," Myla answered.

Witchcraft looked at the intensity of the sword's blue flame.

Prayer.

"Calm down, angel. I am not here to hurt your dupe," he lied, "only to talk to her."

Myla said nothing. He would let his sword do his talking if Witchcraft got too close to his beloved Sharon.

"Sharon," said Witchcraft, "you should have known better than to be shaken so easily. Your faith should not rest on your father, but on Christ. Am I right, Myla?" he asked, smiling. The ugly smile vanished. Witchcraft's vile face intensified in grotesqueness. His eyes bore holes into Sharon. "Go to your mother's closet and look in the brown paper bag!" he thundered.

Sharon put the remote control down and walked to her mother's room, not knowing why she had a sudden interest in what was in her closet.

Myla followed closely. His eyes were riveted to Witchcraft.

Witchcraft's laughter came from deep within.

"Go on virgin. Open the bag. Oh, I'm sorry. You're not a virgin any more, are you. I meant to say *freak*."

Sharon picked it up and started to put it down. This would be the first time she had ever violated her parents' privacy. But there was something compelling about this bag.

She opened it.

There were a few paperback books and some DVDs. Sharon scanned the books. "My God! What is this stuff doing in my mother's closet?"

The DVDs weren't titled. Sharon was afraid to play them. But curiosity urged her on. She closed and locked the bedroom door. The last thing she wanted was for her brother to walk in on a.... Sharon didn't let herself finish the thought. With trembling hands, she pushed a DVD into the slot. She let it play for a couple of minutes.

"Oh, Jesus," she covered her mouth in shame, "I'm so sorry." Tears welled in her eyes. "Please forgive them. Oh...please, God, I...please forgive them." She didn't dare look at any of the others; it was unnecessary.

Sharon was numbed by her discovery and was horrified by the next thing Witchcraft screamed into her mind: "I think it's time you had a pregnancy test!"

Chapter 20

"Are you sure you wrote the address down correctly?" Barbara asked Edwin when she saw the luxuriousness of the homes.

"I have the right address. Jonathan wrote it himself."

"Hmp," said Barbara, still finding it hard to believe that they could live in this neighborhood. "What does he do besides tear up other people's churches?"

"I don't know," Edwin answered, rolling to a stop.

"Well, what does his wife do?"

Edwin thought. "I don't know what she does."

"I hope it's nothing illegal."

"What would make you say a thing like that?" The irritation in Edwin's voice was clearly discernible.

"I don't know," Barbara answered, her tone matching Edwin's. "It's just, how can a preacher afford a house like that? And I don't care what his wife does. It's not enough to pay for that." She pointed an accusing finger at the extra large home.

Edwin rarely got angry, even about things that deserved his anger. But he found himself growing extremely angry at his wife's infantile behavior.

"Barbara, grow up. If this man was white you wouldn't have any problem with this house and you know it." Edwin was shocked that that had come from him.

His wife was even more shocked. "And just what the hell do you mean by that?"

Edwin's head whipped around. This was the first time he had ever heard his wife use such language.

"I told you what happened to Momma!"

"I'm sorry about what happened to your mother, but what has that got to do with this man's house? You're not making a bit of sense."

"You just don't understand," Barbara fumed.

A hurt Edwin looked at his wife. "Yes, Barbara, I do understand. I understand more now than I ever have before." His words carried infinite pain and sorrow. "Eighteen years ago I met and fell in love with the most wonderful lady I had ever met. Her beauty was poetic. Her smile was radiant. Her heart was larger than the ocean, and her capacity to love was just as deep. She was perfect. I married this dream come true."

Barbara's face softened at these words.

"A number of things have happened since we have been together to convince me that my dream is an illusion. Always I made excuses to protect you. I didn't...I wouldn't let anything threaten my belief that you were perfect. But I was wrong; you're not perfect. You're very, very imperfect. Behind your mask of innocence is a lady...a lady..."

He couldn't bring himself to say it. She was a lady capable of more than he could have ever imagined. She was a farce.

"A what?" Barbara inquired insolently.

Edwin was tired, mentally exhausted from the amazing metamorphosis he had lately observed in his wife. "Nothing," he sighed.

"Nothing?" Barbara yelled.

"Drop it, Barbara," Edwin insisted softly. "We'll talk about it later."

"We'll talk about it now!" Barbara demanded.

"I promise you," Edwin tried to placate her, "we'll finish this conversation as soon as we get home. We need to talk." He put his hand affectionately on hers. She snatched it away.

"We'll talk about it now! I mean it, Edwin. I'm not getting out of this car until we put a cap on this." *Put a cap on this? Where did she pick that up? Larry says that,* Edwin mused. "Barbara, these people have invited us to dinner. We accepted the invi—"

"You accepted," she interjected angrily.

Edwin continued as though she hadn't spoken a word. "We're here, and we're going inside."

Barbara protested. "Not until—"

"Now!" Edwin yelled.

Barbara flinched in surprise and not a little bit of fear. "I'm not moving," she said unconvincingly.

"Either you get out of the car of your own volition or I drag you out." Barbara looked into her husband's eyes. There was fire in them. "Which will it be?"

Barbara curled into a defensive ball. Edwin's face hardened. He reached toward her.

"Okay, okay." She quickly opened the door and hurried up the stairs, leaving Edwin behind.

Edwin's heart felt like it would break. He couldn't stand the idea of his wife being afraid of him. He slowly followed her up the stairs. *God, I'm sorry. I didn't mean to yell at her, to scare her like that.*

Jonathan was looking out of the bedroom window. "Honey, they're here."

"Okaaay." Elizabeth took one last nervous glance at the table she had set. This was the first time she would use her gift of bone china. She admired the tableware's brightness and design, the silverware, napkins, and vase with its beautiful flowers. Her eyes landed on a white amaryllis and smiled.

Edwin caught up to his wife and took her gently by the arm. "I'm sorry for speaking to you so harshly. I don't know what came over me."

Barbara didn't comment.

"Honey, I'm sorry for speaking harshly to you. I'm not sorry for giving you an ultimatum."

Barbara did have something to say to this 1920's statement of sudden machismo, but the door opened.

"Hello," Elizabeth greeted them both.

"Good evening," answered Barbara, with a polished smile.

"Nice to see you again, Elizabeth," Edwin said.

"And nice to see you, too, Ed. Glad you could make it. You are going to love the shrimp. They turned out perfectly. Do you like oysters, too?" she asked, as she led them to the living room.

"Yes, I do," answered Edwin.

Barbara admired the spaciousness and decor of their home.

Elizabeth saw that Barbara was impressed with what she saw. "May I take your coats please?" she asked.

They gave them to her.

"I'll be right back. I'm going to get Jonathan."

Barbara smiled. As soon as Elizabeth left the room, she asked her husband in a hushed tone, "Who is she?"

Edwin laughed. "That is Jonathan's wife."

Barbara scooted closer and spoke even lower than before. "She's so young."

"He wanted someone who would outlive him," Edwin joked.

"No, I'm serious, she's probably fifteen years younger than he is," Barbara whispered.

"More," Edwin said, enjoying his wife's shock and conspiratorial whisperings.

Barbara was about to go on when Jonathan and Elizabeth entered the room.

Edwin stood.

"Hello, Edwin," said Jonathan.

They shook hands. Jonathan heartily; Edwin uneasily.

"Fine, fine," Jonathan answered Edwin's tight lips. "I'm going to gain weight tonight, Edwin."

"I hope I don't," Edwin answered, hoping the evening would pass quickly.

The four of them sat and indulged in small talk for a short while. Afterwards, they ate a meal that lived up to its billing. Delicious!

Jonathan took Edwin to his office. It looked a lot like Edwin's home office, only bigger. There were oversized maps on the walls—maps of the U.S. and the world. There was also an expensive looking globe on a fancy brass stand.

Edwin walked over to the bookcase. The number and caliber of books that lined the wall impressed him. There was an entire wall of them. There were several reputable commentaries, Bible dictionaries, Greek lexicons, and various other study aids.

Edwin's eyes widened and his mouth opened in surprise when he saw some of the books. Jonathan had the works of Martin Luther, Jonathan Edwards, Charles Finney, John Wesley, and other famous old time preachers, preachers who Edwin admired greatly, but, of course, preachers who belonged in a different era, when times and spiritual awareness were more primitive.

Jonathan saw the surprise. "Even false prophets enjoy a good read."

Edwin smiled abashedly. "I—"

"You don't have to explain. I understand. You did the only thing you could do, Edwin. You resisted what you thought was false doctrine."

Edwin's smile faded. "Not what I thought Jonathan; what I know.

"That's what I want to speak to you about."

Edwin's body involuntarily tensed up.

Jonathan sat on his sofa and offered his guest the chair at the desk. Edwin's seat was higher than his own. Jonathan had purposefully arranged the chairs this way. Hopefully, this would help Edwin to not feel like he was under scrutiny.

"I owe you an explanation," said Jonathan.

"Well, that's something we both agree upon."

"Where do I start?" Jonathan wondered out loud.

"Try the beginning."

Jonathan slowly nodded his head. "The beginning? Okay, the beginning. Edwin, we are at war." Jonathan's expression and tone was solemn.

Edwin said nothing to this.

"When Satan fell, he took one-third of the angels with him. They became demons, fallen angels, malevolent creatures of infinite wickedness. They no longer have a place in heaven. They live on earth. Actually, their kingdom is just above the earth."

Jonathan looked for some response from Edwin.

Edwin was the perfect stoic.

Jonathan continued. "Their mission is to subvert God's plan."

This evoked a response.

"But God is almighty."

"Yes, Ed, you're right. God is almighty, and He can do anything. However, God doesn't want to do anything. He wants to do what He has planned."

Edwin knew by Jonathan's intonation that he was supposed to ask what that plan was. "And that is...?"

Excitement ignited in Jonathan's eyes. "And that is to witness to the world the excellency of God."

"I can agree with that," said Edwin.

"You can, but you don't." Jonathan's words should have offended Edwin, but they didn't. Perhaps because his words were more imploring than accusatory.

"Would you care to explain?" Edwin asked dispassionately.

"There is only one way to represent God, and that is the way Jesus Christ did it."

Here is where the circus begins, thought Edwin. "I must admit, when I walked in here and saw your collection of books it surprised me."

"I know."

"It surprised me that anyone who espouses the kind of doctrines you teach would have such books in his possession."

"That is exactly what Satan wants you to think. If he can convince you that everyone who prays for the sick and believes God for miracles is an uneducated kook who place more faith in doubtful religious experiences than in the Word of God, well, of course, you're going to be turned off."

"If they are educated, they don't show it. I've never heard so many ridiculous things in all my life than what comes out of the mouth of some so-called faith healers."

Jonathan wished he could brush Edwin's observation aside. He wished he could do like so many other charismatic and full gospel ministers: duck this arrow of truth and call it persecution. But he couldn't do that. He knew that Edwin was correct.

"Edwin, you're absolutely right. There is much in the charismatic and full gospel movement that grieves the heart of God. There is much that deserves His iron hand of judgment, and even punishment. I know personally many of the best known full gospel preachers."

Edwin's curiosity was whetted. "You know some of them?"

"Yes. And many of them do fit that mold, Edwin."

Edwin saw what looked like sadness in Jonathan's eyes.

"They cover up their ignorance of the Scriptures with dubious revelations that are more products of their own warped minds than anything else. I have friends who can teach the devil how to twist Scripture."

Jonathan's apparent passion for integrity moved Edwin to the core of his being. He never knew there was such a thing as an honest faith healer. Could Jonathan be one?

But this mental acceptance of the possibility that Jonathan was any different from the others directly contradicted the louder voice that told him that Jonathan was an advocate of spurious doctrine. How could he admire a false teacher? It didn't make sense.

"Some of them are better liars than the devil. I place them in the same category!" Now there were flashes of anger in his eyes. "I am amazed at the gullibility of God's people. These guys can do almost anything and their followers will still support them. It doesn't make sense. Why are they so blind?"

"Maybe they don't want to see?" replied Edwin, unaware of the significance of his words.

Jonathan looked at Edwin the way a master sculptor would look at a block of marble. He was a work of art in the rough. Soon God would turn this shapeless theological eyesore into a work of resplendent beauty.

"Itching ears," said Jonathan.

"Itching ears," echoed Edwin.

"I see we have more in common than we thought," said Jonathan with a smile.

"That's scary," said Edwin. Something resembling a smile snuck on his face, but he was dead serious.

"It's not that bad being on this side of the fence."

Edwin didn't say anything for a few moments. Then, "How did you come to be on that side?"

"Failure," came the immediate answer.

Jonathan stood up. He went to the map of the world and pointed to a country. "Have you ever been to Kolkata, India?"

Edwin twisted his lips in thought.

“Calcutta. Kolkata was Calcutta until 2001.”

"No. No. I've never been out of country—well, Mexico."

"There is no place on earth like it, and I've been all over the world thrice. It's the most crowded, filthiest, backward, poverty stricken country I've ever ministered in. You've never experienced spiritual oppression until you've lived in Kolkata. Of course, unless you want to consider Haiti.

"Hopelessness permeates every sector of society. It's a stifling, suffocating hopelessness that you can feel in the air." Memories of his past experiences in India surfaced vividly in his mind. "You can see it in the eyes of the little children who survive by scouring other people's garbage."

"How long were you there?" Edwin asked, his admiration of Jonathan growing rapidly by the moment.

"Close to eighteen months the first time."

"Eighteen months? The first time? You've been there more than once?"

"I've lost count of how many times I've been there. However, after I left India the first time I returned a year later and stayed this time for nearly three years."

"You said failure led you into the type of ministry you have." It sounded odd to Edwin's ears to hear himself talk to this man about his ministry as though it was legitimate. He told himself that he was only being polite.

"More than failure, my brother. Miserable failure. I've been a Christian all my life. As a child when other little kids had ambitions to be firemen, nurses, doctors, astronauts, I wanted to be a missionary.

"A missionary to Ecuador spoke at our church. Even at that young age I could tell that he was a terrible speaker. But what he lacked in oratory, he made up for in fire. He did the usual things that visiting missionaries do. He showed us films and slides and that sort of thing."

Jonathan's eyes grew dreamy, like he was looking into a distant land that his heart yearned for.

"As soon as I finished high school, I went to Bible college. The very next day after graduation I was on my way to the seaport city of Kolkata, India."

Edwin sat transfixed, hanging on every word. He tried not to blink lest he miss something.

Jonathan chuckled. Then he laughed, and as he thought about that first debacle of a missionary trip, he laughed uproariously, holding his side.

Edwin joined in the laughter. He didn't know what he was laughing at, but whatever it was, it had to be awfully funny. "What are we laughing at?" Edwin asked amidst his laughter.

Jonathan didn't answer immediately; he couldn't. Finally, his laughter subsided, but not entirely.

"Edwin, you've never seen a bigger fool. I was the Charlie Chaplin of the mission field. When my feet touched down on Indian soil, I looked in every direction and yelled at the top of my voice—I actually yelled at the top of my voice—'I claim this city for the kingdom of God!'"

"You did that in front of everybody?"

"Yep, in front of everybody."

"What happened after that?"

"In short fashion, I failed at everything I did. And I dramatically emphasize everything. I was working with some missionary friends of my father. They were your traditional missionaries. Go to a foreign land, learn the native tongue, preach a little here and there, and hope you win a few converts.

"So I followed their pattern. I learned the language and went to preachin'. I preached and preached and preached and preached some more, but nothing happened. I recall one incident that was endemic of my whole Indian adventure.

"I was preaching to a group of about thirty people. They were nice people. They listened to me courteously, attentively, but nothing I said took root. Now that in itself is not odd. But what was strange was the fact that every single person there wanted Christ."

Jonathan looked Edwin squarely in the eyes—Edwin focused on his nose—and moved closer to him.

"Edwin, they *wanted* Jesus."

Edwin was baffled. Wasn't that what he went over there for? To win converts? "So what's the problem? You had thirty people who accepted your message."

Jonathan prayed that God would help Edwin understand.

"Yes," he said, his voice carrying the excitement that was in his heart. "Thirty people who accepted my message. But thirty people who couldn't accept my Jesus."

Edwin hoped this wouldn't sound as calloused to Jonathan as it sounded in his mind. "You had thirty people who didn't accept Christ. That's not an oddity, even in India, right?"

"No, Edwin. I said, couldn't accept Jesus. These people wanted Jesus, but couldn't accept Him."

Edwin's eyes showed his confusion.

"Something...someone would not let those people give their lives to God. This occurred repeatedly. I'd go to a village, preach the gospel, find a ready audience, and when the time came to ask for commitments everyone acted stupefied. Everyone just got stupid on me. I mean, like they all suddenly became disinterested. I tell you what, Edwin, they don't tell you in Bible college how to deal with an audience that goes stupid on you."

Jonathan stood up. With exaggerated pomp and a failed attempt at a British accent, he stretched forth his hand. "Class, today we will discuss what to do if you are preaching to a group of people who suddenly become nearly catatonic right before your eyes.

"Edwin, I didn't know what was happening until I read Acts 26:16-18: 'But rise, and stand upon thy feet: for I have appeared unto thee for this purpose, to make thee a minister and a witness both of these things which thou hast seen, and of those things in the which I will appear unto thee; delivering thee from the people, and from the Gentiles, unto whom now I send thee, to open their eyes, and to turn them from darkness to light, and from the power of Satan unto God, that they may receive forgiveness of sins, and inheritance among them which are sanctified by faith that is in me.'

"That's when I learned that several things must occur to a person before they can receive Christ. First, he must have his spiritual eyes opened. Second, he must be turned from darkness to light. Third, he must be turned from Satan's power unto God. Only then can a person receive forgiveness of sins."

Edwin didn't understand the full implication of these words, but he felt something happening inside of him. It seemed that his heart was blossoming like a flower. He felt enlarged in his spirit. "What happened after that?" he asked.

"Not a whole lot. I knew what my problem was, but I didn't know how to solve it. A couple of months later I went home broken and disillusioned. I never wanted to see the mission field again."

Edwin couldn't explain it, but he felt a kinship with this strange man. Perhaps it was because he could relate so well to his story. No, he'd never been on the mission field, but he was all too familiar with failure. He knew exactly how Jonathan must have felt.

"How did you get over the failure? How did you recover yourself?" Edwin asked, more for his own benefit than for the sake of moving the story along.

Jonathan perceived this.

"Edwin, I determined that God was right and people were wrong. I determined that God was right and I was wrong. I determined that I would no longer follow in the footsteps of tradition simply because its path was the easiest and most popular. I determined that the Bible would be my ultimate guide."

Jonathan looked deep into Edwin's soul.

"That sounds so spiritual, so cliché-ish, but do you know how hard it is to really make the Bible your ultimate guide?"

Edwin knew that if he had to answer that question out loud, his answer would be no.

"It takes death. It's the reason Paul said, 'I die daily.' Everything and everyone, even Christians, will challenge your decision to obey the Bible." Jonathan pondered several thoughts. "You have to brutally crucify ego and selfishness."

"I searched the Scriptures to see how Jesus evangelized, and Peter and John and the others. Do you know what I found? I found that God never expected them to do a supernatural work with carnal weapons. All of them walked in the realm of the miraculous. Even those who were not apostles."

Edwin felt his parched heart drink in Jonathan's words like they were rivers of life. His mind combatively set up barrier after barrier to divert the flow, but no theological barrier could stop it. The waters overflowed and inundated him with the reality that he was a slave of tradition.

"I went back! To India. Back to Calcutta. This time not as a representative of American Christianity, but as a representative of the Lord of the universe. Edwin, I didn't know what was going to happen. But I was certain that God was with me.

"I had another gospel meeting. Really, you couldn't call the other ones gospel meetings. It's not a gospel meeting unless Jesus shows up. Anyway, this time I spent a day in fasting and prayer. I didn't feel any different, but when I stood before my audience of sixteen, I noticed a difference in the atmosphere of the place. It was...I don't know...it was freer. Yeah, it was free.

"That day when I asked for people to give their lives to Jesus Christ everyone came forward. That was amazing in itself. But something else happened that propelled me into supernatural ministry. I felt an urge—"Jonathan placed his hand over his chest—"a knowing in my heart that I should lay my hands on their sick and pray for their healing."

Jonathan laughed, remembering the awkwardness he had felt that day.

"You know that's in the Bible—Mark 16:18. Anyway, I put my hand on a young man and asked God to heal his eye." Jonathan stared into the past. "The boy was born with only one eyeball," he said slowly. He snatched himself from the past and looked at Edwin. "I watched God create a new eyeball."

Edwin didn't say anything. He couldn't say anything. His mind told him that it was all a lie. Just another charismatic embellishment to give credence to a religion of fanatical emotionalism. But his heart told him it was all true. This was no slick talking television evangelist trying to raise money to build a monument to his ego.

Reluctantly, Edwin conceded that Jonathan was apparently free of ulterior motives. And although he was a stranger, Edwin knew him. Something mysterious had happened to Edwin's heart. He felt that he and Jonathan had somehow become one. One in spirit.

"Needless to say, after that I never lacked a crowd. Word spread fast. The next day I spoke to a crowd of several hundred. And the same thing happened; only this time to more people. From that we were able to build a church. Our first Sunday service we had over five hundred in attendance. We would have had more, but we split the converts up among several pastors."

Just a few hours ago Edwin would not have sat through this story. Now he found himself enraptured by it.

"Jonathan, I don't know what to say. I feel like a little child." Edwin surprised himself with his confession. He stood up and went to the world map. "More like an infant. A newborn baby being birthed into a strange world." He dropped his head. "I've been a fool. I've preached the experiences and prejudices of men instead of preaching the Bible. I've led my people to hell."

This was a real theological departure. Hell—a literal place of everlasting torment for the wicked—was something that he never had accepted. Now instinctively, he knew that hell was real.

Jonathan wrapped his arms around his brother in Christ. "You're right. You have been a fool."

"Are you always so supportive?"

"Okay, you've been a miserable fool. Now what are you going to do about it?"

Edwin's eyes were moist. He thought for a few long moments. "I'm going to do what I've failed to do. I'm going to live for Jesus.

I'm going to preach His Word. I'm going to do what you do. I'm going to pray for the sick!"

"Good! Good!" said Jonathan, slapping him on the shoulders. "There's a whole world out there crying for deliverance from satanic bondage. God is going to use you mightily, Edwin Styles. He's going to do such wonderful and magnificent and awesome things through your hands that you will find it hard to believe it's not a fairy tale.

"First, it begins with your church. God is going to establish his righteousness in your church. Then He will hit Atlanta like a sudden tornado."

Jonathan's words cut through Edwin's euphoria and calmed him down quite a bit.

"I want to do—I mean, I'm going to preach the gospel according to the biblical pattern. But I have no idea what my next step is. I don't know a thing in the world about praying for the sick."

Jonathan smiled mischievously. "That's okay. I'm going to teach you."

They spoke for a couple of hours more and left the den. Edwin didn't want to overstay his welcome.

Jonathan and Edwin walked in on a touching scene. Elizabeth and Barbara were embraced, crying together.

"Don't you worry," Elizabeth consoled her, "it's going to be okay. God is going to work it out. You have to trust Him and let Him do it His way."

"I'll try," Barbara said, "but it's so hard. Sometimes I don't know what to do. I feel so helpless."

"I know you do, honey." She held her tightly and tenderly stroked her hair. "But you're going to have to judge yourself of your sin. Until you do, you're going to remain helpless. God can only help you when you're willing to give it all to him."

Neither of them saw their husbands yet. Jonathan wisely motioned to Edwin and they backed away into the other room.

Edwin was shocked, but happy to witness his wife open up to someone. But he couldn't help but be disturbed that his wife apparently had a sin that she was succumbing to. Everyone had some improvements to make, but from what he saw, it seemed that her problem was of an extreme nature.

After they left, Jonathan received a telephone call. Someone needed help. Against his wife's protestations, which weren't at all of the playful sort this time, he went out into the cold.

Chapter 21

Divorce worked feverishly, but delicately on Jessica. It was extremely hard to maintain this balance, but the three angels that observed his temptations provided the necessary motivation.

Bashnar sent a messenger to Divorce to strongly encourage him to consummate his temptations as soon as possible. The fake deaths of Edwin Styles and his wife had allowed Jonathan to meet and discuss spiritual truths with Edwin unmolested. Jonathan's influence had to be stopped at once!

Divorce formally requested the assistance of a demon of strife and was informed that none were available. Every demon of strife in their region, including the ones who had softened Jessica, was already assigned to Christian churches. A precaution of the Council of Strategic Affairs just in case the revival caught on.

How do they expect me to break up this marriage without strife? Strife is our number one weapon against marriages. Divorce knew that his superiors had the cart before the horse, but he had to make do with what he had. Unfortunately, at the moment all he had was himself.

Divorce wasn't as skilled as a spirit of strife. He almost always came on the scene after the strife spirit had adequately prepared the victim. But he had picked up a few of their tricks.

He magnified her husband's faults. He put the spotlight of satanic criticism on his every weakness, every frailty of his flesh. The inherent pride that Jessica refused to slay made it considerably easy for Divorce to convince her that her harsh condemnatory judgments of her husband weren't condemnations at all; they were spiritual observations.

Finally—and this was his area of expertise—he convinced her that she would be better off without him.

The Spirit of God tried to warn her. He reminded Jessica that God hated divorce, and He told her forthrightly that she had absolutely no biblical right to leave her husband, since her husband was pleased to live with her.

The Spirit of God minced not a word when He told her how wrong she was. How would this man ever get saved? Did she care? His Voice was less than gentle when He told her that her decision to leave was based not on the welfare of the kingdom of God, but instead was motivated by purely selfish motives. She was chasing the elusive god of temporal happiness.

Yet Jessica heard not a word of God's admonition. Her self-will muted His words. She determined to leave the lazy, no good, beer drinking bum and serve her Lord without the ball and chain of an ungodly husband.

*****

Sharon wished desperately that she could undo the evils that had befallen her. She wished that she could somehow reverse them. Yet she knew that her wishing wouldn't change a thing. Her behavior of the past few weeks had busted the dam that had shielded her from Satan's attacks. She now stood directly in the path of a deluge of consequences.

Sharon heard her parents enter the house and make their way up the stairs. The child in Sharon wanted to run to her mother and father and tell them everything. The loss of her faith. The loss of her virginity. Everything. She wanted to ask them what she should do if she were pregnant.

Sharon's fear and gloominess turned into anger as she realized that neither of her Penthouse parents were in a position to tell her about morality. What could they do to help her get out of trouble? They were in as deep as she was.

Myla felt the infinite pain of Sharon. He looked at her with sad eyes. *Oh, that I could trade places with you. That I could remove your grief and give you joy.*

What could he do to help this precious little one? The angel's face brightened with an idea. He touched her eyelids ever so gently.

Sharon felt a sudden heaviness in her eyes. She fought to stay awake, but slumber, sweet, peaceful slumber overtook her fears and worries and put her to sleep.

*****

Edwin knew he shouldn't say anything. He knew that the scene he and Jonathan had stumbled upon was a sacred moment of confidential sharing. He should not let his wife know that he saw or heard anything. But he had to. He waited until they were both in bed before he brought the subject up.

"Barbara, when Jonathan and I left his den we walked in on you and Elizabeth." Edwin's voice betrayed his embarrassment for intruding into what could prove to be a purely female matter.

Barbara's expression was one of surprise and a trace of resentment.

"Uhh, you said something about feeling helpless."

Barbara didn't know whether she should deny it altogether or just tell him everything. "That was nothing; just a little something I needed advice on."

"Nothing serious?" Edwin inquired.

"No, nothing serious."

Edwin sat up. "Jonathan's wife said something about you having to judge yourself of sin."

Barbara's back was to her husband. He didn't see the tears that rolled down her face. "You know how those two are," she answered. "They equate everything to sin. Good night, Edwin."

Edwin knew there was more than what he had been told. He flicked on his lamp. "Honey, I want to help."

"I'm really tired, Edwin."

"Honey, something's eating away at your heart and I want to help."

Barbara rolled over to face him. It was then that Edwin saw her tears.

"Okay, I'll tell you what's eating away at my heart, as you put it."

Her tone of voice made him brace for a verbal assault. It never came. Instead, his wife rolled over on her side, with her back to him, and scooted closer to the opposite end of the bed.

Edwin moved closer and gave her arm a gentle squeeze. "I won't press you if you don't feel comfortable talking to me about it. I know that we haven't been getting along, and—"

Barbara turned towards her husband and kissed him, long and with all the feelings of a lady long denied. "Make love to me," she begged.

Edwin should have been pleased. He should have been excited. He should have been amorously aroused.

He wasn't.

He was terrified.

The spirit that had so suddenly and savagely interrupted the sexual equilibrium of this marriage, and at strategic moments filled Edwin's mind with horrible, emasculating thoughts of unnatural sexual accusations, sprang into action.

He slapped his suction-cup hands on his victim's head and began to massage, hard, but slow—at first. The demon quickened his pace to equal the waves of pleasure that rolled over his crusty body.

Thick, mucous-like yellow slime gathered in the creature's mouth and ran down his long neck. A sure sign that his level of hellish delight was intensifying.

But the waves of pleasure the spirit experienced were to Edwin waves of crushing guilt and shame. A relentless twosome that crippled his male psyche and made it impossible for him to answer his wife's invitation of intimacy.

If only I could reveal to you what happened, he thought.

He remembered the smile of the perpetrator. The smug arrogance of a conqueror to the vanquished. He didn't have to work to remember the pain, the humiliation, the fear of rejection if any of this was ever discovered. These emotions were his constant companions.

Barbara detected his uneasiness right away. Her jaws set tightly. She knew that tonight, too, she would endure further humiliating rejection. "What is it this time, Ed?" she asked firmly.

Edwin was at a loss. He couldn't explain to her what he needed someone to explain to him. He didn't know why his mind and body were being assaulted as they were. *It happened so long ago. And why was I not tormented like this before? Why now?*

Barbara snatched herself out of bed. "That's it, Ed," she said through gritted teeth. "I'm not the smartest person in the world, but I'm not the dumbest either. I told you you'd be sorry," she threatened.

The telephone rang before she could get out of the bedroom.

Edwin didn't hear it ring. He didn't hear anything or see anything, except the shameful pictures of seduction that the helper demon was transmitting to his tormented mind.

I could've done something. I could've...

"Did you hear me, Ed?" his angry wife asked.

No answer. Just a blank look of trouble.

"Ed, I said that was Jessica. She's having some trouble at home and she's going to need a place to stay for a while."

Still no answer.

"Jessica, he said that you are more than welcome to stay here—"she looked sharply at Edwin; she knew that her sister and Edwin didn't get along—"as long you want."

"Oh, thank God. I'll be over in a little bit," said Jessica.

Shortly after their conversation, Jessica arrived after midnight with several suitcases.

*****

The next morning Edwin rose up early. A full two hours earlier than he usually got up on Sunday mornings. The service didn't start until ten-thirty. It was only six-thirty.

Today was supposed to be a normal day. Nothing out of the ordinary. Nothing memorable was scheduled to happen today. As far as the church staff was concerned, their pastor was simply going to continue the theme that he had been preaching on for the past few weeks. *The Day of Miracles Is Over.*

But Edwin knew that he would never preach that message again. It was a lie. He didn't know entirely what the truth was, but he knew—not so much from what Jonathan told him, but from the voice of his own heart—that miracles and healings were for today.

He showered, got dressed, and went to the kitchen and poured himself a cup of coffee. He sipped his coffee and read the Scriptures that Jonathan had asked him to read. Some he read only once, and others he read numerous times.

He closed his Bible in frustration. If one took these verses literally, it would put an awful lot of responsibility on the preacher to set people free. *There is no way I can ever live up to this level of ministry,* he thought. *I'm not Jonathan.*

What troubled Edwin the most was that if he accepted these scriptures at face value—and he knew that he must—he would have to radically change his way of thinking, speaking, and living.

He would no longer be able to hide himself from the hurts and pains and sufferings of the world. He would no longer be able to shield himself from the awful reality of spiritual warfare by subscribing to convenient theological arguments that justified or mystified everything that happened.

The scariest realization was that he would no longer be able to blame God for everything that happened. If there really was a devil, then he and his hordes of demon spirits must be responsible for the evil that is in the world.

Jonathan's words came to his mind. *God has invested in the church what He invested in Jesus: power. Power to deliver people from the power of Satan.* "What Scripture did he give me for that?" he asked himself out loud.

He turned to John 14:12:

> *Truly, truly, I say to you, He that believes on me, the works that I do shall he do also; and greater works than these shall he do; because I go unto my father.*

He that believes. He pondered for several moments, reading those three words over and over. He that believes. He that—yes! He that believes! You have to believe! You have to believe that what God says is true!

A contradictory thought came to mind. *But that was only for the apostles,* it said. But just as quickly another thought burst on the scene. *Stephen was not an apostle, and neither was Philip.*

Edwin looked at the notes that Jonathan had given him and raced to the Scriptures that supported this thought. Acts, chapter six and verse eight. He read them both out loud. "And Stephen, full of faith and power, did great wonders and miracles among the people."

He turned to Acts 8:5-7: "Then Philip went down to the city of Samaria, and preached Christ unto them. And the people with one accord gave heed unto those things which Philip spake, hearing and seeing the miracles which he did. For unclean spirits, crying with loud voice, came out of many that were possessed with them: and many taken with palsies, and that were lame, were healed."

Edwin was awestruck. He slowly closed his Bible. An explosion of biblical insight flooded his caves of theological darkness with a glorious, liberating light.

Being an apostle was not the prerequisite for working miracles or healing the sick, he surmised. Neither of these men were apostles; they were deacons. What did it say about Stephen? He was full of faith and power. That's why the Christian church doesn't work miracles the way they used to. And that's why we don't heal the sick any more. We're not full of faith and power!

No wonder why we have created doctrines to make it seem like God has stopped using ministries of miracles and healings. Either we admit our spiritual bankruptcy to the world or we say that God has changed His methods. God hasn't changed; we have!

Edwin sat for a couple of hours at the little breakfast table. This was so exciting! He felt like an astronaut discovering new life on distant planets.

Someone walked into the kitchen. It was Barbara.

"Good morning, Barbara."

"Good morning, Ed.

Edwin tried to figure out her mood as she fixed herself a cup of coffee. "You can sit here if you like," he said.

"No, that's okay," she smiled perfunctorily. "I'm going to take it upstairs."

Edwin got a clear reading from that response. She never drank her coffee upstairs. It was always at the breakfast table. Leftovers from last night's attitude.

Edwin let out a sigh of exasperation. He drank the last of his coffee and headed for his home office. Despite his wife's standoffish behavior, he felt great. Extremely nervous and ill-prepared for the new course of ministry he would begin today, but he felt great nonetheless. Adrenaline pumped through Edwin's body and fed him an excitement that he had never before experienced for a church service.

He bounced into his office like a child who had just received a new bicycle. He didn't know how to ride it yet, but it was fun just knowing he had it. So what if he was clueless as to what to do with the power that God had invested in His church. Just the idea of God working through him the way He worked through Jonathan was overwhelmingly exhilarating.

Edwin prayed a *God-help-me-preach-good-today* prayer and reached for the doorknob.

That's when the command went forth. The courier angel rushed the message to Myla. Myla opened the pouch: HINDER THE MAN OF GOD SO THAT HE DOES NOT GET AHEAD OF SCHEDULE.

Edwin's hand touched the doorknob. When it did, Myla placed a hand on the small of Edwin's back and one on his abdomen. Edwin felt a sudden intense nauseating feeling take control of his body.

His legs became too weak to hold him up. He knew he was going to throw up. He opened his office door, and he and Myla walked very slowly towards the staircase.

"How are you, brother?" Jessica asked vibrantly.

Edwin heard the voice before he saw the face. He hoped he was in a bad dream. He slowly looked in her direction. Nope. It wasn't a bad dream. It was Frankenstein's little sister.

"What's wrong with you?" she inquired.

"I—ohhh," he said, holding his now throbbing head, "I'm not feeling too well." His voice was scratchy.

"No, no, no," said Jessica. She shook her head and waved her index finger under Edwin's nose. "The devil's trying to keep you from church. You have to speak the Word!" She grabbed him by the head before he could move. "Loose him, devil!" she screamed, and shook his head. She jerked his head back and forth as she accented her commands to the devil. "Let him gooooooohhh, Satan! He's healed by the stripes of Jeeesus!" His head snapped to the right and left.

Edwin winced in pain with each jerk of his head. Jessica seemed to be trying to shake the devil loose. He wanted to make her stop, but he felt so weak, almost too weak to say anything. And she had done it so quickly.

"Jessica," he groaned, "stop it. Please stop it."

Jessica ignored him and instead slapped her palm to his forehead.

It was as though a live wire had been attached to the base of his skull. He snatched away from his looney tune sister-in-law. "What are you doing?" he demanded, wincing from the pain he caused himself by jerking away.

"I'm praying for you."

"Can you pray for someone without decapitating him?"

Jessica pitied her brother-in-law. He was the perfect prototype of spiritual weakness. He didn't know his authority in Christ. *Poor fool,* she thought, *he doesn't even know that Satan has made him sick.*

"Edwin, the Bible says—"

"Yeah, yeah, yeah," he said as he turned and went up the stairs.

When Barbara saw her husband's sickly state, she asked, "Honey...honey, what's wrong?"

"I don't know."

"Sit down," she said. There was a softness in her voice that Edwin hadn't heard in a long time. It seemed like eternity.

He lay down on his back. Barbara quickly removed his shoes and sat down next to him. She put the back of her hand to his forehead to check for a fever. He didn't feel hot.

"Barbara, I'm going to stay here and rest. Call Larry and tell him I'm not feeling well. He'll know what to do."

She looked worried.

Edwin didn't want his wife to worry. Yet his heart was glad at her show of emotion.

"Will you be okay?" she said. "You know—oh, this is ridiculous. I'm not leaving you here."

"Really, I'll be alright," he said.

Barbara bent down and kissed her husband. "I love you," she whispered.

Edwin was surprised and mildly shocked at these words. "I love you, too." His eyes were moist. He pulled her closer and they shared a look of unspoken intimacy. "Barbara, I'm so sorry that—"

She put her fingers to his lips. "Don't...God is...well...let's not talk about the past." She stood up. "I'll get with Larry. You just get some rest and try to sleep off this bug."

Barbara, Jessica, and the boys left the house. Sharon had talked her mother into letting her bow out of going to church. She instead took the car and went to purchase a pregnancy detection kit.

Edwin was flat on his back when the telephone rang. He slowly reached over and picked up the receiver. "Hello."

"Edwin?"

"Yeah." Edwin was embarrassed at how he knew he must sound.

"You sound terrible, brother. Edwin, I just got out of prayer and God wants me to show you something."

"Jonathan, I don't think so. I'm feeling terrible."

Edwin couldn't see the huge smile on Jonathan's face. "I know, brother, I know. I'll be right over."

"I—" began Edwin.

Click.

Jonathan was there in forty minutes.

It took Edwin a several minutes to get to the door. It was torture. Maybe it was the flu.

"Hello, brother!" Jonathan slapped Edwin on the shoulder and walked past him.

Edwin felt like he had just been hit by a bear. "Ohhh, my head..." Edwin closed the door.

"Brother, your apprenticeship begins today."

Edwin walked lightly to the sofa and sat down. "I really don't feel—"the angel took his hands off of Edwin—"up to anything but..."

"But what?" asked Jonathan.

Edwin's eyes were wide. He slowly stood up. He moved his head slowly, then a little faster. Then he jerked it. He blinked his eyes hard a few times. The pain was gone. The headache. The nausea. His burning eyes...gone. Just like that. Edwin felt...he felt...great!

"I'm not sick any more," he said, stupefied at his sudden recovery.

"That's good," Jonathan said, anxious to get the show on the road. "You said you wanted to walk in the realm of the supernatural. Well, today's the day."

Edwin gave his guest a reserved look.

"Don't get dignified on me," Jonathan joked.

"What do you have in mind?" asked Edwin, afraid of what the answer might be. *The sickness left as soon as he came over. Could this be a coincidence? It has to be. Edwin* eyeballed Jonathan. *How could he have had anything to do with my healing? Healing? What am I talking about—healing? But I did get healed. Ohhh, brother, this is way out of my league. I don't know....*

"You mean, what does God have in mind," Jonathan corrected.

"Right. What does God have in mind?"

"We're going to cast out a devil."

"What?" Edwin almost screamed. "Cast out a devil? Is that what you said?"

"Yes. That is exactly what I said."

"That's what I thought you said. What do you mean *we* are going to cast out a devil?" Suddenly this supernatural thing didn't sound so appealing after all. "Maybe you are going to cast out a devil, but I'm doing no such thing."

"Let me slowly repeat myself," said Jonathan. "We are going to cast out a devil."

Edwin looked at the hardwood floor for a long time, intensely studying the lines that separated each light brown strip. *I'm either in or out...in or out. I can't go half-way.* His heartbeat quickened. *Oh, God, what in the world am I getting myself into?*

He thought of the alternative. He could go back to the safety of unbelief. But now as he was being brutally honest with himself, he admitted that this kind of safety was killing him. He was absolutely bored. And since the arrival of Jonathan, he had come to painfully realize that he was absolutely empty. No, he would have to be like the apostle Peter. He was getting out of the boat. He would walk on the water or die trying.

Still, the idea of casting out a devil. He shook his head no as he resolutely decided yes. "We are going to cast out a devil. Me...a ghost buster. I don't believe it."

Chapter 22

Sharon put the pregnancy kit on the counter. Her face carried the strain of a horrible tragedy.

I am not pregnant.

I am not pregnant.

I...am...not...pregnant.

God, I can't...no...I'm not. I am not preg—

"Ma'am?" said the cashier. *Poor girl,* thought the elderly lady, as she held out her hand for the money*, For your sake I hope you're not. Bless her, Father*, she prayed.

"Oh...oh, I'm sorry," said Sharon and handed her the money. She feigned a smile, but it looked more like a grimace.

Sharon picked up the box, clutched it tightly to her bosom, and headed toward the door.

"Young lady, you forgot your change. Ma'am...ma'am, you—"

Sharon turned. "It's okay," she said with tears beginning to roll down her cheeks. "Keep it."

Sharon got in the car and looked wide-eyed at the ceiling. It hit her that she had no place to go to test herself. She certainly couldn't take the pregnancy test kit home. "I wonder if it even works," she said.

Myla lifted his sword with two hands and pointed it at the fast approaching spirit.

It was Witchcraft. He smiled at the angel.

"Neither will our swords lock this time, guardian," he said, and halted several feet away. "I have come merely to offer my advice to your little slut."

Myla's response was a silent, steely-eyed expression of utter resolve. *Just don't get too close.*

"Shaaaaarrroonnn...go to Toni," said Witchcraft. "You can take the test at Toni's house. You need to make up with her anyway."

Myla offered no countering thoughts.

Sharon started the car and merged into traffic.

Witchcraft smiled in smug confidence at the angel. "You have nothing to say? No resistance whatsoever?" He laughed at the hapless angel. "Better that you don't. It would be a waste of time anyway."

He flew away confident of two things: Toni's confession to Sharon—he knew this was inevitable—would destroy any hope of a reconciliation between the two of them. And if the test proved positive, Sharon would finally be his.

Myla watched the wicked spirit leave in admiration. But his admiration was of Captain Rashti. How could he have anticipated the enemy's strategy so precisely? *I wonder what Captain Rashti has in mind.*

*****

This was the second Sunday in a row that Adam and Sherry Chriswell were instructed of God to stay home and pray. They were told to pray against the spirit of witchcraft, which they did. Fervently.

*****

Sharon pushed the doorbell.

It was early, but Toni was already somewhere between high and drunk. She thought that her senses were dulled, that nothing could shock her anymore. But last night's ceremony was especially sickening, even for someone like Toni who had reluctantly grown accustomed to the Family's horrible mini-atrocities. She had never thought they would make her go so far.

How could we do that to an innocent baby?

She tried to drown the voice of her conscience with another straight drink.

The doorbell rang again and Toni snapped out of her limbo. She opened the door. "Sharon?" she said, squinting her eyes. Toni wasn't sure that what she saw wasn't a product of alcohol.

"Can I come in?"

Toni clumsily stumbled out of the way. "Yeah, come in," she said, pulling her by the arm. "I...I'm glad to see you. "What—?" Toni smiled, "have a sit-down."

Sharon didn't sit. "Are we alone?"

Toni didn't see the trouble in Sharon's face. "Yes. Why?"

"I have to ask a favor."

Toni looked at Sharon from head to toe. *Nice dress*, she thought. Her white dress gave her the appearance of an angel. Yet Toni knew that it wasn't the color of the dress that made Sharon look like an angel. It was her sweetness. It was her innocence. It was her honesty. Most of all it was her love.

Toni's thoughts made her self-conscious. She and Sharon were so different. She a daughter of Satan; Sharon a daughter of Christ. She stood and adjusted her robe. "I know I must look terrible."

"Toni?"

"What? I'm sorry, Sharon. What did you say?"

"I need a favor. May I use your bathroom?"

"My bathroom?"

"Yes," Sharon lamented. "May I use your bathroom?"

Her distress was unmistakable this time. "Yeah, Sharon. You know where it is."

Toni put away the liquor and hurried to another bathroom to freshen up. When she returned to the room, Sharon was still in the bathroom. Toni waited ten more minutes then knocked on the door.

"Sharon, are you okay?" Toni heard what sounded like crying. She put her ear close to the door. "Sharon, what's wrong?"

Between sobs she heard, "Toonniii...Toonnii...oh, God..."

Toni was frightened. "Sharon? Sharon?" she knocked on the door. "I'm coming in." She opened the door. Sharon was bent over one of the marble sinks with her face in her hands. "Sharon!"

"Toni...Toni..." Sharon cried, "I'm pregnant."

Toni sobered immediately. She backed into the wall and pressed hard against it. Her eyes were wide with shock and guilt. This was her fault.

"I'm pregnant, Toni. My God, what am I going to do?"

Toni's eyes were tightly closed. Her throat felt dry and parched. She ran from the room and poured herself a drink. She gulped it down and poured another. She drank it and threw the glass against the wall. Toni dropped to the floor in a ball of self-recrimination.

Witchcraft looked at his dupe with satisfaction. She was so pathetic.

Sharon burst into the room. Her chest burned with anger. "Toni, why didn't you do something? Why did—?"

Toni looked up at Sharon, her sad eyes pleading for understanding and forgiveness she knew she didn't deserve.

Sharon stopped in midsentence. Toni's dejection disarmed her.

"I'm sorry, Sharon," Toni cried. "I didn't mean to hurt you. I only wanted to be friends with you. I...." Her voice trailed off.

"Friends with me? Toni...I...what do you mean you wanted to be friends with me? We were friends." This didn't make any sense.

Toni wiped her nose with her sleeve. She looked at Sharon and shook her head slowly. "I didn't want you to get hurt." She burst into tears again.

Sharon wanted to be hard. She wanted to hate the girl who—who did what? She was the one who went to bed with him. She couldn't place all the blame on her. Toni wasn't responsible; she was.

She got on her knees and hugged Toni. "It's okay, Toni." But Sharon knew that it was far from okay.

"No—no, Sharon, you don't understand. I have something to tell you. I, I set you up."

Sharon pulled away. Softly, unwilling to receive the full import of what she had just heard, she asked, "What do you mean?"

"The whole thing was my idea," Toni cried into her hands. "I planned it all."

Sharon was numbed by this revelation.

"I put something in your drink. Some of the stuff they give me at our ceremonies. I told Kevin that you wanted him."

Sharon's mind reeled out of control. Competing thoughts vied ferociously all at once for her attention. Her mental world imploded upon her and buried her reason under the rubble of sanity. How could...? No, Toni couldn't mean... Set her up? Why would her friend do such a horrible thing to her? Sharon shook her head in denial and sought desperately for an explanation that made sense.

"Toni," now Sharon was crying, "what have I ever done to you? What did I do to make you hate me? I've never hurt you."

"You loved me," Toni whimpered.

"I what?" Sharon couldn't have heard her correctly.

"You loved me, Sharon. You loved me."

Witchcraft's dark smile filled the room.

This admission ripped apart Sharon's concept of right and wrong. It wasn't logical to hate someone who loved you.

"Toni, why did you do this?" She strained to keep what little composure she had left.

"Sharon, you're the only one I've ever had."

"So why did you do this? It doesn't make sense."

"It makes a lot of sense to me." The more Toni spoke, the angrier Sharon became. This was absolutely crazy! "You see, I don't have anybody. I've never had anyone. You're the only friend I've ever had. I thought I was going to lose you."

"Lose me? What?" Sharon stood up and paced the floor. "I don't believe this! You destroyed my life because I loved you and you didn't want me to stop being your friend? Are you insane? You don't hurt people who love you!"

"Sharon, I know you don't understand why I did it, but you and I are so different. You have everything and I have nothing. You have parents that love you. You have a family. You have Christ. I knew that even though you were, well, sinning I guess, you would go back to church and all, and I would be left out in the cold."

"But...what—?"

"I thought that if you committed a really bad sin you would be like me, and you and I would be friends. I mean real friends."

Sharon was now more confused than furious. She had never known the bitter taste of such deep betrayal. (Although her father's recent cowardly conduct had come very close.) She wanted to hate Toni. How could she have done something so evil to a friend? Friends don't hurt one another. Without thinking about it, Sharon found herself involuntarily pitying her friend. She got on her knees and cradled Toni in her arms.

"I didn't want to hurt you, Sharon. Really I didn't."

"I know you didn't." Sharon still didn't understand all that Toni spoke. At least not with her mind. But in her heart she understood.

"You must hate me," Toni said, terribly afraid that she had not only lost her friend forever, but that her ex-friend would hate her until death.

Sharon said nothing to this. Instead she searched her heart. The past several weeks had been an emotional roller coaster ride. She had experienced the highs and the lows. Now, at this moment, she inexplicably experienced neither. Yet she wasn't in a void. Thoughts that seemed foreign and out of place rose from what seemed like her belly. Each thought seemed to pull Sharon from beneath the rubble of her calamity.

Sharon couldn't explain the sudden philosophical intuition. But she knew that she was entering a new realm of knowing and understanding God. She was now experiencing true Christianity. Servants of God wouldn't always have things their way. Sometimes there would be hardships, pains, and disappointments. Sometimes there would be betrayals.

Christianity was a strange mix of mountain tops and valleys. Yet even in the valleys, God could be known. His love was the one great constant of life.

"No, I don't hate you," answered Sharon. "I love you, Toni. We're friends." Sharon knew that this was not her speaking. It couldn't be. She wasn't strong enough to love Toni. She wasn't strong enough to not hate Toni. Even now as she felt God's love powerfully and independently flowing through her to her betrayer, she knew in the core of her being—and this was the first time that she had ever realized this—that she was capable of hatred. She was capable of seeking revenge. She was capable of hurting someone. This was a horrible revelation. She trembled at the possibilities of being such a weak person. *Help me, Holy Spirit. You have to help me. I can't do this on my own.*

"Ohhh," Toni exclaimed in relief. "I love you, Sharon."

They talked for a long time, sharing and growing closer than they had ever been before.

This ridiculous reconciliation caught Witchcraft completely off guard. He watched in horror as the whole thing unfolded before his disbelieving eyes. It was such an unthinkable act that he was so paralyzed by fascination of the enemy's strategy that he didn't (or perhaps, couldn't) do anything to stop it. He was mesmerized.

"How could this be?" he asked, not wanting to acknowledge the power of God's love.

Four angels joined Myla just moments before the other demon arrived. They surrounded Sharon.

Witchcraft backed up defensively. *Why are they here*?

"Don't flatter yourself," Witchcraft heard someone say. He turned to his right. Bashnar!

"What are you doing here?" Witchcraft's question was full of contempt.

Bashnar's hands were on his sides. His thick chest stuck out prominently. His bulging muscles weren't clearly defined, but rather appeared as thick trunks of power. Strength exuded from him. Bashnar's black mane had yet to fully recover his scorching. Yet enough of it had regrown to add to his regal appearance.

Bashnar heard the contempt in Witchcraft's voice. He saw it in his eyes. Ordinarily this would have pleased him immensely. A confident opponent, an adversary who looked into the eyes of danger and laughed, an enemy who held his combatant in total disdain.

But Bashnar was not pleased. He was incensed. Witchcraft had not earned the right to display such a haughty attitude. His was not the attitude of a true warrior, but the pompous behavior of a pampered fool.

We will see who deserves direct access to lord Satan, thought Bashnar.

"Unfinished business," Bashnar answered.

"The girl is mine!" Witchcraft spat.

"No, the girl is Christ's." Bashnar's voice was low and even. "Your stupidity has pushed Sharon into the arms of Jesus. Did you not consider her foundation? Your plan is for fools who come to Christ seeking something other than Him: healing, money, jobs, friends, marital bliss. She had no ulterior motives. Sharon came to Christ not to get, but to give." Bashnar's voice raised sharply. "Did you not consider that?"

Witchcraft was insulted that a warrior spirit would question his strategy. "That is none of your business! The Council—"

"Enough!" shouted Bashnar. "I am not here for Sharon." He smiled. "I am here for you."

*****

Adam and Sherry continued to pray against the spirit of witchcraft.

*****

Bashnar looked into Witchcraft's eyes. There was no fear. "You are not afraid. You should be."

"Afraid of what? An overgrown and overrated fighter whose reputation is nothing more than an autobiography of lies?"

"We will see." Bashnar stepped forward.

Myla and the other four angels pulled out their swords.

"The guardians are edgy," said Bashnar. "Would you care to join me outside?"

"With pleasure," Witchcraft answered, excited at the opportunity to close Bashnar's big mouth once and for all.

They went outside.

Witchcraft was first to pull out his sword. "My blade will separate fact from fiction."

Bashnar hated Witchcraft. He didn't want to stick a blade into his gut. No, that would be anti-climactic. He wanted to feel Witchcraft's agony. His rage would settle for nothing less than a hand-to-hand humiliation.

"You are not impressed by the Mighty Bashnar?"

Witchcraft spat at him. "I am impressed only by your great capacity for self-delusion."

Bashnar slowly pulled his sword. "You are afraid of the Mighty Bashnar."

"I'll show you who's afraid of the Mighty Bashnar." He hurried toward Bashnar.

Bashnar threw his sword several hundred feet to his left.

Witchcraft stopped as suddenly as a cartoon character hitting a brick wall. He took a small step backward. *What is he up to*?

"Show our audience you are not afraid of the Mighty Bashnar." Two of the angels sent to reinforce Myla were outside to keep a watchful eye on the demons. "Don't hide behind seven feet of steel."

Approximately twenty feet separated Bashnar from the two swords he had hidden earlier. A precaution just in case Witchcraft wasn't in the mood for hand-to-hand combat.

Witchcraft looked at the angels. His base nature told him to cut his unarmed opponent into a hundred pieces. But he would show all of them that he was not afraid to fight Bashnar in hand-to-hand combat. He threw his weapon away.

Bashnar beckoned him with his hands. *You fool,* he laughed inside.

They circled one another warily.

"I do this for a living," said Bashnar.

"Then you'll soon be unemployed," Witchcraft answered. He swung his long arm at Bashnar's head.

Bashnar didn't move. The intended blow was several inches short. *Tentative fighter,* he surmised. Bashnar jabbed.

Witchcraft's nose attested to Bashnar's speed and accuracy. His eyes watered from the punch. Another powerful jab found its mark.

Bashnar set himself to throw another jab, but Witchcraft caught him with one of his own. A jolt of pain stabbed his brain.

"Can you do that again?" asked Bashnar.

Witchcraft did it again.

Bashnar's head snapped back. The pain acted as a stimulant. Bashnar roared in morbid satisfaction. He swung at Witchcraft with an open palm. His sharp claws ripped flesh away from his face.

The sight of Witchcraft's blood made Bashnar rabid. Witchcraft was no longer an opponent; he was prey. Bashnar rushed in like a wild beast. His claws ripped at Witchcraft's face...his chest...his neck. Blood squirted out.

Witchcraft fought back with the ferocity of a tiger. He sank his teeth into Bashnar's side as they rolled on the ground. The searing pain paralyzed him for a moment. This was enough respite to let Witchcraft stick a thick finger into his eye.

Bashnar pushed him off and Witchcraft scrambled to his feet. Bashnar was on one knee. He tried to clear his burning eye. Witchcraft kicked him hard in the ribs. Bashnar rolled over on his side. He held the place where he had been kicked.

Witchcraft bent over and tried to suck in air to his burning lungs. He should not have done this. The warrior spirit bolted into Witchcraft with amazing speed. Bashnar wrapped his arms around his opponent's belly and back and flew into the side of a brick home, crushing Witchcraft's chest.

They both fell to the ground hard. The combatants struggled to get to their feet. Bashnar was first. His foot whipped across Witchcraft's face. There was an ugly sound. The dazed demon spun against his own bones and fell on his back. Something must have snapped because pain tore through his torso.

Bashnar sank his claws three inches into Witchcraft's chest and lifted him to his feet. Only his toes touched the ground. "You're much too timid a fighter," chided Bashnar. "If I can call you that."

The spent demon's eyes drooped in defeat.

"Who am I?" Bashnar demanded.

"Baash...narrr," Witchcraft gurgled weakly.

"Who am I?" screamed Bashnar, as he crushed Witchcraft's chest unmercifully.

Witchcraft was delirious with pain. "Mi...Mi...Mighty...Bash...nar."

Bashnar looked at the angels who witnessed the whole thing. "Mighty Bashnar!" he roared at them. "Mighty Bashnar!"

He looked at the whimpering witchcraft spirit. *You who mocked my accomplishments! How easily you recant under duress*! "Your weakness disgusts me, Witchcraft. You are a disgrace to the lord of darkness. If Satan knew of your weakness, he would have long ago banished you to the Dark Prison."

Bashnar roared thunderously in victory and tore his victim to shreds.

*****

Sharon went straight to her room to rehearse how she would tell her mother that she was—she paused. She couldn't say it...*pregnant*.

She finally got up enough courage to do it.

Sharon approached her mother and asked to speak to her alone. They left Jessica in the kitchen and went to Barbara's bedroom.

"Mother, I have to talk to you."

"What's wrong, baby? Is something the matter? You don't look well."

"It's about a friend," Sharon told her. "I have a friend who has made a terrible mistake."

"Drugs? Oh, God! They're everywhere. Even in the suburbs. Who is it, dear?"

"No, Mom, it's not drugs. She's"—she looked at her mother apprehensively—"she's pregnant."

Barbara clutched her chest dramatically. "Oh, my God! That's terrible!" She hurried to the door and closed it and sat her daughter on the bed. "I'm not going to force you to tell me who it is, this being such a sensitive matter. But I do want you to stop being friends with her."

"Mother!" Sharon exclaimed unbelievingly.

"I don't mean stop being her friend."

"What do you mean?"

"I mean you shouldn't hang around those kinds of girls."

"What kind of girls?"

"You know, darling. Promiscuous girls. God doesn't like that. Did you know that the Bible calls girls who have sex before marriage—"Barbara looked ashamed at the word she was going to use—"whores?"

"What?" Sharon almost shouted.

"Don't be offended, Sharon. I am not calling your friend a whore. Goodness, no. I'm simply saying that these kinds of girls have whorish tendencies."

"That's a terrible thing to say! You don't even know the circumstances and you're already judging her as a prostitute or something! I don't believe you!"

"Darling," Barbara reasoned with her sixteen-year-old daughter, "unless she was raped, she sinned. She played with fire and got burnt. I know it sounds harsh, but honey that's the way it is."

"For your information, she was raped!"

Barbara's expression conveyed condescending patience with her naive daughter.

"You don't believe me, do you?"

"Did she tell you that she was raped?"

"Yes."

"Where did it happen?"

"At a party."

"At a party? How is anyone raped at a party?"

"She was drugged. She couldn't say no."

"Did your friend drink any alcohol that night?"

"Yes."

"Was she drunk?"

"Yes. I mean no. I told you she was drugged."

"Honey, alcohol is a drug. I don't mean to sound heartless, but this girl, whoever she is, even if she was raped, which I seriously doubt, put herself in that situation. She asked for it. You can't go to a wild party and get drunk and not expect something like this to happen. I bet it's not the first time this girl has had sex."

Sharon headed for the door. "I don't believe this."

"Honey, chastity is a virtue."

Sharon turned. "You're an expert on chastity, aren't you, Mother?"

"What do you mean by that? Sharon—?"

Sharon went to her room and slammed the door. She had tested the water. It was poison.

She wrestled with herself until she was tied up in philosophical and moral knots. She seemed to be now bound to a decision...a destiny. She knew that her decision would affect her destiny. No, *affect* was too mild a word. It would control her destiny. The consequences were fearful. But still, the consequences were in the future. Her situation was in her face right now.

Sharon made up her mind. She had no choice. She knew what she had to do. And nearly imperceptibly in the back of her mind: *Maybe God will forgive me. Maybe His grace will help me back.*

Chapter 23

Jonathan stopped the car. "We're here," he told Edwin.

"What are you smiling at?"

"Nothing."

"Why do I feel like I'm a turkey and this is Thanksgiving Day?" Edwin asked.

"Oh, I don't know. It could be a bad case of mental disorientation malady that causes a deterioration of your space/time/animal/human deducement faculties."

"You ever thought about getting a job as a comedian?" said Edwin.

"Why would I want to do that when I can cast out devils with you?"

They got out of the car.

Edwin looked at the beautiful homes that lined the streets of this plush Duluth neighborhood. Why, the lowest priced home had to be at least half a million dollars.

"Jonathan, are you sure you have the right address?" he asked. He had mentally prepared himself to go to a replica of a haunted house.

The residence he and Jonathan approached was a very large, ultra-modern home that sat on a hill. Winding stone steps led to the front door. There was a huge oval shaped window in the dining room.

Barbara would love that window, thought Edwin.

"I know what you're thinking, Edwin." They walked slowly up the steps. "You're thinking, how could anyone with so much money be possessed with a demon? Am I right?"

"Yeah. I was expecting, well, you know."

"You were expecting to go to a dump and be met at the door by a raving maniac. Only one thing wrong with that picture. Demons don't care how much money you have. They're firm believers in equal opportunity." Jonathan pushed the doorbell. "This lady has been demonized for quite a while, a few years her husband tells me."

Demonized, Edwin pondered. *A lady with a demon. What in the world have I let this man talk me into? What if this lady does have a demon? That's ludicrous...I hope.* "What's wrong with her?" asked Edwin.

The door opened.

A large, but not obese, man greeted them.

"Mr. Banks, come right in."

"Good morning, Mr. Huntley. This is Edwin Styles. He's a pastor. He's going to help me deliver your wife."

"Good, good." He smiled at Edwin and pulled Jonathan to the side and whispered, "I don't mean to tell you how to run your business, Preacher, but I think you're going to need more than one man."

"Oh," said Jonathan, "and why is that?"

"Some people from our church came by to pray for her and she threw them all over the room. They couldn't hold her down."

Edwin overheard that. He inched closer to the whispers.

"How many were there?" asked Jonathan.

"Three people. Mrs. Crevitt—she's a sweet old lady. And Janet Kessling and Murphy Dillon. Good people."

"Have they ever cast out a devil before?"

Mr. Huntley was desperate to get his wife some help, but he still didn't believe in all this demon possession stuff. "Mr. Banks, no one in our church has ever partaken in such rituals."

"That explains it," said Jonathan.

"Explains what?" Edwin asked.

"Pardon me, Reverend Styles," Mr. Huntley apologized. "I didn't mean to whisper."

"It's okay," Edwin answered. "Explains what, Jonathan?"

"Others have prayed for Mr. Huntley's wife unsuccessfully. His church is like yours. They don't believe in casting out devils. Demons don't obey people who don't believe they exist."

"Reverend Banks, I don't know about all of this demon business, and quite frankly I don't care to. But if there is anything you can do to help my wife, do it. Sprinkle all the holy water you want. Just help my wife."

"Mr. Huntley, did you see *The Exorcist*?" Jonathan asked.

"Yeah, a long time ago."

"Forget it."

Mr. Huntley led them to the living room.

The demon who called himself Throne ordered the others to keep silent. "Maybe we can make them think we're not here."

"But Jonathan! What about Jonathan?" said one of the demons.

"I'll take care of Jonathan," boasted Throne.

"Mr. Huntley, I'll need to get some information from you," said Jonathan. His experience taught him that the more he knew about the demonized, the easier it was to set them free.

"Anything," Mr. Huntley offered.

"What exactly is wrong with your wife? Jerry only told me that your wife was being harassed. He feels that she may have been involved in witchcraft." Jerry was the mutual friend who had given Mr. Huntley Jonathan's telephone number

"Witchcraft? That's preposterous!"

Demons. Witchcraft. Where will this end? thought Edwin.

"Yes, Mr. Huntley. Witchcraft."

"Where did Jerry get the idea that Gretchan was involved in witchcraft? This is an incredible accusation." He mumbled something under his breath. "I don't believe Jerry would say something like this."

"We did not come to accuse. We came to help," answered Jonathan. "Listen, Mr. Huntley, I'm going to mention some things and you tell me if you recognize them."

Huntley looked puzzled.

"Tarot cards, palm reading, crystal ball—"

Beads of embarrassment rolled down Edwin's forehead. He found Jonathan's line of questioning extremely discomforting. Why did he ask these questions of such a man? Mr. Huntley was obviously a successful businessman, not a kook.

"Of course, I've heard of crystal balls and palm reading. Who hasn't?"

"Mr. Huntley, what I want to know is have you or your wife been involved, even once, no matter how long ago, in any of the things I mention?" Jonathan continued. "Horoscope?"

This one hit home.

Mr. Huntley tried to play it off.

"Your wife reads the horoscope?"

"Yes, but who doesn't? I mean, I don't, but a lot of people read horoscopes. There's nothing to that stuff." He laughed. "You can get ten different newspapers and each one will give you a different prediction."

Jonathan wrote down horoscope on a notebook.

"Ouija board, séance, New Age—"

"New Age," said Mr. Huntley. "She's mentioned that term before. Several times, in fact. She has several books. Wait here, I'll be right back, he offered with sudden eagerness."

Mr. Huntley returned with an arm load of books.

Jonathan looked them over.

"Edwin, come here." He came. Jonathan pointed to the pile of books. "This is most likely the door that Satan walked through." Jonathan looked at Mr. Huntley. "Your wife is involved in witchcraft."

He opened his mouth to protest. Jonathan cut him off.

"Most people, like yourself, think of witchcraft as a spooky religion of potions and curses, frog legs and puppy dog tails. Witchcraft, basically, is the pursuit of supernatural knowledge or power without the aid of God. Horoscopes are of the devil. If you want to know what the future holds for you, ask God. And the same goes for all this New Age jazz. The only thing new about the

New Age delusion is the package. Satan has put a new face on an old lie. Mr. Huntley, take us to your wife."

"Here they come," Throne told the other two demons.

As they walked toward the room, Edwin whispered, "What's wrong with his wife?"

"You'll see," Jonathan answered.

This terse statement only heightened Edwin's fear. The closer they got to the door, the weaker his legs became. When they walked into the room, his knees almost buckled.

There was nothing about this man's wife that appeared extraordinary. In fact, she was quite ordinary, except she was distinctly pretty. She had large, round eyes and blond hair. She appeared to be European, maybe Scandinavian. But there was something about that room that wasn't right.

"Just pray for her and let's get out of here, Jonathan," Edwin advised.

"Honey, this is Reverend Banks and Reverend Styles," said Mr. Huntley. "Jerry, tells me these men know how to help you."

"Good morning, Mrs. Huntley," said Jonathan.

"Good morning," she answered.

Jonathan nudged Edwin.

"Good morning," said Edwin.

"Good morning."

"Mr. Huntley, could we bring some chairs in here?" asked Jonathan.

"Sure. They're right down stairs."

He and Jonathan headed for the door.

Edwin intercepted them. He smiled at Jonathan. "I'll help Mr. Huntley get the chairs."

Jonathan was tickled. "That's very thoughtful of you."

"Don't mention it."

"Reverend Banks, is it?" the woman asked.

"You can call me Jonathan."

The woman smiled. "My name is Gretchan. Jonathan, what is your formal training? Are you a student of psychology?"

Jonathan detected nothing critical in her inquiry. There was a sweet innocence about her, like that of a child's. "Gretchan, have you spoken to anyone else about your problem? Any doctors, psychologists, psychiatrists, or any other professionals?"

"Yes, many professionals."

A smile came to Jonathan's face. "Where are you from?"

"Copenhagen."

"Denmark?"

"No, Italy," she chuckled. "Of course, Denmark. Have you ever been there?"

Jonathan felt a flash of God's love for Gretchan. He saw in her an innocence being ravaged by Satan. There wasn't a whole lot of difference in the devil and child molesters. They both victimized the helpless and unwary. Jonathan's resolve turned to steel. He knew he would set this lady free. He had to.

"Close," he answered. "I've been to Malmo."

The lady's eyes lit up. "Southern Sweden! That's just east of my home."

"Beautiful country," said Jonathan.

"Yes...yes, it is," Gretchan reminisced.

"What is he doing?" one of the spirits asked Throne.

"I don't know," he snapped. "Just keep quiet and don't do anything stupid to let him know we are here."

Edwin and Mr. Huntley returned with the chairs. Jonathan set three of them side by side and the other faced the three.

"Gretchan, would you sit here, please?"

"Why, certainly, Jonathan."

The sudden familiarity surprised Edwin.

"Mr. Huntley, you sit here on the end. I usually don't allow family members to witness this. Their emotions get in the way. But you need to see this. You have allowed your wife to get involved with something that has destroyed millions of people. After today I don't believe you will allow this to happen again."

The man wasn't offended.

"Edwin, you sit on this end." Jonathan handed him a stack of cards and a Bible. "I've written some scriptures on these index cards. I want you to read them out loud until I tell you to stop."

Jonathan saw the question in Edwin's eyes.

"Because Satan hates the word of God. It weakens him. He has no defense for it." He looked at Mr. Huntley. "Mr. Huntley will be deathly quiet while we help his wife."

The man nodded his agreement.

Jonathan sat in the middle.

"Uh-oh," said one of the demons.

"Shut up," ordered Throne.

"Gretchan, you asked about my formal training. I am a disciple of Jesus Christ, a man of God. I believe the Bible is the Word of God. I believe God loves people and Satan hates people. I believe God is infinitely greater than Satan and that He has given the church power and authority to set humanity free from the devil. I am here as a representative of God. Is that sufficient?"

Gretchan didn't hesitate to answer. "Yes, Jonathan, that is sufficient."

"Do you read the horoscope?"

"Yes."

"Are you involved in New Age philosophy?"

Throne began to sweat.

She didn't answer.

"In Jesus' name, I order you to answer me. Are you involved in New Age philosophy?"

"Yes!" she answered as though she had been holding her breath for a long time. "Jonathan, I tried to answer you, but I couldn't."

"Edwin, start reading those scriptures. Start with Mark 16:17." Jonathan scooted his chair closer to Gretchan. "Horoscopes are satanic. New Age is satanic. What do you think about that?"

Throne tried to keep his composure, but he was as afraid as the other two demons. Hopefully, Jonathan wouldn't press too hard.

"I don't know, Jona—"

"I'm talking to you, Satan!" Jonathan yelled.

Gretchan's body jerked twice and involuntarily stiffened in her seat.

Edwin stopped reading the scriptures.

"I didn't tell you to stop reading."

"Oh...oh." He shuffled his cards. "I saw Satan fall—"

The three demons huddled together.

One of them said, "I wish that he would stop reading the Bible. I hate the Bible! It hurts so badly. Make him stop, Throne."

"Mr. Huntley, touch your wife," said Jonathan. He had to take the man's hand and put it on his wife's shoulder. "What's your height and weight?"

"Six-four, two-thirty."

"What is your wife's height and weight?"

"Five-six, one-twenty."

"Try to push your wife off of her chair."

The man nudged his wife gently.

"Push her or get out of the room."

The man pushed harder...harder...harder. Tears rolled down his cheeks as he pushed with all his might.

I don't believe this, thought Edwin. *That lady won't budge. How...what...?*

"Your wife is afflicted by a devil, Mr. Huntley. You could get forty men in here and all of you together couldn't move her. Do you understand?"

"Yes...yes...dear God, yes," he cried.

"In Jesus's name, let go of this lady," ordered Jonathan.

The lady's eyelids blinked fast. Too fast to be anything but supernatural.

Jonathan placed his hand gently on the lady and pushed her to one side and the other. "Edwin, do you see this?"

"Yes," he answered anxiously. "A thousand shall fall at our side and ten—" he continued to read.

"He knows we're here," said a demon.

"He does know we're here," echoed another panicky demon.

Out of frustration and mostly fear, Throne grabbed one of the demons and started slapping him. "Shut up! Shut up! I know he knows! Just shut up so I can think!"

But it was becoming harder to think, to focus. Edwin was weakening Throne with the Scriptures. Throne shook his head to clear the confusion. This didn't help.

Jonathan looked into Gretchan's eyes. Sometimes he could detect demon spirits in the eyes of the victim. He saw them.

"Let's just leave," one of them said.

Throne would have to do something fast before the others abandoned him. There was strength in numbers.

"Stop reading those Scriptures!" Throne yelled. The voice that came out of Gretchan was a deep, masculine voice. "That doesn't hurt us. Who do you think you are anyway? You don't even believe those scriptures! You're a hypocrite!"

This startled Edwin so badly that he dropped the Bible and index cards.

"Shut up!" ordered Jonathan.

"I know who you aaaarrrrr...." The demon spoke in a high pitched taunt.

"I can't take any more of this," said Mr. Huntley. "Call me when you're finished," he said, and headed for the door.

Throne laughed out loud.

"Edwin, read those scriptures loud and fast. Read them with authority."

"Authority?" Throne asked disbelievingly. "He doesn't have any authority."

"You said you know who I am. In the name of the Lord Jesus Christ who defeated you on the cross of Calvary, tell me, who am I?" demanded Jonathan.

Gretchan's face smirked. "You're a jackass! A nappy head jackass! That's what you are! Heeahh-ha-ha..." he laughed.

"How many of you are in there?"

Immediately the laughter stopped.

A worried look came on Gretchan's face.

"Okay, okay, I'll tell you who you are. You're Jonathan Banks. A man of God. You're a great enemy of our kind. The darkness hates you."

Jonathan turned to Edwin. "I asked that question for your benefit."

The lady grabbed her crotch. "Do you want this?"

"Stop it!" said Edwin.

Gretchan's hand shot from between her legs as though it had touched fire.

Jonathan cocked his head to the side. "Edwin? Did Edwin Styles just command a devil?"

"I...uhh..." he began to read the Scriptures again.

"How many are you?"

Gretchan placed both of her hands over her mouth.

"How many?"

She put up three fingers.

"Who is the strong demon? In Jesus's name, tell me."

Her hands came down.

"The only thing we can do now is to try and wear them out," said Throne. "Maybe we can shake their faith." He instructed the others to take over while he stayed in the background.

"His name is Throne," a demon found himself involuntarily confessing.

Jonathan had been through this hundreds of times. This strategy was nothing new. "Edwin, it's your show," he said.

"What do you mean, it's my show?"

"There are three devils in there, maybe more. The one named Throne is the strong one. You'll have to cast out the others before we can get to Throne."

"I don't know—"

"There's nothing magic about it. Just tell them to come out."

Edwin timidly put down the Bible and his cards. He cleared his throat.

A deep masculine laugh emitted from Gretchan's throat.

"What are you laughing at?" Edwin asked shakily.

"You!" the answer shot back.

"Come out," Edwin asked politely.

"What are you? A male debutante?" asked Jonathan. "You're not talking to Gretchan. You're talking to the spirit inside of Gretchan."

"Come out of her," he said more forcefully.

"No, thank you. I'm not coming out."

"Ask its name," said Jonathan.

"What's your—?"

"You're very polite," Jonathan interrupted.

"In Jesus's name, who are you?" Edwin ordered, this time not at all politely.

"I am Deception."

"Deception, come out!"

The lady screamed and dropped her head.

"That's one," said Jonathan. He felt like he had just taught his son how to ride a bicycle.

Edwin was awestruck. He smiled at Jonathan and put his hands on her shoulders and went through the same routine. This spirit put up more of a fight. After twenty minutes Edwin began to doubt that the demon was going anywhere. He gave a worried look to Jonathan.

"You're doing just fine. Now I'm going to do something to help you."

Thank God, thought Edwin.

"I'm going to praise and worship God," said Jonathan. "I'm going to tell Him how much I love Him. God inhabits the praises of His people. As I sing and pray my love to the Father, continue to tell that thing to come out."

"Make him shut up," the spirit said. "I hate for Christians to worship God. It releases so much power. It hurts us."

Gretchan rubbed Edwin's hand. "If you like me, make him be quiet."

"Come out!" said Edwin.

"Leave me alone!" shouted the demon. "Leave me alone! You're afraid of me! Aaagghhh!" He looked at Jonathan. "Shut up! Shut up! Shut up!" Gretchan's hands went to her ears. "I don't want to hear any more praises! Oh! Oh! The glory of God is filling this place. I have to—aaaaaggghhhh!"

"Okay, Tiger," said Jonathan, "you can take a break. I'll get Throne."

Edwin's heart pounded excitedly against his chest, but this time not from fear.

He waved Jonathan off. "Just keep praising God. I'll take care of Throne."

Chapter 24

Edwin didn't get home until six-thirty that evening. When he opened his front door, even the sight of Jessica didn't dampen his mood. He felt like he had just come from Disney World. Or better yet, Hollywood—where anything is possible.

"Hi, Ed."

"Hello, Jessica. Where is Barbara?"

"She hasn't returned from church yet. Why are you so happy?"

He started to tell her, then thought better of it. "I've just had a wonderful day, that's all. Did you say, Barbara hasn't come home yet?"

"Yeah. She told us to go on and she would get a ride home from one of the ladies at church. She was talking to a lady named Amy when I left her."

Amy, he thought. *That lady can talk. That conversation could last a year or two.*

Edwin headed for the den. He wanted to sit and bask in the glory of the new spiritual world he had discovered. He walked past Jessica and noticed a huge grin on her face. "What's—?"

"Oh, nothing," she answered. "Just wondering what it's going to take to wake you up to the power of God."

Edwin tried to ignore her. "Good night, Jessica."

"This morning you were sick as a dog. I prayed and—"Jessica danced a jig—"look at you now! Healed by the power of God!"

"Actually, Jessica, I doubt that your prayer had anything to do with it."

"Nothing to do with it?" She was insulted. "It had everything to do with it. Edwin, you can have what you say."

Edwin sighed. He knew what theological mumbo-jumbo would follow. Everything in the world was up for grabs to the Christian who believed and confessed the Bible. Lay hands on it, it's yours! Speak it, it's yours!

"Jessica, do you really believe that? That I can have what I say?"

"Of course I do. It's the Word!"

"Then, Jessica, I say leave me alone. In Jesus's name close, your mouth and leave me alone." Edwin went to his den and closed the door. He took off his tie and sat down. *How long is she going to stay here?* he thought.

Someone knocked on his door.

"Come in."

It was Jessica. Edwin did not even try to disguise his displeasure. "What do you want, Jessica?"

She had an arm full of books and CDs. "Here," she said gruffly, "you need to take a look at these. Maybe you'll learn something."

She left before Edwin could say anything.

Edwin laughed. "So this is what guerilla warfare is like. Hit and run before the enemy can react."

He cynically thumbed through some of the books. They were so formulistic. It was like reading a book of magic. One author wrote: "The whole world is yours. Do you see something you want? Claim it by faith! Are you sick? Don't pray about it; speak the Word! God has given you His power! Use it!"

Another writer wrote: "You control the world around you with words. This is going to sound sacrilegious to some of you. But the angels and God Himself must obey your word when it lines up with the Bible."

Edwin read through a number of the books and listened to one of the CDs. He felt defiled, dirty. Like he was eating garbage. Something inside of him told him to give Jessica back her stuff, but Edwin didn't do it. Wasn't that the same close-minded attitude that had kept him from the reality of God's power so long? No, he would force himself to listen to this material. Even though in his spirit he sensed something sinister about it.

*****

The observing spirit handed his report to Bashnar.

"I—"he cleared his throat—"I...the man Edwin has been given our material."

"Good," said Bashnar. "He will become so confused, he will not know what to believe."

*****

Edwin was in bed, but the excitement of the day would not let him go to sleep. Vivid pictures of the earlier drama rolled across the screen of his mind like an endless movie.

The lady's body jerked.

Mr. Huntley pushed his wife until he grunted from the strain. She didn't budge one inch.

"Your wife is afflicted of a devil, Mr. Huntley," Jonathan offered.

"In Jesus' name, let go of this lady," Jonathan ordered the spirit.

Her eyelids batted extremely fast.

The lady grabbed her crotch. "Do you want this?"

"Stop it!" Edwin yelled.

Edwin saw a scene he still could not believe.

"In Jesus' name, who are you?" Edwin asked.

"I am Deception."

"Deception, come out!"

Barbara entered the room. Edwin reluctantly left his mental movie theater.

He got out of bed and walked toward her. "How was church?"

"Fine," she answered, and walked past him, politely spurning his touch. "I have to take a shower."

Edwin sighed and returned to bed.

"I returned those things to Larry," she said from the bathroom.

"Good," a deflated Edwin answered.

When Barbara finished showering, Edwin thought it odd that she wore a nightgown that she hadn't worn in several years. He knew that she didn't like it. It was a gift from her mother. It had a high, fluffy collar and the hem of it touched her ankles. Barbara had joked that it made her look like a sunflower.

She got in bed and turned her back to Edwin. "Good night."

Edwin propped up on one elbow. "Today, after you left, Jonathan and I went to a lady's house to pray for her."

"I thought you were sick."

"I was, but as soon as he came over, I got better."

"That's good, dear," she answered nonchalantly.

"She—"he didn't know how to put this—"was very sick. She had a devil."

"She had the what?"

"She...had a devil," he said.

Barbara wanted to turn over, but dared not. "Did you say she had a devil?"

Edwin cleared his throat. "Yes."

"You mean like at the movies?"

"Yes. Like at the movies."

"And what did you do?"

"I made it leave."

Silence.

"How did you make it leave?"

"I ordered him to leave and he left."

"Just like that?"

"Well, no. He put up a fight. There were three of them. It took a while to weaken them, but they finally left."

Silence.

"Jessica said that you went to Amy's."

"I introduced Jessica to Amy, but I didn't go to her house."

Edwin didn't want to pry, but something wasn't right. "Where did you go?" he asked innocently.

"I told you. I returned those video tapes and books to Larry."

"Yes, honey, but that still doesn't tell me where you were." Edwin was extra careful to sound benign.

"What's the third degree for, Edwin?" Barbara asked defensively. "I had to talk to someone. So when I gave Larry his stuff, I asked him if he had time to speak with me. He was reluctant at first. He said it wouldn't look right. I suggested Piccadilly's. He thought it would be better if we went to his apartment."

Edwin didn't know what to say. He felt better that she was with Larry, but he still didn't like the idea of her going to his apartment. "What was so pressing that you had to go to his apartment?" he asked, knowing fully well what it was.

"Our sexual problems, what else? We have to talk to somebody!" she snapped.

Edwin's anger level rose to match his wife's. "Did it do any good?"

"Yes!" she answered. "It did a lot of good!" She started crying and ran to the bathroom and locked the door.

Edwin waited impatiently until she returned to bed. "I didn't mean anything by it," he apologized. "I trust you, and I trust Larry. I know that neither of you are even capable of—" The thought was so appalling that he didn't finish the sentence. "It's just that it embarrasses me that you feel you have to talk to another man about something so personal."

He touched her arm and she recoiled.

Edwin's lips tightened. He rolled over and made his eyes close.

The door opened. "Mommy," said Christopher.

Edwin and Barbara both popped up.

"Come here, honey," said Barbara.

He walked around the bed to her side. "I don't feel good, Mommy."

She felt his forehead, then his neck. "He's burning up." She put him on the bed and went to the bathroom and came back with a thermometer. She took his temperature twice. "Ed, his temperature is 102.6. We have to get him to a hospital," she said with alarm. frantic.

She rushed to her closet and got dressed. Edwin did the same.

"Take him downstairs," Barbara told Edwin. "I'm going to tell Jessica where we're going."

Edwin carried Christopher downstairs and opened the front door. A blast of cold air greeted them. Chilled drops of water fell from the black sky. Edwin pulled his son closer to keep him warm. A chill shot through Edwin's body, but not from the weather. The car was gone! He took Christopher inside and went straight to the telephone.

"Who are you calling?" Barbara asked.

"Our car," Edwin said angrily. "Someone has stolen our car."

"What?" Barbara was shocked. She hurried toward where the car should have been, then caught herself. "Sharon has the car."

"What? I thought Sharon was in her room."

"No. I let her take the car today. We can talk about that later. How is he doing?"

Jessica came into the living room.

"Jessica, we need to use your car," said Barbara.

Jessica left and returned with the keys.

"Here." She handed them to Barbara. "Have either of you taken authority over the sickness? If your faith is strong, you don't have to take him to a doctor."

"What? Authority over the sickness?" asked Barbara incredulously.

Edwin didn't let his sister-in-law answer. "If you want to conduct religious experiments on little children, have your own."

That statement was like a dog's bite on Jessica's butt. The surprise and pain showed on her face. Edwin knew that Jessica could not have children. But he had answered more out of anger than cruelty. He knew that he needed to apologize, but his anger wouldn't allow him to just yet.

Barbara was momentarily stunned by Edwin's remark. What had gotten into him? First, he had threatened to forcibly make her get out of the car at Elizabeth's. And now he had just said the cruelest thing possible to her sister. She searched his face for a sign of shame or at least embarrassment. There was only hardness. She snatched her attention from Edwin and looked at Christopher. He needed her.

"Let's go," she ordered.

*****

"He looks like a zombie," Marjorie lamented. "What's wrong with him?"

Wallace was as confused as his wife. He didn't have any answers. He felt totally helpless. One minute he and Johnny had been playing a video game and the next minute Johnny was on the floor, apparently in a coma.

If either of Johnny's parents could have seen the demons that were in the room, they would have known why Johnny was in a catatonic state.

A spirit of dumbness gripped the boy's throat. Another spirit, a demon of sickness, wrapped his long arms and legs around the boy's torso and rode him.

"I have to get him to the emergency room," said Marjorie.

*****

Anthony Righetti had become a celebrity since the banquet. He did not know that that evening there was a reporter from the Atlanta Journal in the audience—Bashnar knew. The favorable piece he had written about Anthony, *The Wave Of The Future?* had put into motion a publicity domino effect that eventually resulted in an appearance on *Jasmine*, a national talk show, and an invitation to appear on Oprah.

His appearance on *Jasmine* had been a public relations coup for the Family. The audience and panel could not have been chosen better had he done it himself. Many Wiccans, New Agers, and other softies were in the audience. Their spiritual support was tremendous.

The panel consisted of a Wiccan, a spirit channeler, an official from the Church of Satan, a liberal protestant preacher, an evangelical preacher, and Righetti.

Righetti presented his message as skillfully and subliminally as any master orator. In his hands darkness became light, wrong became right, and the definable boundaries of traditional morality were washed away by the irresistible currents of hedonism. He even led the audience in a chant: "Absolutes are dead. The only thing absolute is my absolute right to be absolutely free from absolutes."

The evangelical preacher had a fit, but he was the poorest excuse for a spokesman that Anthony Righetti had ever seen. He was about as articulate as a rock. More than once the audience booed his pathetic ramblings.

Anthony left that show confident that the only people he did not win were those who were hopelessly tangled up in Christianity's sticky web of deceit.

Ironically, Anthony anticipated today's interview more than his *Jasmine* debut. That was a nationwide event that would give him national name recognition. This was a regional appearance that would be seen only in metropolitan Atlanta. Yet, though this was less exposure, it was more focused. He would be able to appeal directly to the city he was claiming for the Family.

His banquet had won hundreds. A network special in his own city could win thousands.

Anthony smiled at his opponent.

The man returned his smile.

The moderator walked quickly into the room. A sound man was with her. He clipped microphones on their lapels.

"Say something," the sound man told them.

The Christian smiled at his opponent and said, "Jesus is Lord." He repeated that a few times for the technician.

"Okay, now you," he told Anthony.

He smiled at his opponent. "Jesus is dead."

The technician was shocked.

The moderator was delighted. This meant high ratings for the show and a thattagirl for her.

Reluctantly, the technician said, "You'll have to say that again a few times."

Still smiling at the other guest, he said, "My pleasure. Jesus is dead. Jesus is dead. Jesus is dead. Jesus—"

"Okay," the technician said.

"Are you sure?" Anthony asked.

"Yeah, I'm sure," he said with a frown.

The moderator was an attractive black female with aspirations of becoming the next Oprah Winfrey. She sat at a table opposite where her guests sat.

"Gentlemen, I believe both of you have received instructions on the format of today's show. I'll introduce you to our television audience. Each of you will have thirty seconds to say anything you'd like. Mr. Larkin, you're first. Afterwards, I'll ask each of you a series of questions. I'll ask that you refrain from interrupting each other. There will be a five-minute period when you will be permitted to speak directly to one another."

"Sixty seconds to air time," someone shouted.

"Five...four...three...two...one..."

The moderator flashed a smile. "Hello, I'm Daphne Krugle. Tonight I have a special show for you. On March 19th hundreds of people attended a banquet in the Centennial ballroom at the Hyatt Regency in downtown Atlanta. There was nothing ordinary about this event. For in the audience were—"she glanced at her notes—"pagans, Satanists, psychics, witches, spiritualists, voodooists, and other distinctly non-traditional religious practitioners. Tonight our guests will discuss the importance of this startling banquet."

The camera focused on Anthony Righetti.

"Mr. Anthony Righetti is the founder of a group called the Family. His group sponsored the banquet. Mr. Righetti believes Satanism and other non-traditional religions are the wave of the future. He says without apology that Christianity is dead."

The camera focused on the other man.

"Mr. Rob Larkin is a Christian radio broadcaster. He can be heard on over two hundred radio stations, both in the U.S. and Canada. He has written several bestsellers and is considered to be an expert on the subject of Satanism. According to Mr. Larkin, there is no difference in the families of Mr. Righetti and the convicted murderer, Charles Manson."

Daphne smiled at Mr. Larkin. "We'll begin our show by giving you thirty seconds to say anything you'd like."

Mr. Larkin prayed silently for help. "I am here because Jesus Christ is alive, because He is God, because His second coming to Earth is as sure as His first coming, and because it is He who will judge the world of its wickedness. Mr. Righetti is not unlike the Hitlers of our world. His message can only prosper in an atmosphere of rebellion and hate. His message appeals to the base nature of a fallen creation."

"Mr. Righetti..." prompted Daphne.

Anthony looked directly into the camera with a polished smile. "Good evening, ladies and gentlemen. March the 19th signals the death of one era and the birth of another. Christianity is the religion of the past; Satanism and its sister religions are the wave of the future. Christianity offers nothing but strict pleasure prohibiting rules and regulations. Satanism offers you the freedom to enjoy life. The Family is a community of people who have decided to not let Christian bigots dictate their lifestyles." He smiled again into the camera. "Thank you."

Daphne Krugle's insides turned somersaults. She knew she had a winner. Her calm, reassuring professional demeanor hid her excitement.

"Mr. Larkin, was the success of Mr. Righetti's banquet the herald of Satanism's inevitable rise and Christianity's inevitable fall?"

A luminous angelic creature adorned with a kaleidoscopic array of brilliant colors touched the Christian's forehead. "Speak, man of God. Speak forth the words of eternal life," the angel said.

He did.

"Mr. Righetti is parroting the predictions of others who were a lot smarter than him and who had a whole lot more resources to make their predictions come true. Nevertheless, they all failed, and so shall the Family.

"What the banquet does reflect is the fact that evil is growing bolder. This is no surprise. The Bible clearly states in 2nd Timothy 3:13: 'But evil men and seducers shall wax worse and worse, deceiving and being deceived.'"

The moderator was delighted at the friction. "Are you calling the Family evil?" she asked in an attempt to add fuel to the fire.

"Is Nazism evil? Is genocide evil? Of course, the Family is evil."

"Why do you say that? Is it strictly because the Bible says so? What about those of us who are not Christians?"

"Are you not a Christian?" Mr. Larkin asked.

This pointed question about her own religious convictions made Daphne Krugle extremely uncomfortable. She hoped her discomfort wasn't visible.

"What I meant was many of our viewers are not Christians. Those who do not subscribe to biblical absolutes probably see Mr. Righetti and the Family in a different light."

"If anyone sees him in a different light it is only because they are walking in the light of their own darkness. To answer your question, no I do not condemn this man strictly because the Bible condemns him. I condemn him for the same reason that I condemn Nazism and genocide. He is seeking to institutionalize and legitimize behavior that is clearly anti-law, anti-society, and anti-love."

Daphne Krugle interviewed Mr. Larkin for the next several minutes. Now it was Mr. Righetti's turn.

The show was going better than Daphne could have imagined. She put her cards aside and decided to shoot from the hip. "I'm sure you have a rebuttal for Mr. Larkin."

Anthony smiled. "I sure do, Daphne." He looked directly into the camera with the poise of a career politician. "Mr. Larkin has tried to depict the Family as a proponent of aberrant behavior. He has quoted me out of context to give the impression that our belief system is a threat to society. Nothing could be farther from the truth.

"The Family stands for freedom. Freedom to worship whomever or whatever you desire. The Family stands for the rights of the non-traditional. We believe that every person has the right to be non-Christian, without repercussions.

"Christianity boasts of its integrity. It claims to be a bastion of morality, a refuge for the poor, a spokesman for God. Is that why their champions are hauled off to prison for fraud? Is that why their preachers put more money into the purses of prostitutes than into the pockets of the poor and needy?

"I will say it again, Christianity is dead. Its cloud of deception is dissipating into nothingness. We've seen freedom march across the world: Poland, East Germany, Romania, Egypt. Now freedom is marching in America. All over this great country of ours people are rising up and saying, I am free!"

Anthony stretched forth an open hand to the television audience.

"Do you want to be free? Be free. Do you want to enjoy your body? Enjoy it. Do you want to delight yourselves in passion? It's yours—"he closed his fist—"take it."

After Daphne completed her interview of Anthony and allowing the two men to speak directly to one another-*electrifying!*—she reluctantly brought the show to a close. This had been the best show of her career. One thing was certain in her mind: There would definitely be a sequel. Watch out, Oprah!

Jonathan turned off his television.

Chapter 25

Barbara shook her head. "No...no," she said in a disbelieving whisper, trying to deny the doctor's words away. She clenched her fists and screamed in agony. "Nooooo!" She dropped to the hospital floor in shock. Her body convulsed in anguish. "My God," she wailed, "no...no...please...no."

The doctor's words exploded violently in Edwin's ears. "I'm sorry, Mr. Styles. Your son is dead."

Edwin staggered away a few feet to a long window that showed him the darkness of the night. He looked into the blackness of an overcast sky. The twinkles of the stars were hidden behind a concert of clouds. Edwin searched the black void of a starless night to find a semblance of sanity. What he found was nothing. Absolute nothingness.

That was an exact description of what he felt in his soul. A terrible void. A bottomless pit. Eternity's hollow scream. A draining that emptied him of the life force. What was life anyway but the sweet taste of candy that turns out to be poison. A whisper of love that mutates into mocking laughter.

"Why did You do this to me?" he asked God. Those terribly shameful memories that he had tried to bury erupted in his mind. A tidal wave of anger smashed against his heart. "Why do You hate me?" he screamed, and smashed his fist through the window.

A nurse ran to his side and hurried him into a room to stop his wrist from bleeding.

Sharon stepped out of the elevator and went to the right a few steps, then turned around to go the other way. "Where is it?" she muttered anxiously. "Oh, God, please let him be alright."

She hurried down the long hall. From around the corner she could hear someone crying. She turned the corner and saw her mother slumped in a lobby chair. Sharon sat next to her. "Mother? Mother? Where's Christopher? Where's Dad?"

Barbara saw Sharon's face, but her mind wouldn't let her match Sharon's face with an identity.

"Mother," she shook her, "where's Christopher? Please answer me. Where's Christopher?"

Edwin walked up behind her. "Christopher is dead, honey."

Sharon looked up at her father. "He's...dead?" her voice quivered.

Edwin gently lifted his daughter and hugged her tightly. "Yes, Sharon. He's dead."

"But what's wrong with him? What's wrong with him? There's nothing wrong with Christopher."

"Honey," Edwin said softly, "your brother is dead."

The finality of this statement pierced Sharon's shield of disbelief. "He's dead?"

Edwin didn't answer her with words. He gently pushed her head into his chest and ran his fingers through her hair.

When they finally returned home, Edwin called Jonathan. "Hello—Elizabeth?"

"Yes, it is."

"This is Edwin. May I speak to your husband, please?"

Elizabeth detected something wrong. "He isn't here, Ed. Can I help you with anything?"

"Do you know where he is? Or when he'll return? I really need to speak with him. It's an emergency."

"Ed, I don't know where he is. He got a phone call around ten o'clock. Someone needed him to pray with them and he left. Are you sure I can't be of some help?"

Edwin didn't know why he felt his heart harden. "I'm certain."

"I can have him call you when he gets in."

"Don't bother."

He hung up and went to his den. Edwin closed the door and fell to his knees. For a long while he said nothing. The pain was so acute, the burden so unbearable. What was he to do?

*****

The spirit stood before Bashnar, his knees noticeably trembling.

"What is the state of the man, Edwin Styles?" Bashnar asked.

"The blow was sudden—no warning," he answered excitedly. "He is broken, Mighty Bashnar. He doesn't know what to do or what to believe. I heard him accuse God. He said, 'Why did You do this to me?' He also said, 'Why do You hate me?'"

"Excellent, excellent." Bashnar smiled grimly. "I can't wait for little Christopher's funeral."

*****

Through the pain, Edwin pushed the words out of his mouth.

"He was only a boy; a little three-year-old boy. What did he do to deserve this? The doctors don't even know what killed him! Why do You lead us on only to crush us in the dirt? How much can one man stand?" he yelled at God.

He stood up in anger. "I can't take this!" His eyes fell upon Jessica's books and CDs on his desk. He snatched up a CD and read the label. *Confession Brings Possession*. This was one that Edwin had listened to twice.

This famous Bible teacher believed that one could control his world through saying positive things. Failure to do so would inevitably result in tragedy.

"Is this what happens when I don't say the right thing? Is that what kind of God You are?" Edwin slammed the side of his fist into the desk. "Is it!" he yelled. He broke the disk in two and opened his office door and threw the pieces into the hallway. He gathered the rest of Jessica's stuff and threw them out there, too.

"Jessica!" he yelled, "get this trash out of my house!"

Jessica turned the corner and saw her books and CDs—one of them was in pieces!—scattered in the hallway.

"You had no right to destroy my property!"

"Just get it out of my house!"

"If you would have read it, maybe Christopher wouldn't be dead!" She gathered up her treasured books and tapes in a mad huff. Her glare met Edwin's. "You are to blame for this! You are the priest of this house! Satan can only do what you let him, and you let him kill your son!"

Edwin pointed to the door. "Get the hell out of my house!"

The shouting match attracted Barbara, Sharon, and Andrew. Barbara's eyes were red and swollen from much crying. Sharon's appearance was identical. Yet there was a steadiness about Sharon that contradicted her sad countenance. Andrew hadn't shed a tear since he had heard the news of his brother's death. He couldn't. His body had shut down and refused to give him this emotional release. This only added to the pain and confusion of losing his little brother.

"What's going on?" Barbara demanded. "What are you fighting about now? Is it too much to ask that you...?" Her anger's energy suddenly dissipated. She felt her throat constrict. "Christopher is dead," she mumbled through a dry mouth.

Edwin's eyes were piercing. "Your sister is leaving this house now!"

"What—?" Barbara began, but was cut off by Jessica.

"I told this man that he needed to use the power of God."

"And I told you to get out of my house," Edwin interrupted.

"God could've healed Christopher," Jessica said to her sister. "I gave him these books so that he could learn how to use the power of God."

"Are you saying that it is our fault that Christopher died?" Barbara managed to ask.

Jessica didn't want to hurt her sister further, but she had to tell the truth. Didn't God refer to His word as a sword? She rubbed Barbara's face. "If you and Edwin would have had faith in God this wouldn't have happened?"

"That's a terrible thing to say!" said Sharon, who had been quiet up to this point.

The doorbell rang.

Edwin looked at his watch. One-thirty in the morning. Considering their tragedy, it was to be expected that they'd have visitors throughout the night.

"Sharon, get that, please," he said with surprising tenderness.

She went to the door and looked out the side window. Her eyes stretched when she saw the man. Sharon opened the door.

Jonathan looked at Sharon's puffy eyes. "May I come in?"

"Yes. Please come in." It sounded almost like a plea for help.

"You're Sharon?"

"Yes."

"You're as beautiful as your father boasts."

A faint buoyancy surfaced ever so slightly in Sharon's aching heart. She forced a weak smile.

"Sharon, your father called and said there was an emergency. What's wrong?"

Sharon didn't know why, but she buried her face into Jonathan's cold, wet coat and cried, "Christopher is dead."

This chilled Jonathan. "That's your little brother."

"Yes," Sharon cried. "He...he...."

Jonathan held her tightly. "It's going to be okay," he said, his eyes immediately moist.

"Who is it?" Edwin asked as he walked into the room. When he saw Jonathan, he stopped in his tracks.

*****

"Watch out!" warned Trin.

Myla yanked the blade from the shocked demon's belly and turned around. He ducked. Shoooohh! The sword's razor edge whizzed by his head. He recognized the demon that tried to separate his head from his body. It was Coshma. A demon who was as wicked after the Rebellion as he was righteous before the great war.

The yellow-eyed monster rushed his old friend with frenzied abandonment. Myla blocked the silver blade with his own sword.

The next movement was so fast the demon didn't see it. Whooosh! Myla's sword sliced through his opponent's neck.

Three more rabid demons rushed Myla.

Trin swung his sword desperately, cutting through the demon infested air to get to Myla. *I'm not going to make it*," he thought.

A blue flame erupted on his sword. Trin's eyes widened. "Prayer!" he yelled to Myla. Trin gripped the handle tightly as it guided itself to the overmatched demons. The sword slashed with lightning speed and deadly accuracy. The angel tried to anticipate the movements of the runaway sword. He was like a man on a wild bull being jerked and tossed all over. But he managed to hold on to the Spirit empowered sword.

Myla's sword was also blue with Holy Ghost fire. "Who's praying?" he yelled to Trin, as he fought off the wicked spirits who tried to get past Jessica's guardian angel into Edwin's home.

"Adam and Sherry Chriswell," Trin's face no longer anxious by the odds. The odds were now with them. Three angels with prayer against a hundred demons. A hundred demons that had unfortunately chosen the wrong battle.

*****

"What do you want?" Edwin asked Jonathan.

Jonathan was surprised by Edwin's inhospitable tone. "Elizabeth told me that you called. She said it sounded urgent. Sharon told me about your son. I'm sorry."

"You're sorry?" Edwin asked sarcastically. "You mean you're not going to blast me for letting my son die?"

Jonathan knew this was Edwin's pain talking. "No. Who am I to place blame? I don't even know what the circumstances are."

"You want the circumstances? Jessica," he called. "I'll let my sister-in-law tell you the circumstances. You two seem to have a lot in common."

Barbara and Jessica came into the living room. Andrew trailed behind.

"Jonathan meet Jessica," Edwin gestured with his hand. "Jessica meet Jonathan. Between the both of you, maybe we'll find out why my son is dead," he stated bitterly.

Neither of them said anything.

Sharon broke the awkward silence. "Aunt Jessica says it's Daddy's fault that Christopher died," she said to Jonathan.

"Why did she say that?" he asked Sharon.

"I didn't say it. The Word says it," Jessica corrected them both."

"The Word says that Edwin is to blame for his son's death?" Jonathan asked.

"If he would've stood in faith for Christopher, he would be alive right now."

"How do you know this?"

Jessica looked at him as though he had just said the moon was made out of cheese. "Because the Bible says we can have what we say." She quoted Mark 11:23. "For verily I say unto you, That whosoever shall say unto this mountain, Be thou removed, and be thou cast into the sea; and shall not doubt in his heart, but shall believe that those things which he saith shall come to pass; he shall have whatsoever he saith."

Jonathan's face hardened with anger. He understood this lady's theology all too well. A flash of spiritual insight shot across his mind. *Of course*, he thought. *Satan is using her to discredit me. I have to make Edwin understand.*

"Jessica, I know a lot of people like you. Self-professed men and women of faith and power. But in actuality you people don't know what faith is. You laugh at and ridicule other denominations for being weak when you have no idea what God's standard of strength is."

"What makes you such an expert?" Jessica asked smugly.

"Thirty years of preaching in over forty different countries. Have you ever been to Haiti? Nepal? Cambodia? The Amazon? They eat people like you for breakfast."

Jessica wasn't about to let this man talk down to her like she was some kind of spiritual baby. "What do you mean, people like me?"

"People like you are people with no spiritual foundation who get a hold of a few CDs and books and think they've cornered the market on God. You take the promises of God and twist and pervert them for your own selfish purposes. You quoted Mark 11:23, but you don't understand what that verse means."

Jessica was used to talking to people who tried to explain away the scriptures. "It means exactly what it says."

"Wrong. It means exactly what the Bible says."

Jessica twisted her face in utter disgust. "That doesn't make any sense."

"Of course, it doesn't. Not to you. These things are spiritually discerned. You see everything through the eyes of your favorite faith teacher. What it means is this: you don't interpret the Bible by a verse; you interpret the verse by the Bible."

Jonathan knew that she had no earthly idea what he was trying to convey. This didn't matter. The real person he was trying to reach was Edwin.

Sharon listened intently.

"You people pull a Scripture out of context and try to manipulate God with it. How stupid and presumptuous can you get? Is God a puppet that He can be ordered about by His own creation?"

"He's bound by His Word," Jessica countered.

Jonathan knew what she meant. "God has to back up His Word or He's a liar?"

"That's right."

Jonathan marveled at her spiritual darkness. "And who determines if God is backing His Word?"

"We do."

"Your ignorance of the Bible amazes me. Are you familiar with 1 Corinthians 13:9 and 12? It says that we only know in part and that we do not see things clearly. If we don't know everything, and if we don't see everything clearly, how can we judge God?"

There was something else that Jonathan wanted Edwin to hear.

"You know," he said to Jessica, "I've never run into any of your preachers on the mission field. Certainly not in India or Haiti. And do you know why? It's not profitable. Why should they risk their lives for the gospel in a far and distant land when they can live a life of luxury in America? How easy it is to seduce those with itchy ears."

Jessica had suffered enough of this man's rambling. "What do you know about the power of God?" she said as she left the room to pack her suitcases.

Barbara went with her sister.

"Edwin, don't let her steal what God has given you. Satan uses people like her to discredit those who believe in all of God's Word."

"What has God given me?"

"A revelation of Himself."

"No! A revelation of death."

"Death is a part of life."

"Spare me the poetry."

"It's not poetry, Edwin. It's truth."

Edwin's tight muscles relaxed in helpless submission to the confusion that raged in his mind. He lowered his head and said, "I don't know what truth is."

"God is truth," said Jonathan.

"Who is God?" Edwin asked pitifully.

Sharon's heart broke for her father. She knew exactly how he felt and she wanted to say something, but she didn't. She knew that her father needed to hear this man. She did, too.

"God is the Person who gave His life for you. He's the Person who loves you."

Edwin laughed emptily. "If God loves me, why this? Why did He kill my son?"

Jonathan knew Edwin's pain. He knew his confusion. He knew that in Edwin's mind nothing made sense right now. He also knew that Satan would try to paralyze him with questions he could never answer and accusations he could never counter. Love was gentle, but it was also tough. It was time to get tough.

"Don't do that."

"What am I supposed to do?" Edwin was exasperated.

"You're supposed to trust God?"

"Even now?" Edwin asked accusingly.

Jonathan clenched this point. "That's what trust is. Believing God when everything in you, everything around you, tells you not to." He looked into Edwin's eyes. They were dull with painful confusion. "Why do we hold Job in such high esteem? It's because he trusted God in the hard places. He lost everything, Edwin. His business, his health, and his family. Did he accuse God of unfaithfulness or cruelty? No. He said, 'Though He slay me, yet will I trust Him.'

"You have to trust Him like that. If you only trust God when you don't have to, or only when you understand Him, you won't get very far."

Edwin sat on the sofa and held his head in his hands and cried. Sharon sat next to him and put her arm around him.

"Daddy," she said, a lifetime of wisdom compressed into her short sixteen years, "Reverend Banks is right." Her voice was soft and soothing. "We have to trust God even though we don't understand why this has happened. The only thing we can always count on is God's undying love. He loves you, Daddy. He really does."

Jessica and Barbara came into the living room carrying Jessica's suitcases. Barbara tried to get her sister to stay, but Jessica was adamant. She was leaving. As she walked toward the door with her suitcases, she said to Edwin, "I'll see you at the funeral."

Edwin would have recoiled in horror if he knew what that meant.

Chapter 26

Monday was a mournful day of reluctant activity for the Styles. Everyone was red-eyed and zombie-like as they went about the business of preparing for a funeral.

Sharon hurt as much as anyone else. But her pain was vastly different from her parent's. Sharon reeled from the loss of Christopher, but she sensed the hand of God holding her up, already healing her heart. Something deep inside of her—she knew it was God—told her that her brother's death was not an event of finality, but an abrupt transition from earth to heaven. She would see her brother again!

The rest of the family, with the exception of Andrew—he held up amazingly well for a fourteen-year-old—was thoroughly devastated. They didn't see it the way Sharon and Jonathan saw it. The farthest thing from their minds was the biblical promise that to be absent from the body is to be present with the Lord.

Sharon's resurgent faith in Christ again served as the family's spiritual anchor. She coaxed, encouraged, and comforted her family in characteristic resilience, especially her father.

Nevertheless, a stabbing and cruel reality invaded her mind and overwhelmed her heart with a despondency that drained her of her reservoir of inner strength. Sharon suddenly felt weak and vulnerable. Christopher's death had arrested her attention, diverting it from herself to someone else.

Ironically, the peace that freed her from the chains of pity and hopelessness that bound her parents also freed her to think of herself. It freed her to remember that she was pregnant.

She needed to talk to someone. Her mother was out of the question. And although she felt that her father would be supportive, this certainly was not the right time to bring something like this up.

Sharon went upstairs to her bedroom. She closed the door to ponder her fate. She knew girls who had become pregnant. A couple of them had bravely kept their babies. Sharon thought how unfair it was that a girl in high school who had a baby was labeled either a hero or a slut. She certainly was no hero. That left only one thing. She pushed that thought out of her mind. It didn't matter to God what her frame of mind was that night at Toni's. God still loved her and she knew unshakably that he would not hold her sin against her.

She thought of how wonderful it would be to have a little baby, to hold her and nurse her and watch her grow. She remembered how much joy little Christopher had brought to their family. Those little hands and feet. She smiled. Tamara is a pretty name, she thought. I'll name.... "No!" she grimaced and buried her face in her pillow.

If she had this baby, she would destroy everyone around her. Her father would be run out of his church. Her mother would probably have a nervous breakdown. Andrew would be teased at school, and she knew that she would lose the few friends that she had.

Toni! Toni was the only one who would understand. She called her and told her that she had to talk to her. Toni told her to come right over. She would be there in fifteen minutes.

As Sharon rang the doorbell, she suddenly remembered what Toni had said about her involvement in—what was that?—praying to the devil. An icy chill pricked Sharon's skin. *I hope her father isn't home*, she thought.

Toni opened the door and ushered her in.

"Is your father home?"

"No, he's in San Francisco. He won't be back until eleven o'clock tonight."

Sharon got right to the point. "I'm going to get an abortion."

Toni was shocked. "You're what?"

Sharon batted her eyes nervously. "I'm going to get an abortion," she said with much difficulty.

"Do you know what you're saying?"

"Yes, I know what I'm saying. Can you help me?"

"You can't get an abortion, Sharon."

"Why can't I?" Sharon asked with a mixture of anger and fear.

"Because you can't, that's why." Toni looked to the carpet for words. "Listen to me, Sharon. You don't know what you are saying. That's not for you. That's for people like me—the bad crowd. You're a...a...."

"A pregnant teenager! A pregnant teenager who needs help! I can't have this baby!" she yelled. "Will you help me?"

Toni turned away. She couldn't look at her any longer. This whole thing was her fault. *How could I have done something so sick?* she thought. "Alright," Toni muttered. What else could she say?

"Will you help—?"

Toni wheeled around. "I said alright!" she yelled, then apologized. "I'm sorry, Sharon. I just don't want to see you hurt, that's all."

"Have you ever had one?"

Toni wasn't surprised by the question, but she was disappointed. It wasn't something she liked to think about. "Yeah, two." Then to help her conscience, she added, "But that was before I got on the pill."

"Did it hurt?"

"Not physically."

Sharon didn't like the way she said that. "What do you mean by that?"

"I mean it didn't hurt my body."

Sharon heard it again. "Tell me the truth, Toni."

"Okay, Sharon. It was just like the doctor said it would be. Quick and painless. But when I left his office, I knew that I would never be the same again. I'm not a fool, Sharon!" she yelled more at the doctor than at Sharon. "I know what I did. I killed my baby."

Sharon felt a wave of nausea. She sat down quickly. "What month were you in?"

Toni knew that Sharon was groping for an out. She sat down beside her. "What difference does it make? You know as well as I do that a baby is a baby. It doesn't make a difference if he's one day old or one year old."

"But she's only a fetus right now," Sharon offered unconvincingly.

"Sharon, you and I both know that you don't believe that crap. If you're going to have an abortion, at least be honest with yourself about what you're doing."

Sharon stood up and nervously paced the floor, then sat down again. She was pulled in every direction. "What do I do?" she moaned.

Sharon's moan echoed in Toni's heart. She grasped Sharon's hand. "You can keep the baby," she almost whispered."

"What?"

"You can keep the baby. Sharon, you don't know how it feels to know you've murdered your own child. You don't know how it feels to hear your baby scream in agony, and to wake up and find that it wasn't a dream. Every time you see a lady with a baby, it'll bring back memories of your own. You'll hear the voice of your baby crying out to you in every baby food commercial...every diaper commercial."

"Don't you understand, Toni? I can't have the baby! My parents...my mother would have a fit."

"She'd get over it, Sharon," Toni pled.

"My father would lose his church and never be able to preach again."

"Lose his church?" asked Toni. "What do you mean lose his church? What about all that forgiveness Christians talk about?"

The church's double standard was on Sharon's face. "Preachers aren't supposed to have these kinds of kids."

"But that's not fair," said Toni. "It's not your fault." She felt the full weight of what she had done to Sharon. Either way her friend was going to lose. If she had the child, her father would lose his church. If she had an abortion—she knew Sharon—the guilt would drive her crazy.

"It doesn't make a difference whose fault it is. He can't have problems like other people. He's gotta be perfect."

There were several minutes of silence between the girls. Toni found something in the room to stare at. Sharon rested her knees on her elbows and her head in her hands. Each searched her own soul for an answer. Sharon looked up and into Toni's eyes. For a moment neither said a word.

"I know where you can get an abortion," Toni offered reluctantly."

"How soon?"

She reached for the phone. "I'll give him a call."

Sharon became alarmed. "Is this a real doctor?"

"Yeah, he's a real doctor," she said, as she pushed the number. "He's a friend of my father."

A friend of her father?

Sharon hung the phone up. "Do you remember that stuff you told me about your father and all? You know, about praying to the devil?"

"Yeah."

"Does this doctor do that, too?"

"No," she lied.

*****

Rashti was already troubled by Bashnar's success. This report about Jonathan caused him even greater alarm. Apparently the man of God was very close to destruction. If Jonathan was destroyed, the revival would suffer inestimable damage. The man of God had to be saved!

Rashti and a large detachment of soldiers descended with such swiftness on the small Union City farm where Jonathan was ministering that the twenty demons who stalked Jonathan had no time to escape. In a moment, they were surrounded.

The demons pulled out their weapons, but when they saw Captain Rashti they knew their cause was lost.

"Captain Rashti," the leader of the demons called out to him. "You have us outnumbered three to one." He looked at his demons and threw down his sword. The others looked puzzled, then followed their leader. "The great Rashti is a mighty warrior, not a murderer."

Rashti whispered something to Trin, and Trin in turn whispered to a soldier who spread the word among the soldiers.

Mudillus took this as a bad omen.

"Is not the God of heaven a God of mercy?" he said.

Rashti remembered the mistake of King Saul. It was written in the first book of Samuel the prophet, chapter fifteen: "Now go and smite Amalek, and utterly destroy all that they have, and spare them not: but slay both man and woman, infant and suckling, ox and sheep, camel and ass."

King Saul's mistake was that he compromised the Word of the Lord and did not explicitly follow His command. He ultimately paid the supreme price for his self-willed tendencies.

This was a trait totally foreign to the angel the hosts of heaven called the Sword of the Lord. He burned with a holy fire that made it impossible for him to do anything but obey God. Righteousness was his blood, purity his air.

Rashti stood at the front of his detachment. The personable features that made the great holy warrior so approachable were now gone. His emerald green eyes were mirrors of sheer determination, his face hard and resolute. A quiet rage that was discernible to his soldiers emanated from deep within.Rashti slowly pulled out his sword and pointed it toward the heavens. His angels followed suit.

Mudillus's heart pounded hard against his spiny chest. His eyes betrayed his fear. He looked at his sword which he had thrown to the ground. The terrified demon wiggled his long, crusty fingers the way a gunfighter would do before a fight. If he made a move for the sword, the massacre would begin. If he didn't, the massacre would begin.

Forty nervous eyes looked to Mudillus for deliverance. "What'll we do?" one asked anxiously.

"Run," stated an eloquent demon.

"Captain Rashti, maybe we can work something out. A deal. I can give you valuable secrets. Jonathan. I can tell you how the Mighty Bashnar plans to destroy Jonathan. What do you say, Rashti? Can we talk?"

"For the glory of God and the sons of men!" Rashti cried.

There was a synchronized scattering of the demonic host. Mudillus thought that Rashti's command would compel them to their swords. He thought wrong. He was the only one that reached for his sword. All the others took off in every direction, leaving him alone.

He never lived long enough to know he was abandoned. Forty feet separated him from the Sword of the Lord. Three feet separated Mudillus from his sword. He lunged for it. His crusty fingers touched the handle just as Rashti's sword touched his wrist. The demon wailed loudly and yanked his arm away, leaving his hand on the ground. Mudillus scampered to his knees. He did this right before the Sword of the Lord made of Mudillus three where there had only been one.

The other demons met similar fates. Not one escaped.

After the battle, Rashti greeted the mercy angels who were permanently assigned to guard Jonathan. He then studied the man of God for two hours. It was true. He could see it. Jonathan had only a short while before it happened. Rashti's heart broke.

"Watch over him closely," he told the angel in charge. "We can't stop it; it's too far gone. I want to know the moment it happens." He left the little farm wondering how odd it was that goodness was this great man's worst enemy.

*****

"What do you mean, you don't know what's wrong?" Wallace interrogated the young man. "You're a doctor. You go to school all your life to tell me you don't know?"

The doctor had a look of exasperation on his face. "We've checked everything there is to check, Mr. Reynolds." He weighed his words carefully. "This is a most unusual case."

"You can do something, can't you?" Marjorie asked. "You're not saying our boy is going to be a vegetable the rest of his life?"

"No, I'm not saying that at all."

"That's exactly what it sounds like to me," Wallace said angrily. "He's been here three days and you haven't told us anything we didn't already know."

Wallace's continued criticism chipped off a piece of Dr. Shaw's professional demeanor. His face tightened. "I'm telling you for the last time, sir, we have done everything we can to help your son. We have administered every test there is to administer. We have consulted with specialists. There is nothing physiologically wrong with your son."

"Nothing wrong?" shouted Wallace. "He can't talk. He can't hear. What does it take for you people to see that he is sick?"

The doctor sighed and walked away.

"What are we going to do?" Marjorie asked her husband.

Wallace glared at the young doctor as he walked away. "I don't know. I don't know what we're going to do."

"We've got to do something," said Marjorie.

"Don't you think I know that?" Wallace asked gruffly.

"What about that man?" she said.

Their mercy angels rushed to their sides. One went to where Johnny was laid, but he did not touch him.

"What man?" asked Wallace.

"That strange man who spoke at our church."

Wallace looked at his wife in utter shock that she would entertain such a stupid thought. "Are you crazy?"

"No. I'm desperate!"

"We can't take our boy to him."

"Why not?"

Wallace was stumped. "Because it's wrong. That's why."

"It's wrong?" Marjorie exclaimed. "What's right with letting our pride stand in the way of getting help for our child?"

"Marjorie, I am not taking our son to some two-bit faith healer."

"You don't have to. I will!"

"Oh, fine." Wallace threw his arms in the air. "Why don't we ask Benny Hinn to send us a prayer cloth?"

"Say what you'd like." Marjorie was determined. "I'm going to ask that man to pray for Johnny."

The thought was utterly repulsive to Wallace, but he knew that she wasn't going to back down. That mother's instinct was going to make them both look like idiots.

"Okay, listen, why don't we take him to Edwin?"

"Edwin? Why don't we bury Johnny in our backyard?"

"He's our preacher," Wallace reasoned.

"What can Edwin do? Has he ever prayed for anyone in our church to be healed before? No," she answered herself. "And even if he did, it wouldn't do any good. Don't you have to have faith or something? He doesn't even believe in healing."

"And when did you start?" Wallace asked his wife cynically.

"Today."

A mercy angel brought back vivid pictures of that weird church service. Marjorie saw the people fall as in a stupor. She saw that little cross-eyed girl get healed. "God healed that little girl," Marjorie said dreamily.

Wallace shook his head in disgust. The things men had to put up with. *I better hurry and get our boy to Edwin before she takes him to that faith preacher*, he thought. *If word ever got out.* He shuddered at the thought.

Chapter 27

The sky was dark with clouds that moved rhythmically, purposefully, lifelike. They appeared as an orchestra of smoky, black evil, looking down at her, sneering, mocking, threatening. A clap of thunder caused her to flinch in fear.

A sudden gust of cold, swirling wind cut through her clothing. Sharon pulled the scarf tighter around her neck in a vain effort to stave off the biting cold. She wore black from head to toe. Conspicuously absent was a coat for such harsh weather. She took small, timid steps toward the headstone.

A flash of lightning streaked across the sky. She looked up into the darkness and flinched again when the sky roared with thunder. Twenty feet separated her from the headstone. An unfathomable dread reverberated through her soul. The dread grew as she neared the tombstone. She wanted to turn and run away, but something compelled her on, some inner drive.

Another clap of thunder and the sky opened its dams.

She looked down at the stone and read the inscription:

What could have been
will never be
For my giver of life
stole mine from me.
March 19, 2011 - March 28, 2011
Tamera L. Styles

Crying.

Sharon heard the faint cry of a baby. She adjusted the scarf and looked around for the baby. The hollow sound of crying came from every direction. The crying grew more intense. Its decibel level surpassing Sharon's level of comfort. She put her hands to her ears and tried to muffle the crying. The crying stopped.

Sharon removed her hands from her ears and looked at the tombstone, startled. She thought she saw a glimpse of movement.

The stone moved a little, and this time she was sure of what she had seen. Sharon was paralyzed with horror as the ground began to swell. Suddenly, something burst through the grave and grabbed her wrist. Sharon screamed and jerked her arm back and forth, but the thing would not let go.

"You killed me," it said.

Sharon continued to scream. "Let me go!" she begged desperately, still struggling to make it let go of her wrist.

"You killed me, Mother," it said accusingly. "You murdered your own child."

This cut through Sharon's terror. She looked at the thing and recognized it. It...she...was Tamera.

"Murderer," someone spat behind her.

Sharon, trembling and wet, whipped around in the direction of the voice. She saw no one. The closest thing to her was a tree. It was a large, sprawling tree with a myriad of crooked branches and limbs. There were no leaves on it, no signs of life. It was a fitting tree for a place of death.

"Murderer!" it said.

Sharon gasped.

The tree began to move, but not because of the strong, chilled wind that howled through the graveyard. Its branches and limbs stretched forth like arthritic tentacles of malevolence.

Sharon screamed and turned to run away from the tree, but the ground was wet and slippery. She fell in the muck. The creature that burst through the grave still tightly gripped her wrist. Sharon yanked her arm with all the force of a terrified person. Her sudden jerk paid off. The arm went free. She crawled backwards on her butt, her heels struggling for traction in the slippery mud as she clawed at the grass.

"Murderer! Murderer!" the creature from the grave yelled.

"Murderer!" hissed the tree.

Now, underneath her, Sharon heard a chorus of angry voices: "Murderer!" the grass rang out.

The sky's clouds moved ominously into the shape of a small baby. "Murderer!" a deep, angry voice cried out from above.

Accusations screamed out from every place and thing. She covered her ears, but there was no quieting the haunting voices. She scooted backwards in the mud more.

"But I had no choice!" Sharon screamed and popped up in her bed. Her breaths were hard. Perspiration covered her body.

Barbara heard Sharon and rushed into the room without knocking. She was breathing heavily and had a disturbed look on her face. "What's wrong? Baby, are you alright?"

For a moment, Sharon said nothing. Then, "I had a terrible dream, a nightmare actually. I was in a graveyard. I went to visit my...somebody. As I looked at the tombstone, someone burst through the dirt and grabbed my arm."

"Oh, honey, that's terrible." Barbara sat on the bed and stroked her daughter's shoulder.

"Mom?"

"Yes, Sharon?"

"You remember that girl I told you about? My friend?"

Barbara reflected. "No, I don't recall."

"The girl who got pregnant," said Sharon. She dared not look her mother in the eyes as she spoke.

"Oh, yes, her," said Barbara, her disdain noticeable in her speech. "What ever became of her?"

"She...she had an abortion."

"She what?" This was reprehensible.

"She had to terminate the pregnancy."

"No one has to terminate a pregnancy. And it was not a pregnancy that she terminated. It was a baby."

"Well, what would you have had her do?" Sharon asked defensively. "The other day you said she was a whore for having sex before marriage. What if her mother was like you?"

"What do you mean like me?"

Sharon thought about what she was about to say. It was harsh, but it had to be said. "What if her mother was hardhearted? What if she lacked compassion? What if her mother didn't and couldn't understand?"

Sharon's words were flaming arrows that pierced her mother's heart. Barbara responded haltingly, numbed by this revelation. "I didn't know you felt that way about me?"

Sharon saw the hurt in her mother's eyes. She was sorry, but she had to go on. She was hurting also. "What if her mother said it was wrong to have the baby and also wrong to get rid of the baby?"

"That would be unreasonable."

"That's right, Mom. That would be unreasonable."

Barbara was reluctant to continue this conversation for fear that she may be hurt further by Sharon's candor. "Did," she cleared her throat, "her mother do that?"

Sharon's demeanor softened. It was not her mother's fault that she couldn't understand. No one was perfect, and it wasn't fair to expect her mom to be perfect. Sharon hugged her mother. Barbara squeezed her tightly.

"Yes," answered Sharon.

"I'm sorry," Barbara said, sincerely.

Sharon pulled back and looked her mother in the eyes. "It's okay, Mother. I'm sure her mother loves her with all of her heart. She was just trying to protect her daughter."

Andrew entered the room. "Dad said it's almost time to go." The full weight of his little brother's death was on Andrew's face.

"Tell him we'll be down shortly," said Barbara.

It was a full hour before they drove off for the funeral. No one spoke a word the entire trip until Edwin turned onto the church property.

"Dad, why did this happen?" asked Andrew sullenly.

That question was a finger in the eye. Edwin grimaced slightly. "I don't know, son."

Several family members met them in the foyer of the church. Parents, brothers, sisters, in-laws. Edwin spotted Jessica. *And one outlaw.*

Except for Jessica, the show of familial support was water on a parched tongue. Edwin found himself unconsciously thanking God for his family.

"Hello, Edwin," someone in the crowd of well-wishers said.

It sounded like...no it couldn't be.

Edwin turned around. His face registered an eight on the Richter scale of surprise. He looked around to see if Harry Thompson or any of the other behind-the-scene puppeteers were close by. They weren't. Edwin told Jonathan to follow him. He quickly led him to an empty Sunday school classroom.

"What are you doing here?" Edwin asked.

Jonathan didn't like the idea of being furtively whisked away. It had a bad smell to it. A lot like the fear of man. But he knew that Edwin was a man in theological transition. He would try not to push too hard.

"I'm here because friends are there when you need them."

"Friends?" asked Edwin skeptically. "Friends don't lie to friends."

Jonathan's heartbeat quickened at this accusation. "When have I ever lied to you?"

"Everything you say and do is a lie." The words came through clenched teeth.

"Everything is quite an ambiguous word. Would you care to be more specific?"

"You want specifics?" Edwin snapped. "I'll give you specifics. This whole sham about our authority over the devil. Controlling the world around us. Getting the desires of our heart. Is that specific enough for you? Or do you want more?"

"Edwin, sit down."

Edwin's eyes narrowed and he stood taller.

"Please, Edwin, sit down."

He did.

"I don't recall ever discussing any of these subjects with you, except, of course, authority over Satan. And, then, we only discussed how to cast out demons. Or maybe there's no such thing as demons," Jonathan threw in.

Edwin couldn't refute the existence of demons. But to acknowledge their existence was to validate what his crazy sister-in-law said. How could he admit that she was right? How could he not admit it?

Jonathan correctly interpreted his silence as confusion.

"Jessica did a number on you."

"What do you mean?" Edwin asked. "Did she give you anything to read or listen to?"

"Yeah. She gave me some books and CDs."

"And you read the books and listened to the CDs?"

"Yeah, and some of them more than once," he answered guiltily, although he didn't know why he felt guilty. He was only trying to learn the truth. How could that be wrong?

"Edwin, I'm going to tell you what has happened. For some unfathomable reason, God has selected you to roll back the forces of darkness in Atlanta." He tapped him on the shoulder. "You are the tip of His spear. I don't think it's a coincidence that Jessica gave you those books and tapes. I believe Satan is trying to neutralize you by giving you bad doctrine."

"You don't believe that stuff?" Edwin was incredulous.

Jonathan took a deep breath. "Let me explain it to you this way. I am an oddity. I am a full gospel, charismatic preacher who finds that stuff totally disgusting."

"That doesn't make sense," Edwin countered. "The preachers who produced those books and tapes are full gospel."

"No, Edwin, they're not even quarter gospel. The best way to describe them is in first Timothy 1:7, where it says some folks desire to be teachers of things they don't understand. They are blind leaders of the blind. Edwin, this is not some new tactic. Satan's been using this one against the charismatic movement for some time now. Whenever God restores a forgotten truth, Satan distorts it. He did it with speaking in tongues, divine healing, financial prosperity, prophecy, and virtually everything else the charismatic movement is known for."

"That doesn't bring my son back," Edwin added bitterly.

Jonathan spoke softly. "It's not intended to bring your son back. It's intended to help you understand what the devil is doing."

Edwin stood up. "Excuse me," he said coldly, "I have a funeral to attend."

Jonathan sighed. This was going to be harder than he expected. Edwin left Jonathan by himself. For the first time, Jonathan felt like giving up. Why should he continue to waste his time on a man who was so easily manipulated by people and events? Why didn't he see things as he did? Didn't he know that life was fleeting? So very temporary? When would he sell out to God? How much longer would he have to tolerate Edwin's ambivalence?

How long are you going to tolerate Edwin?

Jonathan recognized that thought. "Oh, God, how long am *I* going to tolerate Edwin? I'm so sorry. Forgive me for being so prideful and calloused. This man is at his son's funeral and...and...I...."

Tears rolled down his face. Sometimes he was just too hard on people. Now here he was again praying this same prayer, asking God for the umpteenth time to forgive him for being hardhearted. "Lord, please help me. I don't want to be hard. I only want to do Your will."

Jonathan lightly gripped his face with a single hand and slowly rubbed downward in contemplation. He would stand by Edwin come what may. He stood up, took a few steps toward the door, and collapsed. His muscles strained as he lifted his head and chest off the floor, but there wasn't strength to complete the job. His face hit the floor hard.

*****

Edwin could scarcely make it down the long hall without being stopped by someone offering condolences. Deep down inside he appreciated their concern, but on the surface of his mind, he wished they would leave him alone. No amount of apologies would bring his son back. He nodded politely at the old lady who pinned him against the wall.

"I'm so sorry that you lost your son. I know how you must feel. Arnold and I were married forty-six years before he died. He was a contractor, you know, a fine man. He used to say—"

"Yes, Mrs. Lindsay." Edwin squeezed past her as politely as possible. "I appreciate your concern."

"The Lord giveth and the Lord taketh away," the old lady said to Edwin as he walked away.

Edwin turned around, his face hard with bitterness. "Yes, He does, doesn't He?"

Thirty minutes later, inside the Sunday school classroom, Jonathan began to come around. He crawled to a chair and pulled himself up. He blinked his eyes hard. The dizziness that had caused him to black out was still there, but not as greatly.

Jonathan stood to his feet and leaned heavily against the wall. This was the third time this had happened. He knew that he would not be able to ignore it this time. He felt like a house without nails; he was coming apart. His aching muscles felt unbelievably weak. They held him up only because he made them. His body trembled as he summoned every ounce of strength for the task. He waited until he felt stronger and stepped into the hall.

"It's hard to believe that you're the high and mighty preacher Adam and Sherry say you are," said Jessica when she saw him in the hall.

Jonathan walked past her without saying anything.

"You'll see the power of God!" Jessica said with intense eyes. "You'll see His mighty power today!"

A stab of fear tore into Jonathan's exhausted body—*this lady is dangerous*—but he was too tired to respond to her. Dead tired.

Edwin was grateful and moved that his assistant pastor, Larry McGuire, had asked to conduct the funeral. As he listened to him preach, he realized with renewed admiration that he was a gifted speaker. His speech always seemed so effortless, yet so polished.

Thank you, Larry, he thought, when his assistant complimented his "distinguished fatherhood." Larry was such a good friend.

Edwin closed his eyes. He knew that he had to be strong, if not for himself, for his family. They needed him to be strong. Yet, he fearfully wondered how he would hold up when he looked into the casket and saw his own son. *I wanted so much for you, Christopher. How I wish I could take you fishing just once. Oh, why didn't I do it sooner?* A sudden eruption of muffled whisperings disrupted Edwin's thoughts.

He inconspicuously looked around to see what would cause such impolite behavior in the sanctuary. And at a funeral! It wasn't hard to figure out what the silent commotion was about. His was the only black face among the hundreds in attendance.

Harry Thompson's eyes bulged when he saw him. "What in the devil is he doing here?" he growled under his breath. "Excuse me," he said, as he squeezed past a woman whose figure testified of her hearty appetite. Harry made it to the aisle and told the ushers to get rid of Jonathan.

Jonathan was rapidly coming out of his daze. His faculties returned to a semblance of normalcy. The incredible heaviness he had felt earlier had nearly completely lifted. Suddenly his mind focused on something he had heard earlier. *You'll see the power of God! You'll see His mighty power today!*

"Where did I hear that?" he muttered. "Who—?" Jonathan froze in horror. *No! I can't let her do this*!

A man tapped Jonathan on the shoulder. "Sir, we'd like to speak with you in the foyer." The man had a sour look on his face. Two men stood in back of him like Mafia henchmen.

Jonathan looked to the front of the sanctuary. "There's a lady here who...there!" he whispered to the usher. "Her. She's the one. You can't let her view the body."

Edwin turned in his seat. Many rows of people separated him from Jonathan. But they both were seated on the end, so it was easy to see him. He saw Harry and two ushers talking to him. Apparently Jonathan was raising a stink.

One of the ushers looked at the pastor for guidance. He didn't want to embarrass the pastor. Jonathan saw him looking up front and turned around in time to see Edwin give the usher a mean nod.

Harry spoke up. "Either you leave of your own accord, or I'll have these boys carry you out."

Jonathan knew it was a lost cause. He got up and followed the men down the aisle.

Demons cackling, howling with laughter at the dagger.

When the time came, Edwin approached the casket with dread. He did not want to see his son in a casket. But he was strong. He looked at his boy and held his little hand. "I love you," he said, and walked away when he felt his strength leaving.

Edwin and his family sat and stoically watched the long line of people slowly walk past the casket. One lady who Edwin didn't recognize looked at Christopher for a long time before moving on. Jessica approached the casket, stopped, gently stroked his arm, and mumbled something.

Edwin's heart tightened with apprehension. Something was wrong.

Suddenly, before anyone could stop her, Jessica grabbed Christopher under his armpits and lifted him over her head. "In the name of Jesus, I rebuke the spirit of death! I command that his life return to his body! Let him go, Satan!" she screamed.

Horrified gasps filled the sanctuary. Several women screamed. Who was this lunatic!

"Somebody call the police!" a lady yelled out.

"911," yelled another.

Edwin was momentarily stunned. But he pressed past the shock and sprang into action. He jumped up and ran through the scurrying crowd, bumping into some, knocking over others. He felt like he was running in slow motion. He couldn't get there fast enough.

Jessica saw him coming and became even more hysterical. "Come back, Christopher! Be healed in Jesus's mighty name!" She shook his little body so violently that his head snapped back and forth like it was on a spring.

"Noooooo!" yelled Edwin as he ran up to stop her. He grabbed Christopher's body and tried to pull him loose, but Jessica wouldn't let go. They struggled back and forth. Finally, Jessica jerked hard and when she did the body slipped through her hands and hit the floor.

Two men ran up and grabbed her and dragged her off. She bit and clawed at them wildly.

Several family members gathered around Edwin. He was crouched on the floor with Christopher's body. The tears that he held back earlier now erupted without any restraint. He hugged Christopher to his chest and rocked back and forth. His little body wasn't warm. It was limp. It didn't respond. Christopher was dead. His little boy was dead.

"Charismatic freaks. Charismatic freaks," the demon yelled over and over again. "Charismatic freaks, charismatic freaks...."

Edwin's pain heard the spirit.

Chapter 28

Daphne Krugle was ecstatic. "Are you serious?" she asked the program director excitedly.

"As serious as forty-seven hundred emails can make any director. The phone's been ringing off the hook. Over two thousand calls already and it's still morning."

"That's unbelievable," Daphne said, her mind racing to a plush office in New York. "What? What? Oh, God, that's unbelievable!"

The program director had mixed feelings. Daphne was right. This was unbelievable. No show had ever generated this kind of response. Forty-seven hundred emails! This would probably be the vehicle that carried that little snake to the big leagues. Mr. Gibson didn't dislike Daphne, but he didn't like her either. There was so little to like. She was vain, haughty, headstrong, and the one thing he resented most, focused. Something he lacked terribly. She knew what she wanted and stopped at nothing until she achieved her goal.

The program director's envy wanted her to leave, even if it meant a big promotion for her. But his practicality definitely wanted her to stay. She was good. No, she was better than good. She was excellent. Her name meant ratings.

"I know this is your day off," he said apologetically, "but do you think you could do something to get those two guys together again while the fire's still hot?"

"Yes!" she answered hurriedly. "I'll...uhhh...let me call you back!"

Click.

Daphne stubbed her toe on the dresser and cursed. She quickly showered, dried herself, and dashed into her huge walk-in closet and searched frantically for her newest purchase. She snatched the dress off of the hanger and threw it on the bed.

Less than an hour elapsed from the director's phone call to when she inspected her attire before a full length mirror. *Celebrities—no, stars must look like stars*, she thought. She grabbed her snake skin purse and headed for the door. "Oh, no!" she said in frustration. In her excitement, she had completely forgotten to call either of her two stepping stones to stardom.

"Alice in Wonderland," she muttered, referring to the rabbit in the fairy tale who was always late for an appointment he didn't have.

Daphne dumped the contents of her purse on the white leather sofa. "Where is that paper?" She was like a lady trying to beat a deadline to claim a million dollar lottery. But right now she couldn't find the ticket.

The paper wasn't there. She blasted the living room with curse words. "Why didn't I put the freakin' numbers in the phone?" She paused. "Calm down," she told herself, the elation draining from her expensive bosom. "Just calm down." But she didn't. Her concern was turning into panic. "Where is that paper?" she screamed.

Daphne picked up a small golden container that looked like a makeup case. She opened it. It was partitioned into three parts. Two squares and a long, skinny rectangle. The squares had white powder in them; the rectangle a golden spoon. Daphne dipped the spoon into the powder and put it to her nose. She snorted some of the powder into both nostrils.

Daphne closed her eyes and leaned her head back. Within minutes, the powder was making love to her mind. A rush that felt like a velvet avalanche of psychological pleasure rolled over her senses. Heightening some; deadening others. She opened her eyes to a different world, a world that was subservient to her every whim. A world that rolled out the red carpet to its royal queen. She could do anything.

Daphne put her things in her purse and stood up. "I'll just go to my office and get the numbers," she said confidently. She took the elevator down to the garage and smiled at her new white Jaguar XJL Supersport. *Three hundred thousand dollars a year for a twenty-seven-year-old sister from the projects isn't that bad,* she thought, mocking the poverty that had once made her life so miserable. "But three million a year sounds better." She gunned the engine in park and said, "Just a matter of time. A matter of time."

*****

Familiar spirits were integral and indispensable to Satan's plan to gain acceptance for witchcraft. In primitive lands, he had only to appeal to the fears and superstitions of the culture to gain acceptance. But in countries like America, he had to appeal to the intellect.

These demons were assigned to particular people for the sole purpose of gathering information. This information was used to help the kingdom of darkness plan their offensives. Familiar spirits had also been used profusely to deceive stupid people into believing that dead people are allowed to roam the earth, free to visit and converse with anyone who conjured them up.

However, in the early 1900s Satan had instructed his demons of religion to greatly expand and intensify their delusionary tactics in America. Immediately, the demons of religion ordered the familiar spirits to use the information they gathered to help false prophets gain the allegiance of thousands.

"One day even in enlightened, technologically advanced America millions will follow our prophets," Satan had told his generals.

"Right into hell," said one of them.

Satan laughed. "That's right, general. Right into hell."

The familiar spirit that was assigned to Daphne recorded everything he could. Everything that could possibly be of any strategic value.

Daphne closed her office door and sat down behind her large oak desk. She opened a drawer and pulled out a copy of *Harper's Bazaar* magazine. She flipped a few pages and punched the number.

"I'm sorry, he's in a meeting," said the secretary.

"Tell him it's Daphne Krugle," she said, sure that the twelve-dollar-an-hour secretary would let her through.

The secretary was unimpressed. She was used to talking to celebrities and other public figures. "I'm sorry, ma'am. He can't be disturbed."

The magical white powder took over. "I don't care if he's talking to the mayor. You tell him Daphne Krugle of Eyewitness News wants to speak with him now."

The secretary looked at the telephone receiver and mumbled something under her breath. She started to repeat herself to the belligerent newscaster, but decided against it. The lady's calm insistence sounded a lot like a veiled threat.

"Please hold," she told Daphne. She pushed the intercom button.

Anthony picked up the receiver so that his guests couldn't hear. "Yes, Sheila?"

"I'm sorry to disturb you, sir, but Daphne Krugle is on the line. I told her you were—"

He smiled slightly. "That's okay. I've been expecting her call."

Anthony knew he had the support of the mayor and the two councilmen now. "Gentlemen," he smiled, "listen to this conversation. He pushed the speaker button. "Daphne, what a surprise," he said with the familiarity of an old friend.

Daphne breathed a sigh of relief. Thank goodness! She put on her professional air. "Good morning, Mr. Righetti. I hope I'm not disturbing anything important."

"Oh, no, not at all." He smiled at the mayor. "I was just talking to a few friends about the twin pillars of American society. Money and power," he laughed.

The politicians didn't find that statement amusing at all. They weren't offended at what he said. He was right. They were discussing money and power. It was just that they all knew what an investigative report by Daphne Krugle could do to a politician's career.

"Mr. Righetti—"

"Call me Anthony."

She paused. "Anthony, the response to our special was incredible. We've received thousands of emails and hundreds of phone calls. Atlanta wants to hear more about your Family."

"Is this an invitation to come back?"

"Yes, it is." Daphne crossed her fingers.

Anthony paused. Daphne waited an eternity for his answer.

"Where do you live?"

Daphne was taken aback by this question. But there was something in his voice, something mystical, something compelling that made her give him her address.

"I'll be there at one," he told her.

Daphne hung the phone up. *Why did I give that man my address?* she asked herself. She didn't like the idea of him coming to her condo, but what could she do now? Call him back and cancel? No, this was it. She was going to make it to the top.

At exactly one o'clock the guard called her. "There's a gentleman here to see you. Says his name is Anthony."

"Send him up, Charlie."

Daphne had serious reservations now about letting him meet her at home. "I must be crazy to let this man—"

The doorbell rang.

Immediately, her ambition replaced her fears. Daphne was like a puppy on a leash. She was pulled by an inner compulsion to the door. "Hi, come in."

Anthony stepped inside. "Thank you for meeting with me on such short notice."

"Business is business," she said in an overly professional tone. "Have a seat."

He walked over to the large window and looked at the Lenox mall. They were fifteen floors up. "Every lady's dream," he said. "To shop and watch others shop."

Daphne ignored her feminist compulsion to answer what she considered a sexist remark and forced a smile. She felt more in control of herself now. "Mr. Righetti, will—"

He turned around, smiling. "I thought we both agreed that you would call me Anthony." There was a trace of scolding in his voice.

Daphne became slightly nervous. "Yes, we did, didn't we?" she said, acting as if she didn't notice the undercurrent of control he was trying to establish. "Anthony, will you appear on the show again?" she asked him pointedly, yet politely.

"I am not here to discuss your show."

Daphne's eyes widened. A thought slapped her mind's face. She was alone in her home with a Satan worshipper. "What are you here for?" she asked, trying to conceal her fear.

"Control."

"What is it that you want to control, Mr. Righetti?"

His eyes were piercing. "You," he answered point blank.

A terrible feeling of helplessness enveloped Daphne. She felt like a small child in the hands of a cruel stranger. No one could help her. *Keep your cool. Girlfriend, keep your cool.*

"What, what do you mean by that?" Her voice was steady.

He walked around the white leather sofa where Daphne sat and began to massage her neck muscles. Daphne sat petrified. All of the superwoman crap she had ever heard or read about now seemed absolutely foolish. There was no way a hundred and twenty-pound woman could fight off a large man like Anthony Rhigetti. She dared not move or resist. *Oh, God.*

"You're a beautiful woman, Daphne. You're intelligent and ambitious." Smiling at the back of her head, he put his nose into her hair and slowly breathed in her scent. "You have everything it takes to become the next Oprah Winfrey."

Daphne shivered. She felt like her mind had been burglarized. "That's quite a compliment, Mr. Ri—Anthony." She heard her words and felt like a fool. A frightened fool. This stranger was massaging her and breathing all over her and she was trying to sound as though he was sitting across the table from her in her studio. And to make matters worse, she knew that he knew exactly what was going on in her mind.

"You have everything, except me." He abruptly stopped massaging her neck and sat across from her. Daphne didn't know what to say. "I have what you want; you have what I want."

Daphne summoned all the strength she could. "Anthony, would you please leave?"

"It takes more than beauty and talent to make it, Daphne." He didn't look at her; he looked through her.

She glanced intermittently at his eyes. Each time she did, she felt that she was being x-rayed.

"If you ever make it, it'll be because you stroked the right people. I'm one of those people," he said.

Ambitious curiosity replaced Daphne's fear. What could this man possibly do for her?

Anthony reached into his pocket and took out a piece of paper and handed it to Daphne.

"What's this?" she asked.

"Look at it."

She opened the folded paper: *If this works, I owe you a big one,* it read. It was signed by Walter Simmons. Daphne knew this couldn't be the Walter Simmons of CBS—could it?

"Am I supposed to believe that this is Walter Simmons' telephone number?" Her confidence was returning. He apparently wasn't there to have sex with her. He was there to make a deal.

He gave her his phone. "Dial the number. Use my phone so he'll see that the call is from me."

"You're serious."

"Do it." He smiled darkly.

She did it.

"Hello," answered a man's voice.

"Hello...Mr. Simmons?" Daphne asked dubiously.

"Are you calling for Anthony?"

It was him! She recognized his voice. "Yes, I am."

"Is he there?"

"Yes."

"Put him on, please."

Awed, she handed the phone to Anthony.

He covered the phone with his hand. "I'm going to put him on speaker phone."

"Walter, how are you?"

"Anthony, that scumbag died only two days after the ceremony. Just like you said he would. A heart attack. I have the newspaper article in front of me right now!"

"The Family takes care of those who take care of the Family. I have a friend here in Atlanta who I want to take care of. She's a television newscaster. I emailed you a clip of her."

"Aahhh, yes, yes. Beautiful girl."

"Just as smart as she is beautiful."

"That never hurts."

"She wants to be like Oprah."

Walter laughed. "Her, me, and a million others."

"What can you do for her?"

The man thought about it. He thought about hanging up and forgetting that he had ever met Anthony Righetti. Then he looked at the newspaper clipping.

"How good of a friend is she?"

Anthony looked into Daphne's awestruck eyes. "We're very good friends. She's a good girl. She's got what it takes. She just needs to get before the right people."

"I've got friends at CNN who can give your friend a career boost."

"Good. I'll be in touch." Anthony put the phone in his pocket, crossed his leg, and pushed himself deeper into the soft leather. "Daphne, your call."

Daphne's head was spinning. This man really did know Walter Simmons. And what was it that Mr. Simmons had said? *He died of a heart attack, just like you said he would?* What kind of powers does this man have that he can make another man have a heart attack? She decided that if he had powers like this—which was doubtful, but he had something going on—and if he knew people like Walter Simmons, she would use him to help her career.

"Anthony, I'll be right back."

When Daphne came out of her bedroom, she was clothed with nothing but nature and implants. Anthony's back was turned to her.

"Anthony," she said softly.

He turned around.

She was expecting a smile, a look of lust, a weakening of the aura of power he exuded. She was expecting her nakedness to change him into a mere man, to put them on equal ground. But it did nothing.

He looked her up and down as though he was being delivered a package he had not ordered. She felt like a beggar in the presence of a king. He turned back to the window. "I want more than that." His voice was full of evil intentions.

Daphne was humiliated and confused. He had massaged her, sniffed her, but now that she was standing before him naked, he was rejecting her. A new wave of unexplainable fear swept over her. "What do you want?" she asked, now ashamed of her nakedness.

He turned around and looked her intently in the eyes. She felt something press against her abdomen and enter her when he said. "I want your soul."

*****

Daphne had never been as happy in her life to see someone leave her home as she was when he left. Anthony Righetti was beyond strange. He didn't want her body; he wanted her soul. Daphne was a pure thoroughbred materialist. She didn't believe she had a soul. So what did she have to lose by giving her soul to him in exchange for a once in a lifetime break?

Daphne called Rob Larkin. When he told her that he could not make it, she quickly sat down with nausea.

"I have a friend who wants to do the show," he said.

"Your friend wants to do the show? How could he want to do the show? You've just found out about it."

Rob Larkin laughed. He knew she would find this hard to believe. "I've known about this for two days. My friend told me you would contact me and ask me to do another show."

Daphne was befuddled. "But how could he have known?"

"God told him about it while he was in prayer." Rob had a smile on his face.

"In prayer? Who is this man?"

"His name is Jonathan Banks." Rob laughed. "If Atlanta liked me, they'll love Jonathan. He's a character."

Out of desperation, Daphne took the phone number and hung up. Her ship of hope crashed hard on the rocks. Atlanta wanted an encore of the Family versus Christianity, not some unknown nobody from Stone Mountain. So much could go wrong. What if Mr. Righetti didn't like the idea? What if the guy was a bore? Daphne punched the number. She had no choice.

Daphne let the telephone ring a couple of minutes and hung up. She let out a long breath of discouragement and looked at the ceiling.

The intercom buzzed and she bounced up.

"Yes?"

"Ms. Krugle, there's a gentleman here to see you."

She froze. Was it Mr. Righetti again?

"Who is it?" she asked nervously.

"Jonathan Banks."

Her mouth dropped open. *What's going on here?* she thought. This was crazy, but she had to go with it. "Send him up."

Daphne opened the door. "Come in, Mr. Banks. Won't you have a seat?"

Jonathan sat down. "You have a lovely place here, Ms. Krugle."

"Thank you. Mr. Banks, how did you find out where I lived?"

"God knows where everyone lives."

After Righetti, Daphne didn't know whether to take this man as a prophet or a kook. "Your friend, Rob, said that you wanted to debate Mr. Righetti. Is that correct?" She heard how silly her question sounded. Why else would he be here? "I mean, why do you want to debate this man?"

"I don't debate."

Daphne was flabbergasted. "I knew it." She stood up angrily and went to the large window that overlooked the mall. "I just knew it. If you don't debate, Mr. Banks, why are you here." The mist of professionalism was gone. Daphne saw her dream going up in smoke. Mr. Righetti was going to call Walter Simmons back only after she made him into a local hero. And how could she do that without the special?

"Sit down, Ms. Krugle."

She heard the authority in his voice. It was as compelling as the authority she had heard in Mr. Righetti, only without the dread. *What's with these guys?* She sat down.

"I don't debate; I demonstrate."

May as well go along with it, she thought. "What do you demonstrate, Mr. Banks?"

"The kingdom of God and the glory of His Son."

Daphne's expression hinted at her impatience. "I haven't the slightest idea what that means."

"I know you don't, Ms. Krugle. That's part of the reason why I'm here. What do you know about Christianity?"

"I really don't see the relevance of disclosing my personal convictions."

"That tells me one thing. You don't have any. Or at least you don't have any worth mentioning."

Daphne took that the way she heard it. "What qualifies you to judge me?"

"You do, Ms. Krugle. You don't understand the significance of your position. You're a pivotal player in the upcoming battle between good and evil."

"What battle? You mean the debate?"

"No. The debate is only a very small part of what God is doing. I am talking about a real battle between good and evil. Many lives are at stake."

"Isn't that a bit melodramatic, Mr. Banks?" Daphne asked condescendingly. "You talk like there is going to be actual conflict. A holy war."

Jonathan's eyes were stone. "There is."

"Uh huh."

"Worse than that, young lady. There is going to be judgment."

Daphne was amused. "You mean like Noah's Ark and the flood?"

"Yes."

Daphne's keen mind began to churn. Maybe this guy could cause a commotion. What if she got him to go public with these crazy predictions? There is a good chance that the networks would pick up on it.

"What makes you think these things will occur?"

"I had a vision."

Daphne smiled. "A vision?"

"Yes, a vision."

"What did you see in this vision, Mr. Banks?" she asked with overt ridicule.

"I saw your first debate."

"Was that before or after it aired?" she asked smartly.

"This is no game, Ms. Krugle. Thousands of people are going to die."

"Just a little levity, Mr. Banks. I'm sorry. Please go on."

Jonathan was clearly annoyed by Daphne's arrogance, but he knew that before he left, she would know that God had been there. "Your specials sparked a fire storm of controversy that turned into an inferno of death. Atlanta will be polarized into two camps: servants of Christ and servants of Satan. Those who resist the grace and mercy of God will be destroyed."

"How will they be destroyed?"

"Disease."

Daphne laughed out loud. "You're not the first preacher to predict the end of the world."

"Not the end of the world. The end of Atlanta. Or at least a good portion of it."

"Oh, oh, the end of Atlanta." Daphne shook her head unbelievingly. "I guess I need to put my condo up for sale."

"You have more pressing problems than your home."

Daphne tried to inconspicuously rub at the new pain in her lower chest. "And what would that be?" she asked, smiling.

"Your addiction to cocaine for one."

The smile disappeared.

"My what?" she asked, with an indignation she could barely pretend existed.

Jonathan walked towards her bedroom.

Daphne looked at him crookedly. This fool was waltzing into her bedroom. "What...what do you think you're doing? Get out of my home, Mr. Banks! Get out right now!"

He ignored her.

Daphne had had it with strangers marching into her home and taking over. She went for the phone.

Jonathan came back with her purse. He opened it and took out her case. Daphne watched in shock as he actually went into her purse and opened her cocaine container.

"This."

"I...how did...who?" she stammered guiltily.

"God told me."

All of the air went out of Daphne's balloon of arrogance. "God told you?"

"Yes, He did."

She thought about this for several moments. "But why?"

"Because He loves you. He wants you to stop destroying yourself with this poison."

"My father is a preacher," said Daphne, in a childlike tone. "I remember him screaming from the pulpit about the dangers of dope." She began to cry. "I never thought it would happen to me."

Jonathan hugged her.

"You can be set free, Daphne. All you have to do is cry out to God. Will you do it?"

"Mr. Banks, I can't," she sobbed. "I can't do without it. I need it. My job is so competitive and...."

Jonathan squeezed her shoulders and looked her directly in the eyes. "Do you want out?" His question sounded more like a demand than a question.

"I want to, but—"

"Do you want out?"

"I don't know if—"

He shook her. "Do you want out?"

"Yes. Yes," she cried.

Jonathan pulled her close and hugged her tightly. "It's going to be okay, Daphne. It's going to be okay." He sat her down and wiped her eyes.

She looked at him with desperate and fearful eyes. "Mr. Righetti was here earlier. He has some kind of spiritual power. I think he killed a man with it. He said he wanted my soul. I didn't see any harm in trading nothing for something; so I gave it to him." She rubbed her abdomen. "But something went into me when I did this." Daphne shook her head as she tried to make sense of this. "Can you help me?"

"Who do you want, Daphne? Jesus Christ or Satan?"

She knew that she didn't want Satan. "Jesus."

"Then, yes, I can help you." Jonathan placed his hand on her forehead. "Satan, I cancel this contract that Daphne made in ignorance with you. In Jesus' name, come out!"

Daphne doubled over as though she had been struck in the belly. She fell to her knees and coughed violently for several minutes. She felt like her guts were being pulled out of her mouth. At the same time, something was moving around inside of her head.

Daphne was on her hands and knees, breathing heavily, depleted. "Something's in my head. It says it's not going anywhere."

"Come out!" Jonathan ordered.

Daphne's whole body shook uncontrollably for nearly a minute. Suddenly, she went limp and hit the floor. Jonathan rubbed her face and sat in a chair. It was an hour before Daphne came to and tried to get up. Jonathan helped her to the sofa.

"How do you feel?"

Daphne didn't answer. She had never felt such peace. Her hands slowly raised above her head. Tears streamed down her face. "I love You. I love You. I love You," she said repeatedly, almost oblivious that she was not alone.

Jonathan waited for her to finish praying.

“Ms. Krugle?”

“I feel so light.”

"Ms. Krugle, I need you to go ahead with the debate. I'll be there. Just let me know when."

She wiped her eyes. "What about the disease? The vision you had."

Jonathan smiled. "I'll keep you posted."

He stepped into the hallway. She was both smiling and crying. She hugged Jonathan and cried some more. "Thank you, Mr. Banks."

"I'll send you my bill."

She slowly closed the door.

He took two steps and collapsed to one knee. He waited for the dizziness to leave and pushed the elevator button. *I have to go on.*

Chapter 29

Wallace parked the car in Edwin's driveway. He felt like an absolute idiot. Wasn't he the one who had so vigorously criticized faith healers? He was on record as saying they were all phony. And now he was about to ask the pastor to make a fool of himself. He turned to his wife.

"I am not going to do this!"

Marjorie didn't say anything. She just opened her door and went to the trunk. Wallace popped the trunk and she pulled out the wheelchair.

Wallace sat fuming.

Marjorie opened the back door to get Johnny. His condition had worsened considerably. Now not only could he not speak or hear; he couldn't walk either. Marjorie unfastened the seat buckle and pulled his legs.

"Are you going to help me, or am I going to have to drag our son on the ground?" she snapped.

Wallace wasn't used to being spoken to like that by anyone, especially his wife. But he knew he was in a no-win situation. He got out of the car and slammed the door. He walked around to her side.

"Get out of the way," he said gruffly. He put the boy in the wheelchair and pushed him to the door.

"Who is that?" Barbara called from the kitchen.

Sharon looked out of the window. Her eyebrows raised in surprise when she saw Johnny in a wheelchair. "It's Mr. and Mrs. Reynolds! Johnny's in a wheelchair!" she screamed to the back of the house.

"Oh, my God," said Barbara. She hurried to the door. "Edwin," she called, but he didn't hear her.

Edwin had not bathed or shaved or come out of his office since the funeral two days ago. Barbara and Sharon knew how hard Edwin was taking Christopher's death, so they didn't bother him. And Jessica going berserk at the funeral didn't help any. But this was an emergency.

Sharon knocked on his door, softly at first, then harder when he didn't answer. "Dad, Mr. and Mrs. Reynolds are here. Johnny's in a wheelchair!" She waited awhile and turned the door knob. It was locked. "Daddy, please come out. Mrs. Reynolds is crying." She waited, knocked again, and when he didn't answer, she left.

Edwin sat in a dark stupor. The light was off, both in his office and in his heart. If it was possible, he would never come out of his office again.

Barbara came to the door with a tiny screwdriver. She stuck it in the small hole on the door knob and it opened. She turned on the light. "Edwin, we need you out here. Wallace and Marjorie are here. Johnny's really sick. He can't talk or hear. He can't walk either. They have him in a wheelchair."

Edwin looked at Barbara with red eyes. "Tell them I have the day off," he said bitterly. "I'll get back to them at the next resurrection."

Barbara shook her head in disgust and slammed the door. "OOuuoooo!" she breathed out angrily. "That man is so weak!"

"Where is he?" Marjorie asked, when Barbara returned.

"He's been very sick since Christopher's death," she forced.

"What?" Marjorie exclaimed, hardly believing what she had heard.

Wallace was dumbfounded. He looked at his wife, then at Barbara. "When did this happen?"

"You didn't know?" asked Barbara.

"No," they both answered.

"We've been so tied up trying to find out what's wrong with Johnny that we haven't talked to anyone in the church," said Marjorie. "I'm so sorry. My God, we had no idea little Christopher was sick."

"We called several times, but no one answered," said Wallace. He was embarrassed that he was just learning of this tragedy. He was even more embarrassed that he was here to ask a man who had just lost his son to pray for his own.

He looked at his wife and gave her a strong hint. "You think maybe it would be a good idea to let our pastor and his family grieve the loss of their boy?"

Sharon stepped forward. "No, it's alright Mr. Reynolds. That's what the church is for. To help one another. Christopher is in heaven."

"Thank you, Sharon," Marjorie said graciously.

Yeah, thanks, Sharon, thought Wallace.

"Would you like some tea or coffee?" Sharon asked.

"Yes, thank you, Sharon. Coffee, please." Marjorie turned to her husband. "Would you like some?"

I'd like to get out of here. "No, I'm fine."

Sharon went to make the coffee. Wallace and Marjorie awkwardly, but sincerely, tried to express their sympathy. Finally, they reached a point where there was nothing else that could be said that hadn't already been said.

"Barbara, I know this is not a good time to ask. In fact, it's a terrible time to ask. But we would like Edwin to pray for our son to be healed."

Wallace cringed at his wife's request. Wouldn't Edwin have healed his own son if he had any healing powers? Wallace saw the surprise in Barbara's eyes. "I tried to tell her that this is ridiculous."

"I'll go ask him," Sharon said and left the room.

Wallace cringed tighter.

Sharon knocked on the door. "Daddy, we need you out here." Her voice was resolute. "These people are hurting, too."

No answer.

"Do we have to call Reverend Banks to get a man of God?"

The door opened.

Sharon hugged her father. "I'm sorry I said that, Daddy. But they need help. You're the pastor. They don't have anyone else."

Edwin and Sharon walked into the great room.

"Oh, thank God!" said Marjorie. "Reverend Styles, we're so sorry to disturb you in your time of grief. We had no idea that...well, of this situation. We would've come over sooner." Marjorie looked at her husband, who didn't give her eye contact. He was trying to be invisible. "Johnny is really sick, and we'd like you to pray for him. We know this is terrible timing, but we're at wits end."

Edwin didn't mean to look so cold, but he did. "Funny how humble we get when we need something," he said.

The doorbell rang.

"I'll get it," said Sharon, relieved to leave the room.

Wallace glanced at his wife, then at Edwin. "That was uncalled for."

There was a slight snarl on Edwin's face. "What do you want?" he asked coolly.

"I want you to pray for my son?" Marjorie answered humbly.

"Pray for him yourself," Edwin said dryly. "You're a big girl."

He turned to leave the room and Wallace grabbed his arm. "You can't talk to my wife like that!"

"Get your hand off of me or I'll break every bone in your miserable body," Edwin said through clenched teeth.

Wallace quickly removed his hand.

"Pastor, please," Marjorie begged.

"I'm not your pastor. I quit."

He turned to walk away.

"Edwin."

He stopped in mid step and slowly turned around.

Jonathan!

He walked up to Jonathan and swung at his face. Jonathan had enough time to move so that it wasn't a solid blow. It glanced off the side of his jaw and knocked him off balance. He fell over a lamp and broke it.

"Daddy!" Sharon screamed and ran to Jonathan. "What's wrong with you? He's your friend!"

Everyone was stunned.

Wallace helped Jonathan to his feet, while he kept his eyes on Edwin.

Jonathan rubbed his face and looked soberly at Edwin. "What are you going to do, beat up everyone who has the guts to preach the truth? You're not mad at me. You're mad at yourself."

Edwin stood there empty. Emotionally, he couldn't care less about Jonathan's logic. Or anyone's logic. He was tired of logic. But he knew that Jonathan was right. Shame replaced his anger. His head dropped. "I'm sorry. I...I didn't mean...." He fell to his knees. "I'm a failure," he said, barely above a whisper. "I've failed at everything."

Jonathan got on his knees. He put his arm around his shoulders. "Not yet. The battle's just begun. Everything up to this point has been to prepare you to lead God's army."

Marjorie waited until they stood. "Edwin, will you please pray for our son?"

Edwin looked at Johnny and then Marjorie. "I can't," he said weakly, his faith too small to meet the challenge.

"Will you, Reverend Banks?" Marjorie asked.

"No."

Everyone looked at him with surprise.

"Why not?" asked Edwin.

Before he could answer, Marjorie reached into her purse and pulled out a gun and pointed it at Jonathan.

"Give me that thing," said her husband.

She backed up and pointed it at him. "Stay right there!"

He froze.

"Reverend Banks, you're going to pray for my son."

"I'll pray for your son under one condition."

"What?"

"Your church is having a musical tonight."

"So."

"So I'll pray for him there."

"No way!" said Wallace.

"Shut up!" Marjorie ordered. "Okay, Reverend Banks." She backed up some more so that no one could jump her. "Put Johnny in the car," she said to no one in particular.

They put him in the car. Marjorie got in the back with her son. Wallace and Jonathan rode up front.

"Shouldn't we call the police?" said Barbara, as they followed close behind.

"No," said Edwin. "Everything's going to turn out fine. Marjorie's not going to hurt anyone. She just wants her son healed."

When they arrived at the church, there were few parking spaces. Their church was famous in Atlanta for their quality musicals. It seemed that this evening everyone wanted to see their latest production. Edwin knew that the majority of these people were visitors. Most of his own members had deserted the church.

Wallace found a parking space. Jonathan said to Marjorie, "You can put the gun away now. We're here."

"Please, Reverend Banks," she pleaded.

"I give you my word. I'll pray for your son."

"Get Johnny out of the car first." She didn't trust her husband.

Jonathan got out of the car, but Wallace sat tight. Gun or no gun, he wasn't going in there to make a fool of himself.

"Get out of the car, Wallace!" Marjorie demanded. "You are not going to doom my son to a wheelchair for the rest of his life!"

Wallace didn't budge.

Jonathan didn't say anything. He wasn't taking any unnecessary chances with an armed hysterical lady.

Marjorie put the barrel of the gun to her husband's neck. "So help me God, I'll blow your brains out." Her voice was low and dangerous.

The cold steel against Wallace's skin made him shiver. He looked into his rear view mirror without moving. *She's serious!* he thought. He popped the trunk and set up the wheelchair.

Jonathan reached for the boy and heard a gurgling sound in the boy's throat. "Your days are numbered," he muttered under his breath to the spirit. He put him in the wheelchair and they all went inside.

Edwin, Barbara, and Sharon were only a minute behind them.

*****

The thick mist began to dissipate. Kre'ah, Mudillus's replacement, moved his head from side to side in an effort to get a better view of who the stragglers were. His red eyes widened. A pang of terror shot through his wretched body. Jonathan!

"Tell the others," hissed Kre'ah to a panic stricken soldier.

Everywhere along the perimeter of the church nervous demons prepared for battle. They knew that if Jonathan was here, there would be trouble, big trouble.

*****

Wallace stood by himself as Edwin and the others whispered among themselves.

"Jonathan," said Edwin, "if Harry or any of the ushers see you, you'll never make it in. The ushers are standing in the back." He pointed to the doors to the main sanctuary. "You'll have to make it past them." He glanced at the men's restroom. "You and Johnny wait in the bathroom. Barbara will tell you when to come in."

Jonathan smiled at Edwin. "Did you ever play high school football?"

"High school and college."

"What position?"

"Quarterback," said Edwin.

Jonathan smiled broader. "Figures." He rolled the boy past his father's staring eyes.

"Barbara," said Edwin, "I want you to keep your eyes glued to the window. When you see the lights come on, tell Jonathan to take Johnny to the front of the church."

Barbara didn't know why she felt such love and respect well up inside of her for her husband. She looked him in the eyes with a softness he hadn't seen in her in a long time. She gently stroked his face and said, "I love you."

This momentarily stunned Edwin. He pulled her to himself and kissed her passionately. "I love you, too, honey."

Oh, brother, thought Wallace.

"Sharon."

"Yes, Daddy!" She bounced with excitement. "What do you want me to do?"

"Sharon, I'm going to show you where the fuse box is for the sanctuary and the production." He took her down a long hallway to a small utility closet. He looked at his watch. "Honey, what time do you have?"

"Seven thirty-seven."

"Change it to seven thirty-four." She did. "At seven forty-five turn off this line of lights and turn on these."

"Okay," Sharon answered as though they were playing a game.

Edwin knew the side door entrance closest to the stage was blocked, so he went in through the foyer doors.

Barbara smiled admiringly as he went into the sanctuary.

It was dark inside, except for the stage. Edwin greeted an usher and walked up front to the reserved pew. He sat next to Larry McGuire.

"Hello, Larry," Edwin said, speaking away from his friend, cognizant that he hadn't brushed his teeth in two days.

"Hi, Ed," Larry greeted him warmly. "Good to see you out." Larry's face turned sober. "I'm sorry about what happened at the funeral. That was terrible. I wish I could've gotten to her sooner. She—"

"That's okay, Larry. You did more than enough, and I appreciate it." He glanced at his watch and looked to the back. He saw Barbara's head appear, then disappear.

"How's your wife?" Larry whispered.

"Fine. She's doing fine."

The production lights went out abruptly, leaving the sanctuary pitch black. Then all the sanctuary lights came on. The choir stopped singing in confused embarrassment. Some of the smaller children on stage began to cry.

Edwin hopped up and jumped onto the stage and grabbed a microphone.

Barbara saw the lights go off, then on. Edwin was on stage. She felt a rush of adrenaline. She ran to the men's bathroom and burst through the door. "They're on!"

Jonathan hurried with the boy past Wallace, who was glaring at his wife. Barbara opened the door. "Here goes!" said Jonathan, and ran down the middle aisle with Johnny in the wheelchair.

The first usher he passed took off after him.

"Leave him alone!" ordered Edwin from the stage.

The man stopped in his tracks.

The sight of a black man running down the center aisle with a white boy in a wheelchair shocked the dignified crowd of spectators.

"Nobody leaves!" said Edwin. He saw a lady making her way to the door. "That goes for you, too!"

She stopped and took her seat.

"I have a confession to make to all of you," said Edwin. I've sinned against you, and I've sinned against God. I've sinned against you by preaching a watered down version of the gospel. I let my own prejudices and fears keep me from speaking the truth.

"I've sinned against God by letting men like Harry Thompson and Billy Mitchell intimidate and control me. I let those men and others like them use me to turn this church into a cemetery. For that I am sorry.

"My sins against you are unforgivable. Effective immediately, I resign from the pastorate of this church. I pray to God that He gives you someone who will lead you into the fullness of His purity and power.

"But first, my good friend, Jonathan Banks—"Jonathan smiled and waved to the crowd—"is going to pray for Johnny Reynolds. Some of you know this little fellow. We don't know what's wrong with him. He can't talk or hear or walk. Jonathan..."

"Mrs. Reynolds, come up front," Jonathan called.

She did.

He placed his hand on her back. "This lady's son has been attacked by evil spirits...demons. If nothing is done to dislodge these spirits, the boy will die. How many of you want to see this boy die? And, yet, most of you, maybe all of you, are offended at those of us who pray for the sick and cast out demons!

"I'm going to tell you something: this boy isn't going to be prayed for until every one of you tell me that you want this boy prayed for. If you don't—"he pointed at the crowd—"I'm going home and this boy will die...tonight!"

An old man yelled out best he could, "Pray for him!"

Edwin looked to see who that was. Terrance Knox. Praise God!

*****

"For the glory of God and the sons of men!" the angel shouted.

Kre'ah's eyes bulged with horror. They were surrounded by thousands upon thousands of warring angels. He knew there was no escape. And even if there was, he would not have chosen it. Better to face the host of heaven than the Mighty Bashnar.

*****

A couple of minutes passed. Here and there people timidly began to say, "Pray for him." Soon it seemed that everyone in the church was shouting, "Pray for him! Pray for him! Pray for him!"

Jonathan motioned for the congregation to quiet down.

"I am not going to pray for this child. Your pastor will." He turned to look at a thoroughly shocked Edwin Styles.

"Jonathan?"

"Blitz, quarterback," he said with a toothy smile.

Edwin didn't move. He was frozen with fear.

"You can do this, Edwin," said Jonathan. "Remember the lady you prayed for."

"That was different."

“No difference, Edwin. You can do this. You have to do this. It has to be you.”

Edwin forced himself off of the platform. His knees trembled badly. He looked at the boy. He looked at the congregation. *What if nothing happens?* he thought. He looked at Jonathan for encouragement. He found it in his eyes. Edwin stretched both his arms by his sides and nervously stepped up to the boy.

Two angels descended through the roof and landed in front of Edwin. One of them held a black potbellied container. The other angel had a golden dipper and a jewelry embellished sword.

The angel with the sword lifted it with two hands and cut through Edwin several times.

"Death," a Voice bellowed from the heavens.

The angel with the golden dipper removed the lid from the container. Steam emitted from the bubbling liquid. He filled the dipper and poured it onto Edwin's head. He did this until all of the liquid was gone.

"Life," the same Voice bellowed.

Edwin's face tightened, then relaxed. He felt a hotness come over him. Beads of sweat dripped profusely down his face. It was like standing under a deluge of hot lava. The hot liquid raced through every inch of his spirit, soul, and body. He felt like he had bones of fire!

Edwin gripped the boy's head. "Come out of him!" he thundered.

The response was immediate. "We won't come out! We won't come out! We won't—"

The boy's body convulsed violently and fell to the floor, wriggling and contorting. Edwin instinctively backed up a few feet. He quickly recovered himself, however, and stepped forward. "Come out!" he ordered again.

The body rose horizontally five feet off the floor and slammed back down. It caused a sickening sound. There was no movement. The boy appeared to be dead.

Edwin was as stunned as everyone else who had seen this...whatever it was. What should he do? His first thought was to look to Jonathan. But he made himself not turn around. It wasn’t easy! He took the boy by the hand and held it for a minute or so. What else could he do? At least this way he could buy some time and try to figure out what to do next.

Johnny began to move. He opened his eyes. "Where's Mom?"

"Johnny!" Marjorie shouted.

Pandemonium broke out. Several people ran to the front of the church screaming, "Save me, Lord!"

Edwin led them to Christ in a mass prayer. But he and Jonathan also prayed for some people individually.

"There are still six people in here who need to come clean with God," said Jonathan. "Five women and one man. You will repent of your sin of adultery...now, tonight, or die before the congregation of the Lord."

Total silence.

Suddenly, a lady bolted towards the front and fought her way through the crowd. She buried her face into Edwin's chest. "I'm sorry. I'm sorry." She was crying. "I never planned to hurt you. You have to believe me, Ed. I never wanted to hurt you."

Edwin said nothing. He couldn't. His arms were weak around his wife's trembling body. He slowly shook his head in denial. There was some mistake. Spiritual adultery. That was it. She was feeling guilty about something. Edwin shook his head more vigorously as he convinced himself that his wife could not have literally committed adultery. There simply was no way.

Barbara looked up into the face of her stunned husband. Surprisingly, he felt no anger, only pity for what his wife had suffered. Ed placed his faced next to hers. Their tears mingled. Edwin spoke with a strength he knew was foreign. "It's not your fault. It's all mine. If I would have obeyed God, none of this would have happened."

One by one, the other ladies came to the front. Not as dramatically as did Barbara, but they came.

Jonathan waited five more minutes and stepped off the stage. "These five ladies have all committed terrible sins against their families and their God, but they're forgiven. They've confessed their sins before us all. But the man who seduced them refuses to come forward."

Looking at the crowd, Jonathan walked to where Larry was seated. Beads of panicky sweat rolled down Larry's face. He tried to look as normal and innocent as possible.

Jonathan stood directly over Larry. He looked over the preacher's head to the congregation. Larry fought to control his bladder.

"I am going to count to ten. If the gentleman who seduced these precious ladies hasn't revealed himself by then, I'll do it for him."

Larry put his head in his hands. *I can't go forward. I'd lose my job.*

"Six...."

Maybe he doesn't know it's me.

"Nine...."

I can't do it!

"Ten."

Jonathan looked into Larry's eyes with fiery indignation.

"You filthy child of the devil! You enemy of all righteousness! How dare you tempt the Lord thy God! This very night your soul will be required of you!"

Larry jumped up with indignation of his own. "What's the meaning of this? You can't come in here and destroy my good name! I'll sue you for everything you have!"

He turned and stormed down the aisle. Suddenly, his eyes were opened. What he saw stopped him in mid stride, his leg still lifted off the floor. He stood there on one leg, gaping at the dark mist that blocked his way. The terror that filled his soul shut down his senses. He was in a mental tunnel. Only he and the horrifying mist were in it. Nothing else existed.

But his fixation on the mist was not on its dread. There was something else about this...thing that mesmerized Larry. Somehow he knew that the mist was a person, some kind of evil entity. But it was also a window of some sort. For when he looked into the mist, he could see events happening. Some were single events. Others were episodes of history. Single murders. Entire wars. Heart attacks.

Abortions. Accidents. Plagues. Inexplicably, he recognized every face he saw and knew the unknown facts that surrounded each death he witnessed in the mist. Death! *This mist was death.*

Larry pushed his foot to the floor.

"Larry!" he heard a voice summoning him out of the tunnel.

Larry blinked hard several times, shaking his head. The mist was still there, moving neither forward nor backward. It seemed to be waiting for something. Larry was able to tear his eyes away from the mist and look in the direction of the voice. It was that blasted preacher.

"Larry!"

Their eyes met.

"You have to repent. You have to come clean." Larry didn't hear the arrogance in Jonathan he had heard before. Now the man sounded scared. "This is it. Larry, remember Noah. Remember Lot's wife. You don't have tomorrow."

Larry was on a fifty-mile-per-hour merry-go-round. He was dizzy with troubling thoughts. He looked at the women who had answered Jonathan's call to repent of adultery. Each of them had come to him for help and he had helped himself. These women would no doubt recover. They'd cry and whimper and play the part of the helpless victim and conveniently leave out the details of sex toys, lap dances, and *Frederick's of Hollywood*. Everyone would rally around these kinky little nuns. He on the other hand would never be able to climb out of this hole. This time he had dug it too deep.

The merry-go-round spun faster. What about his wife? After the last time Holly had caught him with another woman, she had told him in no uncertain terms that if he ever pulled that crap again, she would not only divorce him and move back home to Australia with the children, but she would do everything she could to destroy him. She had enough on him to do this ten times over.

Larry looked around the church building. Every eye was focused on him. Some filled with curiosity. Others, he was sure, were filled with judgment. Then he saw one face that sealed his fate. Holly. He exhaled and smiled with resignation.

"Larry?" Jonathan implored.

Larry looked at Jonathan. He said nothing, but Jonathan saw it in his eyes. Jonathan grimaced and slowly walked back to his seat and sat down. He didn't want to see this. He put his elbows on his knees, closed his eyes, and held his head in his hands.

Larry turned resolutely away from Jonathan...away from it all. He looked at the only path he could take. The mist darkened. Its smoke danced excitedly from side to side. Larry stared into its black essence and saw his own story. He inhaled and exhaled deeply and slowly walked his path. He took three steps and dropped dead.

The coroner's report would later list the final diagnosis as rupture of berry aneurysm of Circle of Willis with massive left subdural hematoma, subarachnoid hemorrhage, and secondary pontine hemorrhages. The classification of death would be identified as natural causes.

The congregation was awestruck. Many people were so shaken by God's judgment on Larry that they rushed the altar and fell on their faces. Some cried. Others wailed. Many shook uncontrollably. Even among those who sat riveted to their pews was there behavior that could only be classified as odd. Spontaneous screams. Grown men crying like babies. Professionals rocking back and forth, holding their bellies and mumbling what sounded like gibberish.

Hours elapsed before the crowd began to thin out. It was well after three o'clock in the morning before the last person left. Jonathan and Edwin were exhausted. They sat on the edge of the stage totally depleted. They were empty.

Barbara and Sharon sat on the carpeted floor near the steps to the stage. Wallace and Marjorie sat on the steps. They couldn't discuss enough of what they had seen.

Wallace was stuck on seeing his son levitate and having demons cast out of him. "I have to serve Him. I have to serve Him," he repeated several times. "Can you believe that? Our boy just...." Wallace motioned with his hand to show how Johnny had floated.

Jonathan and Edwin sat at the opposite end of the stage steps. "You know...." Jonathan stopped in mid-sentence and stared at Edwin.

Edwin smiled weakly. He was so tired. "What? Why are you looking at me like that?"

He grabbed Edwin by the arm. "Come on. We have to talk." He took him to the back of the church. "Edwin, you're being oppressed by a demon."

Edwin chuckled. "After tonight...no, I don't think so," he joked.

"No, I'm serious brother. There's a demon on your neck."

When Edwin saw that Jonathan was serious, he said, "Well, get it off!"

"Let's pray." Jonathan took both of Edwin's hands and prayed for several minutes. But he didn't command the spirit to leave. He felt that God wanted to do something else. As he prayed, he saw a little boy being sexually molested by an elderly man. The vision disappeared.

"Edwin, tell me about the little boy."

"Little boy? What little boy?"

"I saw a man having sex with a little boy."

Edwin's knees went weak. He stared at Jonathan with his mouth wide open.

"Tell me about it," Jonathan asked.

"Jonathan, that little boy is me," he said, through a throat constricted with emotional pain. "My uncle sexually abused me as a child. I never told anyone. He said that if I did, no one would believe me." Tears rolled down Edwin's face as he recounted what happened.

"Jonathan, recently I've been having...like nightmares, only I'm not sleep. Whenever I try to make love to my wife something happens. I can't...I can't do it. This voice tells me that I'm not a man, that I liked what my uncle did."

Jonathan waited until he felt Edwin was ready to be prayed for again. He put his hand on his head and said simply, "In the name of Jesus, I free my brother from this harassing spirit and from all thoughts of perversion."

The little demon flinched defensively when Jonathan put his hand on Edwin's head. His three eyes darted in every direction, looking for—

ZAP!

A lightning bolt of heavenly power burned him to a crisp.

Edwin shook his head.

"The tightness is gone. It used to feel like I had a permanent head cold." He shook his head some more. "It's gone. I felt it pop like a balloon. Jonathan," he beamed, "just like that? Just like that? I'm free?"

Jonathan squeezed Edwin's shoulder. "Just like that, Edwin. Just like that."

*****

Harry Thompson had left the church in disgust right after Edwin prayed for the Wallace's son. He punched the telephone number.

"Hello. Mr. Righetti, we have a problem."

Chapter 30

Bashnar could hardly believe his pointed ears. Idiots! How could they have let this happened? Must he do everything himself?

"Dismissed," he told the courier.

The spirit was so nervous that his legs didn't move.

"Get out of here!" roared Bashnar.

This time they moved effortlessly.

Bashnar paced back and forth. Low growls of rage emitted from his mouth. He looked at Jonathan's picture and exploded in volcanic fury. His roar shook the walls. Some of the pictures of fallen preachers fell to the floor. Those that didn't fall to the floor, he slapped off the wall.

Outside his office demons scattered to other sections of the huge fortress.

"I have had it with this bungling bureaucracy!" Bashnar fumed, as he punched a hole in the wall. This was the greatest defeat of his illustrious career. *How could they have allowed such a dead church to break out in revival?* he wondered contemptuously. How could the Council have assigned only one thousand demons to guard the church? Any idiot knew that no less than fifty thousand should have been used, with several lines of defense. Then it dawned on him. *I've been set up! The chairman of the Council set me up! Now I'm fighting enemies inside and out!*

There was only one thing left to do.

Bashnar called an emergency meeting.

The rumors were already out that Bashnar's days were numbered. Jonathan's successful attack on their church, and the amazing transformation of Edwin Styles, was too much for the Council to overlook.

"Quiet!" ordered Bashnar.

The whisperings ceased.

"The dagger, Jonathan, has treacherously destroyed our stronghold. The church is now occupied by the forces of God."

There were gasps in the audience. Many had hoped that the rumors were false. But, now, to hear it from Bashnar himself....

"This is a grave reversal, my colleagues. Many of you have never seen a real revival, and therefore are ignorant of its dangers. Ordinarily, we have been able to give the church substitutes for revival. A musical. A special speaker. A three-night stand. But this is different. This is real. "Real revival brings people face to face with the holiness of God. It penetrates the darkness of sin and cuts away our perversions."

Bashnar looked earnestly at the anxious faces.

"Our power, authority, and influence over this region is in direct proportion to the level of holiness and devotion to God the church exhibits. As they grow weaker, we grow stronger. As they grow stronger—"he paused to give his words added effect—"we grow weaker.

"We have only one chance to stop this revival from driving us from this region: Anthony Righetti and his pathetic Family. I order all of you to serve this man like a slave serves his master. Give him whatever he wants. He's our only hope."

*****

"You did a superb job, my friend," Rashti told Trin.

"Thank you, sir."

"Sit down, Trin.

He sat.

Rashti's eyes were alive with excitement.

"Trin, if this revival catches on in Atlanta, there's a good chance it will be spared judgment."

"And if not, sir?"

The excitement died.

"Then the plague hits," Rashti said sullenly.

"Sir, even if the revival does spread throughout the city, do you think Atlanta will repent?"

Trin saw pain in the captain's face.

"I don't know."

*****

"Mr. Righetti, what are we going to do? We can't let this go unchecked. You should've seen it," said Harry, his voice quivering with fear.

Anthony poured another cup of coffee and took a sip. He looked across the small breakfast table at Harry. "It must have been a sight," he said matter-of-factly.

"It was. It was. I've never seen anything like that. Such power!"

"You sound frightened, Harry." Anthony was smiling slightly, but his eyes were intense with displeasure.

Harry started to agree, but he caught himself. "No. No. Not at all! It's just that, uhhh...I've never seen anything like that before."

"Power impresses you."

"Why, uhh, yes, Mr. Righetti," Harry answered humbly.

Anthony drank some more coffee and sat back in the chair. "Something has happened to me, Harry."

"What's that, Mr. Righetti?"

"Power, Harry. I woke up this morning with...power." Anthony's eyes sparkled evilly. "I feel the darkness of hell. I feel the power of hell, spirits all around me, waiting to serve me, to do whatever I command."

Harry said nothing.

"Would you like a demonstration of this power?"

"No," Harry answered quickly.

"Ahh, but power impresses you, Harry. You said so yourself. And I want to impress every member of the Family. I want them to know that it is better to be with me than against me."

Harry felt hot breathing on the back of his neck. Startled, he turned around. No one was there. "Mr. Righetti," he smiled nervously, "you don't have to prove your point with me. I believe you."

More breathing. Hot. Heavy. Smelly.

Harry moved his head back and forth as though he was being irritated by a fly. "Really, Mr. Righetti, I believe you. Make it stop. You don't have to do this."

Anthony examined his nails. Time to get them done again.

Heavy, hot breathing...hot breathing on his neck.

Harry rubbed his neck vigorously. He flinched when something touched it. "Mr. Righetti!"

The demon grabbed Harry by his old throat.

He fell backwards to the floor, holding the invisible hand that choked him. The veins in his face stood out. He desperately fought and clawed, but the hand wouldn't let go. His eyes bulged as the weight of his predicament drained his hope.

"You see, Harry, the Family is forever. It is not for weak people who are easily frightened. Am I making myself clear?"

Harry nodded his head.

"Can I count on you?"

He nodded his head again.

"Good."

The hand let go of Harry's throat. He rolled over to his side, gasping for air.

Anthony spoke to Harry as he put his cup in the sink. "Don't worry about what you saw last night. I'll take care of them the same way I took care of you."

*****

It was one o'clock in the afternoon, but Edwin was the first one out of bed. He fixed himself a cup of coffee and got the Sunday paper off of the porch.

Barbara joined him shortly. She hugged him from behind and nibbled on his ear. "That was worth the wait" she whispered. "I thought you were tired."

He smiled. "I was."

"I'm going to get a shower. Care to join me, Samson?" she teased.

"Don't tempt me, Delilah." He smiled as he watched her walk away. She was a good woman. *Deliverance ministry*. The thought bubbled up inside of him. A simple command of faith had freed him from the demon that had been tormenting him and making him impotent. Now because of Jonathan, no, because of deliverance ministry, exercising authority over demons, he had his life back. What else was he overlooking or ignoring in the Bible?

Edwin looked at the front page of the *Atlanta Journal Constitution*. "What!" He jumped up and snatched the paper from the table. There was a picture of him at last night's church service. It showed him casting the devil out of a levitating boy.

Edwin could not believe the headline: **LOCAL EXORCIST CASTS OUT DEVIL.** Exorcist. They were calling him an exorcist. He raced through the article. "Ghostbusters...conservative church...musical...Pentecostal camp meeting...hellfire and brimstone...shocking departure from this denomination's doctrinal position...Reverend Styles will become a tourist attraction." Tourist attraction? He kept reading. "The ancient art of exorcising evil spirits prominently displayed...Reverend Edwin Styles prayed for the boy...body apparently flew several feet into the air and slammed down onto the floor...Voices other than his own came from the child's mouth...Hundreds of people ran forward to the altar begging for prayer...Either the Reverend Styles is a genuine exorcist, or he's the religious world's David Copperfield."

Edwin put the paper down and laughed. He looked at the picture again and laughed harder.

Sharon walked into the kitchen. "What's so funny?" she asked, beginning to laugh herself.

Edwin held his stomach. "Look...look..." He couldn't stop laughing.

Sharon picked up the paper. "Daddy, you're in the paper!" Sharon quickly read the article and ran out of the room. "Mom, Dad's in the newspaper!" she screamed.

The telephone rang and Edwin answered, still laughing. "Hello."

Silence.

"Hello," Edwin repeated.

"You and that nigger friend of yours are dead meat."

Edwin sobered.

"What? Who is this? Who—?"

Click.

Barbara and Sharon came into the kitchen.

"What's wrong, Dad?" asked Sharon, when she saw the grim look on his face.

"Someone called and said that Jonathan and I are dead meat."

"Just someone playing on the telephone," said Sharon.

"No, no, this was real."

"Why would anyone want to hurt you and Jonathan?" asked his wife with a worried look.

"I don't know."

*****

Another telephone call.

"Hello," said Edwin.

"Styles," the raspy voice said, "have you thought about what I told you?"

"What are you talking about?"

"A knife in your heart, Christian, if you ever preach again."

"What—?"

Click.

*****

Jonathan heard his wife scream in the bathroom. He ran upstairs and slammed open the shower door. Glass shattered. Elizabeth was crouched, still screaming, and covering her face. Jonathan touched her arm and she went berserk. She fought and clawed him without looking up. "Elizabeth, it's me. It's me," he said.

Finally, she heard her husband's voice. She looked up with terror-filled eyes. Her speech was incoherent.

He got on his knees and hugged her tightly. "It's okay. It's okay." Her body shook with fear. "What's wrong, baby?"

"A man...."

Jonathan glanced around.

"Where? In here?" he asked anxiously.

"Yes. Yes," she cried. "He had blood all over him. It was dripping all over."

Jonathan looked at the floor. He didn't see blood anywhere. But his wife was terrified. She had seen something. A chill ripped through Jonathan's body. *Haiti! This happened to us in Haiti,* he recalled. "Elizabeth, get dressed. We need to get all the saints together. Do you remember Haiti?" he asked, knowing that horrid experience was forever etched in her mind.

"Yes...oh, God, no! I can't go through that again."

"That's why we have to get out of here."

*****

Edwin let the doorbell ring several times before he went to answer it. The curtains and blinds were all closed and all of the lights were off. He peeked out of the window. It was Jonathan and Elizabeth. He quickly opened the door and pulled them inside and locked the door.

"What's going on here?" asked Jonathan.

"Get away from the window," Edwin told him. "Strange things have been happening. Sharon poured some cereal into a bowl and maggots came out. Barbara went to the closet and was attacked by a skeleton." He blushed at how silly and unbelievable he sounded. "I know it sounds crazy. I didn't see anything, but I know it must've happened. It's not a coincidence that both of them saw something."

Elizabeth turned away from the others and grimaced. Jonathan pulled her to him. "That's why we're here," he said. "You're right, those weren't coincidences."

"Were they real?" asked Sharon.

"They were demons," said Elizabeth.

"Demons?" gasped Barbara and Sharon.

"Yeah," answered Jonathan. "I first saw this sort of thing in Haiti. Satan's power in Haiti is incredibly strong. I've seen the voodoo priests there do amazing things. Ordinarily these kinds of demonic manifestations don't happen in our so-called enlightened nations."

"So why is it happening here?" asked Sharon.

"I don't know, Sharon. It could be because the saints here don't pray enough. It could be because Satan sees that revival is coming. I don't know. But one thing is certain. This kind of power is only given to people who are totally sold out to Satan."

"Jonathan, what's the Family?"

"Where did you hear about the Family?" Jonathan asked, alarmed.

"Someone's been call—"

RING!

Everyone froze.

"Let me get it," said Jonathan. He picked up the phone.

"Hello."

"You and your black friend are as good as dead," said the man.

"I have a lot of black friends. Which one are you talking about?"

This confused the caller. There was silence on the other end. "Who is this?" the man asked.

"A servant of God."

"Which servant of God?" the voice demanded.

"Jonathan," he answered the caller. Jonathan heard muffled talk in the background.

"You're dead, Jonathan!"

"I've been told that before."

Click.

"What did he say?" Edwin asked.

"Nothing original. Everyone sit down. We need to go over some details."

Everyone but Sharon sat down. She got them all something to drink. Jonathan waited until she was seated. "We've all been through a lot." He slapped Edwin on the leg. "Haven't we, brother?"

Edwin smiled ambivalently.

"But we're not through yet. Edwin, you asked about the Family. It's a satanic cult run by a man named Anthony Righetti. It's my guess that it was one of his spirit friends that ate Sharon's Apple Jacks."

"Fruit Loops," she corrected.

"How do you eat that stuff?"

"With milk."

Jonathan looked at Edwin. "Oh, she's bright."

"A regular comedian," Edwin added.

"I saw a vision," Jonathan stated routinely.

"You mean like in the Bible?" Sharon asked.

"Just like in the Bible, Sharon."

"Hey, cool," she added.

"I saw a terrible thing. I saw an outbreak of some kind of weird disease hit Atlanta. Tens of thousands of people died."

"My God," muttered Barbara. She was now an earnest believer in whatever Jonathan said.

"But before that happens God will give Atlanta a chance to repent. He always gives us a chance to repent before He judges us for our sins." Jonathan drank some of his tea. "Satan has raised up the Family to frustrate the grace of God. He doesn't want these people to repent."

"What can we do to stop the Family?" Edwin asked.

"I'm going to have a debate with their leader on live television. I don't know what's going to happen, but whatever it is, it's going to polarize good and evil. There will be a clear separation between the two. And if the majority of Atlanta repents, God will spare the city."

No one said anything for a long while. Suddenly, Sharon jumped up.

"That's Toni's father!"

Chapter 31

Anthony Righetti campaigned in Atlanta and the surrounding communities with the fervor of a zealot. His Family, which now numbered in the thousands, passed out flyers by the tens of thousands. His face could be seen on television commercials and billboards, his voice heard on radio, and his phenomenal charisma seen in the conviction of the growing masses that followed him.

He spoke at Piedmont Park and the police estimated the crowds at twenty-two thousand people. They stood in the cold drizzle to listen to a man unfold the glories of self-appreciation and self-indulgence. He extolled the right of women to abort their babies. He criticized the Christian church as a bunch of pie-in-the-sky hypocrites who were criminally insensitive to the plight of females who made such choices. He vigorously defended alternate lifestyles. "Who gave the church the right to tell you what to do with your body?" he asked the crowd. Their response was frenzied enthusiasm. In a few short days everyone in Atlanta knew Anthony Righetti and his Family.

In response, a heavenly mandate was given. *Hold back nothing! Use everything at your disposal to do a quick work in Atlanta!*

Myriads of angels from all over the world were dispatched to Atlanta to reinforce the army already there. Warriors, praisers, worshippers, helpers, healers, couriers, mercy angels and more. They came until there were over ten million of the heavenly host.

Captain Rashti sat upon a white stallion. His eyes burned with the fire of God. He lifted his sword. "For the glory of God and the sons of man!"

And the battle began.

The church's response to Rhigetti's direct attack was at first lazy indifference. But an unprecedented miracle happened. Almost overnight God raised up pastors and gave them courage to boldly speak His Word. Baptists, Methodists, Presbyterians, Pentecostals, Lutherans, and others, all took their religion to the streets. There were a number of nasty confrontations between Righetti's supporters and the church.

A pregnant Christian woman became the first martyr of this movement. She was shot and killed by a drunken skinhead. The lady was the wife of a Baptist pastor who had a very large church and television ministry in Atlanta. Her spilled blood fueled the Christian fire of protest.

Tens of thousands of Christians flooded the downtown and midtown districts with signs demanding the city government to take a stand for righteousness. Surprisingly, this lasted for days. Some were there because of the murdered pregnant lady. Others were there because Rhigetti was so strident in his attacks on pro-lifers. Many were appalled at his militant defense of homosexuality. Still others were there because Rhighetti was the personification of everything they considered evil. He was like the antichrist. Only he wasn't in the Bible. He was in Atlanta.

The mayor assigned hundreds of police to patrol these areas. Not to be outdone, the governor activated the National Guard. Police and military uniforms lined the streets to maintain a semblance of order.

Media from all over America converged on Atlanta for Rhigetti's upcoming debate at *Philips Arena*. There was no way they could ignore the ratings that this polarizing personality would deliver. Many of them treated Righetti with the respect due a head of state. The Christian community, however, was nearly always portrayed as intolerant, over-reactive religious zealots.

Philips Arena was the home court for the Atlanta Hawks. Tonight it was to be the scene of a colossal clash between Anthony Righetti and Jonathan Banks. Unbelievably, all of the 21,000 seats were taken. This was due in large part to Rhigetti's tireless efforts and irresistible charisma. But some media personalities wondered out loud whether the surprisingly large crowd was due to how masterfully he played to the sexual desires of his followers.

Television cameras were everywhere. Technicians worked feverishly on last minute details.

Daphne Krugle was in the building, but not the arena. She was alone in a side room. She wore a dark two-piece jacket and skirt suit with a white silk blouse. A fluffy, red scarf hung around her neck to accent the soft red lines in her suit. Her black leather shoes were decorated with red snake skin.

She looked in the long mirror and began to cry. Everything looked so perfect, but it wasn't. This should have been the happiest night of her life. She was only one step away from becoming a star. Everyone in America would know Daphne Krugle.

But she couldn't do it. She couldn't leave this room. She was scared to death. Atlanta had gone absolutely crazy. It seemed that God and Satan were in a giant tug-of-war, and she was the rope. Now the success she had craved all of her life since her tumultuous West Oakland, California upbringing meant nothing. Tonight she was going to cast a vote for eternity.

Daphne turned away from the mirror in frightened bewilderment. She shuddered when she recalled how evil Mr. Righetti's eyes had appeared when she told him that Rob Larkin was being replaced with Jonathan Banks.

After a long, penetrating stare that stripped away all of her confidence, he had told her, "That's okay, Daphne. You'll take care of Mr. Banks."

"What...what do you mean? What do you want me to do?" she had asked.

"When I give you the signal, you will tell the world that you and Mr. Banks are having an affair."

"But...we're not...my career," she stammered.

He smiled and gently lifted her chin. "Dead women don't have careers."

Daphne had looked into his eyes. They were deep wells of hatred. She knew he would do it. Slowly, grotesquely, his face had changed into the face of a beast. Daphne backed up and screamed, "Stop it!" She covered her face to hide from this evil man.

His face changed back and he smiled. "Stop what?" he asked innocently. He placed his hands on both of her shoulders and put his face close to hers. “I have confidence in you. The Family has confidence in you. You won’t let us down, will you?”

Daphne’s lips quivered the response Rhigetti wanted.

“Smart girl.” He had left, confident that he had Daphne where he wanted her. In the palm of his hand.

After he had left, Daphne tried unsuccessfully to stop shaking. She was shaking now. What kind of man was this? He wasn’t a man. He was a devil, a monster. She nervously paced the floor. What should she do? She hadn't snorted cocaine in days, and only once since Mr. Banks had prayed for her. But now she felt so incredibly weak and hollow. She needed something to help her through the night.

*****

Jonathan and Edwin sat in one of the dressing rooms. Edwin knew he should have been terrified, but he felt incredibly at ease.

"Do you think the Hawks will make it past the first round of the playoffs?" he asked.

"Yeah."

Edwin noted the dryness in his voice. "Is everything okay? You don't have the nervous jitters, do you?" he joked.

Jonathan looked at him intently. "Edwin, I may not be with you long."

Edwin knew that Jonathan traveled extensively and that sooner or later he and Elizabeth would be off to some distant land he couldn't pronounce. But he had pushed that troubling thought to the back of his mind. Jonathan had become more than a friend. He was a savior. Where would he be without him? He owed so much to this strange man. "Where are you off to now?" Edwin asked, his smile covering his disappointment.

"To heaven."

"What? Is it a big secret?"

"I'm serious, brother. I'm going to heaven."

"You're going to die?" Edwin asked incredulously.

"That's usually how it's done."

"What...what...are you ill?" A panicky feeling coated the walls of Edwin's belly.

"Brother, I've sinned against God."

Edwin jumped up. "What? You? What could you have possibly done that you can't be forgiven of?"

"I've worked harder than God," he said with resignation. "I've been bullheaded. Sometimes the smallest indiscretions can cost you the most."

"What...I...."

Jonathan forced a laugh. "I didn't say I was going on the next load." He stood up and good-naturedly nudged Edwin to the door. "Now you go on out there and sit with your family. I'm going to pray a little while longer."

Edwin's alarm lessened, but he was still stunned at this statement. What could Jonathan possibly mean by this? "Okay." He smiled at the man he had come to admire so much. "Okay."

*****

Bashnar approached the perimeter of the angelic armies with his sword drawn. *Even the Mighty Bashnar couldn't win this battle,* he thought, as he surveyed the endless multitudes of angels. The last time he had seen an army this large was at the Battle of Ephesus. Bashnar smiled inwardly. *Chairman, you sabotage my career by sparing me certain defeat. Maybe I'll like Haiti.*

"What is your business?" an angel challenged him as he approached the perimeter.

"I am the Mighty Bashnar," he stated confidently. "Take me to see Captain Rashti."

The angel could hardly believe he was in the presence of this evil legendary warrior. He motioned with his hand and a courier spirit came to him. He whispered in his ear and the courier shot out of sight. He returned and whispered something into the soldier's ear.

"Matraji! Efrinah! Sabboa! Lushan! Escort the Mighty Bashnar to the captain," the angel ordered.

Bashnar walked through the midst of the angels as though he was their leader. He passed the final line of soldiers and stepped into a clearing.

Captain Rashti stood with his sword drawn.

Bashnar looked at the powerful angel with involuntary awe. He took a step closer. "I am the Mighty Bashnar."

Captain Rashti squeezed the handle of his weapon and also took a step forward. "I am the Sword of the Lord."

Bashnar peered at Captain Rashti and thought how wonderful and challenging it would be to fight a real warrior. But he was here on other business. "I am here for Jonathan!"

Several angels unsheathed their weapons.

The captain raised his hand and the angels backed off. "What if I don't let you have him?"

"You will let me have him! It is my right!"

Captain Rashti knew that Bashnar was right. Jonathan had fallen for a subtlety that was not often used. Bashnar knew that the only way to get at him was through the gifts of God. So he had put his career and life on the line by sending great opportunities of ministry to Jonathan. He knew that his compassion was so great that he would never turn down anyone who needed him. The result was that against the promptings of the Holy Spirit, Jonathan had overworked his body, which had never fully recovered from his last trip to Haiti, and taken on more than he was told to do. He was literally working himself to death. But that in itself was not the reason for this moment. The reason for this moment was hidden in plain view.

"I will go with you," said the captain. His resolve as great as Bashnar's arrogance.

Jonathan closed the door behind Edwin and quickly sat down. He was exhausted. He let his head fall back limply and breathed through his mouth. His body felt dead. He tried to pick up his Bible, but his arm would not obey.

Bashnar was like a wild animal who first wanted to enjoy his prey before he devoured it. He watched the hated dagger cling desperately to life.

Captain Rashti was incensed at this humiliation of such a great man of God. "Do it now or get out of my presence!"

Bashnar instinctively flashed his angry eyes at Rashti. The captain glared back, ready to back up his words with heavenly steel if necessary. Bashnar lifted his sword and with one mighty swoop cut through Jonathan with as much ease as cutting through butter.

*****

Edwin, Barbara, Sharon, Elizabeth, and Terrance Knox were all seated together close to where the debate would take place. Adam, Sherry, Jessica, Wallace, and Marjorie sat directly behind them.

Across the arena, Toni pointed to Sharon. "There she is," she told her father's friend. "She's in that first row."

The man gave Toni five hundred dollars and started walking toward Sharon.

"Where's Mr. Banks?" Sharon asked her father.

"He's praying. He should be out shortly."

Sharon looked around the filled arena. She hadn't been there in a long time. There were so many.... Her face went rigid. *My God*! she thought. *What is he doing here? He sees me! He's coming over here!*

"Excuse me, Daddy. I have to go to the restroom."

"I'll go with you," he said, taking note of the rough looking young men she would pass up the stairs.

"Don't be ridiculous, Dad. I'll be alright."

Edwin watched his daughter protectively as she went upstairs. He was annoyed that a lot of guys tried to talk to her as she passed by them. Some of them were either significantly older than his daughter, or they had lived very hard lives.

She waited for the man. "What do you want?" she asked apprehensively.

The man had tears in his eyes. "Young lady, I have just given Toni back her money."

"What?"

"I used to be a preacher and I fell away from God. I became bitter and went my own way."

"But what do you want with me?"

He looked at her guiltily. "You were never pregnant."

Sharon looked at him for several seconds, saying nothing. Shock was written all over her face. She shook her head. “I had an—”

“No, you did not.” The man placed his hand under Sharon’s chin. “I didn’t do anything. It was all to deceive you. I don’t know why they wanted me to do this.” He dropped his hand and his head. "I know it was a terrible thing to do. But after awhile you get used to doing wrong. The more you do it, the easier it becomes."

“But I took a home pregnancy test.”

The man’s expression was sympathetic. “They’re usually pretty reliable, but sometimes they can give a false-positive—if you take it too soon, for instance. Did you wait until you missed your period?”

“No.

“How soon after your encounter did you take the test?”

“A couple of days,” she answered.

Another sympathetic smile, mixed with guilt. “Young lady, even if you were pregnant, your body doesn’t produce HCG that soon. I don’t know why you got a false positive.”

The secret of how this occurred went to the Dark Prison with Witchcraft when he was destroyed by the Mighty Bashnar.

“But you tested me, too,” she said.

His silent response said it all.

Sharon began to cry. She should have been furious at this man's behavior. But how could she be angry at the person who had just given her the best news she had ever received in her life?

"The reason I'm telling you this is because I've come home. I've come back to Jesus." He shook his head in amazement. "Your friend, Toni, led me to the Lord."

"Toni?" Sharon asked through her tears.

The man pushed out a laugh. "Can you believe it? I know. Life can be strange."

Sharon added laughter to her tears. This was unbelievable. A hundred pound weight rolled off her shoulders. "Thank you." She returned to her seat.

"That must have been some restroom," Edwin said to Sharon when he saw the radiance in her face.

She smiled. "It was, Daddy. It was the best restroom ever."

Edwin looked at her strangely and shrugged it off.

*****

Daphne Krugle was escorted to the platform by an Atlanta police officer. He held her hand as she went up the stairs. *I'll hold your hand any time you want me to*, he thought.

Daphne sat down, adjusted her wireless microphone, and looked around. Twenty-one thousand people. There were sporadic flashes of light as people took pictures. She waited for what seemed like eternity, but she wasn't the least bit nervous. When Mr. Righetti sat down, she greeted him professionally and resumed looking at her note cards.

They waited ten minutes.

A man hopped onto the platform. "Daphne, where's your man. We're on in two minutes."

Daphne said simply, "He'll be here."

Anthony went to Daphne and whispered in her ear. "With or without Jonathan, the show goes on."

"Of course, Anthony," she said calmly.

"Where is he?" Edwin muttered.

Ten...nine...eight...seven...six...five...four...three...two...one." The technician's hand came down.

"Ladies and gentlemen, this is Daphne Krugle. We are live at Philips Arena. Home of the playoff bound Atlanta Hawks. Tonight there is standing room only as twenty-one thousand excited people are gathered to—can you believe this?—listen to a religious debate.

"Anthony Righetti has become a household name among Atlantans. A savior to some. A curse to others. An object of bewilderment to others. Do or say what you may. But one thing you will not do is ignore Anthony Righetti."

Anthony loved that last statement. He breathed it in deeply.

"He is the founder of a satanic organization called the Family. This organization purports to be the rightful heir of Christianity. So says Mr. Righetti: 'Christianity is dead.'"

Mr. Banks, where are you? Daphne wondered.

Anthony gave her a look of approval.

"Our other guest is a spokesman for Christianity. His name is Jonathan Banks. When I asked Mr. Banks to do this debate, his words to me were, 'I don't debate; I demonstrate.'"

From the corner of her eye Daphne saw a furtive scowl on Mr. Righetti's face.

"He believes that Jesus Christ is the answer for every problem, the cure for every ill. The purpose for every person. He says, and I quote: 'If Jesus can't fix it, it ain't broke.' End of quote. Tonight our two guests will present two very different perspectives of Christianity."

Daphne's arms were drenched with nervous sweat. *Mr. Banks, where are you?*

"We will allow Mr. Righetti to address the audience first. We'll then call for Mr. Banks," she stalled.

Several thousand people cheered, screamed, and whistled as their hero of ungodliness prepared to speak. He had to wait several minutes before the cheering died down.

"How are you?" he asked?

The crowd roared again. He waved his hands and they stopped.

"I am here because Christianity stinks!"

The crowd was a deafening mixture of cheers from his supporters and boos from the Christians who were brave enough to attend this event. Finally, after much pleading from Daphne, the crowd hushed.

"It stinks with the corpses of its holy wars. It stinks with the corruption of its hypocrisy and greed. It stinks with the corruption of its intolerance and bigotry. It stinks with the corruption of its television evangelists."

Several thousand people jumped to their feet, roaring and whistling and clapping. Some barked like dogs.

"I have a confession to make," he said, with a smile when the people quieted. He whispered into the microphone. "Don't tell anyone I said this. This is a secret just between you and me. Sometimes I wish I was a television preacher. Then I could have all the sex and money I ever wanted!"

The arena rocked with cheers and boos.

He spoke for several minutes more, and when there was no sign of Jonathan he said, "Where is our Christian spokesman? He's probably sleeping off a hangover!"

"Ed, where's Jonathan," asked Elizabeth, now afraid that something was wrong.

"I...I don't know. I left him in the dressing room. He said he wanted to pray a little while longer." Edwin tried to look around all the television and newspaper people who were gathered around the platform. "Sharon, I need you to go to the dressing room. I'm going to debate Mr. Righetti."

"You?" Barbara asked, looking at her husband as though he had lost his mind.

"Yeah, me," Edwin answered, not believing it himself. But he had to do something, even if it was only to make a fool of himself trying to do the right thing. *Oh, goodness. How can Jonathan actually like this stuff?*

"You can do it, Dad," said Sharon. She hugged him and took off to find Jonathan. She expected to be stopped by the guards, but they acted like they didn't even see her. She opened the door and screamed. Jonathan was lying on his back.

"You need a press pass," an usher told Edwin.

Edwin was flabbergasted. He reached into his wallet and pulled out a fifty dollar bill. "Here it is." He pressed it into the man's hand.

The man protested mildly until he saw how much it was. He turned his back to Edwin. Edwin hesitated, then took that as a sign to go on.

Edwin got close to the platform and was stopped by a policeman. "Press pass." It wasn't a question.

Edwin patted his chest and looked down. "I...I don't know where it is, Officer."

The officer looked at him dubiously. "Maybe you'll find it at home."

Edwin sighed and turned around and began to walk away. Suddenly, he stopped and spun around before the policeman could interfere.

"I'll debate you!" he screamed.

The policeman's wide hand gripped Edwin's arm. "Come on. Let's go, mister."

"What are you afraid of, you phony?" he screamed over his shoulder.

Anthony stretched to see who was challenging him. Daphne saw who it was and recognized him. It was the preacher she had read about in Sunday's paper. The one who had exorcised the demon!

"Let him come up," she said into the microphone.

Anthony recognized him too, and smiled. "Yes, let him come up."

*****

"Mr. Banks! Mr. Banks!" Sharon shook him. "What's wrong?" Sharon's mind told her to do a million things, but she couldn't clearly hear any one thing. She looked around the room for...something. Anything! *Oh, God, help me! Please help me!* "What? What?" She shook him again. "What did you say?" She put her ear to his mouth. "The Bible? Is that what you said?" She grabbed it and put her ear back to his mouth. "Okay, okay," she said frantically. She turned to Isaiah 38:1-6 and read it over him:

> *In those days was Hezekiah sick unto death. And Isaiah the prophet the son of Amoz came to him, and said to him, Thus saith the Lord, Set your house in order: for you shall die, and not live. Then Hezekiah turned his face toward the wall, and prayed unto the Lord, And said, Remember now, O Lord, I beg you, how I have walked before you in truth and with a perfect heart, and have done that which is good in your sight. And Hezekiah wept sore. Then came the word of the Lord to Isaiah, saying, Go, and say to Hezekiah, Thus says the Lord, the God of David your father, I have heard your prayer, I have seen your tears: behold, I will add unto your days fifteen years. And I will deliver you and this city out of the hand of the king of Assyria: and I will defend this city.*

*****

The professional term for what Daphne Krugle, newscaster extraordinaire, was doing was improvisation. Daphne called it winging it.

"Some of you may recognize this man." *What is his name? Edward Styles—no, Edwin! Edwin Styles.* "This is Pastor Edwin Styles, another religious celebrity. He's the preacher on the front page of last Sunday's newspaper."

"Good evening, Ms. Krugle," said Edwin.

"Good evening." She hoped it would be a good evening.

Anthony greeted the new guest. "Good luck," he said with a confident smile.

“Luck has nothing to do with this,” Edwin answered.

The men locked eyes for several seconds.

Finally, Anthony turned away and smiled handsomely for those with cameras.

A technician hopped onto the platform and hurriedly pinned a small microphone to Edwin's lapel.

Daphne raised her hands to the crowd in mock confusion. "Live television. What can I say?"

Laughter from the audience.

"Reverend Styles, you've heard the stinging accusations that Mr. Righetti has hurled against the Christian community. What do you have to say to them?" Daphne asked.

Edwin was used to speaking before large audiences, but none this large, and definitely none this hostile. He cleared his throat for words he hoped were there.

"I—" He stopped in mid-sentence. His heart bounced with joy...and relief. "I think I'll let Jonathan address that question," he said confidently. He took off the microphone and put it on the small table and went to meet Jonathan. "Where were you?" he whispered.

"Resting."

"Are you ready?"

"Does Jason wear a hockey mask?"

Edwin patted him on the back. "Go get him."

"Ladies and gentlemen," said Daphne, wondering what the critics would say about the apparent lack of order, "believe it or not, here's our Jonathan Banks." Her voice had a trace of humor.

There was a mixture of cheers and boos, mostly boos.

Jonathan put on the microphone. He took one of the bottles of water off the table and took his time opening it. He took a few swallows. "Am I early?"

"Reverend Banks—"

"Call me Jonathan."

Daphne gave him a business smile. "Jonathan, you're aware of Mr. Righetti's sentiments. Would you like to speak to the audience?"

"No."

Daphne blinked hard.

Jonathan turned to Anthony. "I want to speak to motor mouth."

Anthony's carefully rehearsed smile vanished behind a scowl of contempt.

"Mr. Righetti, you and your Family are a bunch of spiritual buffoons if you believe Satan is greater than Jesus Christ. It doesn't take a genius to see that Satan is a loser." Jonathan took another sip of water and added, "Much like yourself."

Righetti opened his mouth, but Jonathan beat him to it. He spoke directly to the audience. "This man believes that you are all a bunch of idiots. He believes that you don't have the sense to think these things through. You already have the freedom he offers. He offers you free sex. You already have free sex. What has it gotten you?"

Someone shouted, "An orgasm!"

Jonathan waited for the eruption of laughter to die down. "Aids, Herpes, Syphilis, and other filthy diseases. How many of you young ladies have given your bodies to men who didn't love you? It didn't feel good, did it?"

A teenager stood up and shouted, "It felt good to me!"

More laughter from the immense crowd.

"Shut up and sit down, young man," Jonathan said softly. "That's what this man offers you. Life without love. Life without respect. Life without God. He is right about one thing, though. Christianity does have its share of hypocrites and fools. Mr. Righetti hides behind this fact. He hides behind our weaknesses. But our weaknesses are greater than his strengths. We serve a living God who is able and willing to break the power of the devil over your life!"

"You talk about power!" spewed Anthony. "Where is your power? You have nothing but words!"

Some people in the crowd began barking like dogs, signifying their approval.

"The power of God is wherever there is a need and a humble heart," Jonathan answered.

Anthony smiled and pointed to a member of the Family who was planted in the audience. The man wore dark glasses and carried a stick. "This is America," he said to the audience. "The land of magicians and television preachers. What about him?"

"What about him?"

"Can your God heal him? Or is He limited to corns and bunions?"

Thousands in the crowd found this also funny.

"Bring him here," Jonathan said of the man. A man brought him to Jonathan. "Can God heal this man?" he asked the audience.

There were few cheers in proportion to the boos. There weren't many Christians in the arena who believed God would do anything so dramatic. Oh, they knew that He could. But could and would were worlds apart.

"I said, Can God heal this man?"

This time the Christians cheered. Even those who didn't believe the man would be healed. What else could they do? They had to support the preacher. At least he was trying to do something to stand against this wicked man.

"And to those of you who believe my God is dead, what will you do when the man is healed? Will you turn from this man's bankrupt religion?"

The cheers were overwhelming.

Anthony strained to contain his laughter.

Television cameras zoomed in on Jonathan and the man.

"What is it that you desire of the Lord Jesus Christ?"

"My eyes...my eyes...I can't see."

"Out of your own mouth be it done unto you."

The man stretched forth his arms and groped around on the platform for a few seconds. Suddenly, he stopped and snatched off the dark glasses. "I can see! I can see!" he shouted.

At first the arena was completely silent, except for the man. But after several seconds, the Christians went wild with applause. Some shouted. Some jumped up and down. Many cried. They had never seen such a miracle before in their lives.

Anthony and the man let go of their laughter. "He better be able to see," said Anthony. "He drove me to the arena this evening."

This time the crowd laughed for what seemed like forever to the humiliated Christians. Even the police and media abandoned their professionalism and laughed. Although it appeared that most of them were able to stop laughing sooner than the general crowd.

"Jerry is a member of the Family. Everyone give him a hand for his fine acting." Rhigetti was back in control, where he was most comfortable.

Jerry the actor took a few steps and stopped. He stretched his arms out and slowly turned his head in every direction. The encore brought more laughter from the crowd. This was good stuff.

"Anthony," he said, in a low, shaky voice.

Rhigetti was full. Tonight was perfect. The Christians and their ridiculous god were being made fools of. Jerry was milking the moment and Rhigetti loved it.

Anthony!" he screamed. "I can't see! Do something! I can't see!"

There was absolute silence in the arena, except for the news people who whispered frantically among themselves. Rhigetti was now confused. What was Jerry doing? This didn't make sense. How did this improvisation fit into the plan? He had taken the encore too far.

Someone identifying herself as a doctor came onto the platform and looked into the man's eyes. "This man doesn't have any eyeballs!"

This time the crowd was stunned. No eyeballs. Some folks had seen enough. Here and there tiny trickles of people started making their way to the exits.

"What did you do?" Anthony growled to Jonathan.

"The God you mock and say is dead answered his prayer. He asked to be healed and he has been healed. He's been healed of irreverence."

Anthony was stunned, humiliated. Nothing came to mind. No flash of oratorical brilliance. No entertaining deflection of Jonathan's attack. No debater's bravado. Stumped as to what to do next, he sat down, confused by his friend's blindness. He suddenly felt alone and spiritually weak. The power of hell was gone. *Where are my spirits?* he asked himself. He looked at Daphne and nodded. *Now! Do it now*! he told her with his eyes.

Daphne swallowed and tried to regain her composure. No eyeballs? She was way out of her depth. How...what...no eyeballs? She waited a few seconds. "Atlanta, I have a confession to make," she said soberly. "Mr. Anthony Righetti asked me before this show to tell you that I and Mr. Jonathan Banks have been having an affair. This is totally false. There's not a shred of truth to it." She looked directly into Anthony's eyes. "I believe he told me to lie on this good man because he is a liar and a fraud."

"That's a lie!" he yelled. His air of confidence was totally gone now. He had to defend himself. "I never said anything of the sort! This is just another example of Christian trickery!"

"No! She's telling the truth!" a girl in the audience screamed out.

Anthony looked past the lights and dropped his mouth open in astonishment when he saw who it was.

"He is a liar and a fraud! I ought to know! I'm his daughter!"

Flashes of digital cameras erupted from every direction.

Anthony was stunned. He stood up in utter shock. He watched in near paralysis as Toni mounted the platform and took a microphone.

Toni cried bitter tears. She looked at him as she spoke. "My father is an evil, filthy man. He's abused and molested me ever since I was a little girl. He's sick and he's using this Family stuff as a front. It's only a tool to hurt people. Don't listen to him. Don't let him destroy you like he destroyed me."

Anthony looked into the audience and saw the faces of demons. Thousands and thousands of creatures, mocking, jeering, ridiculing. "Fool! Fool! Fool!" he heard them scream. How could this be? They were his servants. Why would they abandon him? Why would they betray him? It didn't make sense. They had a common enemy.

Then it dawned on him. From the very beginning this was never going to be. It was all a game. For some treacherous reason, he had been used as a pawn. But for what? Why would Satan do this to him? A biting thought broke the skin of his crowded and confused mind. *This is exactly what happened to Satan when he tried to take over heaven.* He vividly remembered Scriptures that he had never committed to memory.

> *I saw Satan fall like lightning from heaven...How you are fallen from heaven, O Lucifer, son of the morning! How you are cut down to the ground, you who weakened the nations...Yet you shall be brought down to Hell, to the lowest depths of the*

> *pit...The devil who deceived them, was cast into the lake of fire and brimstone.*

Anthony took a couple of tentative steps backward. He eyed the audience. It was clear that the crowd was not only no longer with him, they were turning against him. He saw it in the stern faces of the cops. He saw it in the ushers. He saw it in the media. But he had never trusted these sharks to ignore blood. So this did not surprise him. Although it was surprising that they would turn on him so quickly.

Then there were those worthless Christians. It wasn't hard to identify them in the crowd, at least those close enough for him to see. They were crying. They were praying. They had their hands raised. They were looking at the ceiling and mouthing off who knew what to that awful god of theirs.

Everyone was laughing at his expense. He had been made a fool of. First, it had been the Christian god with all of his empty promises. Now it was Satan and his disappearance act. To hell with both of them. It was going to end right here. No one would be laughing at Anthony Marcello Rhigetti when it was all over. He reached decisively into his suit jacket and pulled out a black *Baretta PX4 Storm Compact*. The name of the gun was poetically accurate. It was a compact storm in his holster. It's high-capacity magazine could rain twenty nine-millimeter bullets. One was already chambered.

It was all over in a few seconds. But that was enough for the storm. Anthony shot in every direction at the spirits and people who dared to laugh at him. The panic-stricken crowd scurried for cover. Some dove on the floor and hid behind seats. Others ran for the exits. Many were trampled. Harry Thompson was sitting too close for his own good. He tried to hide behind someone, but a bullet tore through his old back and sent him into a fiery eternity.

Daphne ran for the stage stairs. Anthony turned and fired. The bullet found her shoulder and propelled her over the side of the platform.

The policeman who had helped her up the stairs earlier covered her body with his own. Another policeman, a rookie, ran toward Anthony with his gun drawn. "Stop! Stop!" he yelled, with no clear shot because of the fleeing people.

Anthony turned and aimed at the policeman. Four bullets ripped through Anthony's chest. He crumpled awkwardly and fell to the floor on his side. His eyes stared straight ahead. Something appeared in front of him. He struggled to lift his head. The creature moved towards him. Anthony wondered at the demonic beast that stood before him. He wondered even more about the brilliant light that was directly behind the demon and approaching fast.

*Pathetic! t*he Mighty Bashnar imposed on the dead man's mind. *You're pathetic!* He spat upon Anthony. "Death, do your business."

The death demon appeared and yanked Anthony's wailing spirit down to the eternal flames of hell.

Jonathan got up and hurried to Daphne. She was on her back, her eyes open wide.

"Jonathan, I almost went back," she said softly. "God helped me come on tonight without my cocaine."

"Lay still, Daphne," Jonathan said, his eyes watering for his spiritual daughter. "They're going to get you out of here in just a little while."

"The pla...the...plague...what...?

Jonathan tenderly stroked her face.

"Honey," he smiled, "there isn't going to be any plague." He squeezed her hand. "We've won."

The Mighty Bashnar glared at the dagger with hatred and reluctant respect. He was a most formidable foe. "We shall meet again, my friend. We shall definitely meet again."

Bashnar was oblivious to the brilliant cloud of light that was directly behind him only several yards away. He was also unaware of the large, silvery sword that came out of the cloud, and of the powerful angel who gripped it. The angel slowly stepped out of the cloud. His silver sword was engulfed in a blue flame.

Melodic whispers came from the heavens.

Sword of the Lord.

Sword of the Lord.

Sword of the Lord.

Sword of the Lord.

The Sword of the Lord approached the Mighty Bashnar. He lifted the flaming sword.

A thunderous voice spoke from the heavens. "Wait until a time appointed."

The Sword of the Lord lowered his hand.

"Yes," he spoke for Jonathan.

Bashnar spun around. His short and long swords instantly in his thick hands. *Rashti!*

"We shall definitely meet again," promised the angel. Then he was gone.

The End

May I ask you a favor?

Once you read the book, if you find that you enjoyed the story, would you mind going online to Amazon.com, iTunes, Kobo, Barnes and Noble, or wherever you purchased the book and writing a review? Many people determine from book reviews whether or not a story is worth their time. Your review (even a short one!) can help convince others to join the fun!

Let's Stay In Touch!

Join my newsletter at www.ericmhill.com/newsletter. Here's my contact info: ericmhillauthor@yahoo.com or Twitter.com/ericmhillatl.

God bless you!

Other Books by the Author

Spiritual Warfare Fiction

The Fire Series
Book 1: Bones of Fire
Book 2: Trial by Fire
Book 3: Saints on Fire

The Demon Strongholds Series
Book 1: The Spirit of Fear
Book 2: The Spirit of ??? (Coming April 2016)

Other Fiction

The Journey Series
Book 1: The Runaway's Journey (Part One)

Non-Fiction

Deliverance from Demons and Diseases
What Preachers Never Tell You About Tithes & Offerings

Made in the USA
Middletown, DE
24 November 2018